THE DEFECTOR

THE DEFECTOR

HOWARD REYNOLDS

VIKING

VIKING
Viking Penguin Inc.
40 West 23rd Street,
New York, New York 10010, U.S.A.

First American Edition
Published in 1987

Extracts from the songs on the LP *Dark Side of the Moon* by
Pink Floyd are copyright © 1973 Pink Floyd Music Publishers
Ltd., and are reproduced with their kind permission.

Library of Congress Cataloging in Publication Data
Reynolds, Howard.
  The defector.
  I. Title.
PR6068.E956D44   1987   823'.914   86-40256
ISBN 0-670-81528-4

Printed in the United States of America by
The Book Press, Brattleboro, Vermont
Set in Janson

To Valerie and Michael

ACKNOWLEDGEMENTS

The author wishes to express grateful thanks to the following for their help and encouragement: Owen Wilkes, Stockholm International Peace Research Institute; Paul Bannister, Fleet Street West, California; John Morrell, United Newspapers; Clive Entwhistle, Thames Television; Revel Barker, Mirror Group Newspapers; Cliff Hepburn and Gill Edge, CHP Promotions; in the USSR, A.K. and D.S.; and special thanks to Giles O'Bryen at Michael Joseph.

PROLOGUE

SOKOLNIKI PARK
MOSCOW

On Saturday afternoons, the tradition was to quit the city at the end of the ceremony – celebrate the new life amid the birdsong and the breezes.

Szurmanov watched them go by. The bride had a coat with upturned collar. The groom wore a cheap ill-fitting suit. Mechanic, lathe operator – something like that; the tie had been knotted by unpractised hands. The rest of the group followed – young ones laughing, elders more subdued – the last of them a matriarch with moist eyes and clothes solemn and funereal. A small bald man tried to keep in step with her. His face was reddened by fresh air and strong spirit.

Szurmanov tasted the moment, savouring the merriment and the sadness that commingled in the wake of their passing. He imagined them on the other side of the birch grove, holding self-conscious poses while a shutter clicked up frames for memories.

He stepped out then. Through a break in the spruce and larch canopy he could see the distant domes and pavilions of the Exhibition of Economic Achievement and nearer, to the south-west, the soaring tower of Moscow Television Centre. He had often dined there, the Seventh Heaven Restaurant, midway up the gleaming pinnacle, a thousand feet above the city.

Tonight he would go again in celebration. Tonight there would be vodka and finest Beluga and, as the glass and chrome platform turned about its axis, he would once more remark on the wonders of progress and the fact that revolution was now only a word to describe the motion of a Russian restaurant high up in a Russian sky.

1

He clambered down the banking and resumed the footpath. It curved and dipped away through the trees towards the distant bend of the Moskva. He walked a little while longer, then stopped. To his left, the embankment ascended through insubstantial barriers of fern. Ahead and to the right, a small log shelter lay steeped in the shadow of the trees. He waited.

There were two of them.

'You are Pavel?'

Szurmanov debated. 'Who is asking?'

'We spoke last night, on the telephone.'

The boy was in a zippered blouson; shapeless trousers bellied over scuffed toecaps. The girl wore jeans and a green anorak. Its hood shrouded her face.

The boy tried again. 'My name is Dmitri.'

Szurmanov continued to eye the girl. The hood didn't help. She could have been anything between eighteen and forty. He wondered what she was like under the jacket. 'So,' he said, 'you're the girl.'

She frowned, glanced uncertainly at her companion.

'The girl,' Szurmanov repeated. The vapid smile lingered. 'You're late.'

'We saw some people,' the boy said. 'It seemed wise to wait.'

'Waiting is a bigger risk.'

'You have it?' the boy asked.

'In the shelter.' He turned his smile on the girl. 'I should check it. You know the *fartsovshchiki*.'

The boy nodded and moved away. The girl feigned interest in the tree-tops. 'Don't be nervous,' Szurmanov said.

'There are voices.' Her gaze flitted to him. 'I can hear voices.'

'It's only the people you saw before.'

'Yes?'

'An hour ago they were at the Palace of Weddings. Now they come here – a small party, in the park restaurant. It is tradition.' He paused. She looked at the trees again. 'In the old days,' he continued, 'they walked the Lenin Hills; but that was before the stadium and the university and all those little boxes they call houses. Tell me, d'you think it's a good day for a wedding?'

She didn't reply.

'Bright but unseasonal,' Szurmanov continued. 'I think it's cold for August. Well, look at you, your clothes.'

2

The boy returned, carrying a shopping bag of rope and hessian. 'It's short.'

'We do what we can.'

'What is there?' the girl said.

'Two pairs of Lee Cooper.' He glanced at Szurmanov. 'I was promised three.'

'Genuine rivets, though.' Szurmanov was soothing. 'And as compensation I put in a special record for you – best digital recording.'

The girl shook her head. 'Never mind that. Is the stuff there?'

'All of it,' Szurmanov said. 'A half-kilo. The finest, for my friends.'

'Your price isn't very friendly,' the girl said.

The noise impacted without warning, voices loud in the nearby thicket, calling raucously like angry crows. The boy made a move for the girl, but Szurmanov was quicker, clawing at his arm, catching it, dragging him away from the path. The boy still clutched the shopping bag.

They crabbed up the banking. Szurmanov risked a backward glance. He saw the brown and grey uniforms streaming out of the foliage below. There was a lot of shouting and the girl was encircled and she cried out, and the note went so high and so wide everything rang, everything turned bright, piercing, and he felt the upsurge of a wicked joy; and then the Tokarev was somehow in his hand.

He flattened down on brittle ferns and waved the gun and resolved to make it sing.

'No!'

Eyes wide in pallid face, the boy lunged at him. 'You'll get us killed!'

Six rounds in the clip and he felt a powerful compulsion to loose them all. The uniforms were beginning to climb. His right hand jerked convulsively – five rounds now, and answering gunfire; a bullet clipped a nearby branch, sending bark exploding outwards and slashing a white scar in the timber. Four rounds left. The slam of recoil, and now the air was filled with the mad discord of screams and shouts, the hollow crack and slap as the magazine emptied.

'NO!'

Small sounds: the body turned slowly, raggedly, borne downhill on a scree of loose earth and sharp stones. It smeared across the path.

3

The shopping bag, the crumpled denim, the record and an oblong bar in brown paper littered the slope.

The uniforms parted to let the girl through. She raised her hands, moaned behind rigid fingers.

High above, Szurmanov skipped along the upper path towards Poperechny Prospekt, laughing, singing, exulting in the madness of it all.

PART I

CHAPTER
ONE

LENINGRAD

Owen Smith awoke before the alarm call. There was no intermediate stage between sleep and consciousness, and he sat upright with a painful abruptness. Silence lay as heavy as the blankets. He listened to it for a while, alert to its textures, its weight.

He was dressed and ready for breakfast when reception rang: eight o'clock. He thanked them, cradled the phone, then crossed to the window and opened the curtains. The window gave onto the Pirogovskaya Embankment, overlooking the Neva, and the pale morning light was slowly strengthening, gilding the spires and canopies of the city across the river. He craned his head, the better to make out the grey superstructure and triple funnels of the *Aurora*, at anchorage eight storeys below. One warning shot, he thought. 7 November 1917: the cruiser sailed up the wide river and trained her guns on the Winter Palace and everything was silenced by the echo of a single blank round.

His gaze rested for a while as thoughts slowly eddied like the waters around her hull.

Finally, he abandoned the view and sat down on the edge of the bed. His stomach grumbled; the griping presence of hunger surprised him. On the first morning of an operation the brain said there were higher priorities than food. He glanced at his wristwatch: 8.07. His contact had told London they would meet at 8.30 a.m., at breakfast: the Leningrad was an Intourist hotel so the first rule was never talk in the bedroom; the second was never meet in the lobby because that was too predictable a rendezvous point and would be under surveillance. At 8.30 the hotel was likely to be full and in the clatter and clutter of breakfast two more diners would go unremarked.

He hesitated, then shrugged off his jacket and stretched out on the bed. The paperback purchased at Heathrow was dog-eared from the previous day's flight. He thumbed through its pages and found the place where he'd left off. A quarter of an hour to go before he could risk leaving the room – the book would help pass the time, distract him from the nagging imperative of the day.

But his thoughts still roved elsewhere, restless, diffused, and the text kept blurring before his eyes. Outside, the day suddenly brightened. Light came lancing in and the page seemed to shine before his eyes.

Scrambled eggs and a couple of slices of ham; juice, coffee, the ubiquitous bottle of mineral water – the order arrived only moments before Kovotny appeared, a thick-set figure with sagging gut and florid face. Kovotny said something in Russian, paused in innocent reconsideration, then switched to English. 'May I join you?'

For a moment he couldn't think, couldn't remember a single feature of the photograph back in London. 'Yes.' He nodded too vigorously. The cup was midway to his lips and coffee slopped over the brim.

Kovotny sat down and glanced around the crowded restaurant. 'What do you recommend?'

'Depends how hungry you are.'

'I have not eaten since one o'clock yesterday.'

Contact: recognition phase concluded.

One o'clock. A different time and they'd have had to abort; any other hour and Kovotny would be warning of the presence and numerical strength of the opposition.

The Russian picked up the linen napkin and smiled. 'Welcome to the USSR.'

Kovotny beckoned to a waiter and ordered his food. For appearances' sake they exchanged a few banalities as they ate. Smith finished first and struggled to stop himself fidgeting while Kovotny consumed his breakfast slowly and with evident relish.

'We're all right for time?' Smith prompted.

'She knows the arrangements.'

'She isn't working today?'

'No, she has a week's holiday.'

'I see.'

'You wish me to run through it?' Kovotny asked.

'Yes.'

'What did they tell you?'

'The same as you will, I hope.'

'All right.' The Russian splashed mineral water into a glass. 'Yelena Pinsky: pharmacist, aged twenty-five.'

'Does she speak English?'

'Enough.'

'Does she trust you?'

'We met through the Pushkin Society.'

Smith frowned. 'I didn't ask if she was poetical.'

'It is relevant.'

'Why?'

'Romantics are inclined to be foolish.'

'Are you a romantic, Kovotny?'

'Pay me enough and I will be anything you want.' Kovotny paused, then went on: 'Pinsky's involved in samizdat – a small group, here in the city. Usual nonsense, everything from Helsinki to free trade unions. The group leader is one Leonid Guseinov – failed writer, failed everything. He has crusades. Still, they all have.'

'Is Asanov part of this group?'

'Only in so far as Guseinov has adopted him.'

'Why would he want to do that?'

'Out of pity.' Kovotny sipped the mineral water. 'Asanov has not had an easy time. He arrived here in January not knowing anyone.'

'He came here from Moscow?'

'Yes. A rather fine apartment in Zamoskvarechye, the old part of town. Then they moved him to Luzhniki, by the Lenin Hills.'

'And then here?'

'His *propiska* was cancelled.'

'You seem to know a lot about him.'

'London. Also, I make my own inquiries.' He studied the younger man. 'I have worked for your people longer than you.'

'Not just mine.'

Kovotny shrugged. 'The exchange rate fluctuates.'

'Which d'you prefer – sterling or dollars?'

'Swiss francs.'

'Ah.'

'You have to understand, it is not a question of allegiances.' Kovotny set the glass down. 'I am my own country.'

'Tell me more about Asanov,' Smith said. 'Does he know you?'

'He knows only what Pinsky has told him – that she has a friend with contacts in the West.'

'So you've never met him?'

'Nor Guseinov – one day he will go too far, and take everyone with him.'

'Including Pinsky. They could trace you through her.'

'By the time that happened I would have made my arrangements.'

'With London?'

'With whoever permits me to fly first class.'

Smith fingered the cup again. 'Pinsky, is she involved with Leonid Guseinov?'

'Romantically?'

'Whatever.'

'She has a lover, but it is not Guseinov. He is called Vadim Kalininsky.' Kovotny smiled. 'A man after my own heart – and anything else he can find.'

'You know him?'

'Most people in Leningrad know a Vadim Kalininsky. They're all over the city.' He registered Smith's incomprehension. 'Black marketeers, thieves.'

'You know him only by reputation, then.'

'Yes.'

'Why would she want to live with a thief?'

'Perhaps she wishes to reform him.' Kovotny stood up. 'I told you, they all have their crusades.'

Yelena Pinsky descended the crumbling steps of the apartment house, then looked up in vain to see if Vadim was waving goodbye.

The six-storey terrace was in a zone scheduled for clearance. Scraps of litter curled around her feet. Her shoes crunched on broken glass as she walked briskly away from the dark, stained facades. Behind her, at the head of the cul-de-sac, a bulldozer growled and juddered, and an iron ball arced through the air to smash the face of a gaunt, windowless building. She wondered where they would go when their sanctuary fell. Vadim did not believe in paying rent, no matter how insignificant the amount. But then Vadim did not believe in having a permanent address, either.

She reached the junction, where a grey Zhiguli was parked beside a broken street lamp. She opened the front passenger door and slipped inside. In the back of the car was a youngish man – squat, broad-shouldered, with dark hair and eyes – smiling at her.

Kovotny said: 'This, Yelena, is the man I was telling you about.'

Kovotny drove along Gaza Prospekt, angling east towards the centre after crossing the Fontanka. Smith hunched down in the vinyl seat, watching the buildings and the traffic go by. City drivers were the same the world over. No one seemed to bother about speed limits.

Kovotny and the girl talked in Russian, ignoring him. There wasn't much he could do about it. The seating arrangements saw to that. He'd originally wanted the girl to sit next to him, but Kovotny said no, such a configuration only looked proper in a taxi cab, which this was obviously not. In a private car you'd expect two people in the front and one or two in the back, not the other way round. It was best to be inconspicuous; if you lived in the USSR for any length of time, you learned the wisdom of invisibility.

Eventually, she turned in her seat – blue eyes, flaxen hair, a hesitant smile. 'You are from England?'

'Yes.' He smiled back.

'What would you like me to do?' She had a lilting voice, high, sweet; it unexpectedly reminded him of the days of youth, of hope.

'I need to get a message to Piotr Asanov.'

'Okay. You may tell me,' she said.

'It has to be private. No one else must know. Not your boyfriend or anyone.'

'I understand.'

'Tell Asanov he's to be in Rostov-on-Don a week tomorrow: Wednesday. He must go to a place in the city centre, near the railway station. It's called the Tsentralny Restaurant, a few yards down from the Moskovskaya Hotel. At one o'clock he's to have lunch there. Then he must walk down Engels Prospekt to the station. Contact will occur in the ticket hall.'

'Will it be you?'

'No, not me.' Smith reached inside his jacket and produced a calf-skin wallet. 'Can you remember all that?'

'I think so.'

The wallet yielded a folded square of notepaper. He handed it to her, saying: 'Don't lose it. Tell him to destroy it as soon as he's remembered the details.'

11

She opened the paper and read aloud: 'Tsentralny Restaurant, near Moskovskaya Hotel.' She glanced up at him. 'There is no date or time.'

'There's too much on paper already. He'll just have to remember the rest.'

'One o'clock, Wednesday – a week tomorrow.' She pocketed the note. 'Rostov is his home town, I think?'

'There's nothing unusual in a man travelling to his birthplace, going home,' Smith said.

'There is when he has no transit documents.' Yelena gave a wan little smile. 'Or have you allowed for that?'

Kovotny coughed. 'I will give you the papers.'

Yelena was silent for a short time, contemplating the stranger. 'It is sad,' she said.

'He's getting out,' Smith responded.

'You would be happy to leave your country?'

'He'll be all right. There are people waiting to welcome him.'

'Perhaps,' she said, slowly, 'they frighten him more than the people here.'

'It's not a police state.'

'You would say that.'

'Because I live there?'

'Because you are one of the policemen.'

She turned to face the front. Before he could speak again, the car slowed, then nosed into a vacant slot in a parking line. Kovotny half turned in his seat. 'Finished?'

'Not quite.'

The Russian frowned. 'Three people in a stationary car. It is conspicuous.'

Smith felt the snap of an irrational anger. 'Then we'll get out and walk. Or is that conspicuous, too?'

'So long as it is not on water.'

The Zhiguli sped away towards the distant onion domes and crenellations of the Church of the Resurrection. He watched the car merge into the embankment traffic, then turned to her.

The pavement was narrow at this point, little more than a kerb-stone's width; although she was petite, delicate almost, there wasn't enough room for both of them side by side, not with his 200-pound frame. Conversation was impossible. Then he realised that she was disinclined to move anyway. She leaned against the waist-high railings and peered down into the dappled waters of the Griboyedov Canal. Without looking up, she said: 'You have something else to tell me?'

'No, I want to ask you something.'

He rested his hands on a granite upright, felt dust and grit against his palms. He thought how curiously muted the traffic noise had become. They were only inches from the embankment road and no more than fifty yards from the busy thoroughfare of the Nevsky intersection. And yet ... it was as though this girl carried the quality of stillness. He studied her, wondering what sort of people were they – these people and their crusades. She was looking down into the water, watching their two images shifting and fracturing in the ripples of the canal.

'Why have you come here?' she asked.

'To help Doctor Asanov.'

'Because he has something to give you?'

'Yes, and because we have something for him.'

Her fingers traced the narrow grid of the railing crosspiece. 'They sent you here just to give me a message?'

'They sent me here to make sure there aren't any mistakes.' He paused. 'I need to know something. This group of yours, the writer –'

'Leonid, you mean?'

'Yes. The man who brought us here used a curious expression. He said Guseinov had "adopted" Asanov.'

'It is one way of saying it.'

'How has he adopted him?'

'Well ... he writes – pamphlets, letters, protesting at the treatment of Piotr. He campaigns for him.'

'Kicks up a fuss – is that it?'

'Yes.'

'Stupid.'

She shrugged. 'Leonid doesn't care.'

'It'll have to stop, now. The man's looking for trouble. Asanov could go down with him. We don't want that to happen.'

'We?'

'His friends.'

'Ah, those.'

'There's only eight days to go.'

She looked at the canal again. 'If I ask Leonid, he will want to know why.'

'Asanov must tell him.'

'The truth?'

'If he does that, nobody'll be going anywhere.'

CHAPTER
TWO

LENINGRAD

Katerina clung to her father's neck, small hands clasped tight. He did a lap of the living room, ran to the door and back again, then stopped so abruptly she tilted forward, legs kicking at the air.

'*Do dna!*' he called.

'*Do dna!*' A childish echo, silvered with laughter.

Tanya said: 'If they could see you now.'

Forty-one years old, but Yevgeni played with schoolyard abandon. The fair hair was close-cropped and the face unlined and the blue eyes went on laughing long after the smile. She thought again on the improbability of the man-boy with the authority of an ultimate command.

She checked her watch. 'It's almost time.'

He looked at her, frowning. Tanya went to Katerina, still in her husband's arms, and kissed her. Katerina shied away: the game was on, the game was not over. '*Do dna!*'

He put the child to bed, the first ritual of departure. Tanya listened at the doorway as he calmed her, heard the words of an old familiar story about a house and a forest and a bear. She listened until the time came when she sensed, intuitively, the fluttering and closing of tired eyelids. She looked in then. He was kneeling by the small bed, arms crossed on his chest, holding the moment close like a treasured photograph.

The Dvin bottle was centred in the silver tray on the fireside table. He raised it to the light in mock inspection, then poured two tumblers. Tanya took hers to the sofa. They sipped in unison, but she broke off, racked by a sudden spasm of coughing.

15

The drink's fragrance belied the furnace within.

'Go safely,' she said.

'I will.'

'Yevgeni, I know what this command means to you.'

'Thank you.' He smiled self-consciously and shifted awkwardly in the chair. 'Well,' he said.

She smiled back. 'You have everything?'

'I hope so.'

'Give Mikhail my love, will you?'

'Of course.'

'Where are you meeting him?'

'In town.' He paused. 'Do you want a lift to school?'

'It's out of your way.'

'We can detour; it isn't far.'

'I hate saying goodbyes in public.'

She turned her head and gazed at the gap in the curtains where night crowded in upon warm glass. He came to her. Pushed the shoulder-length hair aside, felt it passing through his fingers like soft thread. He was not an imaginative man, but the sensation was inescapable: time was a sieve, through which the seconds were leaking slyly away.

Tanya made her own way to school. The classroom was filling with men and women, squeezing awkwardly into the desks of their children. Tanya stood on a dais by the blackboard. She felt self-conscious. The blue two-piece had come from GUM – there were some here who could have dined for a season on its price tag. Chairs scraped and squeaked on thermoplastic flooring. People spoke to each other – some cheerful, others sombre, nervous. She raised her hand and waited impassively for the coughing and the shuffling to cease. Finally there was only her voice, and the fizzling of the fluorescent lights in the high ceiling.

Another ritual, in a day of rituals: a sleepy coupling at dawn; then lunchtime shopping with Katerina, she holding one hand and Yevgeni the other; the Dvin, glasses raised in farewell; the brief, abrasive touch of his dry lips upon hers ... And now this, the routine mid-term evaluation of her twenty-six-strong class. She praised with detachment, but criticised with vigour, keeping the steel in her voice because that was the way it had to be, the way they expected.

Afterwards she intercepted the widower Grobov. 'A word please, about Tolya.'

'Anatoly?'

The child's father, and she had yet to hear him use the diminutive. Grobov was stiff, hard, unyielding, the oldest parent she had to deal with.

'I'm a bit concerned about him.'

'Why?'

'He's playing truant again.' She paused. 'I haven't put him on report. I wanted to speak to you first.'

Grobov rubbed his jaw. Stubble bristled through the permanent stain of foundry grime. 'I'll deal with him.'

'Like before?' She reached out and touched his arm. Muscles tautened beneath the worn cloth of the seven-seasons coat. 'Beating him won't change things.'

'No?'

'No. There's a reason for the way he is. He hasn't yet got over his mother's death.'

'He has had time.'

'Some children need longer. Look, I'd like to arrange a meeting, with a counsellor.'

Grobov laughed. 'A meeting? You think talking will alter him?'

'We have to try.' She paused. 'It can't go on like this. He runs away. You beat him. He runs away again. Nothing's being achieved.'

'He'll learn.' ·

'Tolya will soon be eight. Which school is he transferring to?'

'Work Polytechnic Middle Thirteen.'

'He'll never settle in. He's in no state to cope with yet another change. But if we could all get together, perhaps talk it through ...'

'There is nothing to talk about.'

'I think there is.' She looked into the seamed face, the flint eyes, and felt the heat of her own anger. 'Damn it, man, we're dealing with a highly sensitive child, a very imaginative child. He feels things deeply. D'you know he's the most creative pupil in my class? You've only got to look at his artwork to see the promise.'

'Artwork.' Grobov's contempt was succinct.

She breathed deeply to steady herself. 'I once asked him what he wanted to do, when he was a big boy.'

'So?'

'He said he was going in the army.'

Grobov shrugged. 'Everyone does.'

'Not as a career soldier. But then, you told him that, didn't you? You told him what he was going to be.'

'It will make him a man.'

'He's not even eight years old!'

'I killed my first Nazi when I wasn't much older.'

'But that was then!' She forced herself to hold his gaze. 'That was then.'

'Has it changed?' He shook his head. 'My son will serve his country, as his country serves him.'

'You believe that?'

'Don't you?' Grobov turned away, leaving the question hanging on the air.

Going out of the building when the last parent had departed, Tanya found herself looking at the mural in the school lobby. Soldiers from a Red Army tank regiment seemed to be guarding the Sino-Soviet border. They were young and tall and very, very handsome. A Chinese combat unit peered at them through a bamboo barrier. The Chinese had open mouths with pointed teeth, slits instead of eyes, and faces of the brightest yellow. The caption read:

> Heroic Soldiers Of The Glorious Soviet People's Army Protect And Defend Us With Ceaseless Vigilance And Unflinching Courage.

Artwork, she thought.

MURMANSK

Yevgeni Ivanitsyn's command waited in the sparkling water, primary generators humming and small wavelets slapping lightly at its titanium shanks. Mikhail Voronikhin stood beside Yevgeni in thoughtful silence, letting his gaze travel slowly over her.

The specification read: Class 661 (Bolshaya), hull number 372; Podvodnaya Lodka Atomnaya Raketnaya Ballisticheskaya - Krylataya; length overall - 160 metres; beam - 18 metres; draught - 9 metres; power - nuclear reactor, steam turbines, twin five-bladed props; complement - 120; electronics - radar (Snoop Tray Model 2), sonar (Whisper, Low Frequency), radio (Zorki-Panaskaya, trawled VLF); armaments - SLICBM, SSN18 (six), SLIRBM, SSNX 22 (eight).

18

Specifications, Voronikhin thought. There is everything on those sheets of paper, and yet there is nothing about her beauty, her strength. Nothing about the men who will make her their mistress.

He glanced at Yevgeni, wondering if he was experiencing the same disturbing mix of emotions, then looked away again.

She filled her pen, towered above it, the sail rising smooth and ebony and threatening. Her sheer size seemed to argue against mobility, yet soon she would outpace the currents, would swoop and turn and soar. Only for a little while longer would she remain becalmed, at rest in a cold haven 200 kilometres north of the Arctic Circle.

'Ready?' Yevgeni asked.

'Almost.' He shook his head. 'She's beautiful, though.'

'You and your women.' Yevgeni smiled.

Voronikhin considered him anew. 'You don't see her like that, do you?'

'Sorry, no.'

'I don't suppose it matters.'

They stepped down from the quay: Mikhail Voronikhin, thirty-nine, newly appointed first officer; Yevgeni Ivanitsyn, forty-one, newly appointed captain.

A benevolent sun warmed the day, lightening his mood as the submarine slid by the squadron pens of Polyarno. Images of Tanya and Katerina still lingered upon the inner eye, but the pain of separation was easing now, receding in the quiet swirl of wake.

The wind plucked at him as he ascended the first observer platform, high up the sail. He stared ahead, oblivious of the cold wind that raced the gulls in from the Baltic. Beyond the prow, the pilot ship steamed sluggishly, a fat grey shepherd tending a flock of one.

Rigging for dive lasted an inordinately lengthy fifteen minutes. Voronikhin mocked: 'What are you, a bridegroom?'

'It's hard the first time.'

'That's what I meant.'

'Ho, ho, ho.' Shevelev hunched further over the console in a gesture of dismissal. He thumbed the solenoids, watched unblinking as duplicated read-outs flashed across the narrow faces of the VDUs. Check sums ran to base as memory parameters computed degree of incidence against relative deadweight. Behind the shimmering glass sequential totalizers spun and held, freezing one number after another until the read-out was static.

He massaged his neck. They had made twelve knots surface passage, using forward scanning to chart a course around the ragged shoulder of the Cape. Now they were going to submerge, and he wanted it smooth and good – that was why the calculus of compensation seemed to be taking forever. Compensation was critical because a miscalculation could make a shambles of the dive mode. Even though he was enfolded by a reliable technology, the spectre of a botched dive refused to budge; going up-bubble, being dragged by the bow weight; down-bubble, being sunk by the stern.

The computer was supposed to mastermind valve flow and ballast ingress, but even so, a computer was fallible because a programmer was fallible, and if it went wrong now there wouldn't be much point in blaming a technician or a wayward microprocessor. Shevelev still believed that if you did not build it then you did not trust it.

Talking ceased. The control room became a tableau – no movement apart from the flexing fingers of the fore and aft planesmen.

Yevgeni descended the surface navigation bridge. Hatch slammed, portal lock spun. The all-stations intercom voiced a final litany: signals, sonar, reactor, fire control, engineering, control room – secure, all secure. Vents opened, flow-rates flashed on monitors, systems telemetry duplicated tumbling figures in rhythmic repetition: check, cross-check, repeat and confirm.

Check and cross-check as the sea rushed into the tanks and positive buoyancy yielded to negative; repeat and confirm as the hull eased down, slowly, gently, beginning to plane, without noise, without fuss.

The waves boiled briefly, then closed over her and denied her existence.

LENINGRAD

Leonid Guseinov's apartment was on the north side of the city, in a residential zone bisected by Primorski Prospekt. Tanya took a centre service to Nevsky, stood indecisively on the wide pavement as the doors hissed shut and the bus juddered away towards Uprising Square. A connection was due at any moment, but she decided to walk for a while and let the air clear her head, lighten her mood.

She skirted Palace Square. Behind her the vast flanks of the Admiralty stretched back in an infinity of shining columns, its stonework golden in the spotlights. Sugar-white doors glistened like the decorations of some impossible confection.

The soft breeze bore the prickly smell of the river. It reminded her of the open sea. Yevgeni would be sailing now. Yevgeni – his was a different world to this set-piece of Czarist empire, this place of palaces and porticoes and floodlit grandeur. She experienced a momentary envy as she moved among the Saturday-night strollers. It was always like this when he went away: the mood lay heavy throughout the first full day of separation.

The Palace Bridge parted to allow the passage of a warship, a shadowy leviathan pierced by hard white lights. It slid by in sonorous majesty, engines humming and bells clanging as the ground vibrated under her feet. She watched it pass, until the bright spangled waters had shivered and calmed, and smoothed back into blackness.

A cab took her to the heart of Leonid's neighbourhood of eight-storey apartment blocks dressed with balconies and window-boxes and television aerials that sprouted like chimney brushes from the flat roofs. She rode the elevator to the fifth floor, registering with surprise the fact that it was working again. In Russia you had full employment because someone built something in the morning, someone else sold it in the afternoon, and then a third person came along at night to repair it.

He squinted against the harsh brightness of the corridor lighting, examined the hallway again, then closed and locked the door behind them.

'Hello, Leonid.'

'Tanya.'

She slipped off her coat, tossed it onto the sofa. His embrace was tight, hungry; it squeezed them together, gauntness against fullness, hard upon soft. She kissed his cheek.

The apartment was cramped and untidy. Papers spilled across the threadbare hearth rug. Books tumbled in disarray over cushions. The furniture pointed up the disorder: an old table, painted white; a typewriter of pre-war vintage; a misshapen sofa; and two armchairs of indiscernible design and uncertain solace.

She smiled. 'I see you've been tidying up.'

'Good help is hard to find.'

She held his hand, so narrow, so feminine. Her grip tightened around his long fingers. He freed himself, cupped her jaw, and considered her silently for a moment. 'Come on, I don't see you for months and then ... Why so miserable?'

'Bad Day at Black Rock.' She moved to the couch, pushed the books aside and sat down. 'I tell myself it's stupid, the little woman left behind, but ... It's having to get used to it again, you know?'

'You never struck me as the little woman left behind.' He smiled. 'Anyway. Happy New Year.'

Her eyes widened with surprise. 'God, Leonid. It's not been that long, surely.'

'Mid-December. I marked the calendar.'

'Liar.'

They both laughed. 'So,' he said. 'How've you been?'

'Fine. And you?'

'Top of the world.' The smile broadened. 'And how's the family?'

'They're well.' She paused. 'How are Vadim and Yelena?'

'A half-hour earlier and you'd have seen for yourself. They were both here. It's Vadim's birthday so he brought me a present.'

'Would you repeat that?'

'I hadn't anything to give him, so he gave something to me.' Guseinov paused for effect and pointed at a box on the table: 'Ballpoint pens – he swapped a batch of faulty fridge thermostats for them.'

'I don't know, the *fartsovshchiki*.'

'They're good pens,' Guseinov said. 'You can have a few for school.'

'School.' She grimaced. 'Don't mention the word.'

'It's only a job.'

'It's supposed to be more than that.' She lit a cigarette and drew deep. 'It was family night last night. Fatstock night.'

'Ouch.'

'Big cow eyes, everywhere. Nobody speaks because nobody dares. Just big cow eyes, staring.'

'You're an authority figure.'

'Don't I know it.'

He was silent for a time, seemingly touched by her mood. Then, as if on impulse, he said: 'Hey, heard the one about the grandfather in 2001?'

She feigned a weary resignation. 'Go on.'

'He's telling his little grandson what it was like in the bad old days. He says: "You're lucky, my boy, you weren't around when there were shortages, when you had to queue for everything." His grandson says: "What's a queue?" "Well, you don't see them nowadays, but years ago people had to stand in line for hours, in a queue. I once queued half a day for a few grams of butter." And his grandson says: "What's butter?"'

Their laughter joined, then slowly subsided. She smoothed the pleats of her skirt and clasped her hands together. 'Well? Are you going to offer me a drink?'

'Can you wait? There's another guest.' He smiled. 'Busy night, eh?'

'What other guest?'

'Piotr Asanov. You haven't met him, he only arrived in January.' Guseinov paused. 'Used to be at Moscow Physico-Technical until they dismissed him and took away his *propiska*.'

'He's lecturing in Leningrad then?'

'No, they've stopped him doing that, too. Anyway, he's calling round tonight – left a note under the door while I was away.'

'You've been ... away?'

'Moscow.' His gaze shifted from her, towards the wall. 'The Writers' Union.'

'The appeal?'

'They turned me down.'

'Oh no ...' A soft, despairing cadence. 'Oh no, Leonid ...'

'They won't forgive the Galanskov piece. Maybe I should've celebrated Sholokhov's anniversary instead.'

'They can't stop you from writing.'

'They can stop me from being published. I had hoped for an audience of more than one.'

Tanya began to tidy the room while he busied himself in the kitchenette, belatedly washing the breakfast crockery. Eventually he returned, saying: 'He's really a scientist, you know, Piotr – audio-electronics. But then he got involved in the refusenik thing.'

'Is he Jewish?'

'No, but he has a Jewish friend, mathematician; the man's been having a bad time of it, what with Pontryagin and everything. So he decided to get out, go to Israel. You can guess the rest.'

She punched ineffectually at a cushion; it refused to assume any identifiable shape. He saw the expression on her face. 'Piotr knows no one here. I have to help.'

She turned away. Anger, explicit yet inexplicable, eddied around her. 'Land of the blind,' she said, and shook her head. 'Land of the blind, Leonid. And you with the one eye.'

He shook his head in slow denial, began to fashion the words of rebuttal. And then Asanov arrived.

She had expected someone small, shabby – a diminutive figure in a suit two sizes too big, someone dressed in shapeless serge, shirt frayed at the collar, and worn, dull shoes. She had expected the darting glance of the fugitive and a bearing that spoke, at best, of a futile dignity.

Instead: tall, confident, blue eyes, astonishingly blue. High forehead swept by wayward wisps of straw-coloured hair. A face of pleasing proportion, the skin naturally tanned. Forty? Fifty? Difficult to tell because the smile was wide and welcoming, and the eyes, the eyes were shining. She wondered how Leonid could be of help to a man like this.

'Doctor Asanov.' Guseinov closed the door behind them.

'Please –' he spoke in a warm baritone, rich with good humour – 'my name is Piotr. And this, Leonid, this is?'

'Doctor Melnikova.'

She smiled in return. 'Please, Tanya.'

With unexpected courtesy, he bent his head, took her hand and kissed it. 'Tanya,' he said.

They sat down, facing each other across the crowded room while Leonid went to make tea.

'I remember,' Asanov said, 'Leonid speaking of you.'

'He has an infinite capacity for slander.'

Asanov smiled. He patted the pockets of the dark brown cord jacket and extricated a tobacco pouch and pipe. 'You are the teacher, no?'

'I'm a teacher.'

'What is your field?'

'Educational psychology. But I made the mistake of leaving the bunker and going to the front.'

'I used to work with children,' he said. 'Deaf children, actually – it was a research programme.' He lit the pipe without fuss. 'But I'm no educator. I couldn't do your job.'

'Leonid said something about . . . audio-electronics? Have I got it right?'

'Dreadful, isn't it? I go to a party and people expect me to mend their record player.'

'You're safe enough here, then. It's a priest Leonid needs.'

They both laughed.

'You're a friend of Leonid's?' Asanov asked.

'Yes.'

'He is a good man.'

Tanya nodded.

'A good writer. I'll be sorry to . . .' Asanov broke off. She waited, but he didn't resume. There was some emotion in his eyes which she couldn't define. His gaze was still on her, but she had the strange feeling she had somehow slipped from focus.

Guseinov returned with a tray bearing tea and three glasses of vodka. 'Everyone all right?'

'I was singing your praises,' Asanov said.

'Louder, louder!' Guseinov tried to manoeuvre the typewriter aside. The tray wobbled precariously on his right palm. She moved to help him.

An insistent fist pounded the apartment door. The frame shivered and woodwork splintered with a deafening crack as a boot went in hard upon the lock.

THE NORTH CAPE

Yevgeni's status was sufficient to merit a respectable minimum of furnishings, yet concession to rank was grudging because living space aboard a submarine was a low priority. Function dictated design. If it worked then it had a place. If not, well . . . The captain's function was in the control room, not his cabin.

He brushed past the edge of the small mahogany desk, glanced fleetingly at the framed photographs of Tanya and Katerina that flanked the miniature bronze cast of the Kremlin Tower. Bought at an airport shop a long time ago, it had been intended for Katerina, yet had somehow stayed with him – a sort of good-luck totem that had not played him false.

He undressed, struggled into the narrow bed and curled up into the foetal position, luxuriating in the softness, the growing warmth. His thoughts meandered as memory revisited the events of the day, then looped back to this small, still place and thence beyond, to the humming, vibrating metropolis all around, the strange steel city inhabited by 120 freemen of the deep.

A remarkable community, peopled by both the fair-skinned northerners and those with the dark complexion of the central Asiatics, a place where men from the woodless tundra of the Arctic shroud found themselves exchanging family photographs with comrades who knew only the blistering heat of Turkmenia and the pitiless skies above the Kara Kum. Men like Svenchsky, nursing his turbines on a journey that would take him far from the mines of the Ukraine; yet not so far as Tahl, who grew up in the Uzhbek cotton fields, or Solokov at SINS, whose childhood navigations had been through the lemon groves of Georgia. So many men, so vast a country – a land where grapes ripened in the Moldavian sun, yet where even the thermometer froze in the long Yakutian winter.

The men from my country, Ivanitsyn thought. Mine. All her people and all her republics and all her songs. My country, with its faults and its failings, but it gave what it could and you took what it offered and the bargain was struck, the bond unbreakably forged: country and countryman, the Russian and his home.

He passed into sleep with the ease of a child, unafraid, untroubled, assured of his world, and of his place within it.

CHAPTER
THREE

LENINGRAD

They were returned to Leonid's apartment late on Sunday morning. They travelled in two militia cars – Tanya in one, Leonid in the other. Twelve hours had elapsed since their arrest; he was astonished that freedom should have been granted so soon, and even more amazed that their captors should provide a door-to-door service to get them home.

He made tea for them, then righted the upturned table; they sat across from one another. He hazarded a weak joke: 'Good job I don't shave.' He touched the long wispy beard with shaking fingers.

She looked away. The beard irritated her; she thought he was a good enough writer without aping Solzhenitsyn.

'What time is it?' she asked.

'Eleven, near enough.'

He sipped the glass of tea. It had gone cold. It should have stayed warm, but then, the glass should have been warmed first. There seemed to be a lot of such thoughts, irrelevancies piled up in the confusion of being back here in the shattered apartment. He reached out, took her hand and said: 'You mustn't worry, Tanya.'

'I have to go.' She felt as if there was a great dam of words within her, waiting to burst. She risked the same four again, pacing them, testing their weight. 'I have to go.'

'All right.'

'They shouldn't have brought me here. Katerina, the sitter – they're still waiting.' Her lower lip trembled. 'This is not my home.'

She closed her eyes. On the retina seared a stark white oblong: the midnight room. The midnight room with its rough-hewn walls and table and chairs and the man sitting opposite her writing it all down

27

... I know your father, Tanya Melnikova. By reputation, of course, not personally, you understand. He has been notified. I think he is in touch right now ...

'Tanya?'

She jolted in the chair. Concern was etched with frightening clarity into the pale, taut flesh of his face. 'I'm all right,' she said.

'Sure?'

'Yes.' A moment's silence, then: 'Leonid, stay away from Asanov. He's the reason they came last night.'

'Not true.' Leonid shook his head. 'The *upravdom* was earning his bonus, that's all. Told them I had a duplicating machine.' A fleeting smile of triumph passed across his features. 'Yelena's the one with access to a photocopier, not me.' He paused. 'Funny, how terrified they are of the printed word.'

After a while she said: 'Why wasn't he released with us?'

'I don't know.'

'They still have him?'

'Either that or he was out first.'

'I don't understand why you have to get involved like this.'

He sighed. 'I met him through one of Yelena's student friends. He told me about this refusenik business. I offered to help.' He spoke briskly: 'Look, he was living in a scruffy hotel, hoping his savings would last till summer so that when they finally threw him out at least the air would be warm. He was alone and lost and it didn't seem to me he should be left that way.'

'So what did you do then?'

'He showed me what he'd written, his ... protest. I polished it up and sent it to *Literaturnaya Gazeta*.'

'And?'

'Nothing. Same with the Academy. I wrote complaining of his treatment and that of his Jewish friend.' He paused. 'They're going to make him a non-person, Tanya.'

She said, quietly: 'Like they're going to make you.'

The sitter had left a note: *Can't wait any longer, have taken Katerina home with me.* Guilt and relief were still convulsing her when she heard the sirens.

She glanced at her wristwatch. Three o'clock. Her father hadn't taken long.

He stood in the centre of the room, a tall, elegant figure in a tailored camel coat, a distinctive mane of silver hair framing the almost leonine features. But the face was haggard, and the grey eyes brimmed with pain.

She looked away, not wanting to see him like this. But the anger and confusion were a brooding presence, pervading and enveloping everything in the room. Wherever she looked she saw her father's face.

'It doesn't make sense,' he repeated.

She had gone to the sofa after letting him in, and hadn't moved since. A cigarette smouldered in the ashtray beside her. Another, between her fingers, trailed a chain of smoke. She looked up at him. He kept rubbing his hands together, as though the skin was cold or dirty.

'I told you,' she said. 'He's just a friend.'

'Who? The second-rate story-teller or the failed electrician?'

'Please.'

Melnikov took a pace towards her. 'Don't you see how it looks? A married woman – in another man's apartment?'

'It wasn't like that.'

'No?' He placed the heel of the palm against his forehead and massaged the flesh with unwarranted ferocity. 'Damn it, child! What did you think you were doing?'

She didn't speak.

'It'll be all over Moscow by now,' he said. He seemed suddenly aware that he hadn't yet taken off his coat. Fingers plucked clumsily at the buttons, as though co-ordination had become inexplicably difficult. He cast the coat down at the end of the sofa, then eased himself into the fireside armchair. He stared at her for a long time, but she did not meet his gaze.

Eventually he said: 'Remember Brezhnev's daughter? Galina? Well, of course you do. You used to know her. That started out in a small way, too. But would they give up? No. And why? Because of who she was, not what she may or may not have done.'

'The KGB aren't involved, Father.'

'They weren't that time, either. At least, not at the beginning. Later on though, well; that soon changed, didn't it?' He broke off, as though mute with disbelief, then continued: 'Can you imagine it, the pressure on them to stop? Even Chernenko got off his arse for once, not that that made a lot of difference. No, they outflanked him all right. Enlisted the Chiefs of Staff – very quiet, very discreet, but very

29

safe. After all, everyone knew what Ustinov thought, and not just Ustinov. It seemed to me the entire Red Army despised Leonid Brezhnev.'

Tanya said quietly: 'I don't see what this has to do with me.'

But he wasn't listening. 'The price of vanity,' he said, and smiled at the irony. 'Brezhnev decorated himself with more medals in a month than Ustinov saw in a lifetime.'

'Father.' She spoke more loudly this time. 'None of this has anything to do with me.'

'You think not.' He replied flatly. 'Galina Brezhnev was arrested for diamond smuggling before her father's body was cold.'

'Because they had a case against her.'

'They had a case against everyone, child. She merely provided the ... opportunity.'

Tanya frowned. 'What are you trying to say?'

'That more goes on in Moscow than you could ever imagine, that's what I'm trying to say.' He continued to stare at her for a few more moments, then abruptly pushed himself out of the chair. He went to the window and stood with his back to her. His hand touched the folds of the curtain, then slowly fell to his side – an absent, meaningless gesture. When he spoke again, the words were somehow muted, the voice curiously distant.

'I am a member of the First Chamber of the Supreme Soviet, a senior deputy with a quarter of a million constituents. When called upon, I advise the Central Committee. There isn't anything I don't know and there isn't anyone I cannot reach.' He paused. 'I spent my life, working for that.'

She waited through an infinity of silence.

He turned then, and this time the words were almost inaudible. 'Why, Tanya? Why?'

She didn't reply, stood up instead and went into the kitchen. There she made two glasses of tea, spooned fruit jelly into his and squeezed half a lemon into her own. When she returned to the lounge he was standing near the door, studying the hazy perspectives of the framed painting. Sea and sky merged into one, drawing him in, bearing him away.

'Is this new?'

'I bought it for our anniversary.' She set the tray down. 'It's by Isaac Levitan.'

'It's like an Impressionist.' He nodded in approval, then turned and glanced about the room. 'You have taste.'

'Thank you.'

'Your mother was the same.'

They drank the tea in silence. Eventually he looked at his watch. 'Katerina isn't coming back yet?'

'Sorry. She's gone to a birthday party – one of her little friends.'

'I'll miss her then.'

'You could stay.'

'There's always a lot to do on Monday. I'll have to get back.'

She ground out her cigarette with slow, unnecessary ceremony. 'Father.'

'Yes?'

'I'm sorry.'

'These things happen.' He paused. 'Once I was your age, too.'

She looked down at her lap and tried to shut it out – the knowing smile, the weary condescension; tried to stall the conversation before its impetus endangered them anew. She squeezed her eyes tight shut, but within the soft red darkness was an oblong bar of harsh white light, spinning nearer, growing bigger: the midnight room, the coldness. And now the noise dinned again: a boot against the door, the room filling with strangers, loud voices, brutal hands, her arm being wrenched behind her as they smashed the table, the chairs, and then one of them lifted up the typewriter and threw it down hard upon the floor. The platen sheared from its mountings and rolled away. *Funny how terrified they are of the printed word.*

Melnikov said: 'You see things differently when you are young.'

She opened her eyes, finding it impossible now to hold back, to conspire in the creation of a convenient delusion: 'That has nothing to do with it!' She felt the pressure of a quickening pulse: 'They came in like savages! They filled the place with their uniforms and their hate!'

'Tanya ... you're still upset. It's only natural to –'

'Will you stop patronising me? Please? Will you stop doing that?' Tears blurred her vision. 'I am not a child. And I never – understand? – never did anything wrong!'

Anger began to eddy around him. 'Yes, well, that's what you think.'

'I don't think. I know!'

'You know?' He was half out of the chair now, fingers splayed wide across the upholstered arms. 'Yes. Of course you do. Your

31

generation, it knows everything. Why? Because it has everything: food, warmth, shelter, luxuries, paintings on the wall, a fridge in the kitchen, a bathroom. And not one room or two rooms but five, five-room apartments! Oh you know all right. You know everything.'

He got out of the chair, seemed ready to confront her, then turned away. 'Your grandparents died here, during the Long Siege. Your grandmother froze to death in a cellar. The last thing she ate was a rat, because that's all that was left to eat in Leningrad. My father, my mother, my brothers, my baby sister; and one and a half million just like them, one and a half million people in this city, dead ...'

She shook her head. 'That's history.'

'No food, no fuel. All the pretty wooden houses – we had to destroy them, just to keep the fires burning.

'I watched my father and my brothers take an axe to my home. The wood went onto the carts. The horses hauled them away, and then there was nothing left of where I used to be.' He turned to her. 'That isn't history, child. That's ... family.'

'But what does it have to do with now?'

'Everything!' He drove his right fist violently into his left palm. 'The enemy was at the gates then and the enemy is still at the gates now. But I tell you something: that is where he stays. He does not come in. You do not bring him in!'

'Is that ...' She stopped. 'Is that how you see me? Some sort of – traitor?'

She went to him and halted so close that their eyes burned into each other's. No movement, only the raging stillness of two un-comprehending combatants, their fast shallow breaths harsh upon the silence.

Finally he stepped aside. Slowly, quietly, he said: '"But know all, listening to these stones: that no one, and nothing, has been forgotten ..."'

She crossed the room with purposeful strides, rummaged through the walnut bureau and returned with a crumpled newspaper cutting. 'Here. Quote that as well.'

He took it from her and stared blankly at the text.

'What d'you think of that, Father?' She stood with hands on hips, head to one side. The challenge and the mockery brought pain and ugliness to her face. 'Amazing, isn't it? The findings of one of Russia's foremost psychologists.'

He didn't respond.

'Read it, Father, go on. It's all about kids – adolescents. Well, you know what they're like, don't you? They get into trouble. They rebel. But it's just a phase. Or is it? Not according to that, oh no. According to that, adolescent behaviour isn't to do with glands or hormones at all. It's caused by something totally different – a strange, secret force. The force of – can you guess? – the force of ... International Masonry! Which is itself part of the even bigger Zionist Imperialist Conspiracy! That's the cause of juvenile delinquency, Father. The Zionists aim a raygun at our children's brains!'

'Where is this from?' Melnikov said.

'*Komsomolskaya Pravda.*' She shook her head. 'Dear God. Twenty-three million children in the Young Communists, and that's their official newspaper. Hey, girls and boys! Watch out, watch out! There's a Jew about!'

He returned the cutting to her without comment.

'Don't talk to me about enemies of the people,' she said, 'when tomorrow you'll make them heroes of the Union.'

That night, as though to disprove the falsehood of a promised spring, winter spread its heavy cape of silence. She awoke to find that the colours of April had fled with the dawn, leaving only a whiteness, spectral and cold.

At lunchtime Tanya took the Metro out to Gorskovskaya Station, emerged with eyes narrowed against the sharp daylight of Lenin Park. Beyond the curve of the snow meadows, larch and beech marched with rigid tread along Kirovsky Prospekt towards the nearby islands. Her gaze followed the tree-line, thoughts flowing alongside, bringing half-forgotten images of Yelagin Isle, the summer celebrations, Yevgeni and Katerina and herself and the bags of roast chestnuts and the band playing and the June evening filled with the noise of the crowds, the seasonal festival of the White Nights of Leningrad.

She plunged into the snow and struck out towards the woodland north of the zoological gardens. Her gaze momentarily fastened upon the heroic architecture of the Stereguschi Memorial. The destroyer's crew had scuttled her in 1904 after a brave single-handed fight against a war fleet of the Imperial Japanese Navy. She angled away from it, wondering why such things were built. They were supposed to be monuments to courage and glory, not the granite guardians of ever-present fears.

She saw Leonid then, his black silhouette seemingly imprinted upon the snowscape like a spindly stick-man, a child's drawing upon a white page.

They found a seat by a rank of fir. He tried to brush it down, but the snow stuck to his gloves. He slapped his hands together and the sound rang out like a pistol shot.

'So much for April,' he said, and smiled. 'I take it, it *is* April.'

'The eighteenth.'

He shook his head. 'The Neva's freezing up again, too. Anyway ... how long've you got?'

'Half an hour.'

'Ah, the joys of full employment.' He laughed.

She studied him thoughtfully. It was impossible to divine his mood. The heartiness jarred and the carefree briskness rang as false as a cracked bell. And then: 'Piotr ...'

She frowned. 'What about him?'

'He's out.'

'He's free?'

Guseinov shrugged. 'Well, he's gone, certainly. I checked this morning. His room's been cleared out and the hotel say they've no idea where he is. He collected his things yesterday afternoon – left in a car with another man.'

She said carefully: 'That doesn't mean ... You know.'

'Doesn't mean anything. Piotr's lots of friends with cars in Leningrad.'

She glanced up at the sky. Sunlight was beginning to filter through, growing stronger with every moment. 'I'm sorry, Leonid.'

'Hey. At least he's got his clothes. In weather like this, a man could die of cold.' He hooked his arm through hers, squeezed them together. 'Don't worry about it, all right?'

A large bird circled the tops of some distant spruce. She watched it in silence, then shifted position, boot heels making short furrows in the snow. 'What will you do now, Leonid?'

'Whatever.' He made a light, dismissive gesture, then turned his head away from her. She suddenly experienced the irrational feeling that they were strangers at a masque, and that he had turned away because the disguise was slipping, that his true identity was about to be revealed.

'Chip chip chip.' The words came out as soft and sibilant as a snowfall, hardly any emphasis, devoid of emotion. 'Chip chip chip.'

'Leonid?'

He still didn't look at her. 'Some they shoot, others they club. Still others they use ice-picks – small, sharp. Chip, chip, chip. I can't write. I can't teach. I can't work. I can't earn a living at anything. Every day they've chipped a little bit more off me.' He chuckled, a sound unnerving in its humourlessness. 'I'm awaiting final demolition.'

'Look, if you take it steady for a while, don't provoke them ...'

'I exist. That's provocation enough.'

She tried again. 'Let the others do something for a change. You've a lot of friends. What about Yelena?'

'She's too busy.'

'Vadim, then.'

'Vadim?' His incredulous laugh soared and echoed. 'Vadim? Come on, Tanya. Vadim's a villain. You know it, I know it. Vadim isn't interested in human rights or refuseniks or Helsinki or anything. He only got involved with us because it's fun, it's stone-throwing at the Establishment.'

'And you aren't doing that?'

'No.'

'Then why get involved?'

'Because I live here.'

'So do millions of other people.'

'They don't seem to know that.' His gaze scoured her, then slowly softened. 'But ...' He reached out, placed his hands upon her shoulders. 'If we keep on, if we keep saying, keep doing ...' The sunlight was growing, bringing to his eyes a look she had never before seen, dark yet bright, shining with a disturbingly messianic intensity. 'My life touches yours, Tanya, yours touches another's – action and reaction, on and on, reaching out, linking up ...'

'I don't ...' She faltered.

'Connections, Tanya. Believe in them. Believe you're not the last human being on this earth, believe there are others, scattered across who knows where. Believe that what you think and feel and do is important, has a meaning. Because one day it's going to happen. And everything will be changed ...'

*   *   *

35

He came, unannounced, at 2.30 p.m. that Wednesday afternoon, stood, politely, by the staff-room table, awaiting the invitation to sit down.

His suit was Western, a medium-weight pinstripe; the shoes were Italian, or a very good Polish copy. He was tall and athletic, with sleek dark hair, an easy smile and a soft, light voice. The only thing wrong was the bronze lenses of the gold-framed spectacles – opaque, impenetrable.

She recognised him even though she had never seen or heard of him before. The midnight man had finally caught up with the midnight room.

His head turned from side to side, the lenses sweeping the narrow, cluttered room, picking up images of chairs and cushions and notice-boards, coats and coat-pegs, files and filing cabinets.

'I'm sorry for the interruption,' he said. 'Your job is very impor-tant. I will keep this intrusion to the minimum.'

She tried to see through the lenses, but registered only herself, in double vision. 'How can I help you, comrade ...'

'Monakhov.'

'You're from the police?'

'I'm from Moscow.'

'Ah.'

'I have some questions, Doctor Melnikova.' He smiled apologetic-ally. 'I hope you don't mind.'

'If it's about last Saturday night,' Tanya said, then stopped. It was unnerving, talking to your own image.

'It's partly about that. But also I wish to ask you some questions about Doctor Piotr Asanov.'

'Oh, in that case ...' She watched the reflection of her smile, then turned away. For some reason it was important not to display any emotion before this man: happiness, sadness, anxiety or, as now, relief. She could not divine the logic; it was as though the place where you lived, inside, needed to be kept locked and shuttered whenever he was around. 'I didn't know him,' she said. 'I only met him for the first time on Saturday.'

'At the apartment of Leonid Guseinov.'

'Yes.'

'So he was Guseinov's friend?'

'Yes.'

'And had they known each other long?'

36

'I . . . I really can't say.' Her throat was suddenly dry. Cognizance had come belatedly, but now she was suddenly aware of the man's total immobility. It impeded thought and speech alike. He sat there as cold and still and stiff as a well-dressed mannequin.

She tried again: 'I think they met in January.'

She breathed in, waited for her nerves to calm. 'Why are you asking me about Doctor Asanov?'

'I thought you knew him.'

'I meant, why don't you go and ask him yourself?'

'Ask him what?'

'Whatever it is you wish to know.' Careful, Tanya, careful. Do not risk a duel when he has the choice of weapons.

'I can't locate him,' Monakhov said.

'But I thought . . .'

'Yes?'

'You still had him.'

'I had him?'

'The authorities.'

'Why did you think that, Doctor Melnikova?'

'Leonid said . . .'

She was blundering on towards the edge of the quicksands, and stopped just in time, but the sentence sprawled on even so. She was fearful without knowing why, because if Piotr Asanov had gone off in a car, well then, what was the harm in saying so?

'Leonid said what?' Monakhov asked gently.

'That he'd been detained.' She hesitated. 'He wasn't released with us on Sunday morning.'

'So you assumed he was still in custody.'

'Yes.'

Monakhov was silent for a time, then he said quietly, without emphasis: 'Where is Piotr Asanov?'

'I told you . . .'

'You told me he was still in custody.'

'Leonid said he was.'

'You believed that?'

'Why shouldn't I?'

Another pause, as lengthy as the last, then Monakhov said: 'Leonid Guseinov is also missing.'

'Missing?'

'He is not at his apartment.'

'You've been there?'

'Yes.'

'When? When did you call?'

'An hour ago.'

Relief flooded over her. 'An hour? Well, I hardly think that makes him a candidate for the missing-persons list.'

'Perhaps not,' Monakhov said.

'Leonid often goes out.'

'Where?'

'I don't know.'

'Yet you do know it is often.'

She sighed. 'Look, comrade . . .' Weariness had finally supervened. 'I don't know where he is. I don't know where he goes. But I imagine he may go out fairly frequently. He is not a prisoner.'

The glasses shone fixedly at her. 'Today,' Monakhov said, 'today is Wednesday, April the twentieth. Doctor Asanov was released at noon on Sunday, April the seventeenth.'

'What of it?'

'From then until now there has been no sign of him.'

She frowned. 'Is it important?'

'It is ... untidy.'

'People aren't always where you expect them to be.' She stood up briskly. 'I can't think of anything else that would assist you.'

Monakhov remained immobile, confronting the space where she had sat. Again she experienced the unsettling eeriness of his lack of animation. Eventually he got up from the chair and made a slight, formal bow. It was so unexpected she could not hide her surprise.

'I'll be in touch,' he said.

MOSCOW

A hesitant wind came off the Moskva. The faint green waters ran before it, slapping against the granite cladding of the high embankment. Areas of snow still lingered, but it was nothing like as cold as he had expected. The air was warm. It brought a smile to the face of the grey capital.

Leonid Guseinov stood with his back to the river and stared beyond the winking traffic lights on Kremlovskaya Naberezhnaya towards the vastness of Red Square. The nearest round tower was but a few feet away, rearing up from the barren verge. Its red-bricked girth seemed massively disdainful. He crossed the road and climbed the stepped pavement edging the perimeter, clutching the hold-all to him. He walked quickly.

A group of tourists clustered around the Minin and Pozharsky Monument. Beyond them, a predictable queue had formed against the Kremlin Wall, its tail-end trailing past the Spassikaya. The gate was dominated by a Gothic tower, with a great clock affixed to the third tier like some giant cartwheel. From here the Kremlin Chimes had pealed out over the last empire. The sightseers craned their necks and squinted against the sky's brightness. For a second, he wanted to stand with them, partake in their levity.

So much *room* – too much of it. They said two *million* people had gathered here for the 1947 anniversary.

He went on towards the mad extravaganza of St Basil's Cathedral, an eruption of pyrotechnic flamboyance: towers shaped like onions, with swirls of green on yellow skin; spheres of rainbow hue with bright serrated spirals; strange confections like whipped cream oozing out of the pink masonry; and finally the central structure, a slender pillar ascending in a succession of unfolding petals, topped by an orb of gold. He hoped God was not colour blind.

A few more steps, just a few more. He stopped, unzipped the bag and set it down on the paving. He took out the home-made banner. Two people were supposed to stretch it out between them, but it didn't matter.

He spread it on the ground and anchored it with the bag.

SOCIALSIM YES GULAG NO
LET THE REFUSENIKS GO HOME

The breeze worried at the frayed edging. He sat down cross-legged and took from the bag a small placard which repeated the words on the banner. He looped the string over his head.

His gaze returned to the people at the Kremlin Wall. The queue moved slowly and silently towards the truncated pyramid of the Mausoleum, where slabs of marble stood out like veined glass amid the blocks of brown granite. The inscription above the bronze doors was picked out in imperial purple.

One word, the colour of emperors, and of God.

A convoy of black limousines emerged from the gateway beneath the Nikolskaya Tower. Red Square was supposed to be traffic-free, but certain vehicles had the run of the place.

He was certain they had seen him. Still, there was probably a little time remaining in which to absorb the world, to soak up its images – a little time to let the mind roam free, because there was sunshine and fresh air ...

Even after all these years, you could still buy meat pie with cucumber from the vendor in Revolution Square Metro. He smiled at the thought.

He examined the faces of the people coming towards him: white, contorted with anger. His life was his only currency, but all he could count was the small change of experience: meat pies with cucumber in Revolution Square.

The faces came nearer.

Laugh, Leonid, laugh.

ROSTOV-ON-DON

He reached the Voroshilovski Bridge and paused to watch the river swirl and foam around the central arches. He had made his way along the wide boulevard of Novocherkaskaya, stopping off at the small and dusty tobacconist's on Engels Prospekt. He still carried its scent: old, dark, sweet.

He studied the bridge, and thought of crossings, from one side to the other.

The river pursued a ragged parallel for another kilometre or so, then swung away. By the time he had regained his course the afternoon was almost gone.

He was still tired. The train journey from Leningrad had taken thirty-eight hours. He hunkered down by the river's edge. The Don plucked at tall, pale reeds, bore them away towards the Azov Sea. He settled in silence, watching the passing of the final day.

Light faded through pink into gold, a warmer light than in the far-off north. He looked across the burning river at the deepening dark of hills that cradled a molten sky.

He closed his eyes and dreamed of yesterday's summer: a paper boat and a fishing line, mother and child in soft haloes of light, a picnic basket and plates and napkins, the sighing of a scented breeze and the humming of bees in the glades of Taganrog, where Chekhov was born, long ago.

Piotr Asanov sat for a long time, waiting for the night.

PART II

CHAPTER
FOUR

WASHINGTON DC

He usually took a half-hour to make it in from Georgetown, but today some kind of accident had occurred and traffic stalled all the way from K Street. He sat impotent and ill-tempered behind the wheel as the wipers batted this way and that across a windshield rendered opaque by a sudden downpour.

He moved off again only to get mislaned on Pennsylvania and wound up behind a tour bus which stopped without warning outside Justice. He sighed. The FBI had shifted headquarters but they didn't seem to have told many people. Perhaps they'd gotten sick of being a tourist attraction.

The dash clock read ten past ten when he finally nosed the car into its basement slot. He took the elevator to the fourth, then switched rides and continued on up in the company of a floor-hop, who was trying hard not to look like Security. The lower levels of the building were rented to an advertising agency, a chrome naugahyde and glass showcase with exotic plants that changed even more often than the accounts. Somewhere within the National Security Agency was a deskman charged with out-station integrity, but the agency couldn't have represented too great a worry because you could hardly make Madison Avenue your temple and Marx your idol.

The doors opened at the seventh to reveal an echoing mezzanine and a central reception area with a corral of desks and banks of CCTVs. The guard signed him in and handed over a plastic-covered ID tag: JOHN GULLIVER.

'Mr Barnes arrived?'

A stubby finger travelled the check-in list. 'Oh-nine-fifty, sir.'

He crossed the hall. Corridors led off like the spokes of a wheel.

The passage going to E Section was carpeted a deep blue, with white panelled doors marching the whole of its length. Decor by Sheraton, he thought; perhaps that's who we're all working for. He strode through his outer office without stopping or speaking and into the inner to discover Barnes sprawled on the day-bed like an effigy of a medieval knight – although the cowboy boots tended to militate against the image.

'Christ, what a morning.' He considered his Tudor friend. 'You ready?'

'Yup.' Barnes didn't move.

'Next time, try not to die with your boots on.'

'Okay.'

'Right then, let's go see the Big White Chief.'

There were four access categories: Restricted, Confidential, Secret, and Most Secret. The Asanov file had top billing. Larson pushed it across the desk and said: 'Bet you thought you'd seen the last of that.'

Gulliver took out a toothpick and tore off the wrapper. 'I quit, Sunday. This is a tobacco substitute.'

'It work?' Barnes asked.

'No. Now I get splinters in the gum as well as pains in the chest.'

'Why bother then?'

'It's a distraction.'

Barnes popped another wedge of spearmint into his mouth, shifted it from one side to the other. 'You want to try these.' He didn't offer.

'Gentlemen.' Larson managed a taut smile. 'May we get on?' He poked at the file.

Gulliver stared at the red vinyl cover. 'Must be nine or ten months since I saw that.'

'There was an unfortunate hiatus,' Larson said.

'Hiatus. Ah.'

'Things didn't work out.'

'That's one way of putting it.'

'You've another way?'

'I'd've said it made the Little Big Horn look like a triumph of strategy.'

'It was,' Barnes said, 'for the Indians.'

'John,' Larson said patiently, 'd'you recall what you read?'

'Some.'

'Did you understand it?'

'I'm not sure.'

'No matter. There's help now.' Larson paused. 'Hands across the sea.'

The toothpick snapped.

'You've an objection?'

Gulliver stared at the tiny shards in his palm. 'I think the Indians just won again.'

'It has to be this way.'

'Wonderful.'

'Last summer we had a conduit, now we haven't. Hence ... our friends.'

'Be a miracle we ever see him again.'

'Oh, we will. He goes to England for orientation, then transfers here.'

'Just like that?'

'It's in the deal. Try and work with them, please? They're doing their best.'

'That's what bothers me.'

'They're bringing some guy in on specialist liaison – civilian. He'll handle the technical end.'

'He's not an expert on paintings, by any chance?'

'Wycliffe's the name. Frank – sorry, Doctor Francis Wycliffe.'

Barnes turned to Gulliver. 'In a field manual once, there was something by an English guy, Francis somebody.'

'Assisi?'

'Camps. That's it, Francis Camps, one of their top pathologists. It was about the effect of gun-shot wounds on various parts of the body.'

'Must've been brief then. The Brits normally shoot themselves in the feet.'

'All right, all right,' Larson interrupted. 'Listen, John. There's a meeting tomorrow in London. Be there. Meet the people. Check 'em out.'

'Tomorrow?'

'Friday, two-thirty p.m. their time, in the office of Rear-Admiral Sir Alec Kenyon.'

'I'm almost impressed.'

'What do I do?' Barnes said.

Larson gazed at the tips of the cowboy boots. 'Mind the ranch,' he said.

JOHN F KENNEDY AIRPORT
NEW YORK

Gulliver stowed his raincoat and grip in the overhead locker, sat down by the window and looked out at the concrete desert of JFK. The 747 was only a third full, the adjacent centre and aisle seats unoccupied. Thank God for that, he thought.

Larson had given him a manilla envelope to open on the flight. He tore off the adhesive strip as the Boeing lumbered skywards. Two sheets of paper and a London Transport Visitors' Guide. Very funny. If these were supposed to be sealed orders, it was one hell of an anti-climax.

The first sheet bore Larson's distinctive scrawl: *A little light reading, John. The Brits kindly forwarded it so don't lose it. It's a photocopy of a routine report by Doctor W. It was for a Cabinet committee meeting last year. That's why it's free from jargon. It seems they need educating too.*

He unfolded the photocopy.

OPERATIONAL RESEARCH EXECUTIVE
MINISTRY OF DEFENCE

On 15 May the gear of an Icelandic trawler in-bound for Hull was fouled by a steel object.
Examination shows it to be a standard TS 904 Soviet sonobuoy, measuring 930 mm with a diameter of 120 mm. Configuration is conventional: a buoyant upper structure with hydrophone array in the lower section.
The purpose of a sonobuoy is to detect the noise of submarines in transit. When dropped from an aircraft – as in this case – the descent is controlled by rotating vanes.
Once in the sea, a radio antenna telescopes to facilitate communication, while a sonar transducer sinks on the end of a cable to a predetermined depth.
Signals are transmitted back to the launch aircraft using discreet VHF probably on the 170–174 MHz band.
Ends report.

When I was a kid, Gulliver thought, I held a shell to my ear to listen to the sea. For some reason, the memory made him sad.

LONDON

The Rear-Admiral had beached himself in an office on the third floor of a rank of buildings overlooking the Thames, a few minutes' walk from Whitehall.

Gulliver went through the revolving entrance door to find himself in a cavernous reception hall. A wide, ornate staircase wound away towards the roof, its treads covered by a cascade of deepest blue. He admired it briefly, then went to the security desk. His heels clacked on the marble floor. The thought occurred that they had probably built this place before America was even colonised.

They wanted to escort him to the elevator, but he pointed to the staircase and insisted on climbing it. They finally relented. They had that look the English always have when confronting foreigners: polite, friendly, and effortlessly superior. And that's only the hall porter, Gulliver thought.

The stairs were steeper than they looked. He took them two at a time, just to demonstrate how brash Americans could be, but no one was watching and the effort left him spent and breathing hard on the second landing.

Room J12, floor 3: an anonymous door, the timber stained so dark it was almost black. He knocked and walked into a room striped with bars of sunlight that filtered in through slatted blinds. White walls, beige carpeting, a desk under the window and a smaller one next to the door at the far end. Presumably this was the ante-room, the secretary's domain.

The woman was tall and striking, dressed in a grey jacket and skirt with white open-necked shirt. She had paused in the act of removing a file from a cabinet drawer. He walked towards her, registering the details: abundant dark hair, long-lashed eyes of as yet indiscernible colour, high cheekbones that lent an almost aristocratic cast. Lips that had parted in surprise now framed a quizzical smile.

'My name is John Gulliver,' he said.

'Ah, hello.' She closed the drawer. 'You found your way all right?'

'Yes thanks.' Too stiff, too formal. He grinned. 'We turned left at Shannon.'

49

She sat down at the desk and fed a sheet of paper into the typewriter. 'Please, take a seat.' Fingers roved expertly over the keyboard.

He pointed to the other desk. 'There all right?'

'Mmm?' She glanced up. 'Oh, yes. It's spare.'

He settled down and watched her progress. She sensed the stare and said without looking up: 'Sorry about this, but it's something that needs finishing.'

'That's okay.'

The machine continued a discreet punctuation of the silence. In the absence of any other distraction, he unwrapped a toothpick. It wasn't something you were supposed to do in polite company, but the urge to light a cigarette was growing stronger by the minute. Perhaps she wouldn't notice. He gnawed furtively, aware of the absurdity of his actions.

Eventually he hid it from sight and said: 'Am I early? It's after two-thirty now.'

'You're on time, Mr Gulliver. It seems everyone else is late.'

'Sir Alec isn't in, then.'

'Not yet.'

'Perhaps he's put to sea.'

She frowned. 'Why?'

'He's a rear-admiral or something, isn't he?'

'Oh, yes.' She gave a crooked smile, as though she was unsure of her response.

'He obviously keeps you busy,' Gulliver said. 'My secretary, she signs the letters while I have to type them.' He smiled. 'I'm sorry, but I didn't catch your name, Miss ...'

The paper jerked free of the typewriter. Laughter in the eyes was broadcast by the voice.

'I'm Frances Wycliffe.'

'Ah,' Gulliver said.

She got up from the desk and ushered him into Kenyon's office, a long, oak-panelled room with windows looking out onto the embankment and the river. They settled into two of the four club chairs that were grouped around the mahogany desk. Gulliver still hadn't thought of anything to say.

Kenyon came in then, moving briskly. He was of medium height, sixtyish, maybe older, with a round, animated face and dark-brown hair receding in an irrevocable tide. The pinstripe suit sported a

Hunter, its gold chain looped from a vest pocket. He seemed to have strayed in from the pedigree herds that browsed the City.

'Frances! Good to see you! And this must be Mr Gulliver!' An enthusiastic handshake; Gulliver had palmed the toothpick without thinking, and now it slipped from his hand onto the carpet. 'Sorry to have kept you both,' Kenyon beamed. 'Sit down, sit down.'

He darted to his chair and squeezed in behind the desk. He keyed the intercom. 'Maggie, coffee and biscuits for three. Cream and sugar – neither of 'em look like they need to diet.' He sat back. 'Well, Mr Gulliver, welcome to London.'

'Thank you.'

Kenyon turned to Frances Wycliffe. 'And how are you, m'dear?'

'Fine.'

Before anyone could see the offending splinter, Gulliver ducked down to retrieve it. Then Kenyon suddenly said: 'Good Lord. You're not trying to stop smoking, are you?'

Gulliver sat upright, smiling in embarrassment.

'Tried the same thing myself, you know,' Kenyon confided. 'Got splinters in the gum, though. Most irritating. I was going to take up the old pipe except that Wilson fellow put me off. Cabinet committees are never very enlightening, but his pipe made things a complete fog. Anyway, tell me: how's Washington these days?'

'It's, it's the same as ever.'

'Delightful town, civilised. See much of the president?'

'President?'

'You know. The fellow in the White House.'

'I don't operate at that level.'

'No?' Kenyon looked disappointed. 'My wife likes his films. He's a good actor.'

'He's stopped acting.'

'Has he really? Good Lord. I didn't know that.'

A woman entered the room with a silver tray. 'Oh look,' Kenyon said, 'tiffin.' He poked at the biscuits on the plate. 'Custard creams – must be Friday.' He looked up at Gulliver. 'And, of course, it is.'

Gulliver stared blankly at him.

'So,' Kenyon said. 'Ready for the off, Frances?'

'I hope so.'

'Mmm. Interesting project, isn't it? Analysis and evaluation – your speciality.'

'I usually do machines,' she said, 'not men.'

'They all come apart just the same, m'dear. Are you with the navy, then?' he asked Gulliver.

He was wrong-footed again. Kenyon reminded him of a squirrel, scurrying here and there, adding kernels to his store of knowledge, then vanishing from sight. You never knew which direction he'd take next.

'No,' Gulliver said, 'I'm from the Defense Intelligence Agency.'

Frances Wycliffe frowned. 'You're a military officer?'

'Yes and no. The rank doesn't matter.' He shrugged. 'We're pretty informal nowadays.'

'And very democratic it is too,' Kenyon said approvingly. 'D'you know, that business you had in Vietnam ...'

Gulliver groaned inwardly. Only the English could make Nam sound like a squabble in a five and ten.

'... I remember seeing your squaddies on TV,' Kenyon continued. 'Some of them had long hair tied in a bow and they called their officers by their Christian names.' He turned to Frances Wycliffe. 'Really.'

She seemed to be having difficulty stifling laughter. Kenyon suddenly grew serious again. 'Right then, to business. Let me explain the situation. As I understand it, this operation is being shared with your people, Mr Gulliver.'

'That's one way of looking at it,' he said.

'And Frances is acting as liaison because she speaks the language – and I don't mean Russian.' Kenyon paused. 'Actually, I'm told this chap's English is remarkably good.'

'Better than mine, probably,' Gulliver said, 'being a foreigner and that.'

'Well, anyway,' Kenyon was unperturbed, 'I want it clearly understood that Frances is only on loan. She's one of my best people and her responsibility is to my department and nowhere else.'

Gulliver sighed. 'Sir Alec, let's not get off on the wrong foot. No offence, but I didn't ask for Doctor Wycliffe's help, and I didn't ask for this to be split both sides of the pond. Far as I'm concerned, this began as a US operation and that's how it's going to end.'

Kenyon beamed unexpectedly. 'Thank the Lord for that. It looks as though it could be rather expensive. I doubt we could afford it.' He lapsed into silence, then went on: 'Shouldn't say it, but really, it's this blasted government and that blasted woman. Entire country's being run by accountants.'

52

'You don't like accountants?'

'In their place, but not here.' He paused, then added mournfully: 'If we ever drop the bomb on Moscow, the Treasury's likely to ask for a receipt.'

At that moment Kenyon's secretary brought two men into his office. The tall one in the leather jacket and blue jeans Kenyon introduced as Martin Leech; the smaller, stockier one in sports jacket and slacks was Owen Smith. Gulliver placed them at around the same age as Barnes, and that was either too young or further proof that he had grown too old. They all stood around while Kenyon made the introductions, then settled into the quilted chairs.

Leech said: 'You're the man from Washington, then.' His accent was neutral, voice pleasant, lightly modulated.

'That's right,' Gulliver said. 'And you?'

Leech smiled. 'I'm the London end. I seem to have been lumbered with the job of organiser.'

'You're in charge?'

'Sort of.' Leech nodded towards his companion. 'This is my number two. It's thanks to him we're here today.'

Gulliver glanced from the one to the other. 'Why?'

'He set up the conduit.'

'It went all right?' he said to Smith.

'Seems so. He's all in one piece, anyway.'

It took Gulliver a moment or two to identify the accent. 'You're Welsh, aren't you?'

'That's right.' Smith winked conspiratorially. 'From the colonies, like yourself.'

Kenyon interrupted: 'Well, this is all very pleasant I'm sure, but time is pressing. Is there anything you're not clear about?' he asked Frances Wycliffe.

She considered. 'I'd like to know more about the arrangements.'

'We've a place,' Leech said, 'in the country – a residential centre for special training, though it's no longer in use. The client will stay there.'

'On his own?'

'Hardly. Owen will be with him, and a back-up team. I'll drop by now and again.'

Gulliver asked lightly: 'How long d'you intend keeping him, Mr Leech?'

'As long as it takes to make him feel at home.'

'Washington can't wait that long.'

'I don't believe I'm accountable to Washington.'

'I am, though.' Gulliver straightened in his seat. 'Look, you people did a good job, but we're the ones who set this up, and we're the ones he deals with.'

'All right. Say ... a month.'

'Say something else.'

'A month's cutting it fine.'

'No, two weeks. After that the property gets shipped out.'

'Forgive me for asking,' Frances Wycliffe said, 'but are we talking about some kind of parcel?'

Gulliver ignored her. 'Two weeks.'

'A month,' Leech said.

'Well, if it's going to be like this ...' She stared from the one to the other. The threat remained unspoken.

Leech said patiently: 'The debriefing's out of my hands. I'm not qualified to set the pace.'

'So who is then?' Gulliver said.

'Doctor Wycliffe.'

She shook her head. 'I hardly think I've the qualifications for this.'

'All you have to do is talk to him,' Leech said. 'He needs to be with someone who understands what he's on about.'

'Me?'

'Well it certainly isn't me. I'm an intelligence officer. What I know about anti-submarine warfare wouldn't fill half a page. Whereas you, you're a scientist; and so is he.'

She glanced at Gulliver. 'He's also a human being.' The American looked away.

'Yes, he's also a human being,' Leech said quickly. 'Which is why it's important to draw him out gently. The Soviets made the mistake of pressuring him. We won't.'

The silence went on for a while. Gulliver continued to stare at the carpet.

Eventually Owen Smith said: 'Staying long, Mr Gulliver?'

'What? Oh. No, just tonight.'

Frances Wycliffe frowned. 'You're not seeing Doctor Asanov, then?'

Gulliver lowered his head again. Civilians – you could tell them the instant they opened their mouths. They threw names out like garbage. 'I'll wait until the transfer to the States,' he said.

'Is that necessary? Surely he's been troubled enough as it is.'

'Unfortunately,' Leech said, 'he does have to go. He's been a decade on the theory; now's the time for practice. The Americans can afford to build to his design, we can't.' He turned to Gulliver. 'Doing anything tonight?'

'I thought I'd find a brick wall to talk to.'

'Seriously, though. Fancy dinner, courtesy Her Britannic Majesty's Government? And perhaps you'd join us, Doctor Wycliffe?'

She hesitated. 'I've rather a lot of work to do.'

'Never mind that,' Kenyon interrupted. 'You go with them. You're all working together, same boat and all that.'

She glanced at him, then back to Leech and Gulliver. 'Really?'

'You go and keep them out of trouble, Frances.'

Leech pushed himself upright. 'That's settled then. Is there anywhere you prefer?' he asked Gulliver.

'We have a McDonald's,' Kenyon volunteered.

'How about my club?' Leech said.

Gulliver closed his eyes. 'I thought you might say that.'

Frances Wycliffe stood up. 'Are women admitted, Mr Leech?'

'Oh yes, we're very broad-minded. We even let Americans in.'

Gulliver absorbed the trappings of the Old World: flock wall coverings and gilt-framed oil paintings, heavy gold brocade and damson carpeting of limitless depth, and individual reading lamps on small mahogany piecrust tables encircled by wing chairs of shining leather. The room was filled with discreet sounds, the commingling of pedigree.

At the next table, an elderly man was asleep with *Yachting Monthly* clasped to his chest.

'Well,' Leech said. 'D'you approve?'

'Depends on the ham on rye.'

'Sorry. We don't serve it. And no one says "Have a nice day," either.'

'Tst tst. And I thought this was supposed to be civilised.' He caught the expression on Leech's face. 'What's so funny?'

'You.' Leech paused. 'The Virginia colonists met here before setting sail for America.'

'Looks like one of 'em got left behind.' Gulliver jabbed a thumb in the direction of the adjacent table.

A waiter arrived with drinks on a silver tray. Gulliver took the small crystal jug and splashed water into a tumbler of Scotch. 'I don't see any women in here.'

'Not allowed.'

'I thought you said ...'

'They can come into the restaurant and cocktail bar, but not the inner sanctum.'

'That why we're here a half-hour early?'

'I thought you might want to talk before she came. You must have some questions.'

'Just one.'

'Go on.'

'Does Frances Wycliffe know the ... background?'

'No.'

'Sure?'

'Not even Owen Smith knows, and he got him out.'

Gulliver studied the younger man. 'That's all right then.'

'It's history,' Leech said.

'No.' There was a prolonged pause. 'It never happened.'

They fell silent again. Then Gulliver said: 'Tell me about her.'

Leech drained his glass and beckoned for a refill. 'Well. Frances Wycliffe: age thirty-seven; Bachelor of Science; defence establishment since university; electronics specialist.'

'But not the only one.'

'The only one with looks like that.'

'She married?'

'Widowed. Her husband was killed in a car crash eight years ago.'

'Boyfriends? Girlfriends?'

'None.' Leech paused while the drinks were replenished. 'She's quite the deep one – lonely, too.'

'I don't believe it.'

'True. There's been no one since her husband: social life, yes; sex life, no.'

'Did she tell you this?'

'Hardly. But the vetting was very thorough.'

'I'm real glad about that,' Gulliver said doubtfully.

He dined on avocado seafood cocktail followed by sole bonne femme, then medallion Rossini with fresh vegetables, then poires Hélène followed by coffee and mints. And brandy on top of

Montrachet on top of four whiskies, three single, one double.

All fuelled up and nowhere to go, Gulliver thought.

He peered around the dining room, letting his gaze range over the old, dark oak panelling, now lustrous in the candlelight. Another brandy materialised. He studied her over the balloon glass. She'd pinned up her hair; ear-rings flared in twin points of fire whenever her head turned. Her dress was black, simple, modestly cut. An elegant woman with an eloquent smile.

With an effort, he tuned into their conversation.

'... and from the Diplomatic Protection Group,' Leech was saying, 'into Special Branch. And finally this.'

'Is it very different?'

'Yes and no. I mean, I'm still a policeman, but I don't arrest anyone any more.'

'Why not?'

'We don't have the power of arrest.'

'I don't believe that.'

'It's true.'

She chuckled. 'So if I said, here I am, a Russian spy ...'

'I'd dial nine nine nine.'

'Really?'

'Well, after you'd paid the bill. First Chief Directorate gets better expenses than us.'

She was about to speak when the waiter appeared at Leech's side and whispered in his ear. He nodded and stood up. 'Excuse me. Bloody phones.'

She watched his departing figure, then remarked, because there wasn't anything else to say: 'That was an excellent meal.'

'Mmm.'

She considered him. He seemed distracted. Perhaps, she thought, it's the drink. He'd consumed whatever went into his glass as though fearful of its imminent evaporation. A curious man, Gulliver. Not quite handsome but, well, presentable: well groomed, medium build, dark eyes and a crop of wayward, greying hair. He wore his age well, until you looked into those eyes. Then you saw memories and secrets and a store of knowledge it had taken fifty and a good few more years than that to accumulate. *Homo sapiens sardonicus*, Sardonic Man. He had been wherever you wanted to go.

'Sorry,' Gulliver said, 'I was miles away.'

'Exactly.'

He frowned, but she didn't elaborate.

Leech returned then. 'Look,' he said, 'I'm sorry about this but I have to get back.'

'Problem?'

'Nothing you need worry about, Mr Gulliver. I mean, it hasn't anything to do with this. A lovely evening,' he said to Frances Wycliffe. 'Thank you.' He took her hand and shook it. 'I really must fly.'

They watched him go. Silence ebbed between them. Eventually Frances said: 'You ... intrigue me, Mr Gulliver. People like you are, well, something of a mystery.' She swirled the brandy around her glass. 'Tell me about yourself.'

'Nothing to tell.'

'No?' A hazy, lingering smile. 'Unlike you, I didn't get a dossier to read.'

'Dossier?'

'How many pages do I merit, Mr Gulliver? One? Ten?'

He smiled back. 'I didn't count.'

'Even so, you know all about me. Whereas I ... I'd like to know who I'm involved with.'

He shrugged and looked away.

'I promise not to tell anyone,' she whispered.

'You don't give up, do you, Doctor Wycliffe?'

'Not if I can help it.'

'And you really want to know?'

'Yes.' She paused. 'How did you get into your line of work?'

He gazed around the dining room. 'Remember Korea? That was my war – between the one they showed at the movies and the one they put on TV. Thirty-eighth Parallel one day, Yellow Brick Road the next.'

'I don't see the connection ...'

'It's how I got into it – Army Intelligence. I'd had enough of being plain GI Joe after Pusan.'

'You transferred to Intelligence?'

'Wasn't difficult. A chimpanzee could've done it – maybe some of 'em did.' He smiled. 'The Red Menace, Doctor. Everyone was paranoid, not just MacArthur and McCarthy.'

'About war?'

'About security.' He shook his head and lapsed into silence. 'The army, air force, navy – we were so paranoid we didn't even trust ourselves. That's how the arms race started. The fleet didn't trust SAC so they wound up duplicating every single Soviet target.'

An eyebrow arched. 'I thought you were the people who claimed to be the good guys.'

'There are no good guys or bad guys. Just ... fools.'

'Is everyone a fool?'

'Only if they're more than five years old.'

'That's your philosophy?'

'That's my conclusion.' He grinned. 'Philosophy'll have to wait.'

'I'd be interested to hear it, when you're ready.' She paused. 'You were saying, about security ...'

'I was explaining how Intelligence became the fashion of the day, military and civil. Old J. Edgar watched Dulles walk all over him, then Dulles watched the Pentagon trampling all over him. They were building empires, Doctor. They still are.'

'And you went in to swell the numbers?' Her head inclined to one side. 'I can't believe that.'

'It was a job.'

'And still is?'

'Well it sure ain't a crusade.'

She studied him for a few moments, then carefully folded the napkin and placed it back on the table. 'End of story, then.'

'I guess.'

'Short, if not sweet? Oh well, thank you for an interesting evening. You'll thank Mr Leech?'

'You'll be seeing him soon enough.'

'And you?'

'We'll meet again.'

She hesitated. 'One last question, Mr Gulliver: the Russians, what will they do about Doctor Asanov?'

'Nothing.' He stood up, chuckled. 'That's the beauty of it all. They don't even know he's defected.'

CHAPTER
FIVE

LONDON

8.00 a.m. The letterbox flap slammed in the door. Frances retrieved the newspaper and carried it back to the kitchen.

The good news: everything was on the up and up; the bad news: that included prices and unemployment and utility tariffs. Abroad: famine in Ethiopia; massacre in India; earthquake in Turkey; drought in the Sudan; war in Lebanon.

She pushed the paper away, feeling a weary resentment. Already the day was jaded. She thought how good it must have been when the world was a big enough place in which to live in ignorance of its ways. You were sympathetic to suffering then. Now, now it paraded itself at the breakfast table, gibbering amongst the crockery.

She glanced up at the pine clock. This morning its ticking seemed louder.

TILGARSLEY
OXFORDSHIRE

The house stood in three acres of grounds, a rambling 1930s mock-Tudor edifice with diamond-paned windows and black and white timber facings. The oak entrance door opened and Leech came down the steps. Behind Frances, the Granada crunched on gravel and sped off along the drive.

'Doctor Wycliffe, hello again.'

'Good morning, Mr Leech.' They shook hands.

He ushered her inside. 'Had a good trip?'

'Yes thanks.' There was an awkward pause, the tempo of their

60

relationship tardy in picking up. 'I didn't expect to see you. I thought your Mr Smith would be here.'

'Oh he is, beavering away behind the scenes.'

He led her across the wide hall and halted outside an oak door. 'Care for some tea?'

'Not just yet.'

'All right.' He smiled. 'Well, I'll leave you to it. Good luck.'

She didn't move, but stood listening to her heartbeat. She watched the reflection of her outstretched hand in the gleaming brass of the doorknob, saw the image reaching out to her. Then fingers parted and closed upon themselves and she went in to say hello to the defector.

She found herself in a high-ceilinged room, thirty feet long or more, on the eastern flank of the house. It was luxuriously furnished with onyx tables and delicate three-piece suites, and unmistakable pieces like the escritoire in one corner and the chaise longue in the other. Standard lamps and table lamps were scattered around, pale gold shades contrasting with the deep red velvet curtains. A bay window arced out towards the front drive; French windows at the opposite end yielded a view of landscaped gardens and lawns. And occupying the furthest corner, near the French windows, was a grand piano of black mahogany.

He was treading down on the pianissimo so that the notes sounded as though they were filtering through gauze. And yet the sweetness still carried the clarity of a simple melody. She waited, not daring to intrude, attuning herself to the slow rhythm of the left hand, the series of chords that blocked progressively in common time, whilst the right hand played single notes, then octaves – high, lilting, haunting.

He sensed her presence then, and the music went away.

He had an open, intelligent face, in which a muscle tightened as surprise stole up on composure. A tawny skein of hair drifted across the forehead. And blue, blue eyes – she had never seen anyone with eyes like that before.

'I didn't want to interrupt,' she said.

'That's all right.' He stood up.

'You play beautifully.'

'No.' It was less a denial, more an expression of regret. 'But thank you.'

She took a couple of paces. 'I'm Frances Wycliffe.'

61

He came towards her, stopped a few feet away. 'And I am Piotr Asanov.'

They lit the silence with awkward smiles. She had the irrational feeling that this was somehow symbolic, this meeting and yet not meeting in the middle of a gilded room. No more than three or four feet between them, but she felt hesitant about crossing it, while he had the air of one who simply did not know how.

'Please,' he said, indicating the nearest sofa.

She sat down amidst the needlepoint covers while he eased himself into a matching armchair.

'I think I'm supposed to make a speech,' she said. 'So. Welcome to England.'

'Thank you.'

He was watching her – cautious, wary; the voice was deep and smooth, but anxiety darkened the eyes. She returned his stare, struggling to remember the words of a half-rehearsed speech.

'Have you been here before? Your English is very good.'

'I learned.' He stifled a yawn, then smiled apologetically. 'Please excuse me. I am still very tired.'

'You came a long way.'

'I'm beginning to realise that.'

'But you've settled in?'

'I am very comfortable.'

She wondered how she could orchestrate the silence, and wished Leech had come in, or Smith.

Finally she said: 'It's a nice morning,' and almost cringed at the banality of the remark.

He nodded.

'It'll be May soon.' He nodded again; she had the disturbing impression the exchange had progressed from the banal to the Pavlovian.

'Is there anything you want, Doctor Asanov?'

'Perhaps we could go outside?'

'I don't see why not.'

'If no one minds,' he added.

She stood up. 'Why should anyone mind?'

'They might be recording this.'

She stared at him, unable to stop the surprise from showing in her face.

'I think,' he said, 'I think they like to do that.'

Smith glanced up. 'What d'you make of that then?'

'Paranoia.' Leech continued to stare at the slow looping of the tape. 'He thinks they're all out to get him.'

'I *know* they're out to get him,' Smith said. 'And I seem to be one of them.'

Leech sighed. 'I don't suppose anyone thought to cover the garden areas.'

'No.' Smith tugged off the headphones and massaged his ears. 'Anyway, who wants bugs in the garden?'

'Very droll.'

Leech went over to the window and looked down. 'They're walking.'

'It's a start,' Smith said. He pushed the chair back and crossed the room to where a card table stood uncertainly by a vanity unit. A tin of biscuits, four mugs, a coffee jar and a kettle decorated the green baize. He moved the kettle aside and located a half-empty bag of sugar. 'Sod.'

'What's the matter?'

'I forgot the milk.'

Leech cast him a sidelong glance. 'I thought you were supposed to be in charge around here.'

'Sorry.' He switched on the kettle and stared around the room as if hoping milk would materialise. They'd shifted the bed and the dressing table out, and shoved a wooden trestle against the wall. Two Sony machines and an Aiwa multi-mode were coupled into a comparator. Six reels spun silent circles.

Leech said, without turning from the view: 'Put 'em on voice activation.'

'All right.'

As the tapes stilled, Smith said: 'Is all this really necessary?'

'Orders.'

'There must be a reason.'

'Yes.' He went to the table and contemplated the kettle. 'They need to know about it if ever he gets close to boiling point.'

'I don't follow.'

'His history, his psychological profile – Asanov is an emotional individual. We don't want him going yonderly like he did in Russia.'

'And the tapes?' Smith persisted.

'Everywhere he goes, everything he says has to be recorded. They're for transcription, and evaluation.' He smiled at his companion. 'Look on the bright side. It's for his benefit. We need to know if he's being pushed too hard.'

'The kettle's boiling,' Smith said.

They reached the southern perimeter of the grounds, the boundary marked by high hawthorn. Leaf was already unfurling, vigorous, shining, filling in the spiky screen.

'You have a garden, Doctor Wycliffe?'

'A window-box. I live in town.'

'Town?'

'London.'

'That's far from here?'

'Not really.' Except ... where *was* here? No one had told her. The driver hadn't spoken during the journey and after leaving the M4 she'd stopped looking at the countryside, immersing herself instead in Asanov's background profile.

'You work in London, Doctor Wycliffe?'

'Yes.' She stopped. 'I don't know if they told you or not – I'm a Scientific Officer, Grade Two, Ministry of Defence.' She waited for some reaction, but none came. Probably, she thought, because a quarter of the scientific defence staff in the USSR were women. It was nothing unusual, unless you happened to be living in a country with an Equal Opportunities Act.

'The people at the house,' Asanov said, 'they are your colleagues?'

'No.'

'They are Intelligence?'

'Security.'

The blue eyes steadied on her. It was like being transfixed by a bright light. 'Why did they send you, Doctor Wycliffe?'

'I'm a scientist.' The wind nagged at her hair. She brushed errant strands from her face. 'I doubt I'm half as clever as you, but I am a scientist.'

'And an attractive woman.'

She laughed. 'You flatter me, Doctor Asanov. I hardly think that's the reason.'

'No?'

'No.'

64

A slight bow. 'I am sorry. I did not mean to cause offence.'

'None taken.'

He nodded. He seemed to be taking a lot of inner decisions. 'What is your field?'

'Marine technology.'

'Strategic?'

'Yes.'

'Defensive?'

'It depends how you define the term.'

He was holding a curl of bark, turning it around in his fingers, inspecting it. 'Perhaps we could go inside now,' he said.

In the bedroom, solenoids activated discreetly at the sound of voices.

'They're back,' Smith said.

In the drawing room, Asanov said: 'I think we are only at ease in our laboratories.'

She laughed. 'Is it that obvious?'

'Yes.' He was sitting in the armchair again, one leg crossed negligently over the other. He looked more relaxed now, she thought. 'So,' he said, 'tell me about yourself.'

'Isn't this supposed to be the other way around?'

'You have a phrase, ladies first?'

'All right.' She wondered if Leech was, after all, listening to any of this. She decided not. There was no point. This man had come as a friend.

She took a deep breath: 'I run a small section – part of the technical division, Ministry of Defence research department. My section is Systems Analysis. Most of the time we look at pictures, photographs of the sort of equipment the Russ ... your people are using. We identify and evaluate. Occasionally we work on the real thing. We had one of your sonobuoys last year.'

'I don't think it was one of mine.' He smiled. 'What did you do with it?'

'Took it apart, to judge if it could do what it was supposed to do; and if so, how well.'

'Am I to be taken apart, too?'

'I don't do people.' The conversation was yielding echoes.

'I am reassured.' Asanov uncrossed his legs. A new air of

purpose surrounded him. 'Now I think we should discuss my terms, Doctor Wycliffe. They are very simple. I ask only to be allowed to work in peace. You must understand, it is like driving a motor car. Two people cannot sit at the same steering wheel, not if only one of them knows the direction of travel.' He stood up and went over to the fireplace, stared at the empty grate. 'I'm tired of working by committee and for committee.'

'You're free to work as you wish here.'

He smiled. '*Svoboda.*'

'Sorry?'

'Freedom.' A brief pause, then: 'I will be ready to begin in a few days.'

'That's fine.'

He glanced up from the grate. 'Doctor Wycliffe.'

'Yes?'

'Tell them. I did not come empty-handed.'

CHAPTER SIX

DZERZHINSKY SQUARE
MOSCOW

Krotov's right hand slipped into the glove with a whisper of flesh against fabric. Fingers flexed then closed upon the grip. He bent lower, eyes narrowed in concentration, aim steady, index finger curling ever tighter.

Melnikov walked in as Krotov pulled the trigger.

'So,' Melnikov said. 'This is how the Second Chief Directorate spends its time.'

Krotov circled the plant, gloved hand catching the wide leaves, sending beads of dull liquid rolling onto the stem. He squeezed the trigger again; the spray cloud misted briefly.

Melnikov closed the door and set a package down on the waxed boarded floor. 'What are you doing?'

'Killing.' Krotov didn't look up. 'Killing pests.'

Melnikov moved to his side and stared at the rubber plant. 'I don't see any, Gregor.'

'Never wait till you see them.' Krotov chuckled. 'I thought you understood how it is around here.'

Melnikov looked away. It wasn't a small room, but somehow Krotov had managed to fill it with so much stuff the place seemed to contract in upon itself. Bric-a-brac dotted every available surface, obscure trophies of forgotten moments. Photographs crowded the harsh white walls, books and folders tilted against each other on shelves above the grey rank of filing cabinets.

A window looked out upon the stark brick face of the opposite wing. Melnikov contemplated it wordlessly, then stared down at the snow-covered courtyard three floors below. 'I thought you'd have moved by now, to the new place.'

'I'm a fixture,' Krotov said.

Melnikov shrugged off his coat and placed it carefully on a chair by the window sill. His gaze ranged the length of the room to the far wall, where a dozen clocks were set in a full-width panel displaying a flat projection of the world together with international and USSR continental time zones.

The word came involuntarily: 'Time.'

'Sorry?' Krotov straightened up.

'I was thinking; it's been a long time.' Melnikov smiled awkwardly. 'We used to walk together over the Krymsky Bridge. This weather always reminds me of the days we used to throw snowballs at each other and arrive late for class.'

Krotov carried the plant to a small side table, already erupting with the splayed foliage of philodendron and fatsia.

'We were supposed to be mature students, too,' Melnikov said.

'After the war, everyone was mature.' Krotov went to his desk, removed the glove, placed it and the empty spray-gun in a left-hand drawer. He studied his guest for a few moments. 'Anyway, it hasn't been that long.'

'Three years ago was the last time.'

'You haven't altered, Nikolai.'

Melnikov smiled again. 'I brought you something.' He motioned towards the doorway, to a small cylindrical container wrapped in newspaper. 'One of those Japanese trees.'

'Trees?' An eyebrow arched quizzically.

'Open it,' Melnikov said. He folded his arms across his chest and watched with amusement as Krotov approached the door almost warily. Gregor and his plants, he thought. The man should've gone to the Botanical Institute, been a horticulturist, been anything, in fact, except ...

You wouldn't believe it to look at him – this small bald figure, this precise little man with his precise little features, the bright eyes, quick smile, careful speech – wouldn't believe that Gregor Krotov, once upon a time of Leningrad, was now a fully-fledged colonel in the KGB.

The newspaper shredded away to expose an earthenware pot containing a small candelabra of branches half-hidden by a canopy of fine green needles. Krotov held it up for inspection. 'It's not

Japanese. *Pirius pumila*: Siberian pine.' He touched a tiny spike. 'It's beautiful. Thank you.'

'I wasn't sure if you were interested in the miniature.'

'Nikolai.' Lips pursed in gentle mockery. 'Obviously I'm predisposed to it.' Krotov moved to the plant table. 'The art of Bonsai,' he said, 'is in the balance. Cut too much off the top growth and the roots fail; too much off the roots and the top withers.'

'You know such a lot,' Melnikov said.

Krotov carefully lowered the tiny specimen. Then he turned towards his guest, considered him with unwavering gaze. 'I also know the strongest branches aren't necessarily at the top of the tree.'

Melnikov gave no sign of understanding. 'I need your help.'

'Tanya?' Without waiting for an answer, Krotov settled in at the desk and withdrew a blue-coloured file from an upper drawer. 'They told me you were coming,' he said. He flipped through the spiral-bound pages. 'Question: What is your relationship with the man Guseinov? Answer: A friend. Question: How well do you know him? Answer: Quite well, but if you're implying we're lovers, think again. Tonight's the first time we've met this year.' Krotov paused. 'It's the militia transcript, the interview.'

'Go on.'

'Question: What is your involvement in the dissemination of anti-Soviet propaganda? Answer: I have no involvement. Question: Are you aware the man Guseinov is a parasite, a dissident, and a professional troublemaker? Answer: I didn't know he'd been that busy.'

Melnikov trudged to the window and stood with his head bowed and hands thrust deep in pockets. 'There is more?'

'It's all like that.' Krotov sighed and closed the file. 'Your daughter has much to learn.'

Eventually Melnikov said: 'I've been making inquiries.'

'So I gathered.'

'Your Major Monakhov –'

'Not mine. He's Fifth Chief Directorate.'

'How come he's involved then?'

'Guseinov's a dissident so he's Fifth's responsibility.'

'Whereas you ...?'

'The good doctor Asanov – Second have a long-standing interest in him.'

Melnikov traced invisible patterns on the window glass. 'This Monakhov. What's he like?'

'Young and ambitious.'

'He figured in the Galina Brezhnev affair.'

'Yes,' Krotov nodded, 'and Sokolov.'

'Sokolov?'

'Manager of Gastronom One.' Krotov gave a thin-lipped smile. 'Get anything you wanted, Sokolov could: Darjeeling tea, smoked sturgeon, Ikra by the tubful – anything ... at a price. An inconvenience fee.'

'I never knew him.'

'No? He was well in with the Brezhnev circle.'

'I wasn't in that, either.'

'Well, you certainly weren't one of Andropov's people.' Krotov put the file away and eased back into his chair. 'Let's stop fencing, Nikolai. I know why you're here. It isn't often one of the Kremlin ruling families drops by.'

Melnikov turned to him, smiling faintly. 'You make it sound like a monarchy.'

'Isn't it?' A slow, lingering shake of the head. 'From where I sit, I see many things. Brezhnev goes, Andropov arrives. Andropov's people sweep out Brezhnev's people. Then Chernenko arrives and his people sweep out Andropov's. Then Gorbachev arrives and his people ... the pendulum swings, Nikolai.'

'What are you trying to tell me?'

'Chernenko was Brezhnev's protégé; Gorbachev is Andropov's.'

'Mikhail is a reasonable man.'

'I hope so. He's here until the millennium.' Krotov steepled his fingers and considered each in turn. 'Why does Monakhov interest you?'

Melnikov hesitated. 'I understand he's less than objective.'

The steeple collapsed. 'You mean you've reason to believe he has his own masters, in the Collegium.'

'It's not unheard of.'

'Quite so. There's many a politician willing to further the career of a rising KGB officer – self-interest, and self-defence.'

'You people,' Melnikov said, 'have a lot of power.'

'Ah ...' Krotov smiled. 'And who is master, and who the mastered?' The smile faded. 'No, Nikolai. You still have the power. That's why you're here. Because you're afraid of losing it.'

'I am here to protect my daughter.' Melnikov adopted a cold, clipped tone. 'They will not crucify her just to get at me.' A glacial silence enveloped them. Krotov waited, saying nothing, watching. Finally, Melnikov shrugged, a gesture combining disgust and dismissal. 'It's all nonsense, anyway. Who cares about this Guseinov?'

'He isn't the problem.'

'Well, your precious scientist isn't, is he? This Doctor Asanov.'

'No?' Krotov steepled his fingers again.

'No, because he's dead; thrown himself in the Neva.'

The right eyebrow inched upwards again. 'Really?'

'They say he was half mad.'

'"They"?'

'People.' Melnikov shrugged again. 'You know.'

'I wish I did. I wish I did and then they could sit here and sort out the mess instead of me.'

Melnikov frowned, seemed about to speak, then changed his mind. He eased himself into a faded moquette chair set at a right angle to the desk.

After a while, Krotov said: 'Piotr Asanov, asset turned liability. Scientist one day, refusenik the next.'

'I didn't know he was a Jew.'

'He wasn't, but a close friend was. Asanov campaigned to get him out.'

'What happened?'

'Nothing. The campaign failed. Result: Asanov grew more and more embittered, antagonistic. Wouldn't work and wouldn't publish. Finally he was shifted to Leningrad, to see if he'd come to his senses.' Krotov shook his head. 'Some hope.'

'Perhaps the treatment could've been more ... sensitive?'

'Anyone else, it would've been food parcels at a labour camp for the next ten years.' Krotov sighed. 'No, you're right. It could've been handled better. Unfortunately I wasn't involved at that stage. The lower echelon ...'

'But now you are involved. Why, Gregor?'

'Because he's missing.'

'Presumed dead.'

'In view of his mental state, yes, that was the general opinion.'

'It has changed?'

Krotov lapsed into thoughtful silence. Eventually he said: 'I remember asking, when this case first landed on my desk, just who this fellow Asanov was. And someone said he was like a man called Kleber a Prussian chemist who lived in the nineteenth century. Kleber apparently devised a universal panacea, a cure for all ailments, a mineral potion made from moondust.'

'Made from what?'

'Precisely. Space travel was mere fantasy a hundred years ago. The man's pretty theories depended upon a technology not then in existence.'

'And Asanov? He fell into the same category?'

'Yes.'

Melnikov smiled broadly. 'There you are then. Half mad, as I said. Unhinged.'

A desk drawer grated open, then closed again; a small leather-bound diary landed casually on the blotter.

Melnikov hunched forward. 'What's that?'

'Moondust,' Krotov said.

Midday came with only the slightest increase in the weary daylight. Melnikov stood at the window, fingers gripping the sill, imagining the scene beyond: the slow crawl of traffic, the slipping and stumbling of pedestrians as winter took yet another unwelcome curtain call.

Finally he turned to Krotov again: 'I still don't understand.'

Krotov leafed through the diary pages and studied the final entries once more.

2 March: Today she finally said, did I want to leave? After all I was not doing any good here. I would never do any good here. They thought I was a troublemaker. They thought I was a lunatic.

12 March: I cannot believe it. It is a hoax perhaps? But after so many years, trying, hoping, pushing myself further and further into a corner. I cannot believe it.

19 March: It is not some fable then. Oh Yelena, my little Yelena. I will never forget this day. THEY EXIST!

23 March: Yes, yes, a thousand times yes! And now I will show them, just you watch. Can't be done? Technologically impossible? You are wrong! They exist. The power is waiting to be used.

28 March: EHE $\times$ 4, or scale down?

Krotov closed the small volume. 'It was found in his hotel room at the back of a drawer under some lining paper.'

'And it's definitely Asanov's diary? There's no mistake?'

'No mistake. The experts have been at it all night: psychological evaluation, technical interpretation.'

Melnikov returned to his chair. 'Even so, they could be wrong.'

Krotov took a deep breath, then said, in a tone of one reciting something learnt by rote: 'Grammar and sentence construction indicate high emotional activity but a rational mind. The emotions are genuine because they are incoherently articulated. Were they synthetic the exposition would be much clearer. Therefore Asanov was not drawing upon delusions. He was writing the truth.'

'But what does it mean? "The power is there." What power?'

'A battery, the technical people say.'

'A *what*?'

'A battery. EHE is apparently some kind of power pack, an acronym for Extra High Energy. Asanov's theories depend upon such a source.'

'And that's the moondust?'

'Yes.'

'Though clearly, it's not on the moon.' Melnikov massaged his jaw. 'Where then?'

'The United States.' Krotov paused. 'I'm told it goes back to 1974. Until then the Americans weren't very interested in electric cars, in battery-powered vehicles. Batteries couldn't provide the range or power of fossil fuels. But then gasoline tripled in price almost overnight, so they set about re-examining the alternatives. The government funded research and public opinion pushed it.' Krotov grimaced. 'Americans – they have these ... crazes: the environment, anti-pollution. They're a consumer society that consumes everything and then grumbles about the results.'

'And our research?' Melnikov prompted.

'Different direction, literally. Solar power and satellite technology.'

'Solar power, then. Wouldn't that have been of use to Asanov?'

'Hardly. His work is underwater technology. There's not much sun down there.'

Melnikov pushed himself out of the chair and began a futile pacing of the room. 'I don't understand. If we knew the Americans were working on this EHE thing, and if we knew it was just what Asanov required ...'

'I know.' Krotov nodded. 'The Americans had an invention without an application; Asanov had an application without an invention. Someone should've realised.'

'But they didn't.'

'That's right. It's happened before. It will happen again. A specialist in one field doesn't understand and very probably doesn't care what a specialist is doing in another. Everything's so big, so complicated. In the muddle, one day, my friend, someone is going to re-invent the wheel.'

'We must have known!'

'About the EHE? The army did. Word was passed to them last year, to the team researching the deployment of long-range remote-controlled tanks. Unfortunately, Piotr Asanov never worked for the army.'

Melnikov halted at the far end of the room and contemplated the clocks. 'Does Monakhov know about the diary?'

'He should do. He found it.'

'Then he understands the implications,' Melnikov said numbly.

'Yes.' Krotov fell silent for a while, then said gently: 'I'm sorry, Nikolai.'

Melnikov didn't turn from the clocks. 'A defection. And my daughter ...' he said, almost inaudibly.

'I don't believe for one minute that she's involved.'

'No, *you* don't.' Melnikov spun slowly on his heel. 'There's been a hero's reception, then.'

'For whom?'

'The young major, bringing home the spoils.'

'The diary came by courier,' Krotov said. 'Monakhov's still up there.'

THE SERBSKY INSTITUTE
MOSCOW

'Good day, comrade. I am Doctor Solovev. Please sit down.'

'Thank you.'

'You are comfortable?'

'I'm all right.'

'Good. Now then, I should like to ask you a few questions. You mustn't worry, it's all quite informal. As you can see, I'm not taking any notes.'

'I'm not worried.'

'You're sure you're comfortable?'

He shrugged. His head no longer throbbed and the wound itself was beginning to itch: a healing sign. But the bruised ribs were irksome. They'd been strapped up at Boutyrky prison hospital by someone with more enthusiasm than expertise. He shifted position. The chair had not been designed for people unable to relax. Pain flamed in his side.

The psychiatrist caught its reflection. 'You had an unfortunate experience, Leonid. Some citizens ... over-reacted.'

'They weren't citizens.'

'No?'

'No.'

'Who then?'

'You know who they were.'

'I'm afraid I don't.'

'Doesn't matter.'

'Who d'you think they were, Leonid?'

'KGB,' Leonid said wearily.

'You think that?'

'I know that.' He paused. 'It's all right. Put it down as a delusion if you want.'

'Well, it's a mistake, certainly. You have to realise that your behaviour upset a lot of bystanders.'

'One of whom happened to be armed with a gun and a cosh.'

'Leonid, really. You slipped, fell down. That's how you hurt your head.'

'And the ribs?'

'An injury in the general mêlée. I told you, some citizens regret-tably over-reacted.' Solovev paused. 'Well then, let's get down to work. What exactly were you trying to do? What was in your mind?'

'I was making a point.'

'It's a very curious way of doing it.'

'It was the only way left.' He stopped and considered for a few moments. 'I don't wish to talk about it.'

'Why not?'

'I don't, that's all.'

75

'Look,' Solovev said, 'this conversation – it's entirely off the record. It does not form part of any medico-legal examination. Nothing you say to me at this stage will go any further.'

'True?'

'Absolutely. This is just between the two of us – no notes, nothing.'

He had to laugh. 'If I thought you believed that, I'd say we ought to change places.'

TRANSCRIPT 2
GUSEINOV L. (8737119)

EXAMINING PSYCHIATRIST   P.F. SOLOVEV
DATE OF EXAMINATION   22 APRIL

If I thought you believed that, I'd say we ought to change
   places.
Why? Would you like to sit behind this desk?
(LAUGHTER) I'd have to be mad to do your job. (LAUGHTER)
You think you know something about psychiatry, then?
I certainly know all about this place.
You've been here before?
By reputation, I mean. Tell me, does Snezhnevsky get a
   copy of this transcript, too?
What transcript?
Does he get one?
I don't know what you're talking about.
Your boss, the Lord of the Mad House.
Doctor Snezhnevsky is Director of the Institute of Psychiatry
   at the Soviet Academy of Medical Sciences.
Well said. Except you forgot one little thing.
Forgot?
The Snezhnevsky diagnosis – you never mentioned it.
You're wasting my time, Guseinov.
No I'm not. I'm helping you. I was going to explain how
   your boss came up with his wonderful diagnosis that
   anyone disagreeing with the Party or the State is
   therefore insane.
That's quite enough.
And he calls himself a doctor. My, my.
The interview is over.
Turn the tape off then.
What tape?

TRANSCRIPT 2 END

Witnessed and approved by: *K.V. Vanovsky*

76

Yevgeni arrived back from Murmansk in the early evening; he greeted her casually, a stranger saying hello. He fussed over Katerina, smiling at her laughter. Tanya said, too brightly: 'Welcome home, Yevgeni.' When he turned to her the smile was gone.

The news bulletin ended with a recap on the latest aggressive moves by the West. The evidence was indisputable: the NATO alliance was an offensive organisation, not defensive. They thrust forth a sword and tried to pretend it was merely a shield. Their plans made a mockery of Western protestations of peace.

The announcer handed over to a woman who talked about the weather, particularly the return of Moscow's winter just when everyone thought it had finally gone. Then came *Today in the World*, with Vladimir Dunayev hunching over his desk, surrounded by bookshelves and trying to look as though he was speaking from home.

Ivanitsyn poured himself a drink. She studied him, thinking he looked somehow older and greyer. She had rehearsed a dozen different openings, but the long empty silence offered no cue. He switched off the TV, remained there, one hand resting on the cabinet. 'I heard what happened.' He spoke in a monotone, as lacklustre as his expression.

'Yes.'

'You were in his apartment the day after I'd gone.'

She continued to gaze at him, seeing the inner pain, the muscular tension, the deepening of the lines and creases in the skin. He went to the sofa and sat down with the excessive care of a man doubting his ground. 'They didn't tell me his name.'

'It's Leonid, Leonid Guseinov.'

'And who might he be?'

'A writer.'

'Ah.'

'The Writers' Circle ...' she began, then stumbled over the fatuity of it all.

'That's what it's called?'

'That's what it is.'

'Really.'

'Local writers, aspiring authors.'

'I didn't know you were an aspiring author, Tanya.'

77

She lit a cigarette, wafted the smoke away. 'Last June they came to the school – Leonid and some others.'

'I was away last June.'

'Yes.'

'Why did they go to the school?'

'We held a literary awareness programme.'

'I see. Catching them young.'

She didn't reply.

'Last June,' he said again, 'while all hell was breaking loose in Vladivostok ...' He shook his head. 'He's a writer, then.'

'Yes.'

'Well known?'

'He would be if they'd let him.' She hesitated. 'He made some mistakes. He wrote an anniversary pamphlet about someone; and a piece about publishing freedom, comparing literary life here with the West.'

'The West? Literary life in the West? In the West a book is only popular if it has more orgasms than paragraphs. Fodder for the dumb herd.' He sighed. 'Your Leonid, he must believe that sort of thing is very important.'

'Don't, Yevgeni ...'

His mouth twisted. 'No. Don't, Yevgeni. Don't criticise the men of letters. After all, what do I know about it? All I do is defend my country, I don't have the talent for anything else.'

'I'm sorry.'

'For me? Or for him?'

'For what happened.'

He drained the glass and brought it down hard upon the arm of the sofa. 'I could have been told, Tanya! I could have been told! I could have heard it from you instead of some flat-faced Bulgar in the Murmansk Commissariat.' There was fire in the eyes, but wetness at the rims, bruising beginning to show on the lower lids. 'A writers' circle,' he whispered. 'You must think me very stupid.'

'Please, listen to me. Leonid was – is – a friend, nothing more. You have to believe that.'

'You were in his apartment.'

'For a drink, that was all, for a –'

'You were in his apartment!'

His anger acted like a fuse, igniting her own: 'Is that a crime?'

'Yes, damn you! Yes!' He sent the glass tumbling to the floor. 'A married woman, the mother of a small child ...? What in hell did you think you were *doing?*'

She let the moment pass: 'You have to believe me, Yevgeni. Nothing happened.'

He stared at her for a long time, gaze unswerving but eyelids moving constantly, blinking back tears. He opened his mouth to speak, then seemed to think better of it.

Tanya said: 'I never mentioned him because, well, people like him – you wouldn't understand them. I don't mean that in a nasty way. It's just that they're different: not better, not worse, just different. They're concerned about the way things are. They're trying to do something ...'

But the words weren't there any more, had ebbed away just when it seemed the current was strengthening.

She shook her head. 'It doesn't matter.'

Surveillance said it was a rooftop apartment in a showpiece block in the new residential district of Polyustrovo, a half-hour's journey from central Leningrad. Surveillance did not know why the subject was there, because it was a reserved residency, made over to local government and local Party officials and their families.

Monakhov got out of the unmarked car, ordered them to watch the exits. He peered up into the afternoon sun. The building was lean, graceful – not the stolid stump of concrete he'd come to expect of high-rise developments. It soared effortlessly up from the ground, foundations swathed in a sweeping fleece of lawn. Quarter balconies, sufficient for one or two people, jutted out beside enormous panoramic windows; evergreen plants trailed and dipped their fronds and foliage over smoked perspex safety fencing. Very elegant, Monakhov decided, and very exclusive.

He walked across the lawn, enjoying the spring of turf underfoot. The supervisor opened the thick glass door for him and passively complied with the request implicit in Monakhov's outstretched palm.

'Kotik,' he said.

'No.'

'But why not?' Vadim spoke softly, the words slurring playfully.

'Because.'

He pressed his face into her hair, nuzzled her ear. 'Because what, kotik?'

79

She rolled away from him. 'I've things to do, Vadim.'

'But you're supposed to be in bed –'

'Not with you I'm not.'

'– resting.'

'Well, there's not much chance of that with you around.' She struggled to free herself of the duvet. Triple-sized bed and triple-sized covers: you didn't so much sleep in this, she thought, as inhabit it. A Leningrad family of five would gratefully share this and still make room for grandmama. By dint of some dexterous manoeuvring, hands clawing behind her back to grasp the pillow, then move it aside, she was finally able to sit upright.

She stared around the room, at the walls with their textured cream coverings, at the integral wardrobes and fitted furniture, gold-leaf traceries standing out in relief upon the smooth, all-white finish. One day a pauper, she thought, the next a prince; living like a fish-wife, and then like a Czarina. With Vadim, you never knew what was going to happen next.

'We shouldn't be here,' she said. 'There'll be the devil to pay.'

Kalininsky smiled at the ceiling. 'So long as someone else is doing the paying.'

She looked down at him and laughed. The outburst triggered a brief spasm of coughing.

'See?' he said accusingly. 'What did I tell you?'

'Give over, Vadim.'

'Bronchitis. I know all about bronchitis.' He wriggled into position alongside her, his shoulders against the soft damson padding of the bedhead. 'Rest and medication, that's the only cure.'

'Warmth. You forgot to mention warmth.'

Vadim turned down the corners of his mouth. 'I forgot to mention warmth. Okay.' Then he smiled again: 'Yelena?'

'No.'

'You haven't heard the question yet.'

'I am going back to the pharmacy tomorrow,' she said patiently. 'I have clothes to iron and things to see to. I am not staying in this bed a moment longer.'

'Marry me, Yelena.'

'No.'

'No?' Vadim said incredulously.

'No.'

'Why not?'

'There's the ironing to do.'

The bedroom door brushed across the deep pile of the carpet. 'What a charming scene,' Monakhov said.

He strolled over to the bed, wrenched the duvet off and backhanded the girl and rammed the muzzle of the automatic so hard into the Georgian's cheek that his head slammed against the padding and he slumped down onto the pillow.

Vadim Kalininsky: the dossier had shown a self-assured young bastard and it hadn't lied. He had jet-black hair, masses of it, dark skin, dark eyes, and a Zapata moustache bracketing the wide mouth – handsome son of a bitch, typical Georgian. But he didn't look too confident now.

Monakhov increased the pressure on his cheekbone. 'Get up.'

He lingered a moment longer, then stepped back to the foot of the bed. His gaze flickered about the room. To his left was the floor-to-ceiling window, a wall of glass against the outside world; between it and the left-hand bedside table was an outsize pillow like a drift of snow on the pale pink carpeting. The girl must have pushed it away during the rites of sex; the air still carried the musky after-scent of love-making.

The girl: one hand was over her mouth, the other had travelled downwards to rest defensively across her pelvis. She had rosebud breasts and a small oval face and blue eyes and flaxen hair. It had been like hitting a doll.

Monakhov stared at the Georgian again and registered the hirsute nakedness, the retreat of tumescence upon the tides of fear. Kalininsky belatedly covered himself.

'Get up,' Monakhov said.

'My clothes ... I can't leave like this.'

'I didn't say anyone was leaving.'

'Who ... who are you?'

'Public safety.' Monakhov smiled. 'And the next question is ...?'

'There's been a mistake.'

'Now now, Vadim. That isn't a question.' He swung the gun around in a slow arc and aimed it at the girl. 'This is a Makarov automatic. In the clip are eight rounds of nine-millimetre cartridge. Muzzle velocity is three hundred metres per second, with an effective range of forty-eight metres.' He paused. 'There are two things I know about in this life, Yelena: people, and guns. Tell your handsome friend that if he doesn't stand up he's likely to become an expert, too. Albeit briefly.'

The Georgian eased himself off the bed.

'Good.' The lenses flashed. 'Now, without turning your head, reach back, grasp the corners of the pillow, and pull.'

Kalininsky's fingers strained, fumbled, and then the pillow whispered across the folds of the sheets, draped itself over the edge of the bed like a broken cloud, and fell to the carpet.

'Excellent,' Monakhov said. 'Lie down again.'

'You thought I had a gun under there.' He spoke partly in disbelief, partly in contempt.

'Come along, comrade,' said Monakhov pleasantly. 'Face down, hands behind your back. You can tell them how you showed your arse to the KGB.'

The Georgian hesitated, then complied. Monakhov moved to the window and stood looking down at the girl. 'And now,' he said, 'we can begin. You can talk to me here, or you can talk to me in another place.'

'I wish to know the reason for these questions. It's my legal right.'

'You have no rights, gozphoza. You don't even have the right to be here.' He paused. 'Yelena Pinsky, you are to be charged with membership of an unlawful organisation acting against the safety and security of the State and people. How do you answer?'

'I don't know what you're talking about.'

'Let's see if I can help, then.' Monakhov smiled. 'Leonid Guseinov, recently the subject of close surveillance: on not one but four separate occasions you were photographed in his company.'

'He's a friend.'

'Let's try another friend: Piotr Asanov.'

'I ... I don't know him.' She lowered her gaze and stared at her hands clasped together in her lap. The whiteness of betrayal showed in the flesh around the knuckles.

'We have a diary,' Monakhov said, 'Piotr Asanov's diary. It's an interesting little book – full of dates, places, names ... your name, Yelena. We didn't connect you straight away but we knew Asanov had been associating with the writer. A check on Guseinov's file produced the pictures I mentioned: Guseinov and Yelena; Asanov and Yelena.'

Yelena said dully: 'I met Piotr through Leonid. Is it a crime?'

'It seems to have led to one. Such a pity. A clever man like Doctor Asanov, highly respected, yet –'

'Don't give me that rubbish! Nobody cared about Piotr. Nobody cared whether he lived or died. He was a madman.'

Monakhov settled deeper into the chair and watched the angry flaring of colour in her cheeks. Better, much better. They get annoyed and they pick up tempo and then – then they trip.

She continued to glare at him. 'Piotr only spoke up for what he believed.'

'Yet he's not even a Jew, is he?'

'You don't have to be, to care.'

'Do you care, Yelena Pinsky?'

She lapsed into silence.

Monakhov surveyed the apartment. 'You humanitarians, you certainly live well.' He paused. 'There was a conspiracy, wasn't there? You and Guseinov and Kalininsky –'

'Vadim has nothing to do with this.'

'Kalininsky and Melnikova; that's right, Tanya Melnikova.'

'No.'

'I forgot to mention the third way we tied you to Asanov. We tapped Melnikova's phone. You came on asking after her, and poor Leonid, and poor Piotr and … So many questions, such a lengthy call. It was traced to the Kirov Apothecary before you were half-way through.'

'Tanya isn't involved.'

'In what?'

'Whatever you're trying to accuse me of.'

Monakhov smiled. 'Where is Piotr Asanov?'

'You took him away.'

'I think not, though yes, he was taken away, thanks to you and your friends.' Monakhov paused. 'I don't know; the lady and the tramp, the pharmacist and the thief. What a combination. You and Melnikova, d'you have a weakness for such men?'

'Leave Vadim alone.' Her lower lip was beginning to tremble, an almost imperceptible quivering that travelled the length of her small body. 'Leave him alone, please.'

'But he's a carrier – of the infection. Oh, didn't you know, treason is an infection?' Monakhov shook his head. 'You're from quite a big family, aren't you? What is it, three brothers? Three sisters? Parents?

Grandparents? Tst tst. That's ten people infected already. Ten people who'll have to be ... cleansed.'

'My grandparents –'

'Are old and sick and it really is a dreadful shame.' Monakhov smiled. 'I've heard it all before.' He reached inside his jacket, withdrew the small silver oblong of an Olympus recorder, and set it down on the smoked-glass table in front of her. 'You've nothing to fear, Yelena. Whatever you say will be recorded, then transcribed. The transcription will be brought to you for signature. There's no question of words being twisted or words being put in your mouth. I do not fabricate evidence.'

He turned towards the picture window. This room was so high up, and his vantage point so distant from the glass that all he could see was blue sky and white cloud, the colours burnished by the lenses. The silence seemed set to course endlessly. Then, haltingly, she said:

'I was contacted ... a man ... he said he wanted me to pass a message to Piotr. I didn't know the man's name.'

'Did the others?'

'No. I told you, it was done through me. No one else knew what was going on.'

Monakhov watched the slow spooling of the tape. 'Asanov knew.'

'It wouldn't have been in his interest to say anything.'

'Not even to his faithful friends?'

'Why don't you listen to me?' she said loudly, anger lending force to the protest.

'But I am listening. And I'm saying, the evidence –'

'You have no evidence!' She stared into her own image. Monakhov remained motionless, showing not even a sign of respiration. The immobility unnerved her, made her think of something glacial, of tributaries of ice instead of blood. The shivering began anew.

'All right,' Monakhov said finally, 'for the record: are you or are you not a friend of Leonid Guseinov, Tanya Melnikova, and Vadim Kalininsky? Yes or no.'

'Yes.'

'State how your involvement began with Doctor Asanov.'

She hesitated, then said: 'January – I think it was January – I met him for the first time. He'd just arrived in Leningrad. He was supposed to be starting a tutorship at the university but the post was withdrawn. He knew no one, had nowhere to go.'

'Were you then contacted by someone with an interest in his welfare?'

'Yes.'

'And this someone – a man, yes? – what did he say?'

'He asked about Piotr – how he was, what were his plans.' She paused. 'I didn't know this man. I still don't. At first I thought he might have something to do with ...'

'With?'

'... with the Israelis. I thought they might want to help him.'

'So you did understand he was a representative of a foreign power?'

'I didn't really think about it.'

'Even though this man wished to help Doctor Asanov leave the Soviet Union? That was what he wanted, wasn't it?'

'That didn't crop up until later.'

'But that was the proposition. You were the go-between, to arrange the defection of a prominent scientist.'

'That's not true!' Indignation drove her to her feet. 'That isn't true! You know what they thought of Piotr, how they treated him!'

Monakhov sighed. 'Stop the tape.'

'I'll have my say, damn you!'

'It's not going to be wasted on this kind of argument.' He pocketed the machine. 'Well. That was to be the gentle approach.'

She eyed him warily. 'What are you going to do?'

'Me? Nothing. But you are. You and your boyfriend are going to get dressed. Then you're both taking a trip into town.'

'Vadim can't help you ...'

Monakhov smiled. 'That may well be the problem.'

He sat down on the low modular dressing table, one shoe resting upon the foot of the bed. Kalininsky tried to speak to her but the gun waved him to silence. Monakhov gazed from the one to the other, saw how she was already distancing herself from the Georgian, as though sheer lack of physical proximity would protect him. As if it mattered.

Kalininsky stood awkwardly by the wardrobes, staring mutely towards the opposite side of the bed. She dressed slowly, keeping her back to him. Monakhov remained motionless until both were fully clothed.

He smiled. The gun came up and three rounds tore into Kalininsky, spinning him, smashing him against the wall, and then the muzzle tracked smoothly across to the left and she was lifted off her feet by the impact, and then the scream and the gunfire and the shattering of glass came together as one.

She went out with limbs flailing, into the sunlight and the breeze, and was broken on the paving stones, while the shining shower of small sharp fragments tinkled and rang all around.

They tumbled and settled and covered her back, and when Monakhov finally looked down he could hardly see her at all.

CHAPTER
SEVEN

MOSCOW

Krotov sat with elbows propped on the desk top, fists balled, jaw pressed down upon knuckles. He considered Monakhov's erect figure with unblinking gaze.

'Well, Major Monakhov, you have been a busy fellow.' His tone was measured, devoid of inflexion. Krotov paused – it was disquieting, talking to a golden reflection of yourself. 'I hadn't realised the weather was improving.'

'The weather?'

'Those glasses.'

'I have an eye condition, retinal sensitivity.'

'You don't like what you see?'

'I meant to the light.'

'The light. Ah.' Krotov nodded. 'And did the light bother you in Leningrad?'

'Comrade colonel?'

'I mean, something must have done. One dead, one dying; a funeral for the girl and very probably another for her lover. Something must have ... troubled you.'

'It's in my report.'

'Mmm, I thought it might be.' Monakhov was standing so still Krotov half expected a plaque to materialise at the man's feet, identifying the sculptor and the reason for his handiwork.

'All right,' Krotov said eventually, 'sit down.' He waited while the statue recomposed itself. 'Vasily, isn't it?'

'Yes, comrade colonel.'

'Vasily.' Krotov leaned back, hands behind head, appearing to digest the information. 'We haven't had much chance to talk, have we? No sooner do I get a call from Fifth than you walk in, walk out again, then head north for exploits of derring-do.' He threw out a brief and inscrutable smile. 'Vasily Monakhov. I've been hearing all about you.' Another pause as Krotov clicked his tongue in disapproval. 'Classic background: five years at Moscow State Institute of International Relations. Family, was it?'

'Family?'

'Father had connections, did he?'

'He was a farm manager in Kazakhstan. I went to school in Alma Ata.'

'He did well, then, getting you into the Institute.'

'I was the token peasant,' said Monakhov simply, without emotion.

'So was I.' Krotov sat up. 'Surprised? Well, I was, though it was different then. Everything was different.' He went on briskly: 'So, why did you want to join the KGB?'

'I was recruited from the Institute. I wanted a career.'

'Career?' The small man laughed. 'Damn me, it's more than a career. This is the good life – power, wealth, status. You're an aristocrat now.'

'I don't think so, comrade colonel.' The lenses flashed. 'My father was employed by the Department of Agriculture. He was a super-visor, when they were reclaiming the north-eastern steppe. He ordered equipment through regional officials. But he didn't know every requisition was being amended by them. For every piece of equipment my father ordered, they ordered another. Loads were intercepted on delivery, the surplus sold on the black market. My father was in a labour camp for three years before the full truth was known. My mother ...'

'Yes?'

'My mother died. Father had been sentenced to life and she ... she gave up.'

'I'm sorry,' Krotov said.

The lenses flashed again. 'That is why I was sent to the Institute, comrade colonel.'

'Reparations?'

'Perhaps.'

'And that,' Krotov said slowly, 'that is why you do what you do.'

'It's a career.'

'No, it's a crusade.' Krotov hunched forward. 'You and that lunatic in Red Square, you're both the same.' He sifted through a sheaf of papers in the wire tray, removed a single sheet. 'Induction, Minsk; special training, Odessa; special techniques, Leningrad.' He glanced up. 'The old place on Nachimov Prospekt – it still there?'

'Yes, comrade colonel.'

'I went on a small-arms course there.'

'I went on nerve-gas weaponry.'

Krotov lowered the page. 'I see you've done Western orientation at Kuibyshev. Some set-up, isn't it? Still got that shopping centre, have they? London, supposedly.'

'They called it the Home Counties.'

'Home Counties, of course. Let's see if I can remember . . . Odeon Cinema, right?'

'It's a place of bingo now.'

'Oh, pity. What else . . . Dolcis shoe shop; pedestrian crossing, black and white stripes with orange beacons.'

'The beacons have gone. They have lights now, with symbols.'

'Symbols?'

'Little green men.'

'Really? I thought that's what we were.'

'Comrade colonel?'

'KGB, major. Aliens.' Krotov was thoughtful again. 'Is it a Marks and Spencers or a Lewis's?'

'Marks and Spencers.'

'With parking meters outside.'

'They've been relocated.'

'I'm not surprised. Marks and Spencers couldn't have been over-joyed with them.'

Monakhov shifted in the chair. 'Comrade colonel, if you don't mind, I have work still to do . . .'

'Oh come on, don't spoil it. This is the first opportunity we've had to chat.' Krotov paused. 'Tell me, were you taught how to order refreshments in a tavern?'

'They call them pubs; and you order by the pint.'

'Very good. You might also like to note that in Ireland they order by the glass; in America it's probably by the quart.' Krotov smiled and tapped the paper. 'According to this you worked for the Twelfth Direction of the Second Chief Directorate. How apt. Graft and corruption in local government – that must have struck a personal chord, Vasily.' Monakhov didn't reply. Krotov continued: 'Then you went to the Ninth and Tenth Directions of the Fifth Chief Directorate. Do you dislike dissidents, too?'

'They're enemies of the State.'

'Yes, but it's not as though they're corrupt.'

'Moral corruption is as bad as anything else.'

Krotov nodded. 'Fifth loaned you out, didn't they? To First, Department A: *Dezinformatsiya.* That must've been interesting. Tell me about it.'

Monakhov's head lowered. 'I ... I can't recall.'

'Try.'

A sigh of irritation, then: 'There were several projects. One of them concerned Jeanne Kirkpatrick, US Ambassador to the United Nations. We fabricated a White House cable ordering Kirkpatrick to be more supportive of South Africa. It damaged America's image with the blacks.'

'Anything else?'

'There was a humorous one. The American trash press said when Armstrong landed on the moon he heard a voice in the rocks. He thought it was God, yet the voice was foreign.'

'God *isn't* an American?' Both eyebrows rose.

'The trash press said Armstrong later discovered the voice he'd heard was that of a Moslem at prayer. So he changed his religion.'

'What did Department A have to do with all this?'

'We embroidered it a little. We said that when NASA discovered their astronaut had become a Moslem, they dismissed him. We circulated the story in every country with a Moslem population. Further proof of American Zionist Imperialist intolerance.'

'How amusing,' Krotov said tonelessly. 'Tell me about Andropov.'

'I don't understand.'

'The London *Daily Express* exclusively reported that Andropov had been shot by Brezhnev's son.'

'I don't remember.'

'Georgi Barancheyev does, your ex-boss. He said you took great delight in discrediting the Brezhnev regime, nationally and internationally.'

'It was corrupt.'

'And is now no more?' The taut smile again.

Monakhov shrugged. 'Perhaps.'

'You know,' Krotov said slowly, 'who Tanya Melnikova's father is.'

'Yes.'

'Someone has discussed him with you, perhaps?'

'No, comrade colonel.'

'No? Well, I am surprised. Here's a juicy tale, better than anything ever concocted by Department A. Here's one of the old guard implicated via his daughter in a defection. You're sure no one has mentioned it to you?'

'I am sure.' The lenses levelled with Krotov's eyes.

Krotov built another steeple with his fingers, then promptly collapsed it. 'Why did you stop the Pinsky interview? Was it because she was about to exonerate Melnikov's daughter?'

'She couldn't very well exonerate someone she had already implicated.'

'*You* say.'

'No. Pinsky said it. Melnikova was party to a conspiracy to achieve the Asanov defection.'

'That isn't on the tape.'

'She said it earlier, comrade colonel.'

Krotov shook his head in a slow, deliberate mime of rebuttal. 'Listen to me, comrade major, and listen very carefully. I may not have a diploma in defenestration, but I do know how things work – including tape recorders. There's going to be an inquiry, Major Monakhov, because I want to know why two unarmed citizens suddenly attacked a KGB officer with a gun in his hand. Until I have all the facts, there's not much I can do about you. But I would advise you to tread very, very carefully. I am running an investigation, not a crusade. You were wished upon me and if I could get rid of you, I would. But for the time being ...'

'I have my orders, comrade colonel.'

'And I wonder what they are.' Krotov stood up. 'Now get out.'

A momentary hesitation, then Monakhov strolled to the door. It closed gently behind him.

Krotov sat down again and stared at his hands. They were trembling.

Later that day, Krotov laid out paper and pens, four of them with different inks: red, blue, green and black. On each one of eight sheets of paper he wrote the name of a city: Washington, Paris,

Vienna, Rome, Oslo, West Berlin, London and Bonn. He lifted the telephone, asked central switch to put him through to the satellite board, then asked the board for clearance to the comm net, and finally sat back to face the long wait.

Eventually the inertia became too much to bear. He stood up, stretched, peered at the panel of clocks, but couldn't immediately make out the one displaying Moscow time. The impressive parade, he decided, was a metaphor for the redundant technology of an over-acquisitive age. He looked at his own watch: 3.55 p.m. And darkness beyond the window, as though they were still in the midst of winter.

Street lamps burned through cowls of ice. He trudged cautiously across the city, not really aware of where he was going, just walking, breathing deep, thinking.

He found himself in Pushkin Square. Framed by its canopy of snow the Rossiya Cinema looked less futuristic than usual. He showed his ID, passed into the warm gloom, and settled down to watch the end of the fifteen-minute newsreel *Novosti Dnya*. The sound was far too loud and the pictures uninspiring. Tractors, he thought, bloody tractors. If it wasn't tractors it was hydro-electric schemes. If they show another one of those I may start throwing things. The final image, of a hydro-electric scheme, faded from the screen, and as the lights went on for the intermission, Krotov removed his hands from his eyes.

The feature was Mikhalkov Konchalovsky's *Siberiada*. Krotov resolved to put everything out of his mind and concentrate on the delicately drawn drama of life in a small Siberian community. He had become a frequent cinema-goer in recent years, and had acquired insights into the language of film, the skills and aspirations of those who made them; he even knew some of the names of those behind the camera. But this time, despite his initial interest, he could not stay awake, and slipped into a deep sleep with the image of the actress Lyudmilla Gurchenko smoothing his way into a comfortable dark.

He awoke to the sound of seats snapping upright. The house lights were brightening. He got up, moved unsteadily into the aisle. Behind him, on screen, the credits unwound. The name of Dmitri Asanov, assistant music editor, was midway down.

He returned to his office. The comm net was now available for scrambled access. He made the calls, then sat back to await results.

Eventually the phone rang: it was Kotcheff in Rome – the first to get the message and seek a briefing.

Krotov was less than explicit. 'I should like you to go sightseeing; a little travelling, around the city.' He cradled the receiver.

Eventually the phone rang again. He answered: another call from another city, no questions or answers, merely the single terse instruction.

Night stilled the tempo of the day, but he did not notice. Only the coloured pens, the coloured cities ...

Paris was the last to come through. Access time to stations varied according to demand and Paris was last because Centre had been hogging it for hours. Krotov knew why. The Middle East desk was worrying about the Iranians again. If you wanted to know anything about Iran the best place to ask was Paris.

When all the briefings had been concluded, he stayed at his desk, labouring on a series of predictive scenarios, only to decide, two hours later, that it was impossible to foretell what would happen. Nothing, probably; the odds were so great. He screwed up the paper and irritably swept the scraps from his desk.

He spent the long night on the floor, huddled in a pile of greatcoats borrowed from the basement lockers. The arrangement was as absurd as it was uncomfortable, but he could not risk being away from the phone. For the first time he regretted having had the old gas fire removed. It had supplemented the meagre heating system, but at the cost of a prized japonica, which had unexpectedly exhibited a terminal distaste for the fumes.

He shivered and wondered how its replacement coped with hypothermia.

At dawn he struggled upright and surveyed the room. Everything was untidy, with paper seemingly scattered everywhere. He loathed it, the disorder, the absence of discipline.

He used a washroom along the corridor, rinsed himself in luke-warm water and rubbed at the overnight stubble as though seeking to scour it clean away. Then he returned to the room, and the clocks, and the RTP.

Random Travel Pattern: you did it when you wanted to be mischievous, to test the wits and strength of the opposition. You did it by sending out a tame fox and counting the hounds that followed. Sometimes, as now, you did it out of sheer desperation, because time was short, and there was no other option to which you could cling.

By noon he knew most of it.

Oslo was out because they only deployed a two-man team; Rome, for the same reason. Obviously they couldn't care less.

Bonn, predictably Wagnerian, had everything apart from the fireworks. Three teams of four. Maracec would not have been surprised to find a helicopter on his roof. So, not Bonn: too much fuss, too much noise.

Paris? Well, Stekovich had been there long enough to know half the SCDF on first-name terms. They kept bumping into each other and making awkward apologies. No, Paris was out: too clumsy.

Vienna? Vienna could have been hot because a conduit still ran through there, but this time it was out because when Tallin stretched out his aching legs under a coffee-shop table he counted not one but three businessmen who were neither meeting their lovers nor eating sachertorte. Not Vienna: too obvious.

Berlin hadn't really counted at all. To contemplate routing a property through there you either had to be a tactical genius or a devotee of Western spy fiction. Nothing happened in reality in Berlin because far too much happened in fantasy.

Krotov stared fixedly at the phone. Only two places left now.

On the wall, the clocks ticked on.

'Hello, Gregor.'

The voice jolted Krotov from his reverie. He glanced up and saw the familiar, silver-haired figure of Melnikov standing uncertainly in the doorway. He took a deep breath, let go slowly and said: 'You want to be careful. That's twice now. Next time they might take you in for psychiatric observation: nobody in their right mind comes here voluntarily.'

'I was worried.'

Krotov shook his head in resignation: 'All right, Nikolai. Have a chair.'

Melnikov trod warily through the litter. 'You seem to have been busy,' he said.

'Mmm.'

'The Asanov inquiry?'

Krotov leaned back, rubbed his eyes. 'You know something,

you're not even supposed to be in here, let alone asking questions about national security.'

The politician settled into the green chair and wrapped the folds of his coat around him. 'I apologise.'

'Yes, well,' Krotov said, then lapsed into silence.

'I wondered,' Melnikov said, haltingly, 'if you'd heard anything.'

'Mmm.'

'Gregor –' no more than a whisper – 'please.'

Krotov gave no sign of having heard. Instead, he stood up, walked slowly down the room and came to a halt in front of the clocks. 'Ten o'clock,' he said. 'How time flies.' Then, before Melnikov could speak: 'Though there's no proof yet, your question, amazingly, seems to have been answered.'

'Question?'

'Is he dead or did he walk.' He turned from the panel. 'Asanov's gone, Nikolai. And yes, your daughter was one of the last to see him before his defection.'

Melnikov seemed to shrink into himself, arms crossed protectively across his chest, head bowed in an attitude of defeat.

'If it's any comfort,' Krotov added, 'everyone's more concerned about what's happening now than what happened in Leningrad. In point of fact, they're so concerned, First have been tied up with GNTK all yesterday and today. I've been running their operation for them.'

'I don't understand?'

'I'm Second, Nikolai, domestic, not international.'

Melnikov cradled his head in his hands. 'A defection though . . . it's unbelievable.'

'Obviously someone appreciated the good doctor's work before we did.'

'Do you know who?'

'There's no proof, as I said, but SIGINT's just finished intensive sampling of Washington–London traffic. Amongst all the usual stuff were five three-second data bursts, priority flashes we'll never decode this side of May Day.'

'So the Americans have him?'

'No, the British.' A wry smile. 'Appropriate, really, seeing how I've been playing the great detective these past thirty-six hours.' By way of explanation: 'Sherlock Holmes, Nikolai, master of deduction.'

'You're telling me you just looked at that map and . . .?' Melnikov came upright, animated by disbelief.

'No, Nikolai. I did not look at any map. I made my own, then peopled it with our employees. They went out into eight different cities and acted as suspiciously as possible. Then they checked for the reaction.'

'And the British?'

'London is very sensitive. Touch it and it tenses.'

'What happened?'

'Nothing.' Krotov smiled. 'Our man completed his task without spotting a single tag.' An admiring shake of the head. 'They must have used a small army.' He registered Melnikov's incomprehension, said: 'He didn't see anyone because he was looking for a face in the crowd. But they were the crowd.'

PART III

CHAPTER
EIGHT

BRISTOL
ENGLAND

The ports were ideal: they saw a lot of passing traffic – itinerants, nationals of all kinds. There were safe houses in Hull and Liverpool, too, places where arrival and departure did not excite comment, where different voices and accents were the norm.

Karodin settled into the sparsely furnished top-floor bedsitter in what had once been a merchant's house. The villa stood in a small terrace of six. It testified to yesterday's wealth and today's indifferent austerity: gardens overgrown, roof-slates lying in scattered fragments across the paths, dark pockmarks in the yellow bricks where the mortar had long since crumbled.

There was a tart on the second floor whose state of repair wasn't much better than that of the house. Centre could have thrown her out, but the cover was ideal: strangers arrived from time to time and no one in the street wondered why. The landlord and his wife were the only other occupants, a Latvian couple who'd been deep for twenty years and had probably forgotten what Riga, never mind Moscow, looked like. He worked on the docks; she seemed to be making a career out of bingo.

When Karodin arrived on her doorstep she asked no questions, merely ushered him inside. He paused in the narrow hall, caught a glimpse of their reflections in a mirror framed with tarnished brass: a stocky, middle-aged man with black hair cropped close enough for monasticity, a small, frowsy woman in shapeless frock with loops of auburn hair resting in improbable coils on her scalp.

She did not ask his name, but stated instead: 'You are the guest, then.'

Karodin nodded.

'London said you were due. D'you need anything?'

'Peace.'

And now he sat in the parlour, offended by the hideous confection of their furnishings: black vinyl suite, orange cushions, green baize card-table spotted with cigarette burns, an impoverished display unit in chipped white melamine and, dominating one wall, a painting of an Oriental woman with a turquoise face.

He resolutely kept his back to her and squatted on a padded stool by the fireplace; the telephone, inexplicably, sat in the hearth.

Polyakov would ring soon. Karodin smiled wryly. One acolyte ringing another, graduates of the Krotov class of '61. Those were the days – you and I, young and fresh-faced and on our first attachment to Centre itself, not knowing what to expect; confident, fearful, brash, anxious ... Going up the steps in stiff unyielding uniforms and being marched into the cluttered room where the small bald figure, silent, impassive, inspected each one of us in turn, then voiced the one question we could never have foreseen: 'Tell me, do you know anything about plants?'

Krotov. All those years ago, even at that first meeting, there was something about his manner that spoke of permanence, of constancy. Colonel Krotov was curiously ageless, changeless – a little man nurturing quiet, elegant schemes.

Karodin sparked a match with his thumbnail, a trick acquired from watching too many American B-movies at the KGB Officers' Club cinema. He lit the cigarette and exhaled lazily. And now, he thought, the young Polyakov is assistant station chief, Washington DC, while the young Karodin is here in England, eighteen months into his second term with the commercial secretariat: acolytes once more, brought together by the enigmatic figure in the third-floor room. It made you feel nervous all over again.

The telephone jangled.

There were no pleasantries; voice modulation processors lent Polyakov's speech a strange, metallic ring.

'You were inquiring about the concert tour?'

'That's correct.' Karodin spoke quickly, curtly: the first call on a new signals route you had to be extra careful, even if the line was tracer sensitive, ready to disconnect at the slightest variation in the electrical resistance.

'How can we help then,' Polyakov said.

'I believe they are over here for rehearsals. One of the players is coming from your part of the world. I can't think of the name, but I'm sure if I saw the face ...'

'We'll attend to it,' Polyakov said. The connection terminated.

Karodin cradled the receiver and lapsed into thoughtful silence again. Still no proof of anything, still nothing more definite to go on than Krotov's gut feeling that it was a joint operation, that there'd have to be a senior liaison man moving between the States and England.

Karodin snapped another match into flame, then snuffed it out and spun it into the ceramic ashtray.

He would be a senior man, a professional, highly experienced; someone who would not make mistakes.

Except the mistake was in the movement.

WASHINGTON DC

Two backgrounders from Central, marked 'J.G. Gulliver - For Information Only', were delivered soon after he returned from lunch. It took him another half-hour to work up enough enthusiasm to read them.

Afghanistan, Update 212 Series B: it reconfirmed what everyone knew anyway - that the Soviets were stuck with the sort of guerilla war they'd been seeking to inflict everywhere else. The irony was delightful.

Moscow, Issue 0358 Series CF: Gulliver groaned. Kremlin factions; more goings-on in the landlocked love-boat. Once upon a time it was hawks versus doves. Now the battle was between cliques, families even, a war between the gerontocracy and the younger technocrats.

Barnes came in then. He was wearing sunglasses. Gulliver waited for him to trip over the water-cooler. Barnes was six-two and built like a quarterback; if he fell they'd hear it on the Hill.

Barnes negotiated the obstacle, sat down and said: 'Hangover.'

'It's mid-afternoon.'

'A big hangover.'

Gulliver studied him. It was just about a year since Barnes had arrived as his deputy. He had the blue eyes and blond hair of a Swede, though he'd actually been born in Montana. But he thought

101

so much yet said so little, and then in such a slow rolling drawl, that Gulliver had originally mistaken him for a retarded Texan, in a wig.

Barnes removed the sunglasses and squinted at him. 'You rang?'

'I wanted to know where you were.'

'I did too.' He stretched his legs, raised them up and thudded his boot heels down onto the desk top.

Gulliver's gaze flicked to the gleaming leather.

Tehran, February 1979: the Shah in full flight and the Ayatollah in full flood; and the Marxist-Leninist fedayeen shooting their way into the compound of the American Embassy. Exactly what Barnes was doing there, Gulliver never did discover. The file wasn't exactly definitive and Barnes's habit of using one word where six would've been welcome didn't promote enlightenment.

A bullet left Barnes bleeding from the shoulder. He wound up in Amir Alam hospital, though not for long. The laughing boys dragged him off to a jail packed with Iranian civilians. They were to be executed at dawn, victims of the People's Revolutionary Volunteer Court. The trial would begin after sentence had been carried out, it was the way they did things in Iran. With no hope of escaping, Barnes opted for a compromise – safe escort back to the Embassy. There was some chance of survival with the rest of the staff and the poor bastards in the Marine detachment. A transfer, Barnes explained, from the jail to the Embassy; not an escape. And in exchange for this shuffling of paperwork, these boots – genuine cowboy, as worn by Glen Campbell. The jailer smiled. His sister worked in the Embassy commissary. They played Glen Campbell tapes all the time.

Thus it was that Barnes returned to the Embassy. Barefoot.

Gulliver continued to eye the replacement pair – Barnes's peculiar idea of what constituted a good-luck charm. He roused himself. 'Asanov's breaking.'

'Wide?'

'He's talking and he's working. The Wycliffe woman seems to be getting through to him.'

Barnes smiled. 'The lady with the amp.'

'Aw, Jesus.'

'Hey, don't knock it. It took a while to come up with that.'

'So long as it was in your own time.' Gulliver reached inside his pocket and withdrew a pack of cigarettes. He caught the accusatory glance and said: 'Don't say a word. It was that London trip. They've an admiral who should've gone down with the *Titanic*.' He inhaled, coughed. 'Our presence is required.'

'For what?'

'A meeting, now. You, me, Larson and some guy from Moffett. The meeting's mainly for your benefit: they've started work on Asanov's designs and you're going out there to check over their security. Seems they understand this thing even if nobody else does.'

Barnes stood up. 'I understand it.'

'Jesus,' Gulliver said again.

They went their separate ways after the meeting. Gulliver shrugged on his coat, left the secure zone and squeezed into the second elevator with a group of home-going secretaries from the agency. He dawdled after them as they filed through the double glass doors and was about to follow when a potted palm walked into him. An apology and then a smiling Japanese emerged from behind the leaves. Gulliver grunted and went on out into the street.

A small delivery truck was parked half-way across the kerb, rear doors hanging open. The scent of dozens of different blooms mingled in sweet intensity. He wondered what slice of the agency's budget got expended on flora. They had a regular park in there, nature on rental, to be rearranged whenever the vista palled.

He stared about him. His own car was in the shop with a blown gasket, its failure irritating, its absence inconvenient. He sighed. No sign of a bloody cab anywhere. Or is that one?

In the fresnel screen the image blurred then sharpened. The lens zoomed, riding smooth on fixed focus. He waved, tried to flag a ride. Before his hand lowered the motor drive came in and the shutter tripped repeatedly.

The Japanese returned and the flower van moved off.

BRISTOL

Five black and white glossies, size ten by eight – they'd come by courier from London, delivered by someone Karodin never saw, the envelope handed to the woman without comment while the car sat at the kerb, engine ticking over.

Karodin fanned them out over the card table, then raised the first print for inspection. Its surface shimmered in the pale light: a tall man mowing the front lawn of a white clapboard house. Karodin turned the picture over. A sliver of paper attached to the back read: George Butler, Assistant Director Eastern 7.

The next one, a bulky figure clambering out of a car: Jonah Delk, Assistant Director Central Europe 3.

A man and a woman emerging from a KeyMart loaded with shopping parcels: Kevin Donnelly, Assistant Director NATO 6.

A man waving obligingly to the camera: John Gulliver, Assistant Director Western 1.

A man leaning against the upright of a tennis net: Roland Cameron, Assistant Director Eastern 4.

Karodin stacked the photographs and drummed his fingers on the top one. All DIA; another assumption but you had to narrow the field. Besides, you could virtually rule out CIA because Asanov was on a military project and, after Powers' celebrated U2 flight, even all those years ago, CIA was still disqualified from Curtain Country. It now played its games in Central and South America, or on the chequer board of Laos, Cambodia and Vietnam.

DIA: it had to be one of them.

WASHINGTON DC

The cabbie placed his bags in the trunk. Gulliver stood to one side and looked up and down the tree-lined avenue, checking parked vehicles on the left, then the right. Everything was fine; every one of them was familiar.

They headed into town. Gulliver opened the *Post*, holding it unnecessarily high to ward off conversation. From time to time he turned to stare out of the rear window. The grey Buick was still there.

From Pennsylvania they turned onto New Hampshire. Gulliver checked again, relaxed: the Buick had gone straight on.

There was a snarl-up around Roosevelt Bridge so they held to the East Bank as far as the Arlington. Gulliver re-checked. A blue Chevy tailgated, hung back, closed up again. He waited. It peeled off along Ohio Drive.

Southbound, now, on George Washington; he lowered the newspaper and looked out at the Potomac. The city looked bright, clean, spreading in tidy grandeur under the warm blue sky.

The sky was the same colour as the third tag, but Gulliver left the survey interval much too long and by the time he checked both the cab and the Pontiac were locked into a traffic stream that could only have one ultimate destination.

The airport was like all airports, a hell of a place for mission feel. Too many stimuli — the brain had to cope with responses and choices and old ladies blocking and small kids jostling. With all that going on, it wasn't possible to do very much apart from pause now and then, try to examine it all, sweep the scene with peripheral vision.

His profile was caught three times by the Minox.

LONDON

Gulliver reached for the phone as soon as he awoke and dialled the number Larson had given him. He sat in the bedside chair, trying to stifle a seemingly unending spasm of yawning. It had been a bitch of a flight. The occupant of the adjacent seat had snored for three hours. When he'd asked the flight attendant if they had no-snoring zones like no-smoking zones she'd merely smiled and inexplicably brought him another piece of cheesecake. He'd stared at it in wonderment; perhaps he was meant to stick it in his ear.

After immigration he'd queued in morose silence while the carousel yielded everyone's baggage but his.

Leech's voice cut in abruptly: 'Hello? Who's that?'

'Me, Gulliver,' he said sourly. 'Who're you?'

'Ah! Mr G! We were just talking about you. I'm with Sir Alec, the line's been switched through. Where are you?'

Perhaps you'd like to send a card to the Kremlin, he thought, 'Mr G arrived safe room 330, Heathrow Hotel, London. Regards, and how's the weather?'

If there'd been the slightest chance of a phone tap, which thank Christ there wasn't, he'd have disconnected there and then. Instead he said: 'I'm at the hotel. Got in early this morning.'

'Right then. Listen: the briefing starts at three o'clock. We'll send a car over at two-fifteen. Black Austin Ambassador, you'll recognise it.'

'I could easily take a cab.'

'Nonsense. You're a stranger in a strange land, have to get the old welcome mat out, you know.' Leech rang off. Gulliver stared at the earpiece for a long time, then began to unpack his suitcase.

He'd expected it to go on to Amsterdam or Australia, but the airport had somehow located it and phoned through to the hotel while he was standing in the lobby wondering what else would go wrong. Exhausted from the flight, he'd decided to go to bed; you never knew how long it would take to get the baggage from terminal to hotel. The instant he'd fallen asleep the porter had arrived and presented him with the suitcase in the manner of one awarding a trophy.

Great start, he'd told himself. Just great.

The call came through at 2.00 p.m. Karodin let it ring three times before answering. London was using digital substitution so he responded as though to a wrong number and waited for them to try again.

Eventually: 'We have the text now. It begins: "Hello who's that query, me Gulliver who're you query" and response.'

Karodin blinked. 'Me Gulliver who're you?'

'Yes.' The voice was as metallic as all the previous callers. 'Text resumes: "Ah Mr G we were just talking about you stop."'

Karodin shook his head. 'Is this a new form of parole?'

'Certainly it is ... singular.'

'Check it,' Karodin said.

Gulliver had expected Whitehall at least. Instead the car stopped outside Great Westminster House in Horseferry Road and Leech led him into the cavernous gloom of what seemed to be an abandoned hotel.

'That's correct,' Leech said, 'one of the best in town before the war.' They waited at the central desk while security made a call. Leech glanced around. 'Walnut and Art Deco, eh? Very tasty.'

'What happened to it?'

'Requisitioned, I imagine. Anyway, the tourist trade rather dropped off in 1940.' He chuckled. 'Actually, things've been dropping off ever since. There was a dreadful flap last year – they thought some masonry had flattened a couple of passing tourists.' He paused. 'Americans.' Then, with only the slightest hint of regret: 'It missed, though.'

Gulliver continued to inspect the lobby. 'Why don't you preserve places like this, spend some money?'

'We would if it was in the Falklands.'

Gulliver frowned, decided to let the remark pass. 'As a matter of interest, what is this place?'

'MAF – Ministry of Agriculture and Fisheries. This is the fish bit. They've a computer, you see.'

'The fish?'

'The department – it monitors all shipping activity in coastal waters; very useful, British technology at its best.'

'Does it use a lot of coal?'

Leech grinned. 'Tst tst, Mr Gulliver. This is a smokeless zone.'

She was wearing a lavender wool two-piece with a white silk shirt. Apart from the mad admiral, she was the only person Gulliver recognised. He examined his surroundings, a long narrow room with pale green walls and furnishings comprising three rows of stacking chairs of a type probably last seen at Buckingham Palace garden parties before the Abdication. He sat down in the third row, exercising extreme caution. Although physical risks were overstated in contemporary fable, field operations sometimes jeopardised the wellbeing of the participants. He did not wish to become a casualty of the Ministry of Agriculture and Fisheries.

His gaze continued to roam: no windows, central-heating pipes angling hither and thither, table at the far end with a blackboard on one side and a projection screen the other. Behind the table were maps of Britain, Europe, and the world. The biggest was the coastal map, the offshore waters split into different zones.

Kenyon went to the table: 'Well, gentlemen. I think we're all here now.'

Heads turned obligingly, faces cast inquiring glances. Gulliver nodded politely and smiled whenever he made eye contact.

'Today,' Kenyon said, 'you're going to be briefed on a development of no little importance. For the benefit of those who don't know their neighbour, suffice it to say this comes within the realm of a Joint Services Committee session. I'm delighted to welcome you all, especially representatives of the Cabinet advisory group and dear Mr Wilby here, from Defence.'

Gulliver turned to Leech. 'Who he?'

'Pain in the arse,' Leech said.

'So without further ado,' Kenyon concluded, 'allow me to introduce a senior member of our scientific establishment – and, if she doesn't mind me saying this, a charming lady too. Gentlemen, Doctor Frances Wycliffe.'

She took it at an easy pace that allowed them to stay level. Gulliver listened attentively, realising the full picture was being presented for the first time but also noting, with a wry smile, the omission of the artist's signature.

'I'm going to begin by talking about ECM,' Frances Wycliffe said, 'our eyes and ears: Electronic Counter Measures. Now, ECM has many applications, but the one we're concerned with today is the submarine. As you're aware, the submarine's greatest asset is its invisibility. Most of them are tracked for most of the time, but considering that just one carries more explosives than the total used in the Second World War, well . . . it'd be remiss not to try to improve things.

'The invention of ASDIC was the first step in the electronic campaign to counter the submarine threat. The subsequent development of sonar has taken us much further along that road. But, gentlemen – and it's an important but – anti-submarine warfare is anything but simple.

'Submarines are like predators stalking through the jungle, hiding in the shadows. Oh yes, there are shadows all right, zones caused by thermal layers which, because they change the density of water, play havoc with active sonar. Cold water reflects, warm water deflects. So an impulse either bounces back before it targets or goes angling off down towards the seabed. Submarines, of course, know exactly where these zones are. They're equipped with hull-mounted sensors for just that job.

'There are other problems, too. Active sonar works best at no more than around twenty-five miles. The only way to extend the search area is to commit so much hardware and so many vessels that one sub can tie up half a fleet. And even then, with so many sensors trying for data, things can backfire. By the time sampling has differentiated between a fish shoal, a sub, or a whale, it can be too late. Of course, you can deploy passive sonar, dunk a mike in the sea from a helicopter and listen. But submarines aren't the noisy old things they used to be.

'The dream, then, of everyone in ASW is to come up with true

108

EAS: Extended Active Sonar. Sonar of great range and accuracy. But that's where the crunch comes.

'If sound is to travel far underwater, then it needs to operate at VLF levels: Very Low Frequency. And that is enormously difficult to generate – and I mean enormously.'

She paused to sip from a glass of water. 'We're using VLF transmitters already, but they're shore-based because of their size. The transmitters are for communication – few people understand how difficult it is to contact something below the sea. To supplement static VLF, there are aircraft roaming the skies right now, gentlemen, trailing aerial arrays well over a mile long. And if you think that's hard to imagine, then consider this: when the Americans tried to develop a world-scanning VLF system for their submarine fleet, their proposed aerial array was 5,837 miles long ...'

Leech whispered: 'She serious? You were actually planning to build something like that?'

'I'd've had help,' Gulliver said.

'So,' Frances Wycliffe resumed, 'that's the background. You can see that if a communication set-up has to be of those dimensions, then a detection set-up has to be, well ... grandiose.

'But what if ECM produced a completely new sonobuoy design? A buoy so small it could actually be dropped from an aircraft, yet could still generate VLF?' She paused. 'That's why we're here today. Because that, gentlemen, is what is now on the drawing board.' She smiled broadly. 'We're moving far beyond state-of-the-art technology – from a simple sonobuoy to what looks, to all intents and purposes, like a ... an underwater windmill.'

Gulliver closed his eyes. Now, he thought, now I've heard everything. Underwater windmills, turning silent sails in inner space.

'We're talking about a structure with six transducer faces,' she continued, 'six paddles, as it were, radiating from a central hub; six ELFTs – Extra Large Face Transducers – in three coupled pairs, in each pair a wide-beam ELFT for wide-zone isonification and a narrow-beam ELFT which will sweep for target definition. We –'

'Excuse me, Doctor Wycliffe.' A man spoke up in the front row. 'I'm getting a little lost here. Have you any pictures of this ... this thing?'

Leech groaned. 'Wilby. Here we go.'

Frances Wycliffe inclined her head towards the right-hand corner of the room. A chair scraped. Kenyon bustled to her side, said: 'Ah, if you don't mind, we'll show the slides later.'

'I think I'd prefer to see something now,' Wilby said.

'They're only sketches – artist's impressions.'

'Even so.' Wilby stood up: he was tall and gaunt, and had a slight stoop, as though he had spent too long poring too closely over a balance sheet. 'Underwater windmills, Sir Alec – I can't recall ever encountering one before.'

'I'm sure the Ministry encounters many wondrous things,' said Kenyon, smoothly.

'Not windmills.'

'Yes, well ...' Kenyon faltered. 'Perhaps a couple of pictures, then. Can't have an unenlightened Ministry, can we?' He raised a hand as though to shield his eyes, like a man searching a distant horizon. 'Mr Greenwood?' A broad figure slowly telescoped from a front-row seat. 'Ah, Mr Greenwood.' Kenyon seemed grateful. 'Are we ready now?'

'The lad's still out,' Greenwood said in a gruff, north-country voice, speech slow and deliberate.

'Oh.' Gratitude vanished in an expression of pain.

'The lad –' Wilby apparently found the term unpalatable – 'is still out for what?'

'A bulb, sir.'

Silence.

'I beg your pardon?'

With the sort of dogged emphasis normally reserved for the hard of hearing, Greenwood said: 'The bulb has gone in the projector –' pause – 'sir.'

Gulliver almost doubled over. Barnes, my friend, you're never going to believe this. He clutched at his side, fought desperately against the spasm. Tears sprang from his eyes. Aw Jesus, Barnes. It's not going to end with a bang or a whimper; we're all going to die laughing.

Karodin was still musing on the oddities of Western relationships when the phone rang again. 'Your friend has gone to a Ministry building. There is a meeting.'

'Do we know its nature yet?' Karodin asked.

'We are trying to establish that; also, who is present.'

'You already have some names.'

'They may not be the principals.'

'Oh, I think you can gamble they are.'

The call disconnected. Karodin sat back again, smiling softly to himself. It had been so easy, and yet it had looked so difficult ...

Chekalkin stayed tight all the way across the ocean then, at Heathrow, his role concluded, he vanished into the predictable mêlée. The others moved in then, a simple baggage intercept the American might have witnessed had he not been jostled by a fellow passenger at the crucial moment.

From then on the problems mounted, beginning with the American himself: he could have been going anywhere, or had someone meeting him; he could have hailed a cab and thus precipitated the sort of tag operation of which nightmares are made, because it was still not dawn, because virtually nothing and no one was stirring in the metropolis; and because you cannot hide a lead and back-up team in a traffic jam composed solely of one United Dairies milk float and one bright red London Transport omnibus.

But instead the American waited, in a tired impotent rage, and argued with the desk staff, and finally trudged to the pick-up stand for the Heathrow Hotel courtesy coach.

Locale: confirmed. Specific locale: pending. First phase ends, second phase commences.

The lead car easily made it to the hotel car park. Simultaneously, Pananyev presented his soulful features to the airport duty desk.

'I am sorry, but I seem to have taken the wrong suitcase.' He held it up for inspection.

'So that's where it is! Been a feller here playing hell.'

'I can imagine, it is so ... distressing. I have found mine now, but the poor man ... Did he say where he would be? Can you get it to him quickly?'

'Just a minute, sir, I'm ringing them now ... Ah, reception? Morning, duty desk here. You checked in a passenger off the BA New York? Gulliver. As in travels. Yes? Well listen, tell him we've located his suitcase, we're arranging to send it over now.'

'Please!' Pananyev interrupted. 'Please! What room is he in? I will ring him after breakfast, apologise personally –'

'There's no need for that, sir. The gentleman –'

'I insist! Ask them what room he is in, I don't want to miss him.'

'All right, all right. Hang on ... reception? Still there? Sorry about

111

that but we're having a right old time of it over here. What room have you allocated to passenger Gulliver? We'll label the bleedin' bag so there're no more cock-ups. What is it? Three three oh. Yes, got it. Thanks.'

Pananyev went briskly to the back-up car and radioed ahead. Specific locale: identified. Second phase ends, third phase commences ...

Karodin slumped further into the armchair, smiling even more broadly. He wished he had been there, except for the fact that it wouldn't have been possible to direct the field operation in situ. Co-ordination, then, had to be from a safe house at a safe distance, where the only thing you could do was visualise what was happening, stay close to the radio link, and finally attempt to think yourself into the target's mind the better to predict his next reaction. In fact, at this stage, you stood the best chance of success by becoming the target yourself ...

So: you are exhausted after a long and tiring flight. A possession has been lost but then you learn it has been found. Natural instinct is to say to hell with everything and go off to bed. Except you've spent a lifetime overcoming predictable responses, you've learned never to dismiss a situation where there's been pattern disruption.

Reluctantly you wait in the hotel lobby, attempting to stir a weary brain into activity, because apart from pattern disruption there's also the other thing, integrity of residence: compromise where you live and you compromise who you are. But logic says you aren't compromising anything, the only thing that's coming into your room is a suitcase. To which training responds – it's been out of your sight in the hands of strangers and now strangers are going to deliver it. What are you, an amateur?

And logic replies: but if the opposition are running interference, how do they know you are here? You took the usual precaution, pre-booked neither the flight nor the accommodation. Besides, there are only two things you can do with a suitcase – bomb it or bug it, and the former isn't applicable and the latter isn't practicable, because they'll realise you're bound to examine the contents on receipt.

Stop waiting; stop worrying. Go to bed. You've been dithering around here for hours ...

Karodin chuckled and thought: actually, my clever American comrade, it wasn't hours at all, but four minutes and fifty-seven seconds.

Not hours, but time enough for the EAS from Technical Support Services to get in and out again, to site the two matchbox-size recorders in room 330, one behind the TV chassis, the other under the bedside shelf, this last with an integral receptor wired to pick up the on-line sound transmitted by the button tap inserted into the telephone earpiece.

Karodin laughed aloud, now.

Ah, comrade Gulliver, what you carried in your suitcase was the one thing we needed and the one thing you didn't know you had.

Four minutes and fifty-seven seconds.

'I thought you handled that very well,' Kenyon said. 'Congratulations, Frances.'

'Thanks.' She pursed her lips in a silent whistle.

Leech and Gulliver materialised at her side. 'The – bulb – has – gone,' Leech said. 'You should've seen your face.'

'How could I?' Gulliver grinned. 'The bulb had gone.' They both dissolved in laughter. It took Gulliver a time to register her expression. 'You didn't find it funny, Doctor Wycliffe?'

'My sense of humour isn't what it was.' She spoke quietly, evenly.

A frown creased Gulliver's forehead. 'Something ... wrong?'

'Piotr. Oh, don't worry. He's not ill or anything. Your precious commodity is alive and well and working flat out, eighteen hours a day.'

'So what's the problem?'

'The problem is he arrived here a month ago and from then until now he's never set foot beyond that house.'

Kenyon shuffled his feet. 'I think I'll just have a word over there,' he announced vaguely.

Gulliver watched the retreating figure. 'What point are you making, Doctor Wycliffe?'

'Piotr needs a break – needs to see some life. He came here as a friend. He's not supposed to be a prisoner.'

'He's not supposed to be a tourist, either.'

'You can still give him some freedom. Otherwise ... I quit.'

Gulliver sighed. 'Aw, come on, Doctor, this isn't something you can organise just like that. A change of scene, a new locale –'

'I'm not asking for that; we're fine where we are. I'm simply proposing that you extend the perimeter.' She gave a brief, knowing smile. 'Oh yes, I speak your language, too.'

113

After a while, Leech said: 'It's possible to extend to the village.'

'Including it or as far as it?' Gulliver snapped.

'Including.'

Gulliver considered her. She hadn't moved, was still calm, composed. But in her eyes a fierce resolve danced on.

'Okay,' he said, 'we'll ease off.'

'Thank you.' A curt acknowledgment; she spun on her heel and walked briskly away.

'Women,' Leech sighed. He shook his head. 'I didn't think you'd agree.'

'Doesn't matter. Let the little dog have its day. Time's running out.'

'Did you notice,' Leech said thoughtfully. 'She said "we". And she called him "Piotr".'

'I noticed.'

TILGARSLEY
OXFORDSHIRE

The stocky Welshman, the one she knew only as Smith, ushered her inside. He seemed surprised. She closed the door behind her and set off for the drawing room. 'Where's Piotr?'

'He's asleep. Is anything –'

'Oh, no ...' She halted in mid-stride. The denial was borne on a weary desperation.

'Went to bed an hour ago,' Smith said. 'He was tired. But if it's urgent, I'll go up and – '

'No!' A sudden embarrassed smile, as though she'd spoken too loudly. 'No, don't bother. It wasn't anything important.'

Smith waited, trying to identify the emotions that played about her face. He watched, and wondered. Finally he asked: 'What d'you want to do, then?'

'Do?' She stared back at him, fatigue in her eyes, and something else too: an acute, painful disappointment. 'I suppose ... I suppose I'd better get back.'

Without any forethought, without understanding why, he found himself reaching out to touch her arm. 'Why not stay for a drink,' he said.

'Drink?' Again the double echo, his word returning to him in an outward sign of an inner turmoil.

'Whatever you want.' He smiled. 'This is my hotel, you know. I'm manager, head cook and bottle-washer.'

Her expression softened. 'A man of many talents.'

'So my wife says – talent for getting out of the shopping; talent for staying out of the kitchen.'

She laughed. 'I didn't know you were married.'

'Oh, I'm married all right. Got the evidence to prove it.' Impulsively he tugged out his wallet and showed her the pictures in their plastic leaves. 'That one's David, he's nine; and that one's Sarah, she's seven.'

'They're lovely. You must miss them a lot.'

'Aye, I do.' He returned the wallet to his pocket. 'Well then, what'll it be?'

She hesitated. 'Is coffee all right?'

'No problem.' He clapped his hands together. 'Cream? Sugar? The works?'

'The works.' She laughed again.

'Right.' He turned away, headed briskly for the kitchen. She called after him: 'Mr Smith?'

'Yes?'

'This is ridiculous. All this time and I don't even know if that's your real name.'

'It is, no kidding.'

'And your Christian name?'

'Owen.' He lowered his voice. 'But I shouldn't be telling you. It's not approved of.'

'It's all right,' she said, 'I'm rewriting the rules today.'

She settled on the sofa and stared around the drawing room. It had been his haven, then his prison, and now ... *Svoboda*, Piotr. How about that?

Eventually she stood up, not wanting the silence any more. They'd organised a small record collection for him; she knelt by the cabinet, fingers flicking through the sleeves.

Owen Smith came in with two cups of coffee. 'Mind if I join you, Doctor?'

'It's Frances to you.'

'Frances.' He gave her a crooked smile.

She watched him set the cups down on one of the small tables, then she returned to the records: Bach, Handel, Mussorgsky, Tchaikóvsky. None were suitable; their weight might break the fragility of her mood. Vivaldi, was there any Vivaldi?

A black sleeve: she withdrew it carefully and stared uncomprehendingly at the cover painting of a prism being lanced by a beam of white light. The light fragmented into the colours of the spectrum. There was nothing else on the cover, no other information.

She lifted it up. 'What's this?'

'That's his.'

'Well, obviously, they all are.'

'I meant,' Smith said slowly, 'that he brought it with him. When they met him at Rostov, he was like a tramp, you know? No clothes except what he was wearing; and no possessions except a shopping bag – with that in it.'

She stared at him, then back to the cover. Her fingertips prised at the corners; the album fell open. She found herself staring at the lyrics.

Two passages appeared to have been underlined with a red felt-tip pen.

The lunatic is in my head
The lunatics are in my head
You raise the blade You make the change
You rearrange me till I'm sane

And if the dam breaks open many years too soon
And if there is no room upon the hill
And if your head explodes with dark forebodings too
I'll see you on the dark side of the moon ...

She gazed up at Smith. 'I don't understand.'

'No.' He shook his head. 'I don't, either.'

CHAPTER
NINE

LENINGRAD

Grandpapa.

She wanted to know about Grandpapa. Was he any better? Was he going into the hospital? Was he coming to stay with them, to get well? Would Mummy be looking after him for long?

Coming back to him like that, the lie, the reason he'd given for Tanya's sudden departure on his return from Murmansk, surprised him, as if Katerina was telling him some unpleasant news. But how could he tell her that Tanya had gone to Moscow to attend the trial of her literary lover, that he didn't know when she'd be back, that she was gone? He dropped down onto his haunches and confronted the pale, serious little face. 'Katerina, Katerina. So many questions.'

They were on the pavement, dappled by the shadows of the trees. A narrow, noisy surge of infants and their mothers swept around them, parting then re-forming like a tide around a rock. He barely noticed them; just the small grave face, the fine-spun hair, the frown that was almost comical, but the eyes which were not – they searched his for truth or falsehood.

'You said Grandpapa was sick.'

'Yes.'

'But that was last week. Mummy went to Moscow last week.'

He eased himself upright. 'Why all these questions?'

'They asked me –' a slow turning of the head in the direction of the schoolyard – 'because Mummy always brings me.'

'It isn't nice, having Daddy?'

The frown vanished. 'Oh, yes!'

He swept her up in his arms and hugged her tightly. His fingers touched the softness of her hair, and he closed his eyes, remembering.

117

Then, almost theatrically, he said: 'Look at the time! You'll be late and then what will they say?'

Unexpectedly, she kissed him on his nose. He laughed. 'Be off with you! Go on!'

A blur of movement, a skipping and a scampering to the gates; a brief look back, small hand raised, waving. He raised his own in return, but she had gone, and the gesture lost its meaning, unnoticed in the bustle of the street.

Ivanitsyn turned on his heel and walked back to the car. It was parked under a beech tree. A few dry leaves of a summer gone still lingered, but elsewhere the branches burgeoned with the greenness of a summer to come. He peered up through the branches, shading his eyes. Through the tree, the sun had a striking, star-shaped aspect. He lowered his gaze. The brightness still seemed to shimmer before his eyes.

He drove slowly back to the apartment, nosed the small Lada into the end garage of the stable-like block. He closed the door and leaned against it for a few moments.

Tanya had chosen this place. This building, this garage, this address – all of it; you touched the timber of a door or the brickwork of a wall and time went into reverse; you expected to turn around and still see her standing there, the maternity dress billowing a little as she arched her back to gaze up at the topmost apartments. And you did likewise, but the sun was too bright, shafts of light interrupted by the overhead branches, the sun a star-burst on a summer's day.

He crossed the courtyard and took the elevator to the seventh floor. He paused outside the apartment door. Here, the first time, he had dropped the key and they had both bent down simultaneously and bumped heads.

Into the apartment, down the narrow hallway: three bedrooms and the bathroom leading off in opposite pairs; he opened the door to the L-shaped living room, closed it behind him, and stood there, contemplating the furnishings and the pictures, and the silence.

He spent a half-hour washing the breakfast crockery, tidying Katerina's bedroom, and fussing needlessly in the living room. He picked up ornaments and set them down again; he ran his fingers over the textures of wood and glass and cloth, needing the assurance of touch.

The telephone jangled with shocking abruptness. He lifted the receiver, surprised to discover that the noise had made him tremble.

'Yes?'

'Doctor Melnikova, please.'

'She isn't here.'

'Oh. D'you know when she will be back, please?'

'Who is this?'

'Major Monakhov.'

He flattened the rest-bar with his other hand and kept it down until he was sure the connection had been broken. Then he lowered the receiver, stared at it, and finally placed it on the table top.

Monakhov occupied his mind for a few moments, just as he had similarly occupied this room. He was discovering many doors inside his head: some could be closed, some could not. He found it curiously easy to shut out Major Monakhov, but the knowledge was bittersweet, for it brought with it the realisation that the cold, still man with the bronze-tinted lenses could very well one day occupy a space larger than any walls or any doors could contain.

He checked the spare bedroom, without any reason or fore-thought, then set about making the bed in their room.

Their room. He sat on the edge of the divan, head bowed, not really thinking, not really seeing. The carpet seemed to wish to absorb him; it wasn't a proper bedroom carpet at all, but one they'd brought from the living room in the other, smaller apartment, which they'd cut up to fit. The pattern made whorls of colour like giant thumb-prints.

The pain that had always been there, in every place and no place, grew sharper now. He got to his feet and retreated back to the living room. The bedclothes remained as they were, barely disturbed by the night's solitary occupant.

He went into the kitchen, boiled the kettle and made coffee. It was the instant kind, imported from Yugoslavia; the taste had gone missing in transit.

He went into the living room again, and sat down on the sofa, cupping the drink in both hands, hunching over it, feeling the steam upon his face.

He sat there until the steam ceased to rise, and remained unmoving as the drink turned tepid, then cold. Eventually he placed the mug on the floor, hoisted his legs up onto the cushions, and stretched out.

Everything was an effort today, as it had been an effort yesterday, and the day before. Everything happened in slow motion, or seemed to, anyway – as though time had become an alien dimension, and try

119

as you might, you were not going to be able to synchronise with it. Time had become space, a very long walk over a very short distance.

He slept away the morning, in a cocoon of dreamless grey.

The doorbell rang distantly.

He rolled off the sofa, stood, unsteadily, blinking against the light, hesitant as to what he should do, as though the sound was familiar but its meaning uncertain. It chimed again.

He moved away, felt an impact against his foot. The mug was overturned, its contents pooling and draining on the beige pile.

A third chime; he shook his head like a dog shedding water and strode purposefully to the living-room door, then down the hall-way, gathering momentum, because the sound had come as a delayed reminder of the shrill descant of a telephone that was now off the hook. Down the hallway and up to the door, heart pumping and driving, breath shortening, quickening, and he reached out and grabbed at the latch and turned and wrenched the door towards him.

She still wore the winter coat she'd taken to Moscow. Even the collar was still upturned. But it seemed larger, somehow, as if the fur had grown or she had diminished.

Her eyes briefly met his, and then were downcast; the pinkness of the lids was the only tint to define itself in amongst all the paleness.

'I didn't know if you were in,' Tanya said.

He felt himself consciously supervising the speech process, laboriously identifying and assembling the words, willing them to emerge in coherent form. 'I was ... lying down.'

'Are you all right?' Quickly, unthinking, her gaze levelling again.

'I ...' The words jumbled, defying articulation. He experienced a momentary helplessness, a numbing paralysis of thought that rendered him incapable of saying all the things he expected to say. His arm dropped to his side.

'I've just knocked the coffee over,' he said.

DNEPROPETROVSK

They told him it had opened in 1968 – the Special Psychiatric Hospital, one of the finest in the country.

He said it's a mistake. I shouldn't be here.

120

They pointed to the thirty-foot-high perimeter wall, coarse grey brick topped by iron stanchions with heavy-duty wire stretched taut.

Look, Guseinov. There's no mistake.

The cubicle contained a bed, a washbasin, a small cupboard with a single drawer. The bed was set in a tubular steel frame. Black leather straps dangled.

The doctor had a soft voice, a soft face. 'There's no mistake, Guseinov.' He sat down on the chair.

'I'm not mad, Doctor. I shouldn't be here.'

'The papers say you should.'

'But I was going to a camp.'

'You want to go to a camp?'

'Yes.'

'That's not very rational, is it? They're not going to get you well there.'

'Nothing's wrong with me!'

The doctor considered him, his completely round face, devoid of any hair, shining with concern and understanding. 'You have residual schizophrenia, Guseinov.'

'No!'

'It's quite all right. The treatment will make you better.'

'I – am – not – ill.'

Gently: 'The patient's lack of insight into his own condition is a common symptom.'

Guseinov closed his eyes. 'No. Please ... No.'

'You must not upset yourself.'

'Then let me go.'

The doctor stood up, walked away. 'We'll start the treatment tomorrow, all right?'

An orderly took away the chair.

When the door closed, Guseinov looked around the cubicle, thought: this is my home now.

He tried to shut it out by closing his eyes, tried to imagine other rooms in other homes, and other people and what they were doing, how they lived. But normality was inconceivable; freedom, unbelievable. To be able to do what you wanted, to be without the fear of the needle, the drugs that would soon invade ...

He opened his eyes, was about to sit down, until he remembered.

The chair. It was not just a chair. The chair was a trophy, a reward earned on merit. In the ranking of such trophies, a chair was second only to a circular mirror of unbreakable glass. You had to be on the eve of discharge to get a mirror. You had to be exceptionally good to acquire a chair.

In the meantime, delusion was support, and sanctuary.

He came in by rail, arriving late in the echoing cavern of the terminal. The journey had taken the better part of two days because of engine failure at Kharkov.

He'd travelled soft, in the deluxe accommodation – private washroom, exclusive use of a two-berth compartment, a small table with its own reading lamp, and above all soft seats, soft bedding. The adjective was now recognised as a particular form of Soviet travel.

There was no one to meet him at Dnepropetrovsk. He went through the double barriers, crossed the deserted booking hall with its clocks and destination boards and grey skittering pigeons high up in the roof. No one to meet him because no one yet knew about the man from Moscow. He raised the bronze lenses with one hand, rubbed his eyes with the other. Then he set off in search of the comfort of a hotel.

'Welcome, comrade major. Welcome to my home.'

Conscious of the golden gaze, he struggled to get up, using the bed frame for leverage. The side bars remained locked in the upright position; only an orderly could release them. It meant that sitting on the edge of the bed was impossible, and getting out an act of consummate athleticism. If you were old or infirm, or too weary to try any more, you lived your life in this narrow bed, tried not to soil yourself, and talked to the faces in the ceiling.

You waited for the day of the Last Treatment, when they wrapped you tightly in canvas, then turned a hosepipe on it and the material shrank and shrank and crushed and squeezed until finally, because your condition was so poor, you died of heart failure.

The Last Treatment – a fairly common end. No visible marks; no signs of violence. The doctor could even show the corpse to your relatives.

Monakhov said: 'You've some explaining to do.'

'Yes?'

'You are going to be co-operative, aren't you?'

'Of course.'

The lenses moved, catching and duplicating the pale overhead orb.

Monakhov sat down on the chair. 'I want to know how you helped Piotr Asanov.'

'Asanov?' Bewildered, off-balance. Hesitantly: 'I helped him ... write things.'

'That isn't what I'm talking about. Asanov has gone.'

'Gone?'

'We're looking for him.'

'Well there's no point in asking me, comrade major. You were the ones who had him.'

'No.'

'But you took him from his hotel.'

'No.'

'I ... I don't understand.'

'Who has him, Guseinov? The Americans? The British?'

'I don't know what you're talking about.'

'The Israelis?'

None of it making sense, not any of it; it was like being pushed onto the stage in the middle of the play, there to portray a character you didn't know in a plot of which you were quite ignorant.

'Piotr's gone to the West?'

'Guseinov –' the word pitched low, dark with warning – 'don't play games.'

'Piotr's defected?' Incredulity drove his voice to the brink of hoarseness; the tears spilled unbidden and he grabbed at the sheet, used its hem to mop his face. 'Piotr. Piotr ...'

Monakhov walked to the washbasin, rested his hands on its lip. 'Tell me about Yelena Pinsky.'

'She's a friend.'

'She's in your samizdat group.'

'No.'

'If you lie to me again ...' Monakhov said.

'Yelena Pinsky is a friend.'

'And she has contacts with Western Intelligence.'

'With *what*?'

'Western Intelligence.'

'But she's a pharmacist!' That, as a rebuttal, sounded more ridiculous than the accusation. He tried again: 'Yelena couldn't possibly be involved in anything like that.'

'Like what?'

'Whatever you wish to call it.'

'You're saying she didn't pass information to the West?'

'Of course she didn't! What sort of information is a bloody pharmacist going to have?'

'But she wrote letters, to Amnesty International.'

'So?'

'I thought my meaning was obvious.'

'It's not a crime to write letters, comrade major.'

'That depends what you put in them. Look, Pinsky was a member of your little group. You were its head and she was your contact point for Western Intelligence.'

'Ridiculous.'

'You and your friends, you were a tool of the West.'

'Totally untrue.'

Monakhov walked back to his chair. 'You know everything that's been going on, don't you? Your little demonstration of April twenty-first, for example. What was that supposed to be – some sort of diversion?'

'I did that on my own.'

'Obviously.'

'I mean, no one else knew, beforehand.'

Monakhov sighed. 'You're going to tell me, you know. You and the girl.'

'Yelena isn't involved in anything and neither am I.'

'Not Yelena – ' a pause – 'Tanya Melnikova.'

'Tanya?'

'Mmm.' Thoughtfully: 'She your lover, Guseinov?'

'Leave her out of it!'

'Why? She another one who isn't involved?' Monakhov shook his head, smiled. 'Tst tst, Leonid Guseinov, you and your women.'

'Leave Tanya alone!' His fists clenched around the bars of the frame, shaking the structure.

Monakhov stared at him. 'I'll bet her money came in handy.'

'Her money?'

'She kept you, didn't she?'

'No!'

'She kept you; I think she kept all of you. But was there more to share besides that? Was there more to share than just the Melnikova money? Come on, you can tell me. How many of them had a go at her? How many shared your whore?'

The chair toppled backwards and the lenses splintered the light and then he was close, very close, leaning over and looking down as the saliva and the hate came spraying and spattering.

'You make me sick! One minute you attack them, the next minute you bed them! You're scum, d'you know that? Filthy, cowardly scum!'

The face slowly receded. Heels clicked across the floor.

Guseinov stared through the bars. 'What do you want, comrade major?'

'Everything.' A whisper, no more.

He lay still for a long time, cradling his head. Names and faces whirled around inside on a carousel of despair: Tanya, Piotr, Yelena. And the others who'd never played much of a part in anything: Yuri and Sacha and Karel and Lenya and, finally, Vadim. What had happened to them?

He didn't hear the door opening.

What had happened? Because if that was what they thought about Yelena, then the rest of them ... And Piotr, the reason for it all. Was it true? Could it be possible? Wait. The message. He came to see me, he was looking for me. He wanted to tell me something. 'Leonid, I'm going to defect.' Nonsense! You don't sit in a chair in a Leningrad apartment and just ... say it.

'Straps, I think,' the doctor said.

'What are you doing?'

Bound tightly, buckles locked. Bound and shackled so firmly he was only able to turn his head from side to side, nothing else. Wide-eyed, staring, disbelieving.

'Stop it!'

Hypodermic rising, a tiny spear glinting in the light.

'Stop it!'

A needle-thin jet of sodium amytal, arcing outwards.

'Don't do this to me!'

Pricking in the right arm. Doctor with the woman's skin and the woman's voice, the mother's concern, doctor bending over him, looking pained, looking gentle: 'There, there.'

'Don't do it!'

Doctor standing up again, smiling.

'PLEASE!'

Everything heavy.

125

He wondered why. The thought shone brightly enough, but he had to chase it, hang onto it like the tail of some erratic comet.

Heavy. The restraints were still there but they didn't much matter, he couldn't move his limbs anyway. Lead. They'd turned to lead. He thought he should do something about that. But still, it wasn't as if he planned to go anywhere.

Monakhov spoke quietly. 'Leonid.'

Someone calling his name. Someone at the end of a tunnel or the top of a well, shouting down, all the way down.

'Leonid.'

Eyelids fluttering, jiggling.

Bright light. It seemed to flood in from all sides. It reflected off bronze-tinted lenses hovering way, way above. But descending now, closer, the face around it swelling.

'I have a message from Yelena.'

'Yelena?'

'You know, Yelena; your friend.'

'Yes.'

'Your friend, Leonid.'

'Yes.'

'Yelena's trying to help Doctor Asanov. Doctor Asanov needs some papers. He needs them urgently, for his work. But Yelena cannot get them to him.'

'Yelena is a very good friend.'

'Well, Yelena cannot help Piotr, because she doesn't know where he's gone.'

'Piotr,' Guseinov said.

'Yes. Can you help Yelena? After all, she only wants to help Piotr. Can you tell Yelena where Piotr has gone?'

'Piotr is a good friend, too.'

Monakhov paused.~

'Leonid, try to help. Tanya knows, but we can't contact her at the moment.'

'Tanya?'

'Yes. She knows, doesn't she? And she would help.'

Struggling to rise: 'Tanya needs help?' Something about restraints, about shackles; something about them, I can't move; everything heavy, pressing down.

'Leonid? Can you hear me, Leonid?'

126

Suddenly, not as heavy, the weight diminishing. Getting lighter, Tanya, getting lighter.

Easing away again into a twilight world, neither hearing the footsteps nor seeing the needle's flash nor feeling the sulphazine, going in deep.

Sanctuary was within the cerebral cavity but nowhere else. No peace, or relief, anywhere else.

Demented signals flashed over the synapses. Light exploded, starbursts scorched his eyelids. He bit his lip and blood spilled. He tasted it, bit again.

Trying now to absorb himself in this pain alone, excluding all the others. Trying now to crowd out the fire in every joint and the terrible compulsion that made shackled limbs jerk wildly in senseless spasm. Moving, always moving.

Trembling, always trembling.

He must retreat into his head and try very hard not to be aware, because that was what they wanted, they wanted him to know about the shuddering room and the violent bed.

The doctor with the woman's face wanted him to know that. The man with the bronze lenses wanted him to know that.

Try very hard to forget yourself, not see yourself as the others did – white and naked, no clothes no pillows no help no dignity, pinioned and sweating and convulsing. No help, all a mistake; no one helps, no one cares, no one listens.

Monakhov stepped aside, looked into the doctor's eyes. 'Have you finished?'

'Not quite.'

'All this ... it is distasteful.'

'One gets used to it, comrade major.'

'Is it necessary?'

The doctor frowned. 'It's standard treatment. It cures them eventually.'

Monakhov studied him minutely. 'You *are* a doctor?'

'Who do you think I am?'

The soft face smiled, a manicured hand reached out for the tray, the fingers closed around the ampoule of haloperidol.

'No! No! No!'

The shout the only consistency in a disintegrating universe.

'No! No! No!'

An endless echo, on and on. The world shuddering, the earth-quake within and without. Bed moving beneath him, shaking, tossing. Head snapping from side to side, muscles whipping, brain loosening.

Far worse than anything that had gone before.

He closed his eyes upon the redness of an exploding sun and saw himself, a tiny figure, whirling around in its screaming centre.

The doctor called early the following morning and made notes upon the record sheet. The investigator, Monakhov or whatever his name was, was still sleeping in an adjacent cubicle. Monakhov had been angry about the absence of a chair. The orderly said chairs were not allowed without permission and Monakhov yelled at him, do you think I'm a patient?

Haloperidol induces major spasm and shock. Under its effect, a patient needs to be reassured that he is not, in fact, coming apart at the seams.

The doctor bent his head to the white, gleaming face.

'There, there, Leonid. It will be all right.'

He came out of it on an insulin surge, emerged with limbs aching and muscles raw and a dryness of mouth and throat as though he'd been lost in the Kara Kum, swollen tongue, matted hair, burning cheeks.

They had taken him on a long journey, but he had never left his bed.

The orderly proffered a tumbler of water. He drank too quickly, gagged, brought it back. He felt the wetness spreading over his clothing.

Clothing. Cotton pyjamas. Broad blue stripes. No collar and the sleeves too short but ... clothing. He picked distractedly at the thin folds.

Monakhov said: 'You got too warm, before.'

He turned his head, a cautious, experimental manoeuvre. The orderly had filled the tumbler, was between him and the man with the bronze lenses.

He drank more sparingly this time. His fingers trembled so he used both hands, like a small child at mealtime.

'I told them to remove the straps,' Monakhov said.

He looked again, saw the weals around the wrists, bright-banded bracelets of angry redness.

The orderly closed the door after him. It rang dully in its frame, the curiously flat sound of steel upon steel.

'What,' Guseinov said, then stopped. Tongue chased moisture into cracked and swollen lips. 'What . . . was it.'

'Say again?'

'What . . . did they give me.' Too tired to force the inflection, so that the question came out wooden, dead.

'A cocktail.'

He drank some more of the water. 'Is –' a deep steadying intake of breath – 'is it over?'

'For now.'

'Why . . . ?'

'Apparently, it's the treatment here.'

'Not ill.'

'It has nothing to do with me.'

'Please . . .'

The tumbler slipped from his hands. It struck the bed frame, bounced onto the cold, tiled floor. He listened to its rolling, waited, until it stopped.

He began to push himself into a sitting position, and then felt sudden rivulets of ice coursing around his neck and spine. 'I'm cold . . .'

'It will pass.'

'Cold.'

'A reaction.'

He had to breathe deeply again; the after-shock was still there, a distant quaking, coming from within. It took several minutes for it to subside. 'Why are you doing this to me?'

'I'm not,' Monakhov said.

'Kill me.' The request was gentle, almost idle.

'No.'

'I should be most . . . grateful.'

Monakhov lowered his head, shifted position on the chair. It was uncomfortably hard. He had brought it from the other cubicle where the overhead light, like this one, burned day and night. More than once he had regretted not going back to the hotel.

Finally he said: 'You have to co-operate.'

129

'I don't know how ...'

'A statement. I can record it.'

'What sort of statement?'

'It's not for me to tell you. It has to be in your own words.' He paused. 'I do not fabricate evidence.'

'What ... What d'you want me to make a statement about?'

'Piotr Asanov.'

'Piotr?'

'Yelena Pinsky, Vadim Kalininsky; oh, and Tanya Melnikova.'

Memory of a distant vista, dimly perceived. He stared at Monakhov, then shook his head again, and this time the movement affected the blur, the recollection sharpened. Piotr, and Tanya.

'Tanya ...'

Monakhov stood up and came towards him, saying gently: 'You're in love with her, aren't you? No. Don't say anything. I can tell. You really are in love with her.'

'What - what about it?'

'Help her, Leonid. Help the both of you. I'll arrange things, fix it so you'll be all right, so she'll be all right.'

'How ...?'

'The conspiracy, tell me about the conspiracy - a simple, voluntary statement. Come on, it isn't much to ask.'

'Conspiracy?'

'You know ... Piotr's defection - the planning, the contacts - you know all about it.'

'I ...' He stopped again, mouth working soundlessly.

'Yes?'

'I don't know anything.'

Still soft, shading out the accusation: 'But you were in it together, you and Tanya. You finalised the plan that Saturday night.'

'No.' A whisper. 'No. You're wrong.'

'Look. You needn't tell me where Piotr went. That can be your secret. I'm not asking you to betray a friend. But you and Tanya, you're implicated. Can't you see that? Now, I already have quite a lot from Yelena. But there are still a few details, little details. So ... come on, Leonid. Make it easy on yourself; a statement, into the tape recorder. That's all.'

He stared mutely at Monakhov, then turned slowly, laboriously, onto his side.

'Damn you, Guseinov!' Shouting, striding to the end of the bed, grasping and shaking the foot rail. 'Haven't you had enough? They're wiping out your brain, comrade. They're ... rearranging you. D'you want that? Is that what you want?'

He moved back around the bed, stared down at the almost foetal image.

'A word from me and there'll be another needle – amobarbital sodium, the truth drug, Guseinov. If you don't make that statement then I'll do it the hard way. I'll do it because I have to, while you've still got a mind to remember with.'

Silence. Stillness. Only the faint motion of the sheet, rising and falling to the rhythm of respiration.

He waited, motionless. Finally he turned away, walked slowly to the door, then stopped and looked back.

'I told them to let you keep the chair.'

LENINGRAD

As soon as they got back, Katerina switched on the TV and threw herself onto the sofa. She hugged a toy bear, a gift from Daddy's friends back in Murmansk, who said the Arctic was full of such cuddly little creatures. This one was Mischa, like the bear who travelled to Moscow for the Olympiad. Katerina now imparted quiet confidences to the large, saucer ears.

Tanya, bringing in the supper tray, almost collided with Yevgeni, emerging from the hall. 'I've done the unpacking,' he said. He settled next to Katerina, with the bear propped up beside them.

Vremya, the nine o'clock news programme, gave way to a retrospective on the life of Tito, as good an excuse as any for a travelogue, for pictures of lakes and mountains and a warm sea creaming silently on a sparkling beach. Tanya gazed longingly at the screen; the past four days in Murmansk had seemed like four months inside a freezer room. She had never felt so cold.

When Katerina had gone to bed, he turned off the set and stood awkwardly in the middle of the room. 'Fancy a drink?'

Tanya nodded. She looked around the room. 'It's good to be home again.' The phrase hung in the air, trailing meanings like banners between them. She closed her eyes on her own thoughtlessness.

He poured two tumblers of vodka. She thought he would sit next to her, on the sofa, but instead he went to the fireside chair. She wondered when, if ever, they would close the distance between them.

'Did you enjoy it, then?' he asked. 'Murmansk?'

'I was frozen.'

A small smile of sympathy. 'You'd soon get used to it.' He waited for a reply, but Tanya said nothing. 'You certainly seemed to get on all right, with the wives.' Another brief interval of silence. 'I know it isn't Leningrad, but the accommodation's good. And there's a theatre, and a cinema, and a good school – Katerina would have a lot of little friends.'

Tanya smiled uncertainly, then looked away. He was so . . . eager. Words of hope, she thought, from a man who was never this garrulous, never this desperate. Yet still she could not adjust to him. He had sustained a sea-change, the mood of bitterness turning to one of conciliation, almost as though he had been the offender. It was the generosity of a man of terrible decency.

She closed her eyes again. It had been an eternity of a week, an eternity beginning outside the apartment door, leaning against the wall and thumbing the bell and thinking over and over, please God let him be there. Yet it was only last Thursday; after that there had been three days of numbness followed by another four days of near paralysis as they inspected the married quarters at Murmansk. She wondered if the coldness had been within her before they journeyed north.

'The wives all get together,' he resumed, 'go into town, on trips.'

'Yevgeni . . .' A slow, helpless shaking of the head. 'Please, I need time. Everything's so confused.' She saw the pain in his face, the return of doubt, anxiety. 'It's such a big step, I mean, for the three of us –'

'Four. There's that blasted bear.'

Words, Tanya thought, words. Both of them were sifting through them, then seizing on the neutral, the inoffensive. She imagined them as skaters, going around and around the same, undeviating circuit, hoping not to score the ice too deeply lest it disintegrate. She struggled to divert the conversation, and said eventually: 'When d'you go back to sea?'

'I don't know.' He sighed. 'Been almost a month, now, and it's still a mess. Shortest commission on record – we'd barely left home

132

waters before the pressure system failed. And now there's metal-lurgists everywhere, analysts – you name it, they're doing it – sonic scans, X-rays, pressure tests. You'd have thought they could have got it right beforehand.'

'Have they said when it will be ready?'

'No.' He drained the glass, peered into it. Quietly: 'I hate this sitting around, waiting. I'm not achieving anything.'

'But if it isn't safe –'

'They'll make it safe if they have to sell the Kremlin.'

She nodded. 'And then,' she said, 'and then away you go again.'

'It's my job, Tanya.'

She looked at him, at the boyish face, the lines etched in by disappointment and frustration. 'You miss it, don't you? Your boat.'

'You make it sound like a mistress.'

Wrong wrong wrong. The word was ill-chosen, calling back echoes and silences; wrong, so brutally wrong; the ice was beginning to crack underfoot.

She organised a small dinner party, something to bring the laughter back to the apartment.

There were two other couples; they lived in the same building. It was a good party; they drank a lot and giggled a lot and finally Igor kissed her a lot saying goodnight.

She closed the door, settled down beside Yevgeni, felt his arm coming around, embracing her. She resisted involuntarily, a sudden brief tensing of the muscles, and then she was clinging to him, saying his name over and over again, melting and yielding as his hands roamed with quick, undisciplined movements that only gradually gentled.

They went wordlessly into the bedroom, and she took him to her, felt the shocking hardness of his flesh. And then the room swung in and out of focus as she closed her eyes upon the brightness flaming within, and they engulfed and consumed each other with terrible urgency.

'Tanya . . .'

'Shhh . . .' She placed a finger to her lips, smiled gently, aware of the signs, the restlessness. He was vulnerable now, as though this was a different kind of nakedness than before, no longer rampant, but spent, no longer dominant because its potency was gone. His was a fire that flashed but did not burn; for him the heat did not ebb slowly away.

Eventually he got out of bed and shrugged on a white towelling robe. 'Just going to the bathroom.'

When he returned she lifted her own robe from its hook, pausing to look around the room. Clothes were scattered everywhere, crumpled reminders of desire, of need.

She was brushing her hair in front of the bathroom mirror when the phone rang. She hurried out, caught it on the fourth ring. 'Hello?'

'Tanya Melnikova? I've a message for you.'

She frowned. 'Who is this?'

'He's being transferred – to Leningrad Psychiatric.'

Something about the voice, something familiar. The frown deepened. 'Who are you? Who're you talking about?'

'Leonid.'

'Leonid?' Loud, disbelieving.

'Yes, your friend.'

'Leonid?' Incredulity drove her voice even higher. A movement distracted her; she turned, saw Yevgeni coming towards her. She spoke hurriedly into the mouthpiece: 'He's all right? He's –'

The receiver flew from her hand, smashed savagely into its cradle. His face was dark and taut and ugly. 'Le-on-id.' Mouth forming each syllable, the sound hoarse, whisper-quiet. 'Le-on-id.' Veins pulsed at his temples, his arm began to rise.

'No, Yevgeni! No!'

His arm was still rising, the fingers of his hand straightening out and she was shaking her head, trying to tell him, trying to speak. 'No ...' Except the voice was not her own.

In the doorway, staring at them, gaze shifting from mother to father and back again, stood Katerina, gripping the paw of a small and amiable bear.

'It woke Mischa,' she said.

CHAPTER
TEN

TILGARSLEY
OXFORDSHIRE

Small and golden in the early light, the cottages appeared after the first bend, nodding to each other across the narrow street. They marked the southern boundary; the schoolhouse, the north. In between stood rows of shops and small comfortable houses fashioned from local stone – flinty grey or pale and warm as buttermilk.

Smith drove slowly, watching history slip by, reassuring and serene: sub-Post Office, hardware shop, another quartet of cottages of diamond panes and lichen stitching, a short terrace with the sharper roofline of the Victorian era, a bakery, newsagent's, and now The Griffin, an eighteenth-century coaching inn, all low eaves and ivy-spangled walls.

A junction was coming up, where the main road dawdled away towards the Cotswolds; he swung the Granada into the left dog-leg, held the shift for the steep ascent. When the road eventually flattened out, he pulled in, stopped, and cast a backward glance.

'Fancy a stroll, Doctor Asanov?'

Warm; warm with the promise of summer, the very air excited by its scent. Asanov strolled along the wide verge, hands in pockets, breathing deep. Far beneath, Tilgarsley offered itself to the morning sun. It looked like a random scattering of toy buildings, stylised, idealised, a child's conception of an English village laid out upon a cloth of green.

Eventually he looked away towards the west. A stream meandered around the bowl of the valley; cloud shadows pressed on the water meadows, travelled slowly over the landscape, delineating the furrows and ridges of ancient strip farming.

After a few moments he walked back to the car, to where Smith stood with arms folded, staring down at the view. 'Beautiful,' he said. 'Exactly where are we?'

'Priory Hill – highest point for miles.'

Asanov contemplated the village again. 'It is very old?'

'Seems so.' Smith smiled awkwardly. 'Be hopeless as a guide, wouldn't I? Although ...'

'Yes?'

'I have been reading up a bit. There's a mobile library, comes once a week. They had a National Trust booklet.' He pointed towards the far-off cottages. 'Lacemakers, they were here first. After that industry died, the women took tiny pieces of bone and turned 'em into buttons.' A sad shake of the head. 'But that's long gone, too.' He moved to the car door.

'No,' Asanov said, 'not yet.'

A shrug of the broad shoulders. 'You're the boss.'

'Piotr.'

'What?'

'My name is Piotr.' Laughter like sunlight shone from his blue eyes. 'Or do you only make friends with the English?'

Smith opened his mouth, then closed it. Finally: 'She's been talking about me, hasn't she?'

'We have discussed you, yes.' The bright gaze held steady, piercing. 'She trusts you, Owen Smith.' He paused. 'And it is Owen, and I am Piotr, and if you argue I will push you all the way down this hill.'

They strolled along in companionable silence, following the crown of the hill. To their left the land shelved steeply away, to their right a wooden sign denoted the perimeter of Forestry Commission land.

Eventually Asanov said: 'You came to Leningrad, did you not?'

Smith stopped abruptly. 'How did you know that?'

'Frances said you organised my ... journey.'

'She shouldn't have said.'

'But it is common knowledge, surely?'

'Well, I hope it isn't in Russia. If I ever go there again, I'd like to come out on a plane, not a stretcher.'

'That is how you see them, Owen? The Russians?'

'I . . . I didn't mean it like that.'

'No, it is all right. My country – it must look brutal to the West.'

'Put it like this: it isn't particularly appealing.'

'Yet we have dreams, too . . .' Asanov turned away, stared out at the valley. 'People are people. There is no difference. Only the bureaucrat is of a different species. The governed are all the same.' He jabbed lightly at his chest. 'Me.' The hand twisted in Smith's direction. 'You.'

They set off again, skirting the edge of the wood. Asanov abandoned the view and crossed over to the trees. They grew close, tight. The outermost were gilded by the morning light, but the shadows deepened quickly towards the interior; he sensed darkness and coolness at the centre. He stooped to pick up a cone, turned it around in his hand. It was warm, brittle. He held it to his face and breathed in.

He took a few more paces, then stopped again and smiled. Smith followed his gaze. To their left a broad strip of unblemished concrete forked from the highway. It seemed newly laid, unmarked, unused, and almost wider than the road itself. Smith peered along the pale, retreating ribbon. It ran straight and level into the heart of the wood. He perceived a clearing in the dimness, an expansion of the concrete into some sort of smooth, flat apron. Beyond it, the trees formed an impenetrable barrier. He glanced around, checking his bearings, frowned. It didn't make sense, building a road on top of a hill, a road that didn't go anywhere.

'Perfect,' Asanov said. He was still smiling. As though, Smith thought, he was remembering something – another forest, perhaps, somewhere else.

'See?' Asanov laughed. 'There is even a place for picnicking.'

Smith hesitated. 'I don't think it's that,' he said quietly.

On their way back to the car Asanov said: 'You were not at Rostov, were you?'

'No. It's the rules, designed to stop you pushing your luck too far.' Smith halted and gave an embarrassed cough. 'Look, Piotr . . . This is going to sound, well, strange. But please don't discuss the operation with me, all right? Anything else, anything under the sun, that's fine; but Russia, my role – no.'

'It is forbidden?'

The Welshman sighed helplessly, rubbed frantically at his face as though trying to stimulate both flesh and brain. Finally: 'You know what an estate agent is? It's a person who makes a living out of the buying and selling of property. Well, I make my living the same way. Skimming the take off things of value.'

'You are saying I am a property?'

'I'm saying whatever you were when this thing started, you're not that any more. You've become a person. Now that isn't supposed to happen, not in this job, but ...' He shook his head. 'Just leave it, all right? I can't talk to you about before.'

Asanov slowly considered, then burst out laughing. 'Estate agent! You know, even in the Soviet Union we hear of the famous James Bond. But all this time, we thought he was a secret one. Not an –'

'Aye, well,' Smith chuckled, 'there's not much difference. We live off what we never own, just like them.'

'Ah! So you do not wish to own me then?'

'You? Hell, Piotr, you're more bloody trouble than you're worth.'

Their laughter floated away from the hill and pealed out across the bright valley.

'That was a delightful meal,' Frances said. 'Shall we finish with coffee, or d'you prefer tea?'

'Coffee.' Asanov feigned dismay. 'Your tea doesn't live up to expectations.'

'I thought we were the people who invented it.'

'Come come, the Russians invented everything, as you very well know.'

The restaurant was three-quarters full. Each table bore a vase with a freshly cut flower and a candle in a cylinder of smoked glass. They sat by the window, surrounded by the cheerful hubbub of voices, the clinking and tinkling of cutlery and crockery. He had acquired a new wardrobe for the occasion, a check sports jacket and dark trousers, a white shirt with blue tie. She thought he had never looked healthier or happier.

'And another thing,' Asanov said.

'What?'

'Your tea.'

'What about it?'

'There's no ceremony to it. Whereas in Russia –'

'Oh no, here we go again ...'

'Don't mock. I was saying, in Russia we do it differently. We make it in a samovar. Then we pour it into a saucer. Finally, we drink it with a piece of sugar held between the teeth.'

'I don't believe it.'

'It is true! The tradition; how all the old ones do it.'

'Ah, so you're an old one, then.'

'Sometimes, I think so. Other times . . .' Boyish mischief danced in the blue eyes. Then he said: 'This . . . excursion. It was your idea?'

'I said you needed – correction, *we* needed – a break. But it was Owen who made all the arrangements.' An indulgent smile. 'I think he has a romantic streak.'

'And Doctor Frances Wycliffe. Is she a romantic, too?'

She didn't reply.

They lapsed into a companionable silence. Asanov stared at the bright constancy of the candle flame, said eventually: 'Just sitting here . . .'

'Sorry?'

'Just sitting here, in a hotel, an English hotel.'

'You make it sound miraculous.'

'It is.' His gaze met hers. 'Nothing to do; no demands to be met; no questions to answer.'

'There is one,' Frances said.

'What?'

'D'you want port or brandy with that coffee?'

In the bar, keeping a discreet eye on the doorway to the restaurant, Smith sat on a stool, cradling a glass of tonic water and thinking again about home. A wife rarely seen the past couple of months; a son and daughter who made jokes about prison visiting hours. He thought: I know a little of what it's like, Piotr, what it's like to be a prisoner.

He also thought there had to be a Newtonian law of motion for salesmen, too: that the attraction of alcohol was in direct proportion to the distance travelled in any one day. His unwanted companion returned from the washroom, then drained the rest of a tankard and ordered another pint of best and a tonic; said, you're sure, only a tonic? I thought the Welsh were supposed to be big drinkers.

Smith studied his benefactor, wondered how he had wound up as a salesman. This one was in his early twenties and acted as though he was en route to the Crusades. Dynamism, vigour, enthusiasm – the radiations were almost tangible.

I'm in confectionery, got a Sierra-ful of choc bars in the car park. What're you in?

I'm not quite sure, Smith said. He excused himself and went outside to find Hawkins half asleep in the car. He woke him and told him to check the car park – Sierra saloon or estate. Supposed to be full of chocolate bars. Hawkins stared blankly after him.

But you couldn't take risks.

The mood was being gentled by the lateness of the hour. Softness had come stealing in amongst the flowers and the candle glow, and voices were lower now.

'I wonder what Owen is doing,' Asanov said.

'On guard duty.'

'Perhaps we should ask him to join us.' His crooked smile belied the thought.

'Perhaps.' She courted his gaze, smiled at him with her eyes.

'He is a good man,' Asanov said.

'Yes.' The smile became laughter. 'Have you noticed something? The more he relaxes, the broader his accent becomes.'

'I noticed.'

'The first time I met him he hardly said a word. Seemed very cool, very professional. Now, though, now he can forget the act.' She paused. 'Funny how many faces we wear.'

Asanov waited, but she didn't seem to have anything else to say. He watched her across the candle flame, seeing the play of light in her eyes, how it sculpted the cheekbones and added further gloss to the cascade of hair.

'I enjoy listening to you,' he said.

'Even after all this time?'

'We have not been together that often.'

'No?'

'Tuesday the twenty-sixth, Tuesday the tenth, Tuesday the seventeenth and Wednesday the eighteenth, Tuesday the twenty-fourth, and today.' He paused. 'You see? How I remember you?'

She had to turn her head and look away. There was something almost childlike about the expression on his face. Quietly: 'Thank you.'

'For what?'

But she didn't reply.

He said: 'If I still had my diary I could tell you –' Braking much too late, colliding hard with unwanted memories.

'You've lost it?' Frances said.

'It ... It will be somewhere.'

Somewhere. A little book bursting with conversations between a man and himself, a little book filled with thoughts, questions and fears, with the man's name upon it, the handwriting an imprint of his ownership. A little book full of dates and places and names.

Tell yourself, Piotr: Yelena is all right. No one knows.

'Piotr? Something wrong?'

He smiled hastily. 'I apologise. I was ... miles away.' He struggled desperately for something to say. Finally: 'This is so very pleasant. What is it called?'

'It's just the hotel restaurant.' Frances shrugged.

'I see. The Grange Hotel restaurant, Tilgarsley, England. I shall remember this place.'

'Actually, we're about a mile out of the village.'

A brittle smile: 'They do not wish me to travel too far.'

Smith got into the Granada. 'You can go inside now, Neil.'

'Thank Christ for that.' Hawkins shivered. 'It's bloody freezing.' He pushed the tartan travel rug aside. 'Done the rooms?'

'Yes. All you need do is sleep.'

'Unless ...' Hawkins said, then sighed. 'Are we getting paranoid or what, Owen?'

'We're getting paranoid.'

Asanov restarted an earlier conversation. Pace was all now, it minimised the gaps between the words.

'You say we have never ... gossiped? But you'd be surprised, Frances, the things we have touched upon during your visits – politics, and history, your culture ... Oh, so many things.'

'We've covered all that?'

'Yes. I have learnt a lot.'

'And the most important lesson so far?'

He smiled. 'I have learned that Doctor Frances Wycliffe is a kind and beautiful lady who should not be living on her own.'

'Oh.' She debated how to respond, decided to go for a lightness that was becoming increasingly difficult to sustain. 'That's it then, is it? That's me all summed up.'

'Well, I don't have a dossier,' Asanov grinned, 'whereas you do.'

'Except that every other paragraph is made up of asterisks, things they don't want me to know. All I do know is –' she ticked off the points on her fingers – 'one, you're fifty-two years old; two, you were born in Rostov; three, you were married and had a –'

Her mouth froze, the words cutting off abruptly even though the echoes dinned on. She closed her eyes, shutting out his face, shutting out the moment; closed her eyes against the crassness of it all, feeling the stifling heat of a furious mortification rising angrily within. Finally: 'I'm sorry, Piotr. That was incredibly thoughtless.' A whisper, voice still choked by her own stupidity. She stared at the candle; it seemed to flare accusingly.

Quietly, reasonably: 'But we can talk about them.'

She shook her head. 'No.'

'Frances, look at me.' She didn't respond. He waited for a few moments longer. 'Did they tell you to stay off the subject?'

'Yes.'

'Why?'

'It's too soon.' She summoned up the courage to meet his gaze. 'I should never have –'

'But it is all right, truly. It is all right.' His gaze slowly lowered. 'I was a lucky man. My wife and my son, Magda ... and Dmitri ...'

She let him assume control of the conversation, let him go into the very area against which she had been so strenuously warned. She could not remember precisely when Leech had cautioned her, when he had insisted on the necessity of keeping the client – my God, the *client*, though – of keeping Piotr Asanov happy and content and unfettered either by unpleasant pressure or unfortunate memories. He's been through a lot, Leech said. What you need to know is in your copy of the dossier.

The dossier: a clutch of censored pages, less than half the Asanov story, and yet, somehow, enough ...

'I do not know what they told you,' Asanov said, 'or what you have read. But it is a simple story. There's no reason to avoid it.' He breathed in deeply. 'In the beginning, I trained to be a doctor, a doctor of medicine. Later I specialised in auricular malformation – conditions of the inner ear. My mother, she used to teach the deaf, so the interest had long been there. I specialised more and more, moved further into pure research. Sound and sound transmission fascinated me; what we hear, what we do not; and why. I learned about everything: frequency perception; spectrum sensitivity; the effect of age upon hearing. I spent time working with deaf children. They were very ... special.' He hesitated, shook his head. 'Special.'

She waited for the tempo to resume.

'Of course,' Asanov said, 'there were other groups, too. The partially deaf, the elderly; and also control groups, children who –' he seemed to stumble over the words – 'who were all right.' He paused again. 'I worked with my own son, with Dmitri.'

The candle flame was guttering; she concentrated on it, willed it to remain.

'Magda died when he was only eleven years old,' Asanov continued. 'We had to manage. Still, people do. He was a beautiful child, Frances – very dark, the hair, the eyes – beautiful, like his mother. He loved music. He even understood it, the miracle of it all. When you think about it, a sound wave, a frequency – yet it is the most eloquent language of them all.

'When his schooling was finished he secured a place at Rostov film studios. Not the visual side, though; Dmitri was more interested in the sound than the images.'

She spoke at last. 'He could write music?'

'Yes, but for his own amusement. It takes a long time to be published, to get a commission.' A prolonged pause. 'His music was beautiful, as you have heard.'

'Heard?' She frowned, framed the words of denial. Then images and echoes came tumbling back. 'That first morning, that piece you were playing ...'

'Yes.' He smiled. 'A piano plays. And Dmitri is ...' The sentence trailed away, unfinished.

She ordered another round of liqueurs. Common sense argued against staying, but decency said otherwise: you cannot leave it like this, you cannot be the cause and then evade the effect.

'He was only twenty-two years old, Frances.'

'Yes.'

'It's not very old, is it?' Asanov's gaze flitted erratically, finally settled on the flower vase. 'In the ... dossier, does it say what happened?'

She swallowed, forced moisture into a dry throat. 'There was an accident. He was killed in a ... a shooting accident, last summer ...'

'That's correct. August, August the twenty-fourth.' Asanov paused. 'We were both in Moscow. I was lecturing; he'd transferred

143

to Moscow Film. They said ... the police said Dmitri had gone with his girlfriend to Sokolniki Park. The girl told them she took Dmitri along for protection.'

'Protection?'

'Yes.'

'But why? I don't understand, Piotr, I don't –'

'This isn't written down, then?'

'Not in the file I have, no.' She opened and closed her mouth, continued to stare at him in mute bewilderment.

Asanov shrugged. 'It is of no consequence.'

'But what happened?'

He hesitated again, then: 'The girl was meeting a dealer, a man who sold drugs. Not that my son was ever involved in anything like that; the girl told them, she said ... Anyway, she wanted to purchase some cannabis – I think it was that. She wanted it for herself, her university friends; but she was so nervous of the dealer, she gave Dmitri his phone number, asked Dmitri to make the arrangements, the appointment.

'And then, somehow, somehow ... the police learned of it. They were waiting. The dealer had a gun; there was shooting. My son died in the cross-fire.'

She let the silence wash over them, knowing intuitively that sympathy was at its best when words were at their least.

'They brought me his things, you know?' Asanov's lips were beginning to tremble. 'Afterwards, in a shopping bag; his things ... blue jeans, a long-playing record –' a brief bitter smile – 'souvenirs of a life, Frances, of a son.' The silence seemed to ebb interminably. 'I don't have the jeans, of course, they meant nothing to me, but the record ... Stupid, no?'

She heard herself say: 'Record?'

'And the shopping bag; when I went to Leningrad I took every-thing I could. When I left, well, there wasn't much time. They would not give me any time. So I grabbed whatever there was – socks, razor, handkerchief, things like that, and thrust them all in the shopping bag and then remembered, remembered what ...' He broke off, shook his head.

Despite herself the question took voice: 'But why a record? Why *that* record, Piotr?' She registered the look in his eyes. 'Owen told me about it. I saw it in your collection. It didn't seem, you know, it didn't look like it would be your sort of music.'

144

'You have heard it?'

'Years ago.'

Asanov nodded. 'It was Dmitri's favourite piece of music. He was always talking about it, its construction, what it said, what it meant. The young – they can be so passionate, yes?'

'So he'd heard it before then, I mean before ... before the park.'

'He knew it by heart. But only on cassette, a ... bootleg? That is what they are called? Very poor quality, from Singapore, I think. He'd always wanted the record, the sound would be far better on a record. But that particular one is very difficult to obtain in the Soviet Union. I even asked people myself, when I was once looking for a birthday present for him.' He caught the expression on her face. 'Frances? Is something wrong?'

'No.' A brisk denial, a quick smile.

But she was hearing different echoes now, and unease was growing within, a chillness crawling amongst inner shadows. Different, meaningless words rang inside her head, and she knew, even though thoughts were still diffused, she knew the taste of a dark foreboding, of something yet to come.

'Was everything to your satisfaction, madam? Sir?'

She looked up, glanced around the restaurant. All the diners had departed and every table had been cleared.

'Good God, Piotr! Look at the time!' To the waiter: 'I'm sorry. We never noticed.'

A polite smile. He folded his arms, stood aside in silent indication of the exit. She winked at Asanov. For the past half-hour she'd struggled to divert him, challenging him with question after question about the sonobuoy, the sensors and the decoupling and the interface and the hydraulics and the computer and anything else that came to mind, anything remotely associated with the project.

When the questions ran out she switched to stories: her own work, the department's, its history. She even regaled him with the tale of Rolls-Royce – how one of the world's most famous names had provided the power for dirigibles that were sent aloft to combat what was then the almost Wellsian threat of the submarine. 1914, Piotr – a Rolls-Royce Hawk engine in a glorified hot-air balloon.

And at last he was clear of the pain and the introspection, and he began to question her: was it really that way? Did they really do that? With rich, deep laughter he remarked on the quaintness of it all.

She pushed her chair back. 'C'mon, Piotr. Time to call it a night.'
'Must we?'
He followed her with obvious reluctance.

Crossing the lobby, her arm through his. Walking side by side to the staircase. Turning to look at her as the drumming began inside, acceleration and crescendo. Ascending the carpeted steps, negotiating the half-landing, continuing the climb.

On the next floor, her arm slipped free. He watched her move ahead and hold open the fire door, smiling. They passed through the doorway and along the corridor; surely she must hear it, he thought, the drumming in my chest.

'Well,' she said, 'it's been a lovely evening, Piotr.'
Has it ended, then?
'What's wrong?' A brief concern, then she smiled again. 'Oh, don't say you've forgotten your key.'
'I think ...' he heard himself say.
'Yes?'
'I think maybe I have too much to drink.'
She laughed. 'It's about time you let your hair down.'
'Frances?'
'Mmm?'
'I enjoyed myself.'
A final smile. 'See you in the morning, then.'
He nodded, and rummaged in the pockets of the unfamiliar clothes for his key.
She moved so quickly the moment flashed out before he could react: a dark sweep of hair, a brief moisture on his cheek, and then her key was grating in its lock and the door was opening and she whispered, 'Goodnight, Piotr,' and closed the door behind her.

Two words: 'Goodnight, Piotr,' and nothing more.
He undressed without thinking, donned pyjamas and cotton gown, and then stood motionless in the middle of the bedroom, looking at the shadows in the empty room.
The drumming inside had peaked and gone. There was only hollowness now, another space amongst all the other spaces, waiting to be filled.
Two words; barely a sentence. But they cast him away, and he had

146

been returned to a private shore, to wait and watch for the cold numbing tide. He crossed the carpet, taking an almost scientific interest in the actions of the limbs – the feet leading and then stopping, a hand that seemed quite remote, disembodied, reaching out, fingers closing upon the telephone.

'Can I help you?' The receptionist seemed to speak from a million miles away.

'I am trying to contact another guest. Doctor Frances Wycliffe, room seventeen.'

'One moment, sir.'

. The extension rang out, stopped. He heard himself say, 'Frances? Is that you?'

'Piotr?'

'I ... I wanted to talk.'

For a few moments there was silence, and then, very faintly, she answered: 'Yes.'

The curtains were drawn back from the window; beyond the glass, he could see a ragged line of tree-tops, a glittering quilt of sky.

She went to him and reached out for his hand, felt the trembling like the fluttering of a small bird, there, in her palm. She led it to its place upon the swelling curve of her breast.

A tremor passed through her body into his; and then came the first hesitant movements, cupping, cradling; she felt warmth at her right breast now, as his fingers spread and flexed and pressed slowly in upon the dark textured circle.

She felt herself arching, wanting to pierce his hands, but suddenly his arms were around her and the embrace locked like a band of iron and he was clinging to her and making small sobbing noises, cries of disbelief, the sounds of release from fear.

They went side by side to the bed. Its covers were pulled back, the creases smoothed from the sheet, a plain of softness. She lay upon the coolness and watched him shed his clothes: an awkward fussing with a button, a brief snap of frustration at a knotted cord.

Then his fingertips were tracing the features of her face, and he kissed her – the gentlest kiss, lips hardly touching before with-drawing. And again he kissed her, and a third time as her hand swept slowly over his body. All the time she watched his eyes, his face – until his head jolted back as the shock ran through him, made him call out.

147

And then he was straining against her in desire and she felt the breath of his sigh, and answered with a smile, and their eyes met and brimmed with the rich conspiracy of the hour.

She imagined herself parting then, mind, spirit and flesh. She imagined his fullness within her, and then she felt him and heard him let out a long, shuddering moan, and answered with a bright, silver cry of her own.

The unit bleeped and the red light flashed. Hawkins stared sadly at the reels.

Apart from the fact that the other Sony was bust and they were having to double-face only one recorder; and apart from the fact that Owen Smith had forgotten the bloody headphones; and apart from the fact that it was fourteen minutes into Saturday morning; apart from all that, none of this had he expected to happen – and to none of this did he want to listen.

She came out of the long dreamless sleep and lay there unmoving for a while. Then she looked at him, as if to confirm the reality of his presence.

'Hello.'

He'd been staring into nothingness, eyes wide and unblinking; the word seemed to jolt him free from wherever he'd gone.

'So you're awake, Frances.'

'Almost.'

She sought out his hand, rested her fingers on his – no pressure, no movement. Everything easy in the shared warmth and the shared silence, in the reassurance of touch and the privilege of privacy.

'What're you thinking about?'

No response, though she was sure he'd heard.

'Piotr?'

'I could not expect you to understand.' He tried to smile away the remark but her eyes remained dark, serious.

She shifted position. 'Piotr, what is it?'

He looked away, then back again. Her gaze hadn't wavered. 'All right,' he said. 'It was the silence when I awoke – it reminded me of something.' He paused. 'During research, I studied two groups of whales – humpbacks and finbacks – how they communicated, the frequencies they used. They are clever fellows, Frances. The humpback, he travels all the way from Bermuda to the Arctic

148

and back again, migrating, mating. And all the time, he sings.'

He halted again. It seemed to Frances as if his thoughts were being seeded by a drifting breeze, and that he was having to pluck at them before they floated beyond reach.

'Singing, Frances, not just one song but many – and each song different, and each song unique to each humpback. That is how they draw themselves together, by their songs.'

She remained silent, continued to stare up at his face. His animation was beautiful and disturbing all at the same time.

'The finbacks also have their songs. But ... we're losing them, Frances ... losing them. Not just because we kill too many too often, but because ... because ...'

His eyes blinked as though stricken by a sudden pain. He shook his head abruptly and then said, with a bitterness that jolted her: 'They want me to make the sea as glass. Did you know that? It is the only thing God neglected to do.'

She pushed herself upright. 'Piotr? Piotr!'

'Oh yes, he has a beautiful song. But his kind, they're so few, scattered so far apart. Does he give up? No! Still he calls out across the ocean and still he waits for the answering cry and still he refuses to admit it, that it's all in vain, that the songs are all in vain ...'

The quaking began then, and she found herself holding him and soothing him and loving him and fearing him. His shudders seemed to echo from a deep well of grief.

His words were quieter now, though the pain in them sounded even sharper: 'If all the ships, Frances, all the ships on the sea; if we could stop their engines, then finback could be heard by finback across two hundred miles. But if we could stop everything, everything, on the surface, below the surface – the ships and the submarines and the scanners and the sounders ... If we could do all that, the finbacks could hear each other across four *thousand* miles. Can you imagine it? Can you imagine what it would be like to give them ... silence?'

PART IV

CHAPTER
ELEVEN

ACOUSTIC RESEARCH CENTER
MOFFETT FIELD
CALIFORNIA

Gulliver said, they've failed, the Brits have failed. So you get out to
Moffett and check security and see how our people are doing, while I
fly over to London for this goddamned conference.

Barnes had been able to piece together what had happened from
the notes. Apparently they'd had a team on it day and night and had
eventually come up with a scale model. They'd loaded it into an RN
Quartermasters' supply truck and driven it to what was left of their
Devonport dockyard.

No funds, few facilities – Gulliver said it was like Great Britain
was closing down.

An Admiralty Research Establishment team locked themselves
away in a massive dry dock and pumped thousands of gallons of
water into a giant tank fitted with a wind machine and wave
simulator. The model went into the tank and promptly sank because
the buoyancy chamber failed. Then the arms – whatever they were –
failed to open so that was no good either.

Even after they'd solved those problems, the upper and lower
sections of the model refused to separate due to a malfunction of the
hydraulics, leaving them jammed irrevocably together.

Washington had been a while in learning of the difficulties.
Gulliver had attributed that to the fact that Washington and London
were two parts of a structure jammed irrevocably apart. The Brits
said they hadn't had enough time, it was only mid-June, less than
eight weeks since the design configuration had been first sketched
out.

Washington sent a message. Mid-June was late enough.

Moffett Field – jammed between the southern end of San Francisco Bay and the foothills of the Santa Cruz. Moffett, anti-submarine base of the Pacific Fleet's air wing, sprawled out across the quaking Bayland mud. You could see the vast dirigible hangars miles away.

A crazy place to site it, Barnes thought. Moffett would be pulverised when the Big One came; after all, the San Andreas Fault lay only five miles to the west. He'd flown into San Francisco International, had a rental car sent up from Burlingame, then headed south through Silicon Valley on Bayshore Freeway. The turn-off was posted soon after Palo Alto and he swung onto the exit ramp just as a P3 Orion came in low and loud.

It settled itself on the shining concrete runway, another eighteen-hour submarine patrol at an end. The P3s ranged as far as the Aleutians. Barnes wondered what it was like, fishing from the skies.

They cleared him through to administration. Reception took a PolaColor of him which was then sealed inside clear laminated plastic. Then an escort guided him through the road network to Building SP 3.

With its rounded roofline and full-height double doors, the concrete block looked like an aeroplane hangar – not as long, perhaps, and certainly not as high, but the similarity was there. It also reminded him of a cinema one of the oil companies had built outside Tehran, where *Funny Girl* had been playing the day the Shah ran away.

He announced himself over the voice box and waited. Then a side door opened and a man in a white coat with breast ID HENNESSY F shook his hand and said: 'Baker's waiting. Go on up.'

It looked like the biggest boxing ring in the world – big enough for the audience, never mind the fighters. A catch fence of triple nylon rope ran all around while at each corner, rising high into the air, stood four arc-lighting towers.

In the ring was the Asanov sonobuoy.

Barnes followed the narrow pathway alongside the wall, then climbed the steps to the control room. He paused and looked down. The sonobuoy was not completely spherical. The only projection from the smooth, shiny casing was the steel stub of an umbilical coupling, from which emerged heavy-duty cabling, twice as thick as the width of a man's hand; it went snaking away into the other corners. The sonobuoy was cradled by scaffolding. So too were the

154

other things connected to the cabling: giant paddles, twelve feet high at least, their surfaces a honeycomb grid. The more Barnes examined them, the more they came to resemble some weird system of microphones.

The control room was a glass-fronted tier running the width of the back wall and projecting out on cantilevered struts. Inside were two men, one tall and gaunt, the other squat and hirsute, and irritable. The gaunt one was in funereal black; the squat one wore open-necked shirt with sleeves rolled all the way up.

'Every year it's the same damn thing,' the squat man said. 'Don't forget, Harry. Don't be late, Harry.' He swung round in the chair. 'Who the hell are you?'

'Barnes.'

'What kind of Barnes?'

'Well, it ain't hay.' He flashed the ID.

'So who gave you permission to come in here?'

'The owner.'

'The who?'

'Uncle Sam.' Barnes smiled. 'I work for him.'

The older man extended his hand. 'Good afternoon, Mr Barnes. My name's Schulmann – from the main contractor.' His gaze roved over Barnes's attire, white sweater under denim jacket, jeans, and boots. 'And you're from . . .?'

'Project security, Washington.' He turned to the other man. 'You're Harry Baker?'

'Yeah. And I'm going to be the late Harry Baker if we don't get on with this thing.' To Schulmann: 'Remember, you heard it here first.'

Schulmann frowned. Barnes frowned. Baker shook his head. 'Jesus H. Four o'clock in the afternoon and here I am with a guy from the mortician's and another out of Marlboro country.'

Barnes peered out through the glass. 'Something wrong, Mr Schulmann?'

'There's been a technical delay,' Schulmann said.

'That's the polite way of saying it,' Baker retorted.

Schulmann looked hurt. 'Considering the little notice we had, considering the time you people gave us –'

'Sure, sure.' Baker sat down at the console. 'That's okay, Mr Schumann.'

'Schulmann.'

'Yeah, right.'

155

A mike sprouted from the instruments panel. Baker thumbed the button by its base. 'Hello? Anybody out there?'

'Nearly finished, Harry,' a voice crackled through overhead speakers.

'How nearly is nearly?'

Pause. 'It's nearly, Harry.' A clicking sound, followed by a muted droning.

Barnes stared down at the ring. There was something alien about the scene, the strange honeycombed paddles in their corners, the smooth black mine with its snaking umbilical cords. The one who'd let him in, Hennessy, was on hands and knees by a paddle, doing something to the cable junction. Finally he slipped through the ropes and jumped the five or six feet down off the dais into a pool of heavy shadow.

The speakers crackled again. 'She's all yours.'

'Okay.' Baker studied the meter display. 'We're ready for scanning. You stay on visual.'

'Copy.'

Schulmann turned to Barnes. 'That's a modified section of the buoy,' he said. 'But it does have the full EHE pack.'

'The EHE?' Barnes prodded.

'It feeds out the power to the transducers – those paddle-shaped things. Of course, in practice it won't look like that. The paddles will be integrated into the buoy proper.'

Barnes pointed towards the mine. 'The power pack and the controls – they're housed there?'

'Can't be anywhere else. You can't plug into the mains, Mr Barnes, not underwater.'

'And all this equipment?' Barnes indicated the console.

'This is the master to the buoy's slave unit. We're locked into the buoy's circuitry. We can over-ride it.'

'I see.'

'Mr Barnes?' Schulmann seemed suddenly agitated. 'This is the first test. But, if it doesn't work, well, my company didn't design this. We can't be held responsible.'

'For what?'

'Failure.'

Barnes unwrapped a stick of gum. 'Nobody's ever been held responsible for that.'

Baker spoke into the mike. 'You clear of that transducer?'

'Clear.'

'Well, make sure you stay that way. That thing topples, your head's gonna be flatter'n a witch's tit.'

Barnes eased into an adjacent seat. 'You take a lot of precautions, Mr Baker.'

'Don't I know it.'

'Why? It's not as though there's anything dangerous down there.'

Baker glanced at him, then away again. 'See the size of that transducer? It's about to get the juice. When that happens, it'll very likely vibrate. And with all that power, and all that vibration, that scaffolding might not be enough. Okay?'

'Okay.'

Baker addressed the mike again. 'Right. Starting . . . Now.'

Spatulate fingers crabbed across the console, throwing keys, punching buttons; telemetry screens shone green. The fingers paused, then hooked around a double-ganged lever, set into the desk like the T-shift of a car. 'Okay, you mother,' Baker said, and pulled.

A red beacon glowed. Barnes wondered if there'd be anything to see. Certainly, there'd be nothing to hear. The output was inaudible. Not like the Grand Ol' Opry coming through loud and clear or something.

'Power gradient on . . . First position. Copy?'

Hennessy's voice, disembodied: 'Copy.'

'Rising steady.' Baker concentrated on the meters. 'Rising . . . Second position. Copy?'

'Copy.'

'Any vibration?'

Barnes's gaze alternated from the meters to the ring below. He began to chew more rapidly.

'Rising three,' Baker said. 'Third position.'

'Copy,' Hennessy responded.

Baker continued to stare intently at the meters, watching the drifting needles as the wavelength grew longer and the frequency slowed.

'Rising four.'

'Copy.'

Steadily, steadily, no movement down there, no noise.

'Fifth position.'

'It's looking good,' Hennessy called.

Power increasing, the intervals between the marks shortening.

157

'Rising six,' Baker said.

Hennessy didn't answer.

'Sixth position,' Baker repeated. 'And rising ... Rising seven.'

The speakers hummed.

'Mark seven,' Baker said. He sighed. 'Hennessy? You copy?'

The humming, the needles, letters and numbers dancing on the green screens – nothing else. Baker said irritably: 'For Christ's sake, Hennessy.'

Then, faintly: 'Harry?'

Barnes frowned. There was a quavering in the voice that hadn't been there before. He looked at Baker but didn't speak.

'Hey! You all right down there?'

'I ... I don't know.' His voice was hoarse, faltering.

Needles trembled, passed through the midpoint of the quadrant. The wavelength undulated, snake-like; power rising eight and climbing.

'I gotta go, Harry.'

'What?' Bewilderment was graphic on the rumpled features. 'What? Say again. I can't hear you.'

'Harry ...' And the voice now sounded as though it belonged to someone with a very bad head cold.

Schulmann said quietly: 'There's something wrong.'

'Hennessy? Are you all right?'

The needles approached, bisected and passed through eight – and rising.

Baker gave an exasperated sigh. 'Of all the times ...'

Breathing amplified with shocking clarity over the speakers. 'I feel sick. God, I feel sick ...'

Schulmann tried but failed to still the tremor in his own voice. 'I'm telling you, there's something wrong.'

Baker turned to him. 'You ever eat in our commissary, Mr Schubert? Don't. The chef thinks he's in charge of chemical warfare.' Into the mike: 'Okay, get out of there. We'll shut down for a while.'

Barnes stood up, shaded his eyes the better to focus through the glass. Everything looked the same – no sound, no movement. Above him, the loudspeakers hummed. Then, below, a white figure, stumbling from the back of the ring, stumbling and twisting, hands squeezing his abdomen. Stumbling again and then falling, rolling into shadow again.

158

To Schulmann and Baker: 'Stay.' Barnes pushed past them and
wrenched open the door. He paused and pointed to the console.
'And turn that thing off.' The door slammed.

'Aw, shit!' Baker's fist slammed down. 'Shit shit shit!'

He pushed the T-bar back up its slot. The red beacon went out.
Schulmann stared helplessly at him, swallowed twice, then began to
tug at the collar of his shirt.

'All this time,' Baker groaned, 'and all this effort and all this
screwing around with a pile of goddamn junk. Jahesus, I mean, what
is it with people these days? Well? You send a guy down, all he has to
do is – what's the matter?'

Schulmann's face was changing, something was coming into
it and the pallor was getting lighter and the lines deepening and
he was staring at the console and the mouth was opening and
working ...

And the needles were leaning further to the right, deflection
continuing, steadily, unhurriedly.

'Wha ...?'

Baker's head jerked from side to side, gaze snapping from one
meter to the next, back and forth, seeing but not seeing, unable to
believe: three pairs, six meters, six quadrants, six needles approaching twelfth position and red.

His fingers scrabbled for the command key, the over-rider, and
hooked around it, knuckles wrapped so tight the whiteness gleamed.
He dragged it downwards, watched the beacon light; he palmed it
upwards, watched the beacon die.

The needles never flickered.

And it was the craziness of all this, the utter unbelievability of it
all, that drove all other thoughts aside, and he found himself suddenly touching his stomach and shaking his head, and not really
knowing why.

On, off. On, off.

The needles swept through twelve and passed into the red zone.

'I don't believe this,' Baker whispered. 'I don't believe this.'

The staircase from the gallery to the floor had seemed a makeshift
affair when he'd first climbed it. Now, half-way down, it felt as
though they'd merely stapled it to the wall. Barnes could have sworn
it was beginning to sway.

He slipped three steps from the ground, went sprawling. He rolled over onto his back, glanced up towards Baker and Schulmann and the glass room. It was shivering.

He shook his head. Got up. Took a couple of paces and felt pain flaring in the right ankle, a couple more and then no further, stopped abruptly by the heat, the heat that came swirling from everywhere and nowhere, heat enfolding like a cloak, heat coming up from the concrete floor, pressing down from the lighting towers high above.

Hot as hell – it didn't make sense. Then the ankle gave way and he flattened out again and found himself staring up at the lights, squeezing his eyes tight against the brilliance. And something inside, rising.

On, off. On, off. Beacon shining, beacon dead. Beacon shining, beacon dead. Backwards and forwards and backwards and then the pain finally breaking through, a sort of grinding, brief, paralysing, a sensation of something grating, way down inside.

Baker glanced up at Schulmann and the cadaverous features were totally white, and the eyes had rolled upwards, obscenely comical, like eggshells bulging, and Schulmann was reeling and clutching his belly – any second he was going to topple and so Baker struggled, struggled against all the weights and the bindings, began panicking, plucking wildly at nothing, got to stop Schulmann from going down.

Then the glass exploded. Windows dissolved in a deafening storm, blowing inwards and outwards, turning the air silver, millions of bright fragments whipped spinning on the gale, giant shards and minute slivers, flying spears slashing and flashing. Telemetry screens crazed and erupted, tearing out black rubber seals that soared and snaked away. Meter glass popped free, small oblong chunks that shot out one by one in split-second sequence, as though flicked fiercely upwards in orchestrated order, some halving, the rest intact, hurtling up into the air.

Hands over his abdomen, Barnes lay there looking up at the lights, a regular firmament shining diamond hard and diamond bright, the reflected heat and reflected glare batting down from the overhead steel latticework. He rolled onto his knees, pushed himself upright.

The silence suddenly blew apart and he staggered, physically assailed by the shock, and saw the front of the control room powdering into a glittering cascade, a splintering crash that dinned on and on.

He could not absorb it, nor believe it; the shock-wave so jolted the optical nerves and receptors that vision geared down into slow motion, the image registering as frame-by-frame pictures of silver and crystals of light, spewing slowly outwards and down like a dam bursting. He stayed there, swaying, transfixed. Then the screaming started.

Reflexes spurred him onwards, towards the sound. Footsteps clumsy, badly placed, but going on because the brain said, you can't stop now, there's a man the other side of this thing, there's a man dying of a heart attack.

Erratically, because of the pain in the ankle, because of this . . . this fullness inside, this strange, ballooning awareness of tactility where no sensation should be, moving on towards the man with a heart attack . . . But who said that? How do you know?

Hennessy was saying a long way away: 'Do something. Help me.'

For Christ's sake, Barnes, pull yourself together. No panic, easy, no panic; left foot, now right foot, one then two and one then two, come on, you can do it, keep going, there's a man you don't know the other side of this, but he's dying just the same.

He stopped dead because the heat had been whipped away, all of it, and coldness was exploding instead, sudden, shocking. Barnes, you stupid sonofabitch, you've got the shower stat on wrong . . . But not in a shower at all, you're here, in this place; and this place, it's in you.

God, but this is *crazy*, this is wrong, this is the deck of a ship in a storm, everything tilting every which way, yawing, lurching, nausea welling and bubbling and beginning to rise; left foot, right foot and then, at last, the fear.

It poured into his skull on a tide of darkness, like the sea rushing in, ice-cold. I am frightened now, God, I am frightened. One step, two step, three step.

He went down on his knees beside Hennessy. He leaned forward to hook his hands under the other man's shoulders, but the inclination was too great, and he kept on leaning, going down, face striking the floor, going down amidst a shivering thunder all the way into a turbulent black.

They placed Schulmann and Hennessy on the first two stretchers, then came back for Baker, and Barnes.

Barnes opened one eye, responding to the unexpected motion. Baker was being carried alongside. He was very still. Half his face was crimson.

Doors clicked shut. The ambulance gathered speed.

Awareness grew slowly: the sensation of travel, the sound of a siren, the nurse bending down, her anxious face pressed close to his.

'Shhh,' she whispered.

'I'm all right,' Barnes said. The words croaked and rasped. He tried again, moistened his lips: 'I'm not scared any more.'

What a crazy thing to say. He wanted to straighten that out with her, but the darkness came again, and this time it was welcome.

CHAPTER
TWELVE

LENINGRAD

'So,' Ivanitsyn said. 'It's farewell again.'

'Yes.'

They'd gone back to speaking like indifferent actors with inadequate lines.

'Well,' they said together, and traded hesitant, embarrassed smiles.

He raised the bottle of Dvin to the light. 'Still some left.'

'It's a new bottle.'

'I hadn't realised.'

Tanya watched him going through the ritual. It had begun to seem slightly absurd, this business of departure; a week ago he'd slammed out of the apartment without any ceremony whatsoever and flown to Murmansk, only to suddenly reappear on Thursday afternoon, almost as though nothing had happened.

No sooner had he gone than he was back again. But something had happened after all: the sub was ready; sailing day Monday the 30th.

'Tomorrow,' she said, not intending to muse aloud.

'Tomorrow.' He raised his glass in a mistaken toast. 'And about time too.'

She took her glass from him, but made no attempt to drink. 'Will it be long?'

'No, forty days, or thereabouts.' A pale smile. 'Forty days in the wilderness – that's Biblical, isn't it?'

Tanya shrugged. 'Everything is ready, at Murmansk?'

'I hope so. I've not paid that much attention.'

'Oh?'

'Two days of non-stop volleyball – trying to find out if I'm still as good as when I played for Leninskiy Komsomol.'

163

'Are you?'

'I'm older.' He paused. 'Still, it was good exercise. My last chance, too. This job, it's so unhealthy. No wonder Mikhail always says we're on inactive service. Forty days and nights with no room to move.'

'So why do it,' Tanya said quietly.

The phrase stayed with him, bringing a memory: Igor, their guest that last Saturday night, had kept asking why – why? Why do it, living a life whose furthest boundary is only a few paces away? Existing for so long in a space so small, the eyes lock in close-focus so that when you come home and step ashore the vista is so wide, so distant, that vision blurs and you feel disorientated, vulnerable, lightheaded.

Why do it? The cry of all those who did not know and never could imagine. Civilians, outsiders – you'd never explain it to them in a million years. Igor had said: I'd go mad being down there, doing your job. Sorry, he'd replied, it's against the rules.

Tanya found herself at the window, staring at the courtyard below. Dusk had yet to turn to darkness. Soon, she realised, soon the transition wouldn't occur at all. She turned to him, said: 'Give my regards to Mikhail.'

'When he turns up.' A puzzled frown. 'I don't understand it; last week he never showed at all.' He remained thoughtful for a few moments, then poured a second shot, snapping it down with a flick of the wrist.

She said quietly: 'Go safely, Yevgeni.'

He nodded. 'It'll be all right this time.'

DIRECTORATE OF OPERATIONS
NORTHERN FLEET
MURMANSK

They ushered Ivanitsyn into a small room along the corridor from the briefing room, then went away again. He stared around the blank walls, not really thinking, not really seeing.

He was still hunched over the desk, head bowed, fingers curling and uncurling through his hair, when the door opened, then softly closed.

A pugilist's face, a weightlifter's build; small, hard eyes, then wide, squashed nostrils and finally the mouth, thick-lipped and moist and bracketed by heavy folds of flesh. The man had impossibly broad shoulders that made the bald, shining head appear in precarious balance with the rest of the structure; his chest muscles strained to burst the fabric of a white cotton shirt.

'I've only just been told,' Ivanitsyn said.

'Administrators.' The voice was unexpectedly light, the smile amiable.

He consulted the personnel roster. 'Commissar Bulgov?'

'Yes.' A slight bow.

'On whose authority is this?'

'This?'

'Your posting. I had my own political officer, before.'

Bulgov gave a huge shrug, the gesture preposterously theatrical. 'I don't know on whose authority. I was ordered here, and here I am.'

'As missile control officer.'

'Yes.'

'Which means you're replacing Yuri Grigoriev.'

'I was not told the name.' Bulgov paused. 'Last-minute transfers,' he said. 'One must expect them occasionally.'

Ivanitsyn stood up and walked to the window. He stared out at the asphalt apron, the grey castellated skyline of distant buildings. 'Mikhail Voronikhin – should I have expected that too?'

Bulgov remained silent.

'Vladivostok, posted to Vladivostok; he couldn't have gone much further. At least, not without an exit visa.'

'I'm not privy to Directorate decisions, comrade captain.'

'What a pity. I thought you, as commissar, would be able to tell me what's going on.'

'Changes.' Bulgov shrugged again.

'Why?'

'I assume they were deemed appropriate.' Bulgov hesitated, then took a step forward. 'I trust we will enjoy our work together.'

Ivanitsyn ignored him. After a while, he returned to the desk, sat down again. 'You're familiar with this submarine?'

'Yes.'

'This is the derivative Delta Two configuration – so which class were you with before?'

'RVSN.' Smoothly; not even a pause.

'What?'

'Raketnye Voyska Strategicheskovo Nznacheniya.' He smiled again.

'You've transferred from the rocket corps to a submarine?' He shook his head in disbelief.

'I didn't seek the transfer.'

'What the hell does a soldier know about a submarine?'

'I was not a soldier.'

Ivanitsyn considered him. 'Well, you certainly weren't a ballet dancer.'

Bulgov sighed. 'I'm with military services section, comrade captain, all branches of the armed forces.'

'Ever been on a submarine?'

'Many times.' Bulgov paused. 'I've done a lot in my career, comrade captain. It is not unusual, though, for Party officers to have a comprehensive knowledge. One remembers the late lamented Leonid Brezhnev. He had great experience of the army and the navy and the air force – if you believed all those medals.'

'I'm not interested in politics.'

'You're a Party member.'

Ivanitsyn closed his eyes. 'I am in command of a submarine.'

'With respect, that doesn't mean you have to forego your other commitments.'

'There are no "other commitments".' Angrily: 'The sooner the Party gets out and stays out of military matters, the better.'

'Spoken just like Ustinov.'

'Actually, I was quoting Admiral Gorshkov.'

After a while, Bulgov said: 'I seem to have misunderstood, comrade captain.'

'Misunderstood?'

'Someone happened to mentioned to me that you were married to Nikolai Melnikov's daughter.'

'What of it?'

'He is a well-respected politician. I naturally thought . . .' Bulgov smiled blandly. 'How soon do we leave?'

'If you don't even know that . . .' Ivanitsyn said, then lapsed into a despairing silence.

'I wondered if there'd be a delay, that's all. There seem to have been many delays where this submarine is concerned.' He moved to the door. 'The sooner we go, the sooner we return. It is a great strain,

166

being away so long from our families, our children, our wives – don't you agree, comrade captain?'

Stukhov walked in five minutes later. He was tall and thin, but there the resemblance ended. Gaunt face and nervous manner, much older than Mikhail, Stukhov had the air of a book-keeper, not a submariner.

He talked endlessly, without pausing for breath. The nervous recital of past achievements and experiences culminated in the observation that, by coincidence, the submarine had the same name as his birthplace.

'There isn't a name, though,' Ivanitsyn said.

'Not to the Admiralty, perhaps.'

'Not to me, either. We should not be ... sentimental.'

It's also a reminder of Mikhail, he thought, Mikhail and his unquenchable romanticism.

'I heard the men had named it,' Stukhov persisted, 'after the prince – the prince, not my home.' He paused. 'Have you ever visited Suzdal, comrade captain?'

'No.'

'It is very beautiful.'

'I see.'

'Tourists come in their thousands. The architecture, it is very beautiful.'

'Mmm.'

'And the river Kamenka, it is –'

'Beautiful?'

Stukhov seemed surprised. 'Yes, comrade captain.'

Yevgeni took a long, slow walk along Lenin Prospekt. The Polar wind funnelled in through the harbour mouth. He turned up his collar, paused to watch the pigeons arguing around the Bredov statue. He trudged on beside the basin where huddled trawlers strained at anchor. The backdrop remained resolutely grey, depressing: cranes, sheds, railroad freight, the ugly sprawl of the fish process factory.

He stopped again and looked back down the Prospekt. A road angled off to the right, leading to a hotel whose name escaped him. One day, after final shore debriefing, Mikhail had asked him to meet there, in the restaurant. There were two sisters, Mikhail had said, working at the Polar Research Institute. They liked uniforms. Two humble junior officers, Mikhail had said, could have a memorable night out.

No, Mikhail. I'm going to Leningrad. You know as well as I do, the wedding's only two weeks away. A final fling, Yevgeni? Before you don the shackles? No, Mikhail. No.

He sighed, retraced his steps. A seagull swooped down, seemed to call out a single word over and over again.

Gone. Gone gone gone.

HEADQUARTERS BUILDING
KGB FIRST DIRECTORATE
MOSCOW

The Volga swung off the quiet highway and sped on through the dense stands of fir towards the spotlit flanks of the new curvilinear building. The fifteen-minute journey from Dzerzhinsky Square and Lubyanka, from the old to the new, seemed much longer to Krotov; not for the first time he felt like a traveller through time, a voyager passing from one century into the next.

The car stopped beneath a marquee of bright light. Krotov glanced up; overhead video cameras appeared to nod in acknowledgment. He adjusted his tunic, shivered in the chill night air, then took the leather briefcase from his driver and strode indoors to meet Monakhov.

'Good evening, comrade colonel.' A slight bow. 'I see we're both working very late tonight.'

Krotov stared briefly into the bronze lenses, then thrust forth his burden. 'Here.'

'Thank you.' Again the inclination of the head, the flash of golden light as the briefcase was accepted. 'Won't you sit down, comrade colonel?'

Krotov hesitated, then settled into a chrome and hide confection which yielded so alarmingly that he wondered if it had been specifically created to diminish the stature of its occupant. When you're disadvantaged to begin with, he thought wryly ...

He folded his hands in his lap and let his gaze roam the wide, soft-lit room. Its resemblance to any office he had ever tenanted was slight. As clean and uncluttered as a set-piece, it featured framed pastel sketches on smooth cream walls, isolated groupings of low-profile Finnish furniture, a white venetian blind that shuttered the length of an impressive picture window, thick beige carpeting that absorbed every footfall and, finally, as enviable a collection of plants as he had yet seen. Centred on the small tables or in colourful aggregation in grey plastic tiers, or ranged along perspex wall shelves, their disposition struck Krotov as anything but random, as though they were a living dimension of the design's dynamic.

As for the desk, it was twice as big as his own, its elliptical construction reinforcing the impression that whoever occupied it was more likely to be from the Politburo than the KGB. The desk and the high-backed leather swivel chair in which Monakhov lounged and the suit – particularly, the suit. It was of pale grey cloth, an expensive weave, exquisitely cut. It was also, despite the Moscow night, a lightweight.

Krotov smiled softly. 'I see you're trying out your new wardrobe. Off on your travels, are you?'

'Yes.'

'Well, everything First needs is in that briefcase.'

'They said you would bring everything I need.' Monakhov placed a slight emphasis on the penultimate word. 'What d'you think of my new home?'

'It's ... temporary.'

'It's civilised.' An arm swept in an airy gesture. 'Andropov did us proud, yes?'

'With Brezhnev's money.'

Monakhov permitted himself a sigh of resignation. Eventually: 'So, you come in person.'

'Asanov's files go back ten years. If Second is to transfer them, then I want to know where they're going.'

'You wish for a receipt?' Without waiting for an answer, Monakhov tilted forward in the chair. A drawer slid smoothly open; Krotov watched impassively as manicured fingers spread crisp white paper over the green blotter. A gold pen was uncapped with a brief flourish; its top rolled away, gleaming in the light.

'One receipt,' Monakhov said, 'so there can be no misunderstandings.'

'There'll be no misunderstandings as long as you realise you're with First now.' Krotov pocketed the paper without scrutiny. 'You're not involved in the Leningrad end.'

'I know.' An idle smile, as negligent as the pose. 'Matter of fact, I've just made my last phone call there. Some news for a certain person - good news.' When Krotov didn't react he continued: 'Anyway, I am indeed out of the Leningrad end, thanks to your brilliant performance.'

Quietly, evenly: 'Comrade major, do not patronise me.'

'But without that RTP we should never have known ...'

'It was a hunch. Besides, Karodin's people did all the work.'

'Albeit that they left it unfinished.' Monakhov leaned back and contemplated the ceiling. 'They could have found him. There was a meeting in London involving most of the principals. Karodin should have had them followed afterwards.'

'How,' Krotov said slowly, 'were they supposed to do that? Apart from the American, no one knew what the others looked like.'

'Yes, well ...' Monakhov said. 'Anyway, it's out of Karodin's hands now.' He paused. 'Washington have identified the American's associate. They followed him to a place called Moffett Field in California. Did you hear what happened there?'

'I heard there was some sort of accident.'

'As a result of which we can now await our quarry, instead of having to stalk it.'

Krotov frowned. 'First has someone inside Moffett?'

'No, but there is someone in the defence contractor handling the Asanov project. That's how we know the test is being rescheduled, this time in the presence of its designer.'

'And you've been selected to handle Asanov's reception.'

'When the word comes, yes. You see, I'm not known to the Americans. That gives me a certain advantage.'

'And the job of field director - ever done it before?'

'That doesn't matter. I have my orders.'

'Is it a retrieval, or ...' The question feathered away.

Monakhov smiled, then stood up. 'Well, thank you for coming -' a deliberate pause - 'and for all your helpful advice in the past. One learns so much from a person like you.'

Krotov arose with difficulty. 'Want to learn some more?'

'Most certainly.'

'That philodendron over there, it's dying.' Krotov smiled equably. 'Get it watered, all right?'

170

JOINT SERVICES MARITIME
SURVEILLANCE CENTRE
PITREAVIE CASTLE
EDINBURGH

Alec Kenyon had been to Pitreavie before, routine meetings involving the armed services and the Ministry of Agriculture and Fisheries and its Scottish equivalent. On several occasions he had sat in the long baronial room and stared out at the conifers beyond and thought how the walls and mullions and turrets of this place made it the most imposing of all the border posts on the secret frontier.

The uniformed marine moved briskly ahead, arms swinging and boots tapping. He determined to keep pace, to stay within touching distance of his escort as they clattered down flights of concrete steps and across various landings and through different levels of operations.

A strange, alien place this, where echoing corridors fanned out in a subterranean web and thick steel doors painted the brightest red were guarded by men with sidearms and lanyards and expressions of grim immobility. Down another flight, and another – Kenyon wondered if anyone had ever heard of elevators – and finally into the inner sanctum.

Air Vice-Marshal Talbot greeted him with a smile and a handshake. 'Welcome to Wonderland.'

'You're right. I do know how Alice felt.'

'Not dropped in before, have you, Alec?'

Kenyon shook his head.

'Part-time warriors,' Talbot said. He chuckled, extended his right arm in a gesture of revelation. 'Well, here we are then.'

A cavernous, echoing room hemmed by glass-fronted galleries, its walls given over to huge perspex display boards, the floor area almost entirely taken up with situ-status desks and computer remotes and plain old-fashioned plotting tables. Uniformed figures, men and women, moved about unhurriedly or sat at their positions, speaking in subdued voices.

'Sort of ancient and modern, eh?' Talbot said, 'white chalk and computers.'

Kenyon glanced at his companion. The light reflected off the other's profile and reminded Kenyon how the tall man had survived

171

a war when plastic surgery was just about as primitive as the weapons which caused the wounds.

He followed Talbot to the end of a white modular console that ran the length of one wall then turned at right angles to it. Three teleprinters were set side by side, the nearest almost teetering over the lip. The middle printer stuttered incessantly, its carriage zipping back and forth. Kenyon glanced in its direction as they passed by, but was too far away to make out the words.

They entered a narrow office, not much bigger than a cubicle, backing onto the Operations Centre. A coffee table and black vinyl chairs and a wall of glass fenced them in from the big room beyond.

'Are you going to tell me what this is all about, Kenneth?'

Talbot hunched forward, discomfited by the chair's awkward confines. He was that unusual combination, tall and broad, with a musculature still firm despite his sixty-odd years.

'You navy fellows, you really are the men of the moment.'

'Senior Service.'

'Those bloody tin cans of yours, beavering about under the sea.'

'Tin cans,' Kenyon said mildly, 'do not beaver.'

'Whatever.' Talbot shrugged. 'Now then. JIC's due for its weekly meeting tomorrow. They'll be studying a report from CIG Western.'

'About what?'

'The new Soviet Prairie-class submarine – the prototype left Polyarno yesterday.'

'So?'

'It's quite a weapons platform: ICBMs plus cruise missiles. They're saying anything we can do, they can do better.'

Kenyon considered him. 'I get the impression we're not completely demoralised.'

'Right. In point of fact, we're rather pleased. We've now got the opportunity to test ourselves, find out how well we can track the opposition.'

'The word is erratically.'

'But what if it was consistently?'

'Then the age of miracles has not yet passed. Unfortunately, or fortunately, depending on how you regard such things, submarines are invisible. Be no point in having 'em otherwise.'

'You're saying it's impossible to track them?'

'To track them all the time, yes. You might hold contact for four or five days. But on the sixth, well, anything could happen.'

Talbot continued to smile knowingly at him.

'Look,' Kenyon said. 'A constant surveillance exercise – it isn't new and it won't prove anything.'

'It would with a sonobuoy like yours.'

'I'd be inclined not to discuss provenance. Besides, it isn't even built yet.'

'No?' The smile widened. 'I hear they're busy in California.'

An eyebrow arched. 'Air Staff seems remarkably well informed.'

'Fleet mustn't expect to hog everything.' Talbot paused. 'Quite remarkable isn't it, this sonobuoy?'

Kenyon stared at him. 'You weren't considering using it?'

'We're doing more than consider. Right now two Nimrods are having their bays modified to cope with it.'

'But I've told you! It isn't built! And no one knows when it will be ready.'

'My understanding,' Talbot said smoothly, 'is that two, possibly three buoys will be ready over the next month or so. Just in time to use against that new sub they've been mucking around with as it comes back home.'

'Next month?' Kenyon's voice scaled the octave. 'Oh yes, I can see the Americans doing that all right. I can just see 'em putting their contractors into top gear, day and night, week after week. They're made of money, aren't they?'

Quietly: 'We're underwriting half the development cost. Though whisper it not, all right?'

Kenyon struggled against an almost inarticulate disbelief. 'But . . . but who authorised it?'

'Defence.'

'And Treasury approved it?'

'Treasury doesn't know.'

'Oh my Lord,' Kenyon said. He lapsed into silence, then went on: 'Tomorrow's meeting. JIC is composing its report to the Overseas and Defence Committee.'

'They won't be mentioning the sonobuoy.'

'But OD already know about it; we had a briefing at Horseferry Road.'

'Knowing of the design is one thing, Alec. Being aware of its development is another.'

'This,' Kenyon said mournfully, 'gets more and more like

Chevaline all over again. Tell me, how does Defence plan to sneak it past PAC?'

'Past who?'

'Public Accounts Committee.' He paused for emphasis. 'Parliament, Kenneth.'

'Oh, that,' Talbot said, and shrugged.

'In that case I dissociate myself entirely. It simply isn't the way to do things.'

Talbot sighed. 'Come on, Alec, please. You know what'll happen. If the accountants don't get ahold of it then the bloody politicos will. They'll form themselves into some glorious all-party sub-committee and organise a free trip for themselves and their wives to sunny California and expect us to hang about while they do the tour of Disneyland.' He stopped, shook his head. 'You weren't in the Falklands thing, were you?'

'Not directly, no.'

'Neither were they. They sat on their arses and mewed while my lot went off with a handful of Harriers – sorry, old boy, can't let you have any more, accounts say they're much too costly – and your lot ran around trying to borrow, borrow, mark you, enough ships to make up a bloody fleet. Don't talk to me about Parliament, Alec. It's full of bloody civilians.'

'I still say we should wait, do it by the book.'

'Too late for that.' Talbot crossed to the printers and took a tear-off from the middle unit. He returned, handed it to Kenyon. 'First entry in the reconnaissance log, the little chronicle we're keeping of that sub's progress. Copies go to the powers that be at naval HQ Northwood and to the maritime liaison group, NATO.'

Kenyon stared numbly at the paper. 'So it's begun,' he said quietly.

Talbot nodded. 'Yes. By whatever means possible we're going to try to pinpoint that sub all the way out and all the way back. And then, when it's in home waters, we're going to use the buoy.'

'But . . .' Kenyon said slowly. 'But they'll know – they'll be able to tell from the signal strength, the range . . . They'll know we have the buoy.'

'Exactly!' Talbot laughed. 'And won't that come as a shock, eh? Won't that scare the pants off old Uncle Joe?'

Kiranovich gazed at each of the displays in turn and listened to the feedback over his headphones. He glanced up when Ivanitsyn walked in, smiled at him. It was not reciprocated. He returned to the SPIS. Integrated with a frequency spectrum analyser, it not only registered active sonar but deduced the nature and range of the transmitter. He nodded towards the screen, to a seemingly aberrant electronic snowflake shining three points to starboard, and said: 'They know we're here.'

'Doesn't matter.'

'It would have been nice to go through untouched.'

Ivanitsyn shrugged. 'We'll lose them soon enough. We always do.' He walked out again.

Kiranovich frowned. Something was nagging at Yevgeni; he wished he knew what it could be.

Ivanitsyn made his way back to the con, where Solokov and Stukhov stood together studying the SINS plotter in an attitude of intense concentration. They did not acknowledge him. All around him the others similarly attended to their work, oblivious to his stern, erect presence. Too much to think about, to deal with. It would only get easier when they reached the warmer waters to the west. Then, the call of the echo sounder wouldn't much matter, and the noises pouring in through the acoustic bow cones would be a welcome diversion: the mewing of porpoise, the clicking of shrimp, the distant thunder of a passing whale; and best of all, the distinctive sound of the humpback heading north for the Arctic.

He stifled a sudden yawn, thought: so far, so good. They'd hugged the ragged coastline of the Cape, nosed silently past the Lofoten and Vesteralen Islands. Now they were weaving around the Moored Surveillance Systems of the GIUK Gap. You had to be very lucky to slip through without your sound signature being identified by the dozens of electronic ears. Fortune and skill – on this battlefield you needed both.

He moved across to Stukhov, followed his gaze to the minute deviations of the SINS plotter. 'Everything is well?' he asked.

'Yes, comrade captain.'

'It draws everything apart from conclusions.'

He wondered why he'd said that. The line was one of Mikhail's, but Mikhail, inexplicably, was not there any more.

He turned away and strode the short distance to his quarters. An MSS update had been placed on the chart table. He studied it for a while, noting the new confirmations, marked with red crosses on the loops and whorls of the chart. They were springing up like weeds, he thought.

With fatigue in his limbs and eyes as sore as though harassed by grit, he lay down heavily on the bed. A brief rest period, a rare break in a crucial phase of duty. He yawned again; it was surprising just how much mental and physical energy drained away in the initial stages of passage. Tired, so damnably tired. Exhaustion had set in long before they'd left Polyarno, what with the strain of an awkward farewell and then Murmansk and no Mikhail; instead, Stukhov, and Bulgov. Things happen, things get rearranged ...

He closed his eyes and lay still, feeling the steady vibration, hearing the muted throb of the turbines, attuning himself to the small world that now replaced the larger one left behind.

Peaks jagged and high, gorges deep, dark. The biggest range of mountains on the planet: four thousand miles long, five hundred miles wide, Mount Pico more than four miles high, forever unscalable. Beyond the mountains, canyons of incomprehensible magnitude where un-named rivers ran, dreadful waterways that pursued paths up to two thousand miles in length at speeds up to fifty miles an hour.

So vast this place – mountains and canyons and rivers spreading out across thirty-one million square miles, from sixty north to sixty south – the Atlantic Ocean.

Yet it was not battalions nor armies that were being thrown into this battlefield, but fortunes: fortunes to make the sea as glass, to render the invisible visible, fortunes to destroy the submarine.

The Americans called it the most desirable real estate in the world and had even produced an analysis to prove it. The report was secret, and might possibly have remained that way, but at least one all-American family had taken it into its collective head to share, for a fee, the nation's anti-submarine warfare classified material with a technologically inferior Soviet Union. The report concluded the total investment by West and East combined added up to fifty dollars per square mile. Fifty dollars multiplied by thirty-one million – a total made all the more awesome by the fact that the statistics were now two years out of date.

Kenyon stared thoughtfully at the print-out on the Soviet sub, imagined strange fleshy ears, Daliesque creations laced with undulating weeds, ears that listened through the stillness and the long dark.

Sub-sea surveillance could just about pick up anything in transit, providing, of course, that it was in range and easily targeted. Some proviso, he thought. The days were almost gone when Soviet submarines used noisy and unrefined echo-sounders for seabed contour navigation. They were getting more clever by the hour, thanks in no small part to the major leakage of Western ASW secrets by the US naval spy-ring. They're catching us up, he decided, and the thought triggered another: to what lengths would they go to get the Asanov buoy?

The unease returned then, the irrational – nay, inexplicable – anxiety about California. There had been only one call from Leech, and a terse one at that: test postponed, a hiccough at this end.

He'd only understood the full implication of the brief conversation after cradling the receiver. *At this end.* It meant Leech was out there; yet Leech wasn't supposed to be going. He had contemplated making further inquiries but security had already said the black-out was on, and the only way to get any light shed on the subject would be courtesy of those with authority to lift the curtain. And I, he thought morosely, can't ask anyone but Leech, or Frances. But she hadn't been in touch either; it was as though the American West Coast was suddenly incommunicado. Leech had promised to brief him that night, as soon as he returned home from Scotland. He wasn't sure if Leech had meant a personal briefing or one via the telephone, but whichever way, the young fellow had some explaining to do. It simply wasn't good enough, not good enough at all.

A familiar voice suddenly cut in: ''Ello 'ello 'ello. To what do we owe this pleasure?'

He turned from the printer, found himself confronting the air vice-marshal. 'Ag and Fish,' he said, 'up top.'

'How did you manage to get in here then?'

'I told them I was on your side.'

Bewilderment made a passing furrow in Talbot's forehead. 'Oh,' he said.

177

Kenyon nodded towards the latest entry in the surveillance log. 'Seems you have everything in hand, Kenneth.'

'So far. Contact's a bit erratic, though.'

'What did you expect?' He paused. 'Keflavik, Brunswick – the Americans are involved then.'

'Naturally.' Talbot smiled. 'Bit like a relay race, eh? One monitor centre hands over to another as the target passes through its area.' He bent down to study the print-out. 'Heard anything from the West Coast?'

'Not really. You?'

'Only that there's been a delay – something technical, I can't get the details.' Talbot hesitated. 'You don't think it's serious, do you?'

'Wouldn't have thought so. Anyway, they're supposed to be letting me know tonight.'

'Good.' Talbot straightened up. 'Be a mite embarrassing, it all went wrong at this stage. No point in doing all this if we've nothing to chuck at the target.'

'Are you sure we have?'

The smile returned. 'Faith, Alec, have faith.'

Kenyon slowly nodded, then moved towards the centre of the big room. Once again he was beset by a sense of unreality, as though the clocks and maps and large rectangular tables had anchored the place in a different time and a different war. Though the technology seemed sophisticated, and some of it downright futuristic, it would not in the least have surprised him to suddenly hear a Home Service broadcast by the Savoy Orpheans, or to encounter some RAF type talking about Big Wings.

A young man of studious aspect was hunched over the nearest plotting table. He looked up from the pins and skein of multi-coloured threads that marked the target's course. Kenyon bent down to examine the assortment of plastic tokens, fashioned in the various shapes of different sea-going vessels, drawn together in a clutter at the left-hand corner of the table. 'So where's the get-out-of-jail-free?' he said.

'Sorry sir?'

He jabbed a thumb in the direction of the tokens. 'What're they supposed to be?'

'They're us. And this –' the young man presented a toy submarine for inspection – 'this is them.'

'Clever stuff,' Kenyon said admiringly.

178

The token was returned to the table top. 'This,' said the young man, 'is the sea.'

'Good Lord. So that's why it's blue.'

The young man stared uncertainly after Kenyon as he made his way back to the printer console, where Talbot stood with arms folded, surveying the scene with an attitude of patent self-satisfaction.

'Impressive, eh, Alec?'

Kenyon nodded. 'No expense spared, Kenneth.'

The air vice-marshal sighed. 'I wonder what they're thinking about down there.'

'I wonder what we're thinking about up here,' Kenyon said.

CHAPTER THIRTEEN

LOS ANGELES
CALIFORNIA

It came in low over the neon fields of the city. The earth shimmered a cold green, as though the 747 was dropping into some vast electronic pasture. Three hundred feet above La Brea and Frances could see it all: the freeways, the intersections, all the glittering striations of the pulsing, sparking grid.

There was a predictable queue at immigration; she yawned; as the queue began to move, she shuffled her attaché case forward with her right foot. In her left hand she carried a yellow plastic bag, 'Heathrow Duty Free Say Hello to the Good Buys', containing two hundred Bensons – a thankyou gift to Gulliver for taking care of Piotr on the journey over.

At passport control came the inevitable question: 'Business or pleasure?'

Pleasure. She collected her baggage from the carousel, located the Sheraton phone and asked them for a courtesy coach. Then she gathered her belongings and walked out into the warm California night.

Barnes waited until the coach had gone, then went back inside the terminal and rang Gulliver.

'She's clean,' he said.

Sunlight made rainbows in the spray as the ocean surged against outcroppings of rock. Piotr Asanov sat unmoving, listening to the sea, to the distant barking of elephant seals in their rookeries. Tall cypresses surrounded him; bright blossoms splashed vibrance in amongst the green.

He shaded his eyes and tried to make out the California coast, but the helicopter remained the sole point of definition, coming in low from Miramar Naval Air Station.

He felt himself a part of this place yet not of its time, as though this was an imposed dimension. When he closed his eyes the Pacific receded and instead of its glistening thunder there came something gentler, something more comforting in its less flamboyant harmonies. The Don, the reeds being carried down to the Azov Sea, the peace, and the sadness.

The olive-coloured Navy saloon met Frances at the pad, then wound its way through the cypresses to a gravel apron in front of a half-dozen white-painted bungalows. Her escort ushered her inside, out of the heat; she stood indecisively as he carefully set her baggage on the floor, saluted, then got back into the car and drove off.

She wandered onto the back patio, beyond which a manicured lawn framed a large rectangular swimming pool. Miniature palms fringed the bright blueness. It seemed that everywhere she looked, brilliant colours flared and blazed, as though she'd become a character in a Hockney landscape.

She turned slowly on her heel. A tall figure stood in the shadows of the room.

'Hello, Frances,' Piotr said, and opened his arms wide.

It was, Frances decided, a ridiculous thing to attempt, what with the heat and the aftermath of transatlantic travel.

She stopped for breath. 'How high did you say it was?'

'A few hundred feet.'

'You're not planning on climbing all the way, I hope.'

'No. Just a little further.'

181

'I must be mad.' She burst out laughing.

The path took them higher. Their footsteps stirred the dust, sent a million flakes of gold dancing in the spoked beams of sunlight. She was aware of birdsong beyond the juniper, and the chattering of cicadas, and, here and there, the kaleidoscopic columns of butterflies, dancing in quiet places.

He led her to a bench near the lip of a soaring stack of rock. She looked down upon the dark green of the island canopy, and then beyond it to the cobalt blue of the encircling ocean.

'And you were the one who didn't want to leave England,' she said.

'No one told me it would be like this.'

'Would you have believed them if they had?'

He smiled shyly, shook his head.

She watched the swallows darting nearby, small sure acrobats disporting on the thermals. She didn't speak for several minutes, feeling the warmth of the sun on her shoulders, the touch of his hand on her own. Eventually: 'You've settled in then, Piotr?'

'Now that you are here ... yes.'

'Flatterer.' She laughed. 'Anyway, you've had Owen's company, haven't you? I mean, he did come with you?'

'My young Welsh friend?' A wry chuckle. 'Oh yes, Owen came with me.'

'Where is he now?'

'He thought we would be better on our own.' Asanov squeezed her hand and seemed about to lapse into another easy, companionable silence; but then his brow furrowed, and he slowly shook his head. 'I should have come here before. I should have been at the test.'

'You couldn't have done anything. From what I hear, there was nothing wrong with the transducer or the power unit. It was the external control system that malfunctioned.' She saw the doubt in his eyes. 'It wasn't your fault.'

'People were hurt. I have not done all this to hurt people.'

'It was an *accident*, Piotr.' She leaned towards him and kissed his cheek. 'Hey, everything's all right now.'

'Is it?' He breathed deep, exhaled slowly. 'I don't know, Frances. So much haste; so little time. Rush, rush, rush; the Americans are like small children, they see something in a shop window and cannot wait to get their hands on it.'

182

'Well, they were half-way there to begin with. In theory, it shouldn't be that difficult to marry their efforts to yours.'

'In theory.' A light, mocking echo. 'That is the problem. Theoretically everything can work. But then Moffett –'

'An external system, not your design.'

'The integral system isn't much better.' He paused. 'Did you know, they've fabricated the complete unit?'

'No, I didn't.'

'It's ready for full prototype testing, all except the computer program for sensor control. They're having to rewrite it yet again.'

'So?'

'The program is crucial. If the computer fails to service the sensors, then they won't work and cavitation will destroy everything.'

'It'll be all right, you'll see. Now I'm here we can tackle the problem together.'

'The Sorcerer's Apprentice, Frances?'

'That's right. We'll give 'em all the gold they want.'

'It isn't gold they wish us to create, though. It's glass.' He stood up. 'Come, I'd like you to meet my friends.'

'Friends?'

'Yes.' He smiled. 'The seals.'

CARIBOU BAY
SOUTHERN CALIFORNIA

Monakhov gave up contemplating the glittering breakers and trudged back across the wide beach. He walked around the side of the clapboard to a forecourt of sunbaked earth. The road was at its narrowest here. It ran straight and flat, a sea-level blacktop perpetually powdered by sand.

He turned from it and confronted Bridies Store. Palms laid drooping shadows over blistered white paint. A bright red fridge bearing the Coke logo hummed and shuddered by the entrance. He bought two bottles and sat down on a bench near the door. Heat burned into his buttocks. It had to be eighty-five degrees and climbing.

He swigged the first Coke dry, tossed the empty into a trash basket, then started on the second. Sweat dripped from his forehead.

The bottle almost slipped from his grasp. Cautiously he transferred it to the other hand.

Opposite him, a county road climbed away from the blacktop. A four-storey house with exaggerated corner bays overlooked the junction. The bays projected in a kind of tower going up from ground level to roofline. Monakhov had rarely seen anything so ugly.

His gaze shifted back along the perspective of the blacktop. Caribou Bay: you drove through at much over the limit and you'd miss the place completely. A few stores selling bait and seashell trinkets – except they were little more than flyblown shacks, bowed by the heat, propped up by the rental surfboards stacked outside. Apart from the shacks, there were a half-dozen pink and cream washed houses on the landward side, faded, tired, blinds permanently drawn against the searing day. Summer pads for UCLA professors, for extra-mural activities after the sun burned out beneath the Pacific.

Caribou Bay: sole attraction – a bright red fridge with geriatric heat exchanger. Caribou Bay: one way in, one way out.

Monakhov got up from the bench, walked over to a Mustang parked on the forecourt and unlocked the trunk. Inside was a container, only twelve inches square.

He remembered watching an American gangster film at the KGB club cinema in Nijinsky Street. Everyone in it seemed to carry a violin case.

Twelve inches square: the butt, stock and magazine nestled in velveteen niches, clingfilm wrapped tightly around the greased steel and gunmetal. The double-frame butt was longer than the actual pistol, though both together couldn't have been more than nineteen or twenty inches; and lightweight, too – three kilograms, if that. Another container, a circular affair with button-down flap like a long lens case, housed the silencer. He didn't know what effect it would have on range; theoretically it was supposed to endow the shotgun characteristics of wide sector spread. San Diego had also added ten banana-shaped boxes, each holding a magazine of twenty rounds of 7.65 mm. The boxes were tied together with broad plastic tape, the loose ends welded flat by a metal punch.

Quite what a contractor was doing with a VZ 61C escaped him. But specialists were notoriously unpredictable; one hired by the Bulgarians turned out to have a preference for the crossbow which, considering that circumstances called for an SMG, was singularly inappropriate.

Monakhov checked his Rolex, then climbed into the Mustang and headed away.

The rendezvous was an amenity area off the southbound carriageway; he slotted the car into a vacant bay, eased himself out and almost cringed at the heat. He slung his jacket over his shoulder, sauntered around the single-storey block and entered the washroom. The mirror image was decidedly unflattering: cream shirt stained with sweat, trousers concertinaed, tie half undone. The tie was a damned nuisance. He sighed and straightened it, ensuring that the Rotary International motif was in plain sight.

Another time check: one minute left. He emerged into the heat and leaned gratefully against the cool wall of stone and slate. Then he crossed to the observation area that jutted out over the sand, where gulls picked amongst black chains of seaweed. The noise was much greater here; the Pacific broke purposefully upon the beach, besieging it with enormous barricades that shattered and re-formed and shattered again. He closed his eyes and momentarily experienced a strange sensation, of being within some tumultuous organ as the diapason swelled.

When he opened his eyes the specialist was smiling at him.

He wore a fawn sports jacket and slacks and a dark tie over a white shirt. Not a mark or stain anywhere. His face was strong, handsome, burnished by the sun; hair almost albino white; posture erect, yet without stiffness or effort, confirmation of military pedigree.

Stitched into the tie was an emblem – a tiny wheel.

'Pleasant day,' the Englishman said. The accent was expected but Monakhov was diverted nonetheless.

He struggled to complete the role. 'It is better than being in the city.' An inward groan: he must must must remember the contractions of this language.

The man looked at his tie and said: 'I see you're a member, too.'

'I am – I'm from San Diego.'

'Really? I live in London.'

Check it: the line was supposed to be Paris, I live in Paris.

'Though I live in Paris now.' The man chuckled. 'Damn fool business, don't you think?'

Monakhov hesitated. But there was no choice – he had to go for second reference.

'I've never been to Paris.'

The man convulsed in a bout of rich laughter. 'Look, old son, you want to go through the whole thing, perhaps we should step inside the shade.' He paused. 'All right. You have never visited Paris. To which I say: well, you should, it's far more civilised than San Diego.' He shook his head. 'Who writes this stuff? Buggered if I couldn't do better myself.'

'It is procedure.'

'It is farce.' He peered at the bronze lenses. 'Did you select this place? Tell 'em it's too good. Bloody ocean. I can hardly hear myself think.'

'The noise stops anyone from overhearing.'

'What did you say?' Then he laughed again. 'Come on, get it over with.'

'It's a place called Caribou Bay.'

'I know it.'

'They will drive through there, once the traffic's been rearranged.'

'You're spending the dickens of a lot of money. I hope it's worth it.'

'It will be if you do your job.' Monakhov paused. 'They're taking the lunchtime train, Los Angeles to San Francisco. To get to the station on time, they will pass through Caribou Bay at around eleven hundred hours.'

'One car?'

'Two. Possibly three.'

'Possibly?'

'We do not have a contact, where they are at present.'

'That's not very good, is it? They could change their travel pattern and you'd never know.'

'We have a source.'

'Reliable?'

'Reliable enough to provide details of the schedule.'

'It's four hundred miles from here to San Francisco. Why not fly?'

'The subject does not like flying.'

'I can see him going off cars, too.' He paused. 'All right, we'll manage. Which car will the target be in?'

'That won't be known until departure. There is mobile surveillance on the Interstate; the unit will advise you over the radio.'

'It's a bit match and mend, isn't it?'

'Say again?'

'Doesn't matter. We'll just have to hit everything. You brought the things I need?'

'In the car.'

'White Mustang, isn't it?'

'Yes. I assume you have brought your own keys?'

He made no response, as though the question wasn't worth an answer.

'And your vehicle?' Monakhov prompted.

'Maroon-coloured Pontiac, eighth down the line, nearest the verge. There's a sign.'

'Sign?'

But the specialist was walking away.

Monakhov located the Pontiac, climbed in and started the engine. He was about to shift into reverse when a Toyota camper muscled into the rear-view mirror, all pennants and stickers and CB aerials, with surfboards lashed to the roof.

He waited for it to manoeuvre into a bay. His gaze flitted from the mirror to the windshield. The specialist was standing on the margin of turf. He looked cool and relaxed, hands in pockets, staring up at the sky.

The sign was next to him. Monakhov focussed on it and found himself confronting a strange conjunction of images. On the triangular plate was a thick black squiggle. Beneath it, a warning notice read:

> There may be rattlesnakes in this area. Rattlesnakes are
> active at night during the summer. They will seek out shady
> places during the heat of the day. Children should be
> warned not to go near any snake. Reasonable watchfulness
> should be sufficient to avoid snake bite.

The specialist looked in his direction, and smiled.

INTERSTATE FIVE
SOUTHERN CALIFORNIA

'Unit one to unit three. How goes it?'

'Looking good. Over.'

Gulliver returned the mike to its clip.

They were driving north at a steady fifty in the Oldsmobile.

187

Ahead of them Smith's Buick clung to the nearside lane. She could just about make out Asanov in the back of the car. 'I hope he knows where he's going,' Frances said. 'Owen, I mean.'

'I hope he remembers which side of the road to use.'

She gazed out of the windshield. The heat haze formed a shimmering curtain. 'I understand you're not going to join us for the re-run. Might I ask why?'

'Apparently the last test was like the San Andreas coming apart.' He glanced at her. 'Feel like enlightening me?'

'The signal strength was too great. You push it out at that level and there's a chance it'll interfere with the controls. They used to fiddle petrol that way in England, using the power amp of a CB radio – I think they call it the burner. If you turn it to maximum output the signal upsets the pump's metering system. People were putting ten gallons in with the pump only registering five.'

'And that's what happened at Moffett?'

'More or less. The cut-out failed because it misread the output. The over-rider failed because the circuits went haywire.'

Gulliver was thoughtful for a while. 'My deputy said the control room blew up.'

'A singer can do the same with a wine glass.'

'Breaking a glass is one thing, Doctor. Making someone think he's flaky is another. That sort of effect, it's pretty terrifying.'

'Infra-sound,' she replied.

Smith risked a rearward glance. 'You all right back there?'

'Yes, thank you.'

'Not exactly Oxfordshire, is it?'

Asanov laughed. He contemplated the purple-brown hills. 'There isn't much grass out here.'

'Don't you believe it. It's just that they smoke it instead of growing it.'

'You've been here before?'

'A couple of times.'

'There is a song,' Asanov said, 'I left my heart in San Francisco.'

'You'd better not leave anything, or Leech'll murder me.'

Asanov eased himself deeper into the cushioning. 'This is very pleasant, Owen.'

'Glad you came?'

'Yes. To be able to travel, go where you want, to have freedom of choice –' he smiled – 'you'll never know how good it feels.'

There would be time to empty three, maybe four, magazines down the diagonal, but anything more and exit would be a problem. The upper storeys of the house overlooking the junction had no fire stairs and there was only one escape route – out the back, through the yard and into the alley where the Mustang was parked.

The specialist finished assembling the Skorpion, then used a small cotton rag to wipe the oil from his hands. He approached the task with the air of one fastidious in all things.

He moved aside the window blind and stared down on an unchanging scenario: blacktop running straight and true, the narrow county road angling away from it. A dusty black LTD was parked at the junction – the intercept, with passenger and driver. The specialist was using two vehicles, the second of them a Chevrolet stationed further along the blacktop. But it was the LTD that worried him. Two people in a parked vehicle ... On a burning hot day like this no one would sit in a car unless its wheels were turning and the air conditioning was stemming the sweat of travel.

He turned from the window and let the blind clatter back, then crossed the big, dusty room to the transceiver, conscious of the creak of timber, the old house complaining of its emptiness. He settled down by the communications pack. Two or three cars, the man with the bronze-tinted glasses had said. You will be advised. As though on cue, the unit suddenly bleeped.

Gulliver overhauled the Buick and took the point position. 'So what's infra-sound, then?'

She hesitated. 'Well, it's high-energy, low-frequency sound.'

'That explains everything. Thanks.'

'If you're wondering about your colleague, he suffered an extreme side-effect. Anxiety, disorientation, nausea – they're all classic symptoms.'

'The way you're explaining this, I get the impression it's happened before.'

'That's correct.' She frowned, trying to summon forth the details. 'Ten or twelve years ago, in France, they were bench-testing the engines for the French Concorde. The power reached such a peak even the ground started vibrating. The vibrations set up infra-sonic waves. They travelled from the test area and saturated an adjacent admin building. People began to feel sick and dizzy. Some of them developed anxiety states.' She paused. 'It happens with earthquakes, too.'

'How d'you mean?'

'The preliminary stages of a quake cause massive vibrations underground. A very low-frequency signal results. We can't hear it, but animals can – they can even feel it. Dogs are particularly well attuned. Long before anything happens, they detect the infra-sound. They start barking, running around. It's an anxiety response.'

'I never heard of an anxious dog before.' He chuckled. 'If I ever have to move to San Francisco, Doctor, remind me to live near a kennels.'

Sunlight fragmenting on its side, the Porsche pulled out too late and too wide. The Kenworth artic was already swinging across three lanes when the anti-jackknife fractured and the tractor unit decoupled and rammed the centre armco. The rig whipped broadside in a screaming arc but then momentum lifted the wheels and destroyed the centre of gravity and the thing went over on its side and skated on down in an explosion of sparks.

Ground impact burst the locking bars and the loading-bay doors tore open and sheared away. Steel and metal scrap decanted and cartwheeled and disintegrated. The following traffic weaved and skidded as drivers instinctively ducked low on account of all the stuff suddenly coming down from out of the clear blue sky.

When the dust finally cleared, the highway north of the Doheny Park split was completely blocked off.

'Is this Steinbeck country?' Frances asked.

'You're a mite premature. Monterey's way to the north.' He nodded towards the monotonous folds of arid hills. 'But that's Korea all right.'

'Korea?'

'Where they filmed "M.A.S.H." There, and behind the Hollywood Hills.'

The radio interrupted: 'Unit three to one.'

'What is it?'

'There's a wreck.'

'Where?'

'Doheny Park.'

'Bad?'

'A truck's been totalled. Nothing's getting through.'

Gulliver sighed. 'Okay. We'll take the Caribou Bay route.'

'What has happened?' Asanov asked.

'There's been an accident and the road's jammed. We'll have to divert.'

'Won't that take longer?'

'It might.' He smiled. 'But it is the scenic way.'

Gulliver gripped the wheel more tightly now, hoping she wouldn't notice the whiteness around the knuckles. It would have been better had she travelled in the back, like Asanov was with Smith. Traffic was heavy as they funnelled into the coastal strip, but then it gradually thinned out as local stuff diverted onto eastbound county roads.

He watched the rear view for a while, then slowed down and signalled Smith to overtake. The Buick surged by. Smith waved. Gulliver re-checked the rear view. Nothing. Not a damn thing.

'Everything all right, Mr Gulliver? You seem preoccupied.'

'I don't want to miss that train.'

She leaned back in her seat. The car felt inexplicably hesitant, pressing forward then easing back. Even more curious, Smith's Buick was maintaining the gap, duplicating their uneven progression.

'Where's unit three?' she asked.

'Sorry?'

'Unit three. You keep talking to it. Is it your base station?'

'Not exactly.'

'Where is it, then, ahead of us or behind?'

'Neither.' He glanced at her. 'There's nothing to worry about.'
The car slowed again as he concentrated on the rear-view mirror.

'I'm not worried.' She checked the dashboard clock: 11.07.

'Not long now,' Smith said.

'I was almost asleep.'

'You should've said if I've been boring you.'

'Boring me? Nonsense.' He paused. 'I've been thinking – I can get it to work all right.'

'Good,' Smith said.

His gaze flitted to the rear-view mirror again. Gulliver was still holding flank, checking, monitoring.

Bad as each other, we are. Candy-bar paranoia all over again. So, all right, there was pattern variation. So what? As if anything could happen now. Besides, fat lot of good you'd be, Owen Smith – not even armed.

Caribou Bay. Gulliver eased back as Smith slowed for another urban limit, another unkempt oasis of brick and clapboard and shingles, surfboard rentals and tackle and bait. The left-hand verge was widening into a sunbaked forecourt running parallel with the road. A handful of stores leaned into the heat, blanking out the blue. He slowed again, matching the Oldsmobile's speed to that of the Buick.

A panorama of light and shadow moved lazily past the window. Tall trees and tinder-dry shrubs sprouted from terracotta tubs; a big red fridge proclaimed Coke.

Abruptly the Buick swung out of line, slewing over towards the right-hand kerb.

'Get down!'

The LTD came out with heart-stopping suddenness; common sense said to swerve far over to the left, across the crown of the road and onto the forecourt, but instinct clamoured instead and so Smith spun the Buick broadside on and stopped. The black car flashed by and out of vision.

The specialist watched from behind the blind. The LTD should have emerged shallow, angling in alongside the target and squeezing it into the shore strip, but they'd sat too long with nerves too taut and in the moment of release had floored the gas pedal too hard, so that it went snaking onto the blacktop with more wheelspin than traction.

He lifted the Skorpion to his shoulder.

Gulliver stabbed the brake and the hood dived. Though he aimed for the gap, reaction time was inadequate and he could only yell at Frances and hang on to the wheel.

They hit the Buick and shunted it aside. Metal buckled, chromework snapped loose, a wheel trim went scything through the air like a bright silver discus.

He was aware of skidding past a stationary car and having to

192

compute that as well as the black saloon. If this was an accident then they were okay, but if it wasn't ... Then the windshield crazed over with a deafening crack and the air burned briefly around him. Orientation gone now, vision cancelled as they bucked and crashed on the corrugations of the forecourt and finally stalled as the dust cloud came whirling all around.

On the shoreside, the specialist could see the herdsman climbing out of the Chevrolet and then crouching behind the driver's door, going for second pressure on the Smith and Wesson. On the forecourt of the clapboard store, the Oldsmobile lay stranded in its own dust cloud. It had a number on its roof, but it was not possible to decipher that yet. Roughly twenty-five yards north of the target vehicles, the black LTD straddled the crown of the blacktop.

A perfect view, he decided, of an imperfect configuration. The Buick was not only on the wrong side of the road, it was much too close in to the vertical. Instead of aiming along the diagonal, he'd have to open the window now and lean right out and sight down the perpendicular. He shook his head and reached for the casement catch.

After the moment's tumult, the squeal of tyres and jolting bang of collision, everything stopped, no movement, no sound – stunned, frozen. Smith watched his fingers fret with the harness clip, felt nothing there, saw them flexing without purpose, trembling.

Asanov said: 'Owen? Owen!'

Gulliver leaned across Frances to uncouple the belt, but his own had locked up and he had to punch out the release. She freed herself then and reached for the door handle and it was obvious she was going to step out, step right out into the middle of it. He grabbed her left arm, ignored the cry of protest as he dragged her over the centre console so that they tumbled out almost together, limbs colliding on the hot earth.

The Smith and Wesson, sighted through the Chevrolet's door frame, vectored in on the prime target, then tracked back to the secondary.

An unexpected choice of targets, with the Oldsmobile the better bet. It had stopped with its tail swung out, so the line of fire was going to have to be oblique, but even so; the noise of the shot

193

smashed through the silence and melded with the explosive fragmentation of the rear lights.

There was a .357 in a lateral clip beneath the steering column; Gulliver reached up with fingertips straining. But then he heard gunfire behind them; the Oldsmobile shuddered, glass tinkled. The whine of a ricochet as another bullet spanged off the fender. Gulliver threw himself flat and rolled aside.

Three maybe four seconds into event and at most three maybe four seconds remaining – because there was frontal impact now, and they were under crossfire, herded in from the rear by the Chevrolet, boxed off at point by the black LTD.

He glanced at Frances. She was breathing fast, eyes wide, mouth open ... and then face contorting, head turning, as the air split apart and a shower of fragments rained down from above.

He got onto his knees again and clawed for the gun. The herdsman was going to give up soon on the glassware; he might be on an oblique to the Oldsmobile but that could easily be changed; only a few short steps and he'd have his sight line perfect for the kill. In the meantime, all they had was an open door for frontal defence and nothing more substantial than a prayer for rearward shield.

There were two of them – dark suits, dark glasses – out in the open by the Ford LTD, the furthest of the pair concentrating on Gulliver's car, the nearest turning this way now. Sunlight struck off the chamber as the revolver levelled and the muzzle flashed – once, twice, three times.

Belt snapping free, Smith moved at last, kicking the door open and ducking down onto the warm asphalt, then crabbing frantically away from the line of fire. A forward glance took in the silver and maroon Chevrolet, driver's door open like a wide shining blade, with a figure just discernible beyond the window frame.

He was boxed in, front and back. The realisation punched him flat and for a second he lay still, bewildered by its numbing impact. With a final despairing effort he picked himself up and scrambled around the tail.

He tried to drag himself upright but things were happening all at once. The rear door opening, Asanov starting to get out ... The Buick was rocked violently by a shattering staccato of automatic fire; and now Smith had a third factor to contend with – the numbness spreading, chasing wetness all along his spine.

Twenty rounds of 7.65 at a muzzle velocity of nearly a thousand feet per second and the magazine was empty, the Skorpion's high-toned song cutting off, the jabbing backpush of recoil abruptly ceasing. The specialist straightened up, almost staggered back into the room, then reached down with gloved fingers and scooped up the second magazine and heard the click of alignment as it locked in.

He returned to the window and leaned out so far the perspective was almost vertiginous; and then the Buick was dancing again as its roof erupted anew in a pattern of jagged holes.

Half in and half out of the car – his position didn't bear thinking about. The door was fast disintegrating as rounds passed clear through only millimetres from his skin, but his fingers still strained, twisted, slipped, tried again. Gulliver felt the lower edge of the clip and gave a last desperate push against the spring release, hardly able to think with all the noise. The spring was beginning to move. Push, damn you, push! But then he felt his hand withdrawing, an involuntary reflex he could do nothing about. Never mind, try again ...

The Magnum toppled, smacked his collarbone with bruising force. He twisted, dived for it, rolled away and felt the sting of dirt as bullets kicked the earth beside his face. Safety off and he was raising the gun straight-armed, two-fisted, swinging it, and then the recoil hammered through him with the first wild shot.

Thirteen maybe fourteen seconds into event.

Come on Barnes, for Christ's sake, come on. He didn't know if he was saying it inside or shouting it aloud, but anyway the thunder finally came. A lethal sibilance chopped at the sky as the helicopter crested the gable of the corner house, hung so low the downdraught rippled the roof tiles and lifted them and sent them spinning in an artificial gale.

Sweet Jesus. The bloody cavalry.

'Lower. Steady. Lower.' Barnes spoke quietly, assuredly, because it was important to keep the pilot calm; at this speed and height they could clip the trees or the masonry and fireball on out into the Pacific.

He cradled the Armalite, held it tight, knowing what it could do but also aware of what it could not do. Accurate fire from the

195

pitching deck of a helicopter ranked high in the latter category. They were hovering above the Buick, the rotor only inches from the prominent bay window of the corner house. Looking down, Barnes could see no evidence of the roof number now – but then there wasn't much evidence of the roof, either. Wisps of smoke were beginning to rise from the interior where incandescent metal had fired the upholstery.

The Bell pirouetted again, and brought him into unexpected confrontation with the startling image of a suntanned face thrust towards him almost on a level with the deck of the helicopter. Then the face vanished and he glimpsed something very small and very silver in amongst the shadows and the shape registered immediately.

He snapped the adjuster to Auto and loosed off a stream of fire that smashed into the room and then traversed across the facade, sending woodwork and rendering powdering outwards in grey-white stars. But now they were turning away, dancing, going backwards tail first over the rooftops. Two figures stood below them by a black saloon, but he had no chance to do anything about them because the vista tilted and there was nothing but sky now out beyond the perspex screen.

Frances had squeezed herself under the car, unable to see anything except the floor pan and axle. There was nothing Gulliver could do for her or himself; he had to find a safer corner of this erupting battlefield and just hope to God Barnes didn't pile straight into the blacktop.

There was only minimal view, and even though the only cover was the most garish imaginable, he had to go for it. Moving like a sprinter off the block he zigzagged the short distance across the forecourt and hurled himself at the unlikely sanctuary of the big old bright red fridge. The impetus took him too far and too hard and he slammed into the woodwork before going down, just as everything came apart in a blizzard of flying splinters and dirt.

Gulliver saw him then – a slim figure in a dark suit, in the middle ground between the LTD and the house. He wedged himself as solidly as he could and with both hands clamped tight got the angle roughly right and after that there was only the boom of the Magnum and the violent, wrist-snapping aftershock of its recoil.

Three rounds, two virtually wild, but in amongst them a positive – a straight chest shot that slammed into the target, lifted it clean off the ground and hurled it back a dozen or so feet before it tumbled and rolled and sprawled and lay still.

Gulliver moved out, towards the Chevrolet.

The old house was shaking, but already the specialist had mentally distanced himself and nothing mattered now except exit.

The fusillade had stitched so deep a pattern in the wall that brick as well as plasterwork had sprayed over the room, and as he'd gone down a ricochet had slashed like a white-hot broadsword from the nape of his neck almost to his throat. Pain flashed and burst within and the Skorpion went skittering somewhere in the gloom as he rolled and thrashed upon the floorboards. He pushed himself into a sitting position, reached for the gun, and slammed another magazine home. It was only now that he saw the second wound and the tiny dark red fountain that pumped and spurted high up in the left thigh.

The herdsman had evidently had enough; it was one thing to tackle a defenceless target, but quite another to take on an airborne battle-wagon.

Gulliver reached the Chevrolet just as the short squat figure made to get into the car. Without registering a face or a weapon, he threw himself down and emptied the Magnum in a final reflex burst, then watched as the car and the figure blew apart in a spray of redness and metal and glass.

Above him, the helicopter was going south in a juddering arc; it completed the circuit, then came in at one hundred feet above the Caribou Bay limit. Barnes could see it all laid out below in incongruous symmetry. Northbound and southbound traffic beginning to jam up at both perimeters of the kill zone.

He prepared for the run-in, struggling for position and trying to think straight amid all the noise because even with the headphones in place the wind-rush was deafening. In peripheral vision he saw the pilot's hand, index finger jabbing in frantic forward motion. Barnes nodded.

The black LTD was wheeling round, trailing pennants of smoke. He couldn't work out what was in the driver's mind, because instead of coming forward the LTD suddenly went into reverse and shot backwards a hundred yards or so before slamming into a small Datsun that had inadvertently blocked its escape. He glanced to his left and saw small frightened figures running across the beach, away

197

from the clapboards ... And then another one, it looked like a woman, rolling out from under Gulliver's stranded Oldsmobile.

No more time now; they were into the approach, and wire was quivering on each side, shining filaments ready to tear out the rotor, trees crowding in as the Bell dropped lower and the blacktop rushed upwards, getting wider, getting nearer.

The LTD lurched forward, then accelerated rapidly over its own newly laid tracks. The helicopter swept towards the LTD, range down to two hundred feet now, and the sunlight was dazzling on the radiator grille; one fifty feet and the helicopter's locust-like shadow was striping the windshield; at one hundred he steadied the Armalite; at fifty he squeezed off a final burst, just as the Bell seemed to stand on its tail before screaming vertically away into the high bright blue.

For a brief moment, Gulliver thought the LTD would run straight over him, but then the chopper came clattering overhead and the Ford's windshield vanished, glass, frame and all. It swerved violently to its right, bounced onto the forecourt and into the Oldsmobile, and then flipped over onto its side and seemed to hurdle the last few feet before vanishing in an ear-splitting maelstrom of splintering timber.

He was still staring dumbly at the dense, rolling dust cloud when, with an almost genteel exclamation, Smith's Buick finally went up in flames.

They set down on the beach only inches from the wreckage of the clapboard. He jumped out, Armalite cradled to his chest, and sprinted carelessly over the shattered spars. He was aware of round white faces coming towards him, but continued on at breakneck speed and paused only once when he reached the forecourt and found himself confronting the beacon that was Asanov's car.

He ran around it, felt the heat against his face, then shouldered open the door of the house and took the stairs two at a time, thinking all the while – it's too late, too late to even bother.

He had no idea of the layout of the house and the zigzag landings only compounded his confusion. But instinct was screaming at him as he gained the third floor. The man hobbling towards him, one hand pressed over an arterial wound and the other holding a small SMG, could only stare in disbelief as the Armalite stammered its last deafening burst.

Barnes walked out of the house and into the sunlight, then stood with legs planted wide apart and breathed deeply to steady himself. So many people. He had never seen so many materialise so quickly, groups of them scattered all around, silent, staring, motionless. He glanced to his right, to where the Buick was burning brightly. Somehow he'd expected the fire to sound louder, to feel hotter. He turned left and walked slowly towards the little group huddled beside the kerb, Gulliver on his knees, the Wycliffe woman stooping low.

Spectators ranged themselves in a mute semi-circle that spilled out over the blacktop. Someone saw him approaching; eyes widened at the sight of the Armalite dangling almost negligently from his left hand. They moved out of his path with quick nervous steps. He eased himself down beside Gulliver, the manoeuvre made unexpectedly awkward because of an uncontrollable trembling in his leg muscles.

Gulliver glanced up, his face white and taut. Barnes couldn't decide if it was shock or anger; he had never seen Gulliver with such an expression before. The Wycliffe woman continued to stare helplessly at the ground. His gaze followed hers.

They lay together on the sidewalk, the Russian's face a mask of crimson, a darkening stain continuing to spread across the chest of Owen Smith.

CHAPTER
FOURTEEN

SHERMAN OAKS
LOS ANGELES
CALIFORNIA

The drive was banked high with the glossy leaves of a laurel hedge. They angled in off Canyon Avenue and wound up the slight gradient to the point where the hedging stopped and the grass began. Sprinklers turned lazily over the glistening lawn.

Leech was out of the car before the driver had time to get to the door. His gaze swept briefly over the landscaping, then he strode purposefully towards the house, a white neo-Colonial affair with portico and fluted pillars, and windows composed of small square panes, fussy embellishments on an already chaotic facade.

Gulliver stared impassively from the open doorway. 'You made it then,' he said. Leech climbed the steps without answering. After a few moments, Gulliver turned on his heel and led the way into a grandiose hall. The door closed behind them with the slightest of sighs.

'I don't know how it happened.' Gulliver lit another cigarette and dropped the match into an overflowing ashtray.

'You must have some idea,' Leech said. 'They were in your care.'

'Having just come from yours.' He settled deeper into the armchair and considered Leech through a spiralling plume of smoke. 'They had to have time to set it up, which means they must have known the schedule.'

'Well, they didn't get it from us.'

Gulliver sighed. 'Look, Asanov hadn't been here a week. More to the point, he hadn't been on the mainland more than a few hours. San Clemente is –'

'An island? Yes, I do know that.'

'I was going to say, is a damn sight safer than your chocolate-box village.'

'The place wasn't exactly uninhabited.'

'Near as makes no difference. They shut Wilson Cove a while back.'

Leech closed his eyes. 'I've had a hell of a time these past few days. Kenyon nearly went spare when he finally got the full picture.' He refocussed on Gulliver. 'It comes down to the fact that they knew Asanov was here.'

'Well, they didn't find out from us.'

'So what was it, Gulliver? A freak coincidence? They stuck a pin in a map and said ah, that's it?'

'San Clemente was secure.'

'And Moffett?'

'Likewise.'

Leech rubbed his forehead and gazed around the book-lined room as though seeking answers in the gilt-blocked spines. He pushed himself out of the armchair and walked slowly to the door.

Gulliver stubbed out the cigarette. 'Leech.'

'What?'

'I'm sorry.'

'Yes, well.'

Leech found himself encompassed by a salon chair, its leather quilts already warmed by an obliging sun, in a huge room where Hollywood met Versailles and reproduction pieces bobbed about on a rose-pink tide. Brocade merged with flock and the frozen cascades of indelicate chandeliers, a Fragonard hung on one wall but a Primitive on the other, while on another, like bricks of black and grey, were framed ranks of monochromes of yesteryear, Graumann's Chinese Theater with Lana Turner being young. Beside the wide expanse of patio window was a Yamaha baby grand; beyond, a lawn pricked by croquet hoops was being patrolled by Gulliver's team. Leech watched their dogged perambulations for a while, then closed his eyes.

'I can get them to make up a bed if you like.'

He snapped awake, blinking rapidly against the brightness. She smiled softly. 'Don't get up.'

'Doctor Wycliffe,' he began, then stopped, hand clamped hard against lips in a futile bid to stifle a yawn.

'I hope you didn't row all the way,' Frances said. She sat down in the sister chair, smoothing the fabric of her cream linen dress, and stared at him with quizzical gaze. 'Welcome to my home, Mr Leech.'

'It's ... it's quite something.'

'Gross is the word you're looking for.'

He smiled. 'I suppose it is a bit de Mille.'

'You've seen the bathrooms, then?'

'One of 'em. Though only water came out of the tap.'

'Apparently there's a shortage of goat's milk.' She stared about her. 'William Wallace Blankenberg, the man who owned all this, made a fortune out of armaments. So much money he didn't know what to do with it. So he came here, for the good of his ... wealth.' A slow, private smile. 'And now we're here; so appropriate.'

Leech hesitated, then said gently: 'I'm sorry for what happened.'

'We're getting over it.'

'Don't push too hard. It'll take time ...'

'Funny – sometimes it seems long ago, other times ... is that how it is? You lose track of the hours?'

'I don't know.' Leech faltered. 'It's never happened to me.'

'There's this feeling of ... numbness. And then the ridiculous part, when you can't stop talking about it – to yourself, to anybody, to the walls, even. I've gone over it so often it's becoming more unreal. More and more vivid yet less and less believable.'

He smiled awkwardly, but didn't reply.

'I watched the TV news,' Frances continued. 'Strange, their lack of curiosity. I mean, it was the main item but even so, they ... Oh, I don't know. It's as though they believe the impossible out here.'

'Well, it is California,' Leech said.

'Perhaps everywhere will be California one day ...'

He struggled for something to say. Eventually: 'Who thought up the organised-crime angle?'

'Gulliver.'

'Not bad.'

'Not bad? I thought it was preposterous. Just watch, he said, watch what they do with it. After Watergate nothing is incredible in this country.' She paused. 'They had a reporter, from the network –

the Organised-Crime Man. Can you imagine that? The way he talked, you'd've thought he had a diploma in it. They're so articulate, between the commercials.' She stopped again. 'D'you think there's such a thing as a threshold of belief?'

He shrugged. 'Perhaps.'

'I think there is. And I think it's getting lower every day. I used to be disturbed by shrieking headlines. Now it's the shrinking ones I worry about.' She stared unwaveringly at him. 'Will it all end in the small print, Mr Leech?'

He smiled awkwardly again, feeling embarrassed for her, for the confusion and the shock. 'The small print,' he said. 'It's an interesting thought.'

Somewhere in the house a clock tolled the quarter with echoing chime. 'So,' Frances said, 'you're to be my escort home.'

Leech nodded. 'That's right.'

'And if I don't wish to go?'

'It's your decision, naturally, but it would be better if you came back. You said yourself you had a department to run.'

'There's too much to do here.'

'Forgive me for saying so, but I thought it was more or less wrapped up.'

She stared at him, grey eyes bright with amusement. 'Tell me, d'you really understand what we're doing?'

He smiled back. 'I'm trying.'

'It isn't simple, you know. It isn't straightforward. We're not talking about a one-man band any more. Piotr may well have mastered the design but right this minute there are dozens of technicians and engineers, scattered throughout this country, working flat out to ...' She stopped, shook her head. 'It's a huge operation – one main contractor, two sub-contractors, two consultancies, four naval agencies, and all stations from Honeywell through to Rockwell.'

'Well, so long as it hasn't gone to the lowest tender ...' Leech said. They both laughed. He stood up, then paused uncertainly. 'How is he? Piotr?'

'Very well. His old self again.' It was her turn to hesitate. 'And Owen ... Is he going to be all right?'

Leech nodded. 'It'll be a long job, but ...'

'Thank God for that, at least,' said Frances.

Gulliver was still in the library when Leech found him, sitting with legs draped over the side of the chair. 'Took you long enough,' he said.

'Couldn't be helped,' Leech replied.

'You could've told her straight that she has to stay.'

'What she has to do,' Leech said slowly, 'is think it's her decision.'

'Freewill, huh?'

'That's what it's all about, isn't it?'

SAN PEDRO
LOS ANGELES
CALIFORNIA

Frances and Piotr strolled in silence through the sun-dappled peace of Whaler's Wharf, past elegant timbered houses, behind whose Georgian casements the Pacific breeze stirred white drifts of lace.

A comforting panorama unfolded all around: roof tiles and chimneys gilded by the light; cream picket fences and the lazy swing of open gates, little paths to panelled doors, each one of them of different hue; and here and there grey-green shadows, cast by ironwork curlicues of Victorian lamps. In between the quiet houses, rising above a curious harmony of Cape Cod simplicity and English Regency, peering down impassive and improbable, the California palms spread their leaves like wide dark feathers to brush against the wash of blue.

They found a small restaurant off the Wharf and settled down to tea and cakes; confronted by the linen's crispness, the cutlery's sheen, they thought themselves nostalgic for places which had never been.

'The suntan suits you,' Frances said. 'I hadn't really noticed it till now.'

'It is my camouflage.' He laughed. 'I don't wish to stand out in the crowd.'

'How's the war wound?'

'I don't even know it's there.'

War wound. Funny how you made memory more palatable by undermining it; a touch of the ridiculous always made pain easier to bear. Frances remembered that moment in the sun – a mask of redness, a feeling of utter helplessness, stooping down, leaning over, wanting to help but unable to touch; and thence to a hospital brisk, clean and bright as a Park Lane office block.

'Lacerations, Doctor Wycliffe, that's all. Scratches.'

'I wonder how Owen is feeling.'

The question was so close to the echoes in her mind that for a moment she didn't know if she'd heard it or merely recalled it. Asanov frowned. An erratic tracery of discreet sutures stood out in miniature corrugation on the left side of his face.

Frances patted his hand. 'I was thinking about Owen, too.'

'He'll be home now.'

'Martin Leech came as escort.' She paused. 'He wanted me to go as well.'

He looked away, slowly shook his head. 'They make their plans and devise their schemes and to their astonishment it actually works.'

'What does?'

'You and I. Two elements brought together to make a useful alloy.'

'I think you're misreading the situation.'

He laughed. 'Listen, I come from a place where you only get at the truth by misreading the text.'

'Well,' she faltered, 'that's over there.'

'Here is different?'

'Hopefully it is.'

'Hopefully what?' A familiar voice sounded in her ear. The chair scraped and Gulliver sat down with a broad smile. 'I trust I'm not interrupting anything, but ...'

'You were just passing?' Frances smiled.

'Yup.'

'Just passing. I see.' She paused. 'Piotr has a theory that we're under surveillance. Does that account for your just passing?'

'Theories, theories,' Gulliver said. 'That all you people do all day? Sit around theorising?'

She chuckled. 'You haven't answered the question.'

'I'd rather you answered one of mine.' He lit a cigarette and hunched forward with elbows on the table. 'Something I've been wanting to get straight.' He addressed Asanov: 'Those paddles of yours – transducers. Barnes was on the receiving end of that infra-sound thing and it damn near sent him crazy.'

'So?' Asanov frowned.

'So if it can happen in, well, in the laboratory, what's to prevent it from happening, you know, down there, in the sea? I thought I'd ask now while you haven't got your heads down. This whole thing is galloping ahead and I'd like to understand it better.'

'There's nothing to understand,' Asanov said. 'Air and water are different media, Mr Gulliver. You can shout very loudly in a room, but try doing it underwater – all you achieve is cavitation, bubbles. There's no acoustic interface.'

Gulliver sighed. 'Putting it simply, you're saying it can't happen.'

'That's correct,' Asanov said, 'it can't.'

WASHINGTON DC

The Potomac tidal basin spread itself in a still and sparkling plain, cradling the inverted image of the Jefferson Memorial. Gulliver rested his forearms on the topmost railing, leaned forward as though to secure an even better view. From this vantage point at Cherry Trees, the building seemed to shimmer as much as the image.

He counted the pillars underpinning the canopy, the ascending ridges of the saucer-smooth cupola, but try as he might it was impossible to believe the substance or the reflection, to view this as anything other than a vista out of time.

'When a man is tired of Washington ...' Larson began.

'... he is tired of lies. I know, I know.'

Barnes looked at each of them in turn. 'So what happens now?'

Gulliver continued to gaze at the memorial.

'What I'd give to have an office in there,' Larson said.

Barnes shrugged and popped another wedge of gum into his mouth. 'It's okay.'

'Okay? Good God, it's more than okay. It's pure, noble. A man reaches a certain age, Mr Barnes, he yearns for things like that.'

'It's a memorial.'

'I don't care what it is –'

'You don't have to be a certain age for a memorial. You have to be dead.'

'I was making the point that all around there is, well, detritus – waste and want and detritus. It's brutalising. Finally, a man gets to the stage where he ... D'you always chew gum?'

'I tried tobacco once.'

Larson turned away, the look of repugnance etched deep.

Without shifting his gaze Gulliver said: 'When d'you want me to go?'

'Oh.' Larson hesitated. 'Sooner the better. He's just about ready.'

'He could stay on.'

'After what happened, I don't think he should. Anyway, it's been decided.'

'Ah.'

Larson turned back again. 'And you, Mr Barnes, you get yourself back up to Moffett.'

'I'd rather go to London.'

'I'd rather you didn't, all right?'

Gulliver said: 'I've finished the transcripts. He seems to be managing.'

'Yes, well, they're still taping and there's still a need for security.'

'How impressive.'

Larson said patiently, doggedly: 'The screw-up was on our side, not theirs.' He raised a hand to forestall the expected protest. 'No more arguing, John. Barnes has the job of determining what went wrong. You have the job of ensuring it doesn't happen again.'

'But there's no point, damn it. Going over there, where the man's got more nursemaids than I don't know what. It makes no sense at all.'

'Look at it this way, then: you're representing our interests.'

'We can't be that interested if we're letting him go.'

'He has to go there,' Larson said wearily, 'for the same reason he had to come here. That thing they're building, they want to try it out as soon as possible.'

'Jesus. Not another test.'

'Actually, I think they've finished testing.' Larson smiled and began to walk away.

'Hey,' Gulliver called, 'are you going over?'

'Sorry. Too much to do here.' He didn't look back.

'Well, have a great time doing it then.'

'Oh, I will, I will.'

LONDON

The buzzer sounded. She sighed and got up from the table. Ten o'clock at night – not the best hour for receiving unexpected callers.

She thumbed the intercom. 'Yes?'

'Doctor Wycliffe, it's Martin Leech.'

'Surprise, surprise.'

'I hope you don't mind but –'

'No – ' a weary resignation – 'I don't mind. Come on up.'

He stood in the doorway, staring beyond her at the apartment: a large split-level room, cool, contemporary, spotlit from a variety of sources, the furnishings modern, simple.

'You can come in.'

'Oh. Sorry.' He made for the sofa. 'I was just –'

'Passing?' She leaned against the door. 'Of course you were. I don't know, it's been ten hours since I got back, that's all. Come to share my duty free?'

'That wasn't why . . .' He smiled. 'Thanks, whisky would be fine.' After she had poured their drinks he said: 'I've been with Sir Alec. He wondered how you were.'

'Didn't Neil Hawkins say?'

'He seems to be suffering from jet-lag.'

For some reason that struck her as absurdly funny. When the laughter had subsided she said: 'There was no need to send him half-way around the world.'

'You had to be escorted.'

'Who's bringing Piotr, then? Gulliver?'

'No, it'll be one of our people. Gulliver's coming independently.'

She watched the bubble spires forming in her glass. 'How's Owen Smith?'

'Getting better.'

'And you're sure there's no permanent damage?'

'Well,' Leech said, 'the bullet went just about everywhere – clavicle, ribs, sternum. But no, nothing permanent. A millimetre either way, though . . .' He shrugged.

She said, quietly: 'Who were those people?'

'Opposition, KGB sub-contractors.'

'God, you make it sound almost mundane.'

'It's the way it is.'

She stared at him, then looked away. 'So, what can I do for you?'

'I wanted to see how you were.'

'Checking on the property, is that it?' Her sardonic smile faded slowly. 'I'm beginning to hate this, you know, the constant feeling of being watched.'

'You'll be all right.'

'My nerves aren't at their best, Mr Leech.'

He drained his glass. 'Tell me, how's the project going?'

'It's going fine.' She frowned. 'There's a rush on to get it finished, to use it against some Soviet submarine or other.'

'I know.'

'Two months. That's all they've had on it so far.'

'Well, there isn't much longer,' Leech said. 'That sub, it's just turned for home.'

After breakfast the next day, she took the Tube to Kensington High Street and fought her way through the crush of tourists to the street. Tall buildings had created an artificial canyon through which the wind gusted; she turned up her coat collar and walked briskly over the crossing towards Church Street.

Clear of the junction, she paused in front of an antiques shop. The images reflected in the plate glass showed a fractured world of splintered people swirling past, heels tapping the pavement, punctuating the traffic's swelling drone. So much turmoil, so much urgency; briefly she longed to be somewhere else, somewhere wide and serene and empty.

A man in a fawn summer suit stood by a telephone kiosk, lighting a cigarette. He could have been about to make a call; he might even be expecting one. But the kiosk remained unoccupied, and the man shivered outside. She went inside the velvet silence of the shop, let her unseeing gaze range over the paintings and bric-a-brac and cabinets and chairs.

The woman asked, 'May I help you?'

'I ... No, no thank you.'

'Just browsing?'

'Just passing.' The words snagged somewhere within; she almost winced.

Out on the pavement again, Frances strode along, following the curve of the road, squeezing between other pedestrians, almost stumbling over shopping trolleys and small children. She found herself heading towards Kensington High Street again, but dared not turn back. Instead she walked up the inclined driveway to the Royal Garden Hotel. The climb exhausted her last reserves of strength; she stood in the lobby breathing weakly, rapidly, feeling tremors run through her. Impossible, all of it, impossible – as though life had somehow shifted gear, pitching her into a different dimension where uncertainty ruled absolute and aberration was the norm.

She stared around her, absorbing the scene: crowded foyer, scattered seating, a busy reception desk, pamphlets posters clocks wall calendar WEDS JUNE 29. And then the lobby phones – as soon as she saw them, she understood why she had come here. She stumbled into one of the booths and dialled Leech's number.

'Call them off.'

'Doctor Wycliffe?'

'Call them off, damn you!'

'What's happened? What's going –'

'Leech, listen to me. I don't want any more. D'you understand? I'm tired and confused and I don't want any more. Your watchdogs, call them off.'

Finally, reluctantly, Leech said: 'All right.'

'There's a man in a fawn suit; when I got off the Tube he followed me, he was by a telephone kiosk and –'

'Not one of mine.'

'By a telephone kiosk –'

'He probably wanted to make a call.' A brief pause. 'I'm sorry about this.'

She felt it then, a sudden inexplicable slackening deep inside, tension diminishing so unexpectedly that muscle and sinew began to tremble violently. She slumped helplessly against the perspex cowling, eyes squeezed tight, fingers struggling to maintain their grip on the receiver. After a while she heard herself say: 'Everything seemed to be closing in. Nobody said it would be like this, Leech.'

'It's all right, Doctor Wycliffe. You'll be okay.'

'Will I?' She felt the rising thrust of a revived hysteria. 'Well, that's good then. I mean, I'm standing here and I don't know that, I don't know if I'm okay or not.'

'I'll send a car for you.'

'No.'

'Only be a minute, you stay –'

'Leech, no. Just ... Just leave me alone.'

She put the receiver down and walked slowly back along the High Street. A distancing effect seemed to be at work again, and she felt numbed, anaesthetised. She was tardy in recognising the first heavy drops of a summer squall; by the time it registered, the storm had impacted with full force, making kerb and tarmac sweat and gleam.

She hugged her coat to her and lunged for the sanctuary of the nearest shop. The doorway was already crowded. She struggled inside. Racks of records paraded their garish covers along each wall. She edged down a narrow aisle, gradually orientating herself to the new surroundings. A girl here, a youth there, each in bright colours that argued against the desperate monotony of the music pouring from hidden loudspeakers. She examined them wonderingly, urban parakeets in a monotone jungle.

An errant thought brushed against her like a wayward strand of hair: I'm getting too old, Piotr.

Blocked by a girl with red hair strident as a fire alarm, she turned to contemplate the nearest rack. L to P, like an encyclopaedia. Her fingers flicked through the polythene covers: nothing recognisable, nothing familiar, a wasteland of pouting faces and empty smiles, of the undeclared, the androgynous and the obscure, a wasteland shining row by row. Suddenly she was arrested by a black cover, a prism lanced by light.

Back in her apartment, Frances put the record on the player and sat down to listen, the sleeve open on her knee.

> Us, and them
> And after all we're only ordinary men
> Me, and you
> God only knows it's not what we would choose to do
> Forward! he cried (from the rear)
> And the front rank died
> And the general sat, and the lines on the map
> Moved from side to side ...
> Black, and blue
> And who knows which is which and who is who?

She sat with eyes closed, unmoving, listening intently, finding new and personal echoes in phrases that would usually have meant nothing to her.

> And if the dam breaks open many years too soon
> And if there is no room upon the hill
> And if your head explodes with dark forebodings too
> I'll see you on the dark side of the moon.

As Frances listened, an image occurred to her – a scene in a park in a faraway city, a moment of which she had never been part, yet a moment that was still of this place and this time. The image went skittering away, but with a conscious effort she brought it back, turned it over in her mind. And as she did so, fragments from Asanov's file came to her, and she remembered also the gaps in the copy Kenyon had given her. It all fell into place then, and she knew with a sudden bleak insight what had happened to both Dmitri and Piotr Asanov. The knowledge was so bitter it seemed to turn her to stone and pitch her into a well of unendurable darkness.

PART V

PART V

CHAPTER
FIFTEEN

LENINGRAD

In the background, the simple eloquence of a lone guitar, the soft cadences of Janna Bichevskaya. Tanya listened, smiling sadly at the harmonies. Protest songs, they used to call them in the West. But it seemed they had nothing to protest now; their music was as unfocussed as their beliefs. She watched the water beginning to bubble in the percolator, then carried a tray of crockery from the kitchen into the living room.

Vadim smiled at her. He still seemed to be having difficulty finding words, using them. Nods and smiles, that was the vocabulary of the moment, a body language more articulate than speech.

Finally he said: 'Music's nice.'

'Sound better with a new stylus.'

'No problem then,' he grinned. 'Got boxes full.'

She laughed delightedly. 'Oh, Vadim ...' She paused, then asked: 'How is Yelena?'

Vadim's face abruptly contorted; she saw bewilderment and disbelief. 'Vadim ...?'

'You don't know, do you?'

'Know what?' She went over to him, still carrying the tray from the kitchen.

'Yelena.' His breath rasped in the silence. 'She ... She's dead.'

After the initial jolt, only the numbness, sudden, freezing, rendering her incapable of speech or motion.

'I thought you couldn't have known,' Vadim said.

Yelena. The name dinned in her brain. Little Yelena. Fragile as a doll but strong as a, strong as a ... She shook her head, felt the word being torn from her yet heard it issuing in the merest whisper:

'No.' And then, feeling the futility of her denial: 'Why, Vadim?'

'Why?' His voice was dull. He sighed. 'I keep asking myself the same question, over and over again. I've had plenty of time to ask.'

A noise intruded then: it was a cup clattering in front of her, dancing against a plate on the tray. She willed her limbs to stillness and, with elaborate care, placed the crockery on the carpet, then slowly straightened up, considered him anew.

It had been obvious from the moment she'd found him waiting outside her apartment that this Vadim was not the same as the one of old. Still the dark eyes, the tanned skin, and the Zapata moustache a flick of defiance, but the vitality missing, some inner animation dimmed. He seemed smaller too, not just physically, though there certainly wasn't the robustness of before, but smaller in a different way, diminished, somehow, moving with steps instead of strides, making hesitant gestures with the hands instead of the old wild exaggerated flourishes.

She heard herself ask: 'What happened?'

Vadim seemed locked within a memory; it was a while before it released him.

'It's a long time now,' he said. 'April, April 26th. We were at Grundvik's, house guests, as it were. Well, he doesn't mind. The way they live, some of them – so much money they don't ... You know? Yelena hadn't been well. We were talking, I don't know what about, and then he came straight in, straight in and left me there and interrogated her and after that he just, he just ... I try to remember, Tanya. I close my eyes and I kind of see it, but it's over so quickly, like the way it was. Quick, sudden, finished. There's a gun in his hand and something is hitting me and hitting me ...'

She stared at him, dazed, still in the paralysis of shock. She wanted to go to him but felt incapable of movement. Words dribbled softly in meaningless invocation. 'Dear God. Dear God.'

'I didn't even know myself,' Vadim said, 'about Yelena. That's funny, isn't it?'

'Vadim, I –'

'Hey, it's okay.' He tried a smile, maintained it with painful discipline. 'I survived.'

She listened to the mechanics of respiration, hers and his, and then he suddenly whispered, 'Monakhov,' and the name remained the loudest sound of all.

*   *   *

216

Later, when she had consumed two glasses of vodka – a Finnish label ripe and raw – and the smoke was uncurling from yet another cigarette, she was able to look at him again, and believe. 'You're certain, then.'

'Yes, Monakhov.'

'The same one who's been to see me.'

'The man from Moscow.' A sardonic smile, as if that said it all. 'He used to come a lot, to the hospital. Those glasses, I remember looking at them and seeing myself, seeing how small I was. He said we'd resisted arrest.' Vadim shrugged. 'It's almost possible.'

'But is it true?'

'No.'

She held his gaze for a few moments, said quietly: 'You're having to deal, aren't you?'

He nodded and sighed. 'That's worse than anything else.'

'I know.'

'I only wish you did. Nobody knows, not really.'

'But if you wanted to make a stand, Vadim, tell the truth ...' The sentence foundered on its own absurdity.

'It's too late for that.' He hesitated. 'I've had to make a statement. In return for Monakhov saying I wasn't involved – that Yelena attacked him and I got hit, accidentally – in return for that, I've said I don't remember anything.'

'So you both walk away from it.' Tanya shook her head. 'It's a poor bargain, Vadim, and I doubt he'll keep to it. What I still don't understand is why it happened?'

'He came to Leningrad because of some kind of conspiracy, a conspiracy to arrange the defection of Piotr Asanov.'

'Defection?'

'That was my reaction. Obviously it makes no sense to you, either.'

'It's ridiculous! What does he mean, defection?'

'Well,' Vadim said slowly, 'Asanov has gone.'

'Yes, but I thought he'd been, you know, re-arrested, or taken back to Moscow.'

'Monakhov says he's in the West.'

'But how? Why?' Angrily: 'Oh, this is stupid. Stupid!'

'Monakhov also says Leonid was involved, and Yelena. And you.'

217

'How could I be involved? How could I be part of something I know nothing about?'

'It's all right,' he said, 'you don't have to convince me.'

'Well, I certainly don't have to convince that bastard.'

'Tanya –' quietly, carefully – 'watch out for him, hey?'

'You're the one who should be watching. That sort of man, Vadim. He can't afford to let someone like you ...' She shrugged. 'You know what I mean.'

'Don't worry,' he said softly, 'I'm ready for him now.'

STATE PSYCHIATRIC HOSPITAL TWO
ARSENALNAYA
LENINGRAD

He sat across the table from her, an avuncular man of hearty voice and portly build, the round and dimpled face suffused a cheerful pink. The smile embraced her, seemed to encompass the entire room.

'Naturally you're concerned. We all are.'

'Then I can see Guseinov?' Tanya asked.

'His assessment, you know, it shows he has considerable talent, considerable.'

'May I see him, please?' She lit another cigarette, watching her fingers tremble. 'I don't have long.'

He smiled understandingly. 'You're a teacher, aren't you? My daughter's a teacher, in Kharkov.'

'Comrade director –'

'Assistant director.'

'I've come to see Leonid Guseinov.'

The smile communicated instant regret. 'I'm sorry, but ...' His hands spread wide. 'It isn't possible today.'

'I've written authorisation. I showed it at the door.' She reached for her handbag, nails scrabbling at the catch. 'I have it –'

'That's all right, your pass is in order.'

'Then why can't I see him?'

'He's in treatment.'

'But they said ...' She shook her head. 'Any Friday, any Friday you can come and visit. Two weeks ago I saw him, but then last Friday ... What's the point in lying to people, in telling them lies?'

'Oh come now, no one is telling lies. There's been a little mix-up, that's all.'

'Then why couldn't I see him last week? And today, why can't I?' She had to look away; the round face was so full of sympathy, understanding, that she felt in danger of being seduced. Her gaze travelled to the paintings, the fir trees and the snow, the horses and the troikas. Prints, not originals – convincing counterfeits like the smile on the face before her.

She glanced at her wristwatch. 'I have to get back soon.'

'I wish I could help you, gozphoza, truly I do.' He sighed. 'But it's treatment day.'

'For Leonid?'

'This is a hospital.' He spoke gently, without a trace of condescension. He leaned back, folded his hands over the swollen waistcoat of the three-piece pinstripe suit. 'Sad, isn't it, how often this happens? People of talent, it's as though their powers are too great for them. As we well know.'

She didn't reply. He waited a few moments, then went on: 'I was speaking historically, you understand. I meant, here we are, in Leningrad, Pushkin's city. Was there ever a finer writer than Pushkin? And yet look what happened to him. One of the finest fencers of his generation, yet he was killed in a duel, by a pistol shot. And he had the choice of weapons. Why didn't he choose a foil? Why pistols? Did he want to kill himself?' A prolonged, ruminative pause. 'Talent is a terrible possession, gozphoza. It roosts too often in an insubstantial nest.'

Quietly yet emphatically, the words evenly paced, Tanya said again: 'I want to see Leonid Guseinov.'

The man eased himself out of the chair. 'Come back next Friday.' A conspiratorial wink. 'I'll see what I can do.'

She stared up at him. 'You're playing with us, aren't you?'

'Playing, gozphoza?' The smile shadowed away. 'No one is playing.'

Tanya left the building and retrieved her car from the hospital parking lot. Lunchtime traffic dawdled along the Nevsky, careless of crossings or pedestrians; the only obstacles that merited negotiation were the buses, the double-jointed, ochre-coloured single deckers that weaved this way and that, and the white trolley buses which seemed to stop no sooner than they had started. She tried to manoeuvre out of a stationary queue of vehicles, then abandoned the attempt and wearily pushed the gear shift into neutral.

Thoughts pushed and pummelled like the throb of noise around her; she closed her eyes, saw Leonid's face. Leonid, with his dreams and his foolishness and his bravery and his laughter.

'Tanya, why were Adam and Eve Russian?'

'I don't know.'

'Because they had no clothes to wear, only an apple to eat, and thought they were living in Paradise.'

'You have to try, Tanya,' he had told her. 'You're not alone. People you'll never know, never meet, different people in different places – yet it all connects. One day, it all connects.'

The traffic moved off again. She engaged first and felt the car lurching forward, then glanced up for a routine check in the mirror.

A black saloon was squeezing in from the nearside lane, making space for itself behind her; a black Cajka.

She accelerated, steered towards the crown of the road, and saw the car begin to swing out in pursuit. An oncoming military truck was virtually upon her before she reacted; lights flashed and a horn blared and then it rumbled by, its wheel-arches almost scraping her roofline. She ducked back into the stream of traffic, watched the Cajka follow, then everything came to a halt again as another bus made its stop. She clung to the steering wheel and stared fixedly through the windshield.

Lunch-hour in the Nevsky; say to yourself this isn't happening, cars and people all around, the world going about its everyday business, its little concerns. It isn't happening.

You're playing with us, aren't you? Playing, gozphoza? I can't live like this, Leonid. I can't, I can't, not day after day, not hour after hour. *No one is playing.*

Her helplessness yielded to a desperate rage: so where are they then, Leonid, all the people in all the places, where are they? You think they're going through something like this? You think we're all reflections of each other, one great lake of glorious humanity? There's only one reflection now: a black saloon with opaque windshield tailgating remorselessly all along the wide boulevard.

The traffic began to move. Her foot slipped from the clutch; the car stalled. Hand on ignition key and turn, turn, damn you. Engine catching, missing, firing, dying, key twisting savagely back and forth.

In the rear-view mirror, the driver's door was slowly opening, opening wider. Turn, turn, turn, then a flood of relief as the engine started, and she was speeding away with the accelerator flat down towards the next intersection, shifting gear and hearing the transmission crash and then hauling opposite lock, hard over, over! Her vision jolted as her head struck the roof-lining, wheels bounced across the sidewalk, people scattered, people blurred ...

She was through. Wider than an alley but narrower than a road, the anonymous backs of buildings either side rearing up and rushing by, boxes and cartons and litter everywhere and the Lada weaving in and out. An ornate wooden cart coming up on the left, a flower vendor's.

She felt the car slewing hopelessly, saw the trash cans a half-second before ramming them head on – a jarring, jangling impact, something cartwheeling away, something else smacking at the roof, glancing off, but clear of it now, going past, going on.

The Cajka had made the turn and the headlights were on, twin orbs burning bright. It was making ground, but the trash cans were horizontal now, and he'd know they'd tear out the suspension so he tried for a gap that wasn't there and ploughed into the flower cart and everything fragmented in an explosion of splinters and blossom.

Tanya braked, the Lada nose-dived, but it was too late because a high-sided van swerved into vision. She braced herself and cried aloud, and then her voice was cut short as the force of impact drove the breath from her lungs.

For a heartbeat, there was no sound or motion, nothing at all. Then awareness began to seep back: vibration, the trembling of the shift, engine still running, car still moving on.

She was almost oblivious to the burning at the back of her throat as she struggled for oxygen, breasts heaving, neck muscles straining. Metal clanged and rang somewhere, accompanied the sensation of something buckling, tearing, peeling back. The car was picking up speed, and outside it was all beginning to blur again.

Suddenly, she was out of the alley: sharp left-hand turn, mercifully through a gap, and merging into city traffic, dense, slow, slowing, stopped. In the rear-view mirror, nothing.

A heavy truck halted in front of her with an audible hiss of air brakes. She inched the Lada up close, focussed on the drip of oil spattering from the massive rear axle, willing the truck to move. Another expulsion of air and wheeze of hydraulics, the thunderous clatter of a power plant revving up, the impossible corrugations of giant tyre treads beginning to roll.

In the mirror, she saw a black saloon slewing fast out of the alley, one headlight shining, the other blind.

The Lada seemed to move out of its own volition; she found herself confronting a view of the middle of the road, with oncoming traffic glaring and hooting. But the ridiculous part was that the indicator was on; her hand had reached out and put the indicator on and the beacon was blinking merrily away just as it always did. She turned the Lada in an almost lazy curve across the face of the steel tide, a strangely muted kaleidoscope of light and colour. And there ahead was the orbital road, the western highway out of the city.

Three lanes of traffic were filing in both directions, but it didn't matter. Tanya saw nothing but the broad, shining ribbon of road ahead. She felt no inclination now to look for the Cajka, but concentrated on keeping it steady and following the westbound highway.

A suburban junction came up; the lights were in her favour. She turned past a block of shops, into a narrower road and accelerated away. The road unwound leisurely, dipping and rising and swinging right then left, utterly peaceful, empty, serene, nothing at all except the rushing of the wind.

The verges widened on either side; beyond them, concrete towers rose towards the sun. The pavements were crowded with mothers, children, babies – going shopping, pushing prams. And the quiet road swept on and on.

In the mirror, a small shadow appeared, dark, gaining.

She thrust the Lada up an incline, overtaking slower vehicles. As she came level with the crest of the rise, she saw that the traffic had halted at a crossing. People were walking slow and unheeding across the road: an old man, a young woman, a child, a pram ...

No time to brake, no room to stop; she wrenched the steering and felt the response, and then all the sounds erupted simultaneously. Vision spun, shone bright, then whirled away into night.

CHAPTER
SIXTEEN

LENINGRAD

It was parked tight against the kerb, all six metres of it; no sign of the driver or passenger. Vadim waited a moment longer, then moved from his vantage point by the garage wall. He approached warily, glance darting this way then that. When he reached the car his hand stretched out involuntarily and caressed the warm sheen of metal.

A Zil 117, in standard nomenklatura dress: black body, white-walled tyres, tinted glass, twin headlights, chrome fenders and wheel arches, gleaming, glittering; behind the wide radiator, a V 8 seven-litre power plant. He walked its length, envy overcoming caution. The driver's window was still wound down. He leaned in to taste the scent of wealth and power: auto box, air-conditioning unit, stereo, centre console with electric window controls and telephone. Behind the front seats was a partition of smoked glass, half open to reveal quilted headlining and contoured seats of pale oyster leather.

He walked away with soft reluctant tread, wryly wondering if the battle against imperialism was the better for having carbon-copy Cadillacs leading the charge.

A white Zastava swung into the forecourt seconds after he had concealed himself. Body pressed tight against the garage wall, he peered around the pointing and watched as a small bald man clambered out of the miniature saloon, paused beside the Zil, then strode briskly towards the lobby.

Vadim debated briefly, then turned slowly on his heel. Today would not be a good day to visit after all.

Tanya said: 'I can't think. I can't feel. I can't even function any more.' Her gaze held his. 'Can you understand that, Father?'

Melnikov didn't respond. He sat with body hunched forward, elbow propped on the arm of the sofa, hand cupping jaw, eyes staring steadily, unblinking.

'I don't know what you expect,' Tanya said. 'They're my friends.' Melnikov caught the faint tremor in her voice.

Eventually he said: 'It's not a case of expecting anything.'

'No? I thought that's why you were here – the questions, the concern.'

'You're my daughter.'

'Your liability?'

'I love you, child,' he said quietly.

She had not anticipated that, words spoken without hesitation or ceremony. They were not an answer to any question but the refutation of a glib and thoughtless jibe. Because of that, and because of his stillness, the stoic calm that silently promised to remain undisturbed no matter what was thrown at him, there was nothing she could do now except let the tremor rise and break into tears.

'No one is telling you how to run your life,' Melnikov said. 'No one is telling you how to do this or do that.' He paused. 'I would rather have silence than noise, Tanya. I would rather stay away than fight you.'

'But you are ...'

'Fighting you?' Sadness lit the leonine features, brought a brief and haunting animation. 'No, child, it is you against yourself.'

The doorbell rang. She watched him get up and move woodenly to the door. Voices sounded distantly from the hallway, then Melnikov ushered in a small man she had never seen before. He had a bald head, dark bright eyes and cheeks in which something of the cherub still lingered.

'This is the friend I was telling you about, Tanya,' Melnikov said, 'Colonel Gregor Krotov.'

'Gozphoza.' He gave a slight inclination of the head, a gesture of courtesy neither formal nor elaborate.

She didn't look at him, didn't speak.

'Gregor is from Moscow.' Melnikov hunkered down beside her chair. 'He's come to help.'

Krotov glanced from one to the other. But you didn't need eyes to perceive, he thought, that pain danced attendance upon both of them, the silver-haired man and the woman of pale countenance.

'Gozphoza,' he said finally, then stopped. Tanya's face was tilted towards him, eyes dull despite the moisture. 'At the risk of being presumptuous,' Krotov began again, 'might I have a glass of tea?'

She busied herself in the kitchen, preoccupied with the arrival of the little man with the quiet demeanour. There was something about him – hard to define, but something empathic nevertheless, encouraging trust, inviting friendship. There was a conciliatory air about Colonel Krotov, an openness which, given his job, argued of a subtlety that could still prove deadly: after all, the KGB did not employ people for their finer qualities. For the first time in a week, her spirits began to lighten.

She returned with the tea and set the tray down. Krotov moved to her. 'Let me help.'

'No, it's all right.'

He took the glasses even so, carried one to her father, then politely waited while she sat down before doing likewise.

'This,' he said, 'is most welcome.' He smiled at her. 'You're feeling better now?'

Tanya nodded.

'You were fortunate to escape in one piece. It must have been a frightening experience.'

'I've known better.' His funny smile made her smile back involuntarily, then she grew serious again. 'Why was I being followed?'

'Obviously someone is interested in you.'

She hesitated. 'My father says you're in charge of the investigation.'

'He's right. But it's not my style to cause havoc on the public highway; so amateurish.'

'There is a man, a Major Monakhov ...' Tanya said cautiously.

'Well, it certainly wasn't him. He wasn't even in the country last week.' Krotov paused. 'If I might explain something to you, yes?'

'Please do.'

'You said in your statement that you were being followed by a black saloon, possibly a Zil. Despite what you may think of the KGB's influence, we do not have access to such vehicles, or even cars which resemble them.'

'I don't understand?'

'I've got enough from the eyewitnesses to identify the car as a Cajka. It's smaller than a Zil – for smaller Party officials.' He turned to Melnikov. 'Someone in Moscow is feeding information to

Leningrad, Nikolai; and someone in Leningrad is making sure the pressure stays on.'

'D'you know who?'

'No. Nor do I see any point in trying to find out. People with Cajkas are only one step down from people with Zils. They're clever, they have power, and they're operating on home ground.'

'So this was local, then.'

'Yes, and personal.' He turned back to Tanya. 'You have to appreciate, gozphoza, that you are not the prime target in all this. They have your father in their sights, not you.'

'They?'

Krotov shrugged. 'People.'

'How Kafkaesque.'

'They're people who resent your father's power base. The distinction between a family and a regime is not perceived in the Kremlin.'

Her gaze flitted to Melnikov. 'I have my own life, Father.'

'You're not being asked to change it,' Krotov said. 'Merely to be more ... circumspect.' He sighed. 'Look, gozphoza, I'm recommending no further action in your case, not because of who you are, or who your father is, but because of the facts – or, to be accurate, the lack of them. There will be no charge against you because there is no evidence against you.'

'Then I'm free to do as I wish?'

'I don't issue licences, gozphoza.'

Tanya stood up. 'My father has just lectured me on the company I keep. D'you wish to do likewise?'

'I wouldn't presume.' Krotov considered her with frank, unwavering gaze. 'But I would say this: merely because you see things in a certain way, do not make the mistake of thinking your viewpoint is unique.'

'I hardly think we share it, comrade colonel.'

'Why? Are we not of the same species?' He shook his head, then looked away. 'No system is perfect, Tanya Melnikova. But even so, there is room for the individual, for truth.'

'I can't accept that.' She picked up her glass and took it to the tray. 'After everything that's happened, I can't accept what you say.'

'Then what,' Krotov said thoughtfully, 'will you do to change it?'

'I don't know yet.'

He nodded, as though her answer confirmed a conclusion already reached. 'Gozphoza, a word of advice.'

'Yes?'

'I've studied your file. The records show you're a fine teacher.'

'So?'

'So you're more powerful than your father could ever be. He has charge of his generation, but you have charge of the next.' He gazed steadily at her. 'Abandon what you have now, and the future will be as the present.' He got out of the chair and moved to within a few paces of her. 'Think about that, mmm?'

MOSCOW

Monakhov was waiting when he got back. Krotov walked in to confront golden images of himself and it was an effort not to let the surprise show through. Instead he said: 'You've brought the file, then.'

'On your desk, comrade colonel. They said you wished its return.'

'Yes, since you've finished with it.' He continued on past Monakhov, feeling compelled to maintain a brisk momentum. Damn Monakhov. At this hour of the night! Damn the man.

Behind him the velvet voice said: 'I understand you've been in Leningrad.'

'You understand correctly.'

'How is the investigation going?'

'Who's asking?' He turned to stare at the younger man: still the lightweight suit, the expensive shirt and tie, the shoes forever unobtainable in Moscow no matter who you knew.

Monakhov was frowning. 'Comrade colonel?'

'I said, who's asking. You? Or your masters?'

'I have no masters, comrade colonel.'

'I have no masters,' Krotov almost snapped at him in disgust. 'My, my. You're here at half past one on a Tuesday morning and I'm supposed to think it's out of honest curiosity.' He retraced his steps, stopping at the chair where Monakhov still negligently lounged. 'Thank you for the file, comrade major. You may go now.'

'I may be asked to continue the inquiry,' Monakhov said.

'I think they're wanting someone with a better record of success.' Krotov paused. 'Enjoy America, did you?'

227

Monakhov shrugged almost imperceptibly. 'It could have been better.'

'That's one way of putting it.' Krotov walked across to his desk and sat down. The thick ring-bound file covered most of the blotter. He reached into a drawer, saying: 'I'll give you a receipt.'

'That's not necessary.'

'In that case –' he closed the drawer – 'good night, Major Monakhov.'

'I thought you might have some ... queries?'

Krotov resisted a sudden impulse to shout at the man. Instead, he closed his eyes, ran a slow mental count until the timing synchronised with his own respiration, then leaned back into the chair. 'Queries, comrade major? Oh, I've one or two. Such as why a Cajka is now a pool car of the KGB. Such as why witnesses in my investigation are being pressurised and harried and damn near killed. Yes, I've one or two queries. But I'm not looking for answers from you.'

'With respect, I don't know what you're talking about –' he smiled as though to point up the deliberate pause – 'comrade colonel.'

Krotov made no response other than to slowly steeple his fingers.

'It's just that if you're picking up where I left off,' Monakhov said, 'if there's anything you still need to know ...'

'Rest assured. If – and I emphasise the word – *if* there's any reason for this inquiry to continue, then it will probably proceed very much as you planned.'

Monakhov got up. 'Thank you, comrade colonel.' He paused as though waiting for some further acknowledgment from the small man, then walked slowly to the door. 'Good night then, Colonel Krotov. It was good to see you again.'

Krotov let the silence wash over him for a long time, then leaned forwards, opened the dossier and skimmed quickly through it. The Asanov material remained intact. The Melnikova/Guseinov appendices were not. He smiled wearily; the young major and his juvenile games; letting you know that whatever you did he remained unaffected; letting you know that he could have had the pages photocopied but had chosen instead to fail to return them. So predictable, Vasily, so amateurish.

He stood up, stretched, yawned. Mind games at this hour of the morning, though: if I'm not too old for them then I'm certainly too damn tired.

Tanya eased herself off the couch and walked stiffly across the room to answer the telephone. Katerina materialised in the kitchen doorway, looking questioningly at her. 'I can manage,' Tanya said. She lifted the receiver. 'Hello?'

'Tanya Melnikova? This is Stelyavich, assistant director at Leningrad Psychiatric.'

Her pulse accelerated. She waited.

'The patient Guseinov – he's being released.'

'Released?' Incredulity made her voice almost inaudible.

'The programme is over. The papers are being prepared now. That's why I'm ringing you. The release document has to be signed by the responsible party. He can't be discharged otherwise.'

'But he's ... he's a prisoner!'

'Not here, gozphoza, I can assure you of that.'

'I meant before he went to hospital, before he came up here ...'

'The custodial order has been suspended providing he complies with the conditions of licence.'

'What does that mean?'

'It's all been explained to him, gozphoza. He understands the terms. Now, are you prepared to act as the responsible party?'

'I ...' She shook her head as though trying to pummel clarity into the midst of confusion. 'Isn't there anybody else?'

There was a lengthy pause; when Stelyavich spoke again he sounded as though he was reading from something. 'Guseinov, L. No fixed address. No known relatives. Next of kin: not posted.'

'There must be someone, surely.'

'Doesn't seem so. All you have to do is receive him.'

Like a parcel, she thought. 'Am I also expected to look after him?'

'Gozphoza?'

'His accommodation, comrade – he certainly can't stay here.'

'There is somewhere else, then? His friends, perhaps?'

'I don't know.'

'Ah.' The interval of silence lasted so long she began to wonder if he had quit the phone. Then: 'Without a permanent address ... I am sorry.'

'You mean you won't discharge him?'

'He can hardly walk the streets. No, we will have to return him to the custodial authorities.'

'But you said I had only to receive him.'

'Well, there is the matter of accommodation.' Stelyavich paused again. 'I seem to have wasted your time, gozphoza. Please, my apologies. Unless you can resolve the domiciliary question ...'

She replaced the receiver and made her way back to the couch. Katerina, still in the doorway, said: 'I've washed them all and dried them all and put them all away.' Not so much a statement as a recital.

'Good girl.'

'Are you all right?'

She nodded, closed her eyes. Faces bobbed like lanterns in the darkness. A voice that was her own yet not her own set a trickle of words coursing meaninglessly through her head: *no more, I can't; no more, no more* ...

'Hello, kotik.'

Eyes opened wide. 'Vadim!'

'The same.' He grinned broadly and bent down to kiss her cheek. 'No, don't get up.'

'I never heard the doorbell, I never heard ...'

'It wasn't pulled to.'

She glanced at Katerina. 'How many times must I tell you? You always close the door, always.'

Downward stare, shuffle of small feet. No reply.

'She's been doing some shopping for me,' Tanya said.

'You are a good girl, aren't you?' Vadim said.

Katerina looked up. 'I don't know you.'

He laughed. 'I'm Uncle Vadim.'

'I don't have an Uncle Vadim.'

'You do now.' He went to her and settled on his haunches at her side. 'Hello, Katerina.'

'Hello.' The brief acknowledgment was eloquent with suspicion.

'Would you like to do something else for your mother, Katerina?'

She studied him with head cocked to one side.

'I bet your mother would really like some tea,' Vadim said.

Wearily: 'I'm never out of that kitchen.'

His lips compressed in an effort to stifle the laughter. 'Here,' he said, reaching into a jacket pocket and producing a small cardboard box with a flourish. 'A present, for the hostess.'

She glanced uncertainly at Tanya, then back to the dark features again. 'What is it?'

'Open it.'

Fingers tentatively took the box from him and pried hesitantly at the lid. 'It's a watch!'

'A special watch, for a special person.' He pointed to the tiny dial. 'See those circles, on its face? They're Olympic circles.'

'It's a souvenir?'

'More than that. It was official issue for the junior athletes at the 1980 Moscow Olympiad.'

'I have a bear,' she said cryptically.

'Yes, well ...' He shook his head, then stood up.

'What d'you say, Katerina?' Tanya prompted.

'Thank you.' A solemn smile. 'Thank you for the present.'

He ruffled her hair. 'You'll make some tea, then?'

She walked away, still looking at the watch, nodding in silent assent.

'Vadim,' Tanya said, 'you shouldn't.'

'Why not?'

'You shouldn't, that's all.'

'Hey, I've boxes of them. Traded a couple of hundred windshield blades, old Wartburgs – no good to me.'

'Is it valuable?'

He laughed again. 'To the fartsovschchiki, Tanya, everything has a value.' He settled into the armchair. 'Curiosity value – a few roubles, no more. You short of anything yourself? I've a nice line in *tiubeteykas*; you should see the stitching.'

'Do I look like an Uzbek?'

'Lace then, genuine handmade Vologda? Glassware? Finest Khrustal?'

'No.' Laughter sparked the pain in her ribs again, the bruising sustained in the smash flaring with a heat that made her wince. 'Please, Vadim, don't ...'

'Records? Jeans?'

'Vadim!'

He spread out his palms in an attitude of supplication. '"Who does not work, shall not eat."'

Patiently, painfully: 'Vadim ... What did you want?'

'To see you.' He removed the black leather jacket, folded it carefully and placed it on the floor. 'I came yesterday but it looked like you had very important visitors.' He paused. 'I heard what happened.'

'You don't miss much.'

'No.' He smiled, grew serious again. 'So. How are you?'

'All right. A few bruises here, the odd scratch or two there. I'll survive.'

'Want to tell me about it?'

'Not at the moment.' She nodded in the direction of the kitchen. 'Katerina thinks a tyre blew out. Anyway, never mind me. You're looking well.'

'Never better.' The laughter returned. 'Walking wounded, eh, Tanya? We must be keeping the hospitals in business, what with me and you and –' He stopped abruptly.

'And Leonid,' she finished for him. She studied him for a while, then: 'I've had a telephone call, Vadim.'

CHAPTER
SEVENTEEN

LENINGRAD

Spenssky unclipped the handset and attempted to pass it back. The cord snagged against the gear-shift; his fingers scrabbled to free it. A gloved hand brushed his neck and snatched impatiently, stretching the cord taut. 'Control to Unit One.'

'Unit One receiving.' Metallic syllables crackled through the dash speaker.

'Situation?'

'Static – target still on station, Arsenalnaya, driver with vehicle.'

'Very well. Stand by.'

An audible click, then a rush of static filled the car. Spenssky half turned and reached backwards with his right hand. He could not see the occupant of the rear seat, but the other's irritation was manifest. The handset jabbed his shoulderblade.

'Next time,' Monakhov said, 'make sure the wire's free.'

There were only so many times you could read the GDR anniversary magazine, only so many times you could share in the joy of the farmer, bricklayer, engineer and doctor, celebrate with them the thirty-five years of peace and prosperity achieved through union with Soviet Russia. Tanya put it aside and checked the time again: 10.05. She had been waiting an hour now, in the cool green room. Nine o'clock or so, Stelyavich had said. She'd arrived, been taken to his office, given the discharge papers to sign, then led back here while administration set about the slow processing of the documentation.

She lit another cigarette, heard the noise then: footsteps echoing along an unseen corridor, growing louder, drawing nearer. She pushed back the chair and stood up.

He broke free of the orderlies, ran towards her with arms out-stretched. 'Tanya!' Their bodies melded in warm collision, a tight, stifling embrace. She stepped back and smiled in disbelief. 'Leonid, Leonid. Let me look at you.'

He performed an elaborate about-turn. 'Well?'

'Some mannequin.'

'Some patient.'

She shook her head. 'And to think I've been worried sick.'

'But I'm fine!' His eyes were bright and animation suffused every aspect of his appearance. Even the clothes were new and fresh: sweater, cord jacket, black denims.

She hooked her arm through his. 'Vadim's waiting. Let's get out of here before they change their minds.'

Drained almost completely of colour, brick, concrete and granite indistinguishable, their textures washed a uniform tint of pearl – the White Nights of Leningrad. Beneath an opalescent sky, the twilight city seemed to lack both shadow and substance, a one-dimensional imprint upon a pallid, quiescent landscape.

Leonid craned his head this way and that, fidgeting restlessly in the back seat as he stared out at the pale city. 'Look at it, though,' he said, 'look at it.'

Tanya squeezed his hand but didn't speak. His gaze settled on her, the intensity dimming as moisture filmed over. 'Thank you, both of you.' He turned away again, considered anew the steady sweep of the city as the little Polski-Fiat continued on its journey. Eventually he asked: 'Where are we going?'

'The Warren,' Vadim said.

'The Warren?'

'That's right.' Vadim risked a backward glance. 'Why so surprised?'

'It's been pulled down, nothing's there any more.'

'I'm there.'

'In a field?'

'Not quite.'

'The Warren.' Leonid spoke in a sustained note of wonderment. 'I haven't been for years. The canal, does it still flood?'

'It still floods, Leonid, as bad as ever.'

'And people still live there? They must be mad.'

*   *   *

Spenssky came in off the west orbital, following the long curve past the electronics factory, then straightening out again beyond the agricultural museum.

The proximity of ancient and modern struck him as incongruous; at other times he would have commented on the contrast of architecture and intent.

'Comrade major.'

'Yes?' Monakhov said curtly.

'Two more kilometres.'

'I know.'

'Oh? I hadn't realised you knew Leningrad.'

'Evidently.'

'Can be very confusing for a stranger – very big.'

'Not as big as Moscow.'

'No, not as big as Moscow.' A feeble response but he could think of nothing else to say. He glanced up at the mirror, wondered if the image would encourage further small talk. Opaque lenses stared fixedly back at him.

The Warren: an angular landscape of sharp, jagged peaks, of rubble and twisted paths festooned with telegraph wire, of pale swathes of mud randomly slashed in amongst the cinders and the dirt. Ascending tiers of shattered brick and stonework stood with their feet in pools of glimmering water; the slow shelving of fallen masonry, fractured lintels and broken friezes reminded of another time.

Once, the mansions stood in baroque splendour, six-storey terraces for the noble or the opportunist. Once, fanlights spilled gold upon the stoops, gilded the impossible filigree of iron railings, forged in respectful imitation of the Emperor's own balustrade. Once, carriages drew up either side of the street and gentlemen called in hats and tails; brass knockers rapped and panelled doors yielded; small white visiting cards were accepted with a bow and borne inside upon shining salvers. Once upon a time in Saint Petersburg.

But then Nature began to call, too, knocking with wind and rain. The engineers returned and considered and finally understood that you can make only so many channels and only so many ramparts before earthly forces overwhelm. Too many holes punched in too tightly stretched a fabric: the Neva backed up, bringing unexpected tides; the wild wind blew in from Finland, to be concentrated by artificial canyons of brick and stone. The fabric began to tear.

The paupers arrived when the princes departed.

For a time it was all right, it was possible to put new branches into the canal system, relieve the pressure, dissipate the currents' energies, redesign the ramparts, renew and reinforce them; for a time it was even possible to build more and more ranks of houses. The land was not over-developed; the poor needed a home, and the absent rich wanted an investment.

For a time it was possible to live a whole life in the Warren. But now only one terrace remained – crumbling steps up to yawning doorways, dark halls, empty rooms. To its left stood the last remaining facade – nothing behind it at all, a gaunt and battered rectangle no thicker than a course of brick.

Behind the terrace, the wasteland spread in aching monotony, an expanse of flattened earth ribbed with splintered beams and ruptured piping, the perspective lent depth only by the heaps of rubble and receding tides of broken roof tiles.

Vadim parked the car alongside the centre house of the terrace.

'Wait here for a couple of minutes, then come in,' he said. 'I have to get ready.' He winked delightedly, then jumped out of the car and ran up the steps to the front door of the house. They watched him unlock the door and disappear inside.

'He obviously has a surprise for us,' Tanya guessed.

'And where would Vadim be without life's little surprises?'

'Well, we mustn't spoil it for him.'

They waited impatiently for a while, looking out over the eerie, broken landscape of the Warren. Then Leonid said: 'Come on. I've been waiting around for the last two months and I'm beginning to lose my taste for it.'

They got out of the car and walked up the steps together. Vadim opened the door as they reached the top. 'Be it ever so humble ...' he said, and led them upstairs by the light of a pencil torch. Only Vadim could have a pencil torch, thought Leonid. They reached the fourth-floor landing, and with a flourish Vadim threw open the big double doors.

Candles: Tanya had to blink against the shocking dazzle, the myriad points of brightness that flared and sprayed and flickered and spired; candles, dozens of them, not one or ten but dozens – on fluted stems, on silver branches, in single, double, triple tiers, by the hearth, on the dresser, on the tables – a dancing brilliance, everywhere.

She closed the door behind them. 'I don't believe it.'

'Believe what, kotik?'

'All ... all this.' She turned questioningly to Leonid.

'I think,' he said slowly, 'they should call him Aladdin.'

She made her way to the hide sofa and slumped heavily into its rich embrace. Leonid remained by the door, fingers still pushing abstractedly into the bristle of beard. 'Vadim, where on earth did you get all this?'

'Around.' Vadim knelt before a walnut escritoire, extracted three tulip glasses from a drawer. 'Sorry, no cocktail cabinet.'

'Look at it,' Leonid said. He moved his arm in a slow, sweeping gesture. 'That cabinet, those chairs, the candles ... I've never seen...' He stared helplessly at her. 'Tanya, say something.'

She shook her head, feeling a fluttering in her breast, the teasing convulsions of a fast-rising hysteria. The laughter broke then, laughter of relief and disbelief, of amazement and amusement, driving her back against the cushions, breath going and eyes squeezing tight on a firmament of stars.

Monakhov opened the car door and gingerly stepped out of the Moskvich. He checked his watch: 10.32 p.m., Thursday 7 July. He bent down and peered into Spenssky's rubicund features. Over-fed and over-paid – if this was the calibre of the Leningrad operation, then better to close down now and allow the militia sole domain.

'Stay.' One word, carefully enunciated, as though spoken to a dog. He considered the frantic nodding of the anxious face, then turned slowly on his heel and walked towards the stoop. A thin man emerged from the hallway and stood to one side like an usher. Monakhov cautiously climbed the steps, paused at the topmost to contemplate a flat Mongoloid face. 'Yes?'

'Fourth floor, end room.'

A quick upward glance, grazing across the boarded windows – no light, no sign. 'Sure?'

'Yes, comrade major.'

'And Viktor One?'

'Arrived a moment ago.' His index finger pointed across the street. 'Behind that ... that wall.'

'Tell them nobody moves.'

'Yes, comrade major.'

'Nobody in or out, nobody away from the cars until I say so.'

He hesitated. 'You're Shadrin, aren't you?'

'Yes.'

'You're a long way from home.'

'We're a long way from anywhere.'

'But I don't understand where you've got it all from. It's like you've ransacked GUM.'

'It was like this when I got back,' Vadim said. He saw the deepening frown on Leonid's face and added hastily: 'I've been away, too – business. You know how it is.'

'Did Yelena have anything to do with this?' Leonid asked.

'Yes.' No hesitation. They had agreed that Leonid should not know of Yelena's death. Tanya watched the unwavering smile and inwardly marvelled.

Dank and dark, with a stench of foetid dilapidation; Monakhov paused on the first landing, breathing through his mouth, unwilling to taste the air any more. It was almost pitch black here; he felt nameless shapes beneath his feet, the texture of fungus at his fingertips. He wrenched his hand from the bannister.

He continued to climb the high stairs, movements wary, limbs tense. Something seemed to drift against his leg – the lightest touch, then gone. He shuddered, skin crawling with revulsion, then frowned at himself for this infantile foolishness. An old newspaper, frightened by an old paper.

He made the final ascent in a mood of angry determination – because of the fear and the shame, but above all because of the people who sat in the fourth-floor room who had brought him to this foul place. On the landing he listened to the sound of their voices from within, identified the pale outline of the doors. He clasped the handle and turned it. Three faces spun round in unison as he walked into the room.

'One more for the party,' he said.

He sat down on the sofa and smiled at each of them in turn. 'Please, don't mind me. I was in the neighbourhood and thought I'd drop in. How are you then, Vadim? Feeling better?'

Leonid started, his bewildered glance darting towards Monakhov, then back to the Georgian.

'Get out,' Vadim said, words snarled rather than spoken, welling up on a tide of disgust. He managed a couple of paces towards

Monakhov before Tanya grabbed at his arm, half shouting, half whispering: 'Leave it! Leave it!'

Monakhov studied them, the clash of wills, the pointless, silent, angry struggle. He let his gaze wander around the room, resting it briefly here and there – on the furnishings and the pictures and the configuration of candles. Voice silken, he said: 'Looks like you exchanged one Fools' House for another, Leonid.'

Leonid sidestepped the other two and came towards him. 'What're you doing here?'

'No.' A slow shake of the head. 'It's what are *you* doing here?'

Tanya returned Monakhov's stare, her eyes glittering. 'Well, well, well. To what do we owe this honour?'

'Oh,' he said lightly, 'I think you can guess.' He watched Leonid slowly subside into an armchair. 'So, the Leningrad Literary Circle is in session, eh?'

Eyes still bright, voice even colder than before – she felt absurdly confident of herself, shored up by a freezing anger – 'I asked why you were here.'

He sighed. 'All right. Vadim Kalininsky, Tanya Melnikova, Leonid Guseinov. In the name of the Russian Soviet Federal Socialist Republic you are to be individually and severally charged that, on this day Thursday the seventh of July, in the Hero City of Leningrad, you did wilfully and knowingly conspire in the escape from custody at State Psychiatric Hospital Two –'

'What?' Leonid, galvanised into action, stood upright, face white with anger and fear.

'State Psychiatric Hospital Two, Arsenalnaya, in the aforementioned Hero City, the patient-prisoner Guseinov, contrary –'

'What are you talking about?' Leonid shouted. 'Escape?'

'How else d'you explain it?'

'I've been *released*!'

A sad, slow shake of the head; Monakhov watched the shadow of despair pass across Leonid's face.

'But the papers . . . All the papers.' He seemed on the verge of tears.

'False.' He contrived an air of regret. 'Forged.'

'It's all right,' Tanya said, 'there's nothing to worry about.' She got out of her chair and walked towards Monakhov.

He delved into his coat pocket and withdrew a transceiver. 'Shadrin, you may come up now.' The unit slipped back inside. 'I'm not alone, gozphoza.'

'Hired hands, comrade major?' Tanya paused, arms folded across her breasts. 'You are sure of yourself.' She went to the hearth and stood with her back to him. 'I was asked to sign those papers. The hospital asked me.'

'No.'

'There is no conspiracy, Major Monakhov.'

'Like last time, eh?'

'So how did we do it then?' Her voice was devoid of even the slightest inflexion.

'The papers are counterfeit, the signatures are forgeries.'

'Not Stelyavich's. I watched him write it.'

The lenses flashed in surprise. 'He knows nothing about it.'

'He was the one who asked me to sign.'

'And you can prove that, gozphoza?'

She nodded almost imperceptibly, as though answering a wholly different question. Eventually Tanya said: 'And what of the other "forgeries"?' She emphasised the word with contempt.

He shrugged dismissively. 'The initials of an assistant secretary from the RSFSR Penal Department - not a very good copy, though.'

'And?'

'Another forgery - the signature of the Deputy Chief Examiner, Review Committee, City of Moscow Judicial College.'

'That it?'

'No. There has to be a counter-signature.'

'By whom?'

'The senior Party official who happens to be available at the time.'

Tanya inhaled, laughter clipping the back of her throat, then began a leisurely pacing, wandering past the hearth, the cabinet, fetching up in the right-hand corner of the room. She reached up to pluck at the fabric of a wall-hanging - a broad swathe of gold satin that flowed in convoluted folds from ceiling to floor.

'My father.' No emphasis - a conclusion simply expressed.

'It is his signature,' Monakhov said.

'But ... a forgery.'

'That's the oddest thing, gozphoza. It's so good, it could even pass as genuine.'

She looked at him then, and the smile was glacial, feral, so vicious that it twisted and transformed her face.

A fist rapped twice upon the double doors. He continued to stare at her, the lenses golden, fixed, unmoving. Finally he said: 'All right, Shadrin.'

The door opened.

'Hello, Vasily.'

Monakhov turned as Krotov politely bowed.

The colonel crossed the room with small, quiet strides – no fuss, no further acknowledgment of Monakhov's presence. He halted in front of Tanya. 'Gozphoza.' He gave his slight bow again.

'Comrade colonel.' She smiled, aware of the flexing of facial muscles, and wondered why this was the only sensation she could feel when now was the moment when relief should have come flooding in.

'My apologies,' Krotov said. He gestured towards the door. 'I do so hate the theatrical.'

'Where is Shadrin?' Monakhov asked casually.

'Reassigned.' The small man turned to Vadim. 'You're Kalininsky, aren't you? I recognise the face.'

Vadim's nod of affirmation was hesitant, uncertain.

'They didn't tell me,' Krotov said, 'you were a candlemaker.' He took a step towards Leonid. 'And you must be Guseinov, yes?'

Leonid stared back at him, wide-eyed.

Tanya gazed at them, each in turn – statues in a tableau, no movement, no sound.

Eventually Krotov said: 'I kept my word, comrade major. I promised I'd continue where you left off.' He turned slowly, impassively, to confront Monakhov. 'The Melnikova tap ... You should have remembered your own thoroughness.' He stared into the lenses, the shining fire dance. 'Technology, Major Monakhov. You never know when it will trip you up.'

'The comrade colonel has no authority to –'

'I was with Chebrikov this morning. He has a tape of the call from our friend Stelyavich to Doctor Melnikova. He also has a release document bearing forged signatures, one of them that of a Politburo member. Quite a conspiracy, Major Monakhov. And if you hadn't tapped that phone we would never have known about it. So careless of you to get caught in your own trap.'

Vadim found voice at last. 'And what will you do with the evidence?'

'Enough.'

'That's supposed to be an answer?'

Krotov considered him. 'I don't have to account to you.' His gaze fixed again upon Tanya. 'I tried to tell you – things are not as they seem. Chebrikov is not Beria.'

'Meaning what?'

'The KGB is not a law unto itself.'

She returned his stare for a moment more, then knelt down by Leonid's chair and reached up to take his hand. She saw someone move out of the corner of her eye, but then Krotov was speaking quietly again: 'There's nowhere to go, comrade major.'

Monakhov halted, the door half open.

'Better you walk with me,' Krotov said. 'My people ...' A small smile, a slight shrug.

She found herself looking into the lenses again and the smooth, fire-lit face; his mouth opened and closed, tongue sliding almost sensuously across lower lip. 'You knew.' Two words – nothing more.

With an effort of will she turned away from Monakhov. Leonid's long slim fingers lay inert within her grasp. 'I couldn't tell you, Leonid. All that's happening, I couldn't tell you. But it's for the best – for you, for all of us.'

He nodded, a mime of comprehension. Emotions made a shadow flutter across his features.

'Hey,' Vadim smiled. 'Don't worry, it's over.'

'Over?' The frown deepened in spreading corrugation.

'You're free.'

'In time,' Krotov said quietly. 'There's the question of sentence.'

Vadim's dark eyes scoured Krotov, then searched Tanya's face. She looked away. 'What does he mean?' He took a step forward. 'What is he talking about?'

Krotov sighed. 'Your friend isn't free yet.'

Vadim took another step, closing in on her. 'Tanya?'

'Please, Vadim.' She breathed the words, head bowed, eyes closed behind the fall of hair. 'Please ...'

'But they've let him go!'

'Kalininsky –' Krotov began, but the Georgian was past him now, standing before Tanya with fists clenched and mouth working.

'What does he mean, Tanya? Damn it, answer me!'

'He means ...' She hesitated, started over. 'Leonid has to go back.'

'No.'

'It won't be like before though, Colonel Krotov's promised to –'

'No!' A violent shake of the head. 'He's free!' He stared at her as though she was in only erratic focus. 'You tricked me.' His voice was full of disgust.

'No.'

'You tricked him, too.' Vadim motioned in Leonid's direction, body trembling, respiration a series of sharp quick breaths. 'You said if I let him come here everything would be all right. You said if I went along with it ... What have you done, Tanya?'

'I haven't done anything!' She was on her feet now. 'Don't talk to me like that, not after all I've been through, don't start accusing –'

'All you've been through?' His laughter scythed at her. 'You? You haven't been through anything!' He spun around, moved with furious footfalls to the hearth, and stopped with his back to her. 'God above, what *you've* been through ...'

Krotov coughed embarrassedly. 'This isn't helping anyone.' He paused. 'Look, Kalininsky –'

Vadim swung round again, face dark, wild: 'No, you look! You look! I thought you'd come to help, I thought she'd fixed it so it was all right. But instead, instead ... what? You stage a pantomime, a pantomime for the benefit of that bastard over there!'

Bronze lenses tracked back from Krotov and levelled on Vadim.

He gazed into them. 'You laughing, Major Monakhov? Enjoying it? You should. I'd enjoy every second of it if I were you.' He stopped, breathing raggedly. 'You win after all, don't you?'

'It isn't like that, Kalininsky,' Krotov said icily. 'And if that's what you think then you're a bigger fool than I took you to be.'

'Ah! But of course! That's all Kalininsky is – a fool! Got room for one more, Leonid? You and me, share a bed, eh? Well, why not? I mean, look at him, look at Kalininsky. Street boy. No brains, no background. What does he know about anything? What does he care? Him, he can't even sign his name!' He moved towards them. 'Except, except ... Vadim Kalininsky never betrayed anyone in his whole life.'

'There's no betrayal,' Tanya said, but the protest was muted by a numbing incredulity. 'Vadim, you have to understand –'

'Hey, kotik, tell Leonid. Not me.'

Krotov shook his head. 'I think we'd better be going ...'

'That's right,' Vadim said. 'You go. Lock him up again and leave me alone.'

'Forget it, Vadim.' The words dropped so quietly in amongst them it took her a second or two to realise who had spoken. 'Forget it,' Leonid said again. He stood up. 'You did well, Tanya.' A forced, fragile smile. 'And I had a ride out, eh?'

She clung to him, body pressed tight upon the muscle and sinew of his angular frame. His hand stroked her hair, let the strands smooth out between his fingers. Eventually he broke away, stood back, cupped her jaw. 'I'm all right now.' He glanced at the Georgian. 'I was never going to be free. Can't you see that?' he said softly.

'If they'd chosen to –'

'No, Vadim, no. It's not a question of choice.'

They stared intently at each other. Finally Vadim stepped aside, stood limply, silently, all energy spent. When he spoke the words barely carried: 'There's always a choice, my friend. For you and me and ... and all of us; there's always a time, to decide.'

Tanya walked quickly to the window to hide her tears. Desolation stretched before her, an infinity of ruin. To her right, the last remaining facade stood like a raddled face, pockmarked, punctured, in terminal decay; through the glassless windows, she could see the pale wash of sky, like cataracts filming across a hundred eyes. To her left, fencing off the street, was a barrier made from old doors and slats of timber. The narrowing perspective of the crazed, abandoned street slashed through the frozen spillage of masonry and dirt.

Below her were the cars – five of them, dark, anonymous, a grouping of predatory beetles with eyes that dully shone. Beside and in between them, Krotov's men stood patiently to attention, shadows in shadowland.

Three others were waiting outside Vadim's room; the one called Ivanovich shepherded her and Leonid downstairs. She paused at the top of the steps leading down to the street and breathed deeply of the soft night air.

'Some reception,' Leonid said. She felt the grip of his hand on her own.

'Will you forgive me?' she said.

'That's a strange question.'

'I've hardly slept, wondering if it could have been different. It seems ... cruel.'

A wry, gentle smile. 'The cruelty would've been knowing how to stop Monakhov but doing nothing about it.'

She nodded, gnawed her lower lip. 'I can still visit, then.'

'Well, hospitals aren't the best of –'

'You're not going there. The colonel has spoken to someone in the prisons department. They're transferring you.'

'To where?'

'He hasn't said yet.' She looked at him and tried to smile. 'It'll be better. He's going to make sure you're all right.'

He cocked his head to one side. 'You believe him?'

'He's not like ...' She shrugged.

After a while, Leonid said: 'Don't worry too much about Vadim. Yelena will straighten him out.'

The name jarred her; she opened her mouth to speak but said nothing, fearing a tremor in her voice might betray her.

Ivanovich squeezed his bulky frame between them and halted midway down the steps. 'Gozphoza? If you'll come with me ...'

'Please ... I'd like to ride with my friend.'

Ivanovich considered the request, then said: 'Very well.' He gave an unexpectedly rueful smile. 'You can both show me the way.'

Leonid frowned. 'You're not from Leningrad?'

'No, comrade, we're not from Leningrad.'

They heard footsteps behind them and turned to watch the others crowding out: Krotov, Monakhov, the two escorts. Despite herself, her gaze locked onto Monakhov. So still, so silent. She had not known what to expect of this night, but there should at least have been some element of confrontation after Krotov's arrival, some protest or denial. Instead it was as though Monakhov had withdrawn into himself. Mannequin-stiff and golden-eyed, he stood motionless at the top of the steps; the aspect was of machine, not man, the impression of circuits temporarily switched off while others continued to compute, calculate.

'Come on, Leonid,' she said.

They followed Ivanovich to the Volga saloon. As the driver opened the door, Tanya paused this last time to look back across the ruined street to the crumbling house and the fractured steps and Monakhov and Krotov together on the sidewalk, approaching the nearest car. And then the quiet finality of the scene was disturbed by a sudden clatter in the doorway as a figure appeared, arms outstretched.

'Vadim!'

Her scream tore through the silence as white fire stabbed from his

245

hands two-fisted around the gun. Then his arms convulsed from the recoil before the searing brightness and noise split the air again and Krotov threw himself sideways as Monakhov, in mid-stride, was punched, lifted, hammered against the car.

Vadim was still there on the topmost step, a cloud of gunsmoke writhing around him. Then the gun flashed a third time and Monakhov toppled like a stricken marionette. He lay silent and unmoving, the crazed lenses spinning golden webs upon the rigid face.

A cannonade of gunfire erupted then, and the doorway fragmented and Vadim fetched up hard against the woodwork and shuffled and slid and sprawled and finally was stilled.

Tanya made the steps without consciousness of flight, raced up to the doorway and threw herself down beside him.

The light in his proud eyes was waning, receding.

She felt a breathless presence abruptly at her side – Krotov's face, mouth working but she heard no words, only the thick, painful rasping that struggled from the Georgian's lips.

'Vadim,' she said.

Lips parting, half snarl, half smile, a whisper travelling back from a faraway place. 'Kotik.'

Her hair tumbled forward as she pressed her face against his, her arms around him, cradling, holding, keeping him, shielding him, covering him, staying him.

Resistance beneath her, some last monumental effort of will – she sensed it, eased back, stared deep into his face, his eyes, and the light that dwindled even as he spoke.

'I ... decided ...'

'Shhh, it's all right, all right.'

'Yelena and –'

The shudder passed through him and into her and she lifted him then as a mother nurses a child and meaningless words fell softly upon him as she gently rocked back and forth, back and forth.

Krotov coughed. 'He's gone.'

Back and forth, back and forth.

'Gozphoza ... ' Krotov looked away, got up slowly. The trembling at the back of his legs was so violent that he had to struggle to stay erect.

'Please,' he said, and again, 'please ...'

No movement, no response. It was as though she was pinioned there in the pale light.

Then carefully, haltingly, she lowered his body to the ground. Her fingers reached out and closed his eyes. She stood up, turned and faced the street.

'It didn't have to be,' she said.

'Gozphoza?'

She rounded on him with sudden savagery: 'There was no need!'

He stood helplessly before her fury, unable to defend himself with even the simplest of denials.

Moments elapsed one by one, then at last she felt the rage beginning to fade, and she breathed in and out in a steadying tempo and the flat dull words were finally no more than a whisper.

'I trusted you.'

The Zil drew up then.

The door opened even as the limousine halted short of the line of cars, and the silver-haired figure of Melnikov emerged.

'Tanya.' He held out his arms in beckoning embrace; his voice was low, husky.

His gaze flitted this way and that, taking in the silent figures and frozen gestures, the parked cars striped with pallid light, the debris and destruction fanning out either side. She stepped into the middle of the road and stared at him without speaking.

'Tanya . . .' He let his arms collapse like a scarecrow wearied of its trade.

'What do you want?'

'Come home.'

No indication that she had even heard him.

'It's over, Tanya.'

Too elegant, she decided – the coat, the shoes, the proud head of hair – he was too richly costumed for this particular stage. She jerked her head like a dog shedding water, tried to focus herself and confront the demands of the moment. Melnikov took a step towards her, halted awkwardly, impotently. 'I came for you.'

She lowered her gaze, concentrated on the broken ground at her feet, and then, with quickening pace, turned away from him, walked briskly to Ivanovich's car, to where Leonid still stood.

'You mustn't,' Leonid said. His face was white, spectral, seemed to hang eerily in her vision. She stared fixedly at him, hands reaching behind her for the doorcatch.

'No,' he said, but the door was open now, and she was standing aside, and the driver had started the Volga's engine and Ivanovich was coming towards them.

'No,' he said again, but it was impossible to resist her and he clambered into the back seat.

She settled beside him. He studied her, the skein of hair, the dirt-streaked face, the crumpled coat raggedly parted, the dress with its dark stains. Everything seemed wrong, somehow; the impression was of a refugee running from war.

She said, quietly: 'I'll wait for you.' She wasn't looking at him, preferring instead to concentrate on the windshield and the empty vista beyond. He fumbled for words, couldn't find them.

Ivanovich slid into the front passenger seat and closed the door.

'It can't be like this,' Leonid said. 'You can't just ... leave.'

'I'll sort it out.' She was calm, impassive.

'But what about your husband? Your daughter?'

'Yevgeni will be all right. And my father – for the time being he can take care of Katerina –'

'No, Tanya! No! You haven't thought it through!'

She turned to him, speaking even more softly than before: 'You don't know what I've thought.'

He made a final attempt, sensing its futility before the sentence was half complete: 'Where will you go? What will you do?'

'Wherever they take you, I'll be near. And I'll find others, others who're like us.'

He sighed gently, regretfully. 'You're ... you're too naive.'

'Isn't that how we have to be?' She slumped back in the seat. 'Drive,' she said.

The Volga moved off, bumping and jarring across the camber, nosing carefully past the gleaming length of the Zil.

The elegant silver-haired man seemed to slip slowly by, face taut, mouth open, and then was gone.

She turned to look back at the scene, but already it was receding, and the dwindling figures were no more than shadows under the pale glare of the white Leningrad sky.

PART VI

PART VI

CHAPTER
EIGHTEEN

TILGARSLEY
OXFORDSHIRE

'Where you staying?' Leech asked.

'Grange Hotel.'

'Comfortable?'

'It's okay.' Gulliver gave up on the view from the window and walked slowly back into the centre of the room. He halted by the fireplace, yawning. The big house seemed steeped in a sort of pervasive somnolence that embraced whoever inhabited it. 'Leech,' he said. 'I didn't ask to come back.'

'It doesn't matter.' The younger man finished his coffee, set the cup and saucer down on the table. 'I don't mind.'

'I do, though.'

'Joint ops.' Leech shrugged. 'What's mine is yours.'

'So how is he?'

'Asleep. He landed at Lakenheath at two o'clock this morning.'

'And Frances Wycliffe?'

'She flew in the day before yesterday. They're all coming home to roost.'

Gulliver gazed thoughtfully at him. 'I take it there are no problems.'

'Minor one, yesterday – nothing to worry about, though.' Leech paused. 'She doesn't understand about protective surveillance, got herself in a right state.'

'That's all we need.'

'No, it's all okay. Medical forewarned us. She's being monitored as well as Asanov. Everything's recorded, transcribed, analysed. We need advance warnings more than ever now.'

'Is he showing signs of turning into a flake?'

'He's holding up very well – considering.'

An ornate telephone suddenly jangled. Leech strode briskly to the corner table. He listened for a few moments, then returned the receiver to its elaborate stand. 'Seems we have a visitor,' he said, 'the lady herself.'

'She's here?'

'She just turned off the M4, heading north.' He massaged his jaw. 'Funny. She never rang through or anything.'

Gulliver shrugged. 'Come to wake our Sleeping Beauty, I expect.'

She turned too quickly into the driveway and almost lost control on the gravel – tyres spinning, chippings spraying out over the lawn. She braked hard and the Capri went into a slide, leaving dark furrows in its wake.

She clambered out as Leech arrived on the doorstep. 'Where is he?'

'Doctor Wycliffe?' Alarm and bewilderment corrugated his features.

'Damn it, where is he?'

'Piotr?'

'Gulliver – has he arrived yet?'

'Yes, but ...' Leech gestured helplessly. 'What's the matter? What's happened?'

She went briskly up the steps and brushed past him into the hallway. He followed her in. 'Just a minute! What the hell d'you –'

She went straight to the drawing-room door and pushed it open. Her impetus carried her on into the middle of the room.

'Mr Gulliver ...'

He pushed himself out of the chair and stared blankly at her.

Behind her, Leech said: 'What in the name of Christ is going on?'

'I was just about to ask the same question.' Gulliver continued to stare at her.

She took a step forward, stopped a few paces from him. 'You ... bastard!'

His mouth worked pointlessly, lips parting, closing. Finally he managed to say: 'What is this? What're you talking about?'

'Moscow. It was you, wasn't it? You killed Dmitri Asanov.'

Birdsong sounded from beyond the window; a fleece of cloud drifted above dark treetops. Leech shook his head, turned from the glass and eased himself into an armchair.

She was still in the middle of the room. Gulliver said slowly, deliberately: 'I'll say it again, Doctor Wycliffe. I didn't kill anyone.'

'You knew.'

'So maybe I knew. That doesn't mean I had anything to do with it.'

She turned to Leech. 'Did you know, too?'

He nodded.

'And Owen?'

'No.'

'He went out there.'

'Not then, not last August.' Words of denial followed haltingly: 'It wasn't our operation. We weren't involved.'

'We weren't involved. I see.'

Gulliver sighed. 'How did you find out?'

'The record – the one he brought with him, the one Dmitri was given.'

'Either I'm not following this properly or –'

'Piotr told me that Dmitri had a favourite piece of music; we were talking, I can't remember how it cropped up ... *Dark Side of the Moon* it was called. He'd always wanted a decent copy, Dmitri – a decent recording. Even Piotr had tried but ...' She paused. 'And then, by a complete coincidence, a total stranger made a present of it that day in the park.' A brief, bitter smile. 'Except it wasn't a coincidence, was it?'

Gulliver didn't respond.

'No,' she resumed, 'it wasn't a coincidence at all. Somehow someone knew every last detail, every last jot of personal information about Dmitri Asanov. Why? Well, there's only one reason I can think of: his father, Piotr Asanov. Which meant that someone also knew every last little detail about him, too.'

She took a deep breath, let go slowly, then moved across to the sofa and sat down. 'Someone,' she repeated, 'someone knew. But who? Who, Mr Gulliver? Who was taking that sort of interest at that time? The Soviets? Hardly. They were all set to exile Piotr to Leningrad – he was an embarrassment, an expensive failure. So, if it wasn't them, then ...' The cold smile returned.

Gulliver lit a cigarette, took time out to inspect it very thoroughly. Finally: 'That it?'

'No. There was Piotr's file, the dossier. I could understand why some of the technical data was blanked out, the detailed references to his work. I mean, you were using it to brief other people, weren't you?'

'Government advisers,' Gulliver said, 'mine and yours.'

'Yes. That's what I meant, that I could understand the security considerations. What I couldn't fathom was why Dmitri's death was treated in such a cavalier fashion. "Killed in a shooting accident in Moscow" is all it says. Something as major as that, probably the real reason why Piotr went off the rails last year – but that's the only reference to it.'

'So?'

She shifted position, stared at Leech. 'When you gave me the file, and I read that part, I asked you what it meant. All you said was something like – Oh, what a tragedy, Doctor Wycliffe. Such a *terrible* accident. Remember?'

Leech nodded.

'Well, I don't remember,' Gulliver said.

'It was before you came on the scene,' said Leech tightly.

'Christ Almighty, it wasn't supposed to say anything!'

'Oh? So what would've happened if she'd steamed in that first morning without knowing? Hello, how are you, how're the folks back home? That'd really have made his day, wouldn't it? Done his peace of mind no end of good.' Leech was half-way out of the chair, seemingly propelled by the sudden explosion of anger. 'She had to be told! We had no choice!'

Gulliver breathed heavily. 'Priceless, Leech, just priceless.'

Leech hauled himself upright. 'The only thing that's priceless round here is you! As a textbook example of how not to do the job ...' He broke off, inarticulate with fury, then turned to her. 'Don't ever let 'em tell you that he and I are on the same side. He's a bigger threat than the bloody Kremlin!'

The door slammed shut behind him.

Gulliver dragged deep on the cigarette, stared fixedly at the ceiling cornice. Eventually: 'Anything else, Doctor Wycliffe?'

'No.'

'You mean you just looked at a line in a dossier and thought, Ah, it's them damn Yankees again.'

'Don't be so stupid!'

He continued to gaze into the air, impervious to the scorn in her voice. 'Every time ... Every time I have to deal with you people, I get the impression ...' He sighed.

'Oh for God's sake, Gulliver.' Frances felt weary with exasperation; the sentence barely carried across the room.

He stubbed out the cigarette and nodded slowly as though concluding some private, inward debate. 'What exactly did Leech tell you?'

'I've just been through all that.'

'There must've been something more.'

'He said it was an accident, I've told you. And then he said he hadn't time to go into the details, and they weren't relevant anyway. The main thing was to stay off the subject, it would only distress Doctor Asanov and that was the last thing any of us wanted.'

'But you were curious, surely.'

'I've been curious about a lot of things, Gulliver. That was only the first. After that I got to thinking about your involvement, because that didn't make any sense, either. Your people didn't get Piotr out, didn't organise it, didn't do anything. You had no claim to him ... unless it was a prior one.'

He considered her for a few moments. 'Anything else?'

'Yes. He was always going to have to work with you – meet you, be with your people. Yet you stayed out of the way. You came to England because of him but refused to go anywhere near.' She paused. 'What were you afraid of? Did you think he suspected?'

'It seemed best to get the debriefing over.'

'In case I picked up on anything?'

'Yes.'

'Because he'd confide in me?'

'Yes.'

She held his gaze through the intensity of the silence, then looked away and said quietly, evenly: 'You used me.'

'You're no different to anyone else,' Gulliver said.

Leech paced impotently in the hallway, almost collided with Hawkins as he spun around to retrace his angry path.

'Martin?' Hawkins' boyish features tightened with concern. 'What's going on?'

'Nothing.'

'Doesn't sound like it.'

Leech stopped. 'Don't say you can hear it all over the bloody house.'

'No, it's just the tape, I was –'

'Tape? You switched on the *tape*?'

'Well, she is here, and he'll be coming down soon, and there is this thing about monitoring and ... Well, I happened to slip on the headset – just to check.'

'Key.' Leech held out his hand.

'But it's back on VA, it'll switch off soon as they –'

'You think we want that down for posterity? Christ above, Neil!'

Hawkins thrust the key into Leech's extended palm. 'You never heard anything, Neil. You never heard a single word, all right?'

'If you say so.' The words were delivered with obvious reluctance. Hawkins gazed uncertainly at him.

Leech turned and sprinted up the staircase. He strode briskly to the door at the end of the landing. Fingers fumbled with the key, it refused to seat correctly the first time, then he felt the pressure of the tumblers and a voice said: 'Good morning, Mr Leech.'

Hand on doorknob, key in lock, Leech felt trapped like a guilty schoolboy. 'Hello, Doctor Asanov.' He turned slowly, leaned negligently against the door. Asanov stood a few paces distant, hands in the pockets of his dressing gown, bright-eyed and smiling.'It is like being home, Mr Leech.'

'Did you sleep well?'

'Very well. But then, I'd taken enough tranquillisers to stop an ox.'

Leech nodded. 'Sorry about the flight but ...' He tried a smile, wondered if it had managed to surface. 'So. You're awake.'

'Mmm.' Asanov paused. 'Is everything all right?'

'Sorry?'

'You seem ... preoccupied.'

'Me? I ...' He swallowed, started over: 'Everything's fine, absolutely fine.'

'Good.' Asanov smiled broadly. 'So, what's for breakfast?' He set off towards the staircase.

I don't believe this is happening, Leech thought. He drew level with Asanov and said: 'Breakfast is on its way.'

'You are so kind.'

'It had nothing to do with me,' Gulliver said. 'You have to understand that.'

'Try me.'

'A different department started out with it, two maybe three years back. Asanov's name cropped up so they slotted in an AIP – agent in

256

place – to make contact. But despite working in the same establishment, a technical assistant or something, he couldn't get near. So he bided his time, listened to the gossip. Eventually he picked up on the story of Asanov's friend, a Jewish mathematician elsewhere in the same facility. This man wanted to leave, to go to Israel, but his exit visa was blocked. Asanov totally over-reacted – he went straight to the barricades with a crusade that ran all the way to Academy level. Anyone else and they'd never have been so indulgent, but as he seemed to be on the verge of something special – Anyway, he finally overplayed it. Research stalled so the crusade stalled too. His friend got internal exile and Asanov got the hard word. But as he's an obstinate kind of guy that didn't do the slightest bit of good. He was damned if he'd work under duress.'

'Did you approach him then?'

'Yes. The AIP talked about opportunities in the West.'

'America.'

'First phase – you never get into the specifics.'

Like a masque, she thought: strangers in brief partnership, moments shared, identities withheld. 'Go on.'

'Asanov didn't react one way or the other – not hot, not cold. But by now we'd got a better idea of his research programme. We'd been hoping to go in the same direction too, but it was obvious now that we needed Asanov to guide us, otherwise we'd waste years going up blind alleys. The Asanov file had everything in it by that stage: subject, family, associates – every last detail, in the small print. Washington reassessed it and decided to go for Dmitri as a way in.'

She frowned. 'But why?'

'There was some sort of bust-up at Rostov Film, where he worked. Dmitri got mixed up with a gang of change-the-worlders, writers, musicians, reactionaries. The KGB arrested the whole lot – except Dmitri. He was transferred to Moscow instead. Carrot and stick; they'd bounced Asanov and got nowhere, now they were trying the gentle touch through the son.'

'What happened then?'

'Same thing, more or less. Dmitri Asanov wound up with a group not unlike his one-time Rostov friends, plus some students, from Lomosonov. That's how he met his lady friend.'

'Tell me about that day in the park,' Frances said.

Gulliver lit another cigarette. 'There was a scene going – nothing too heavy, but the girl was involved. We had a pusher on tap, tame, eager to please as long as the price was right. We decided to work him. An auxiliary was then brought in to cultivate the girl. Eventually he let slip he knew a source, Mexican gold, quality stuff. Dmitri was still trying to impress the lady at that stage, so he got roped in. He was given the number and told to make the arrangements.'

'But it was a trap,' she said dully. 'How though? Why?'

'Leverage. The intended deal was: You're in trouble, Doctor Asanov, and your son's in trouble, and it's only going to get worse. But we can help both of you.'

'Both? Wouldn't Dmitri have been in prison?'

'Arrested, yes; prison, no. Maybe a couple of days' interrogation, then he'd have been out while they went looking for our auxiliary, who by that time was well away.'

After a few moments Frances said: 'This pusher, what was supposed to happen to him?'

'Nothing. He carried insurance. The fartsovshchiki have a lot of connections; the black economy can't work without them.'

'So he's still in business, then.'

'No, we had to close him out.' Gulliver didn't look at her.

She stood up and walked unsteadily to the window. 'So what went wrong?'

'He'd become a user.'

'And you employed him?' Frances asked disbelievingly.

'Nobody knew. They should have but ... He was high when he arrived at the rendezvous. What happened after that was crazy man's stuff.'

'Why the record?'

'Christ knows. It would be part of his style, largesse, something to show how important he was.'

'I meant, why that particular one? Dmitri's favourite?'

'It must've cropped up.' He paused. 'You tell someone he's going to be pitched into a risk situation with a total stranger, chances are he'll ask what the other party's like.'

Slowly, with mounting incredulity: 'And that led to a discussion about records?'

'No, that led to a discussion about how Dmitri Asanov was the son of a brilliant scientist and how this entrapment was the end phase of a half-million, three-year investment. Jesus Christ! What d'you think they discussed? He probably asked what the kid was like? And our

258

people probably told him he was okay, not a flake or anything. Next question: So what does he do? Answer: He's some sort of musician. Inevitable comment: Anything in particular? I do a neat line in ...' Gulliver shrugged.

'And then someone remembered the small print.' A crooked, sardonic smile. 'My, oh my.'

'It happens.'

'Don't tell me! Don't tell me that any more. I've had enough of your world-weary rationalisation.' She sat down again, body slamming hard against the cushioning. The thudding of a violent pulse seemed to fill the room.

'It was an accident,' Gulliver said quietly.

'Which you contrived.' She gazed unwaveringly at him. 'It might've been better if you'd killed Piotr.'

He waited through the long silence. When she bowed her head, Gulliver said, 'You going to tell him, Doctor Wycliffe?'

No response; she was hunched forward, hands cradling her jaw, just sitting there.

'It wouldn't do any good,' Gulliver said.

'Don't!' One word, jabbing; a haggard, contorted face glared up at him, eyes shining, dark, moist.

The door opened abruptly. 'He'll be down in a minute,' Leech said. 'I tried to insist on breakfast in bed but ...' He glanced from Gulliver to Frances, saw the pain, the anger. 'Great,' he said.

She pushed herself upright and dabbed a handkerchief at her eyes, at the stains and streaks on her cheeks. 'It's all right. I'm going –' a brittle laugh – 'I can hardly see him like this.'

Gulliver stood up. 'I'll drive you.'

'Getting out of the way?' Her voice carried a high note of hysteria. 'Can't face him?'

Gulliver ignored the taunt and turned to Leech. 'Does he know she's here?'

'No.' He paused. 'Doctor Wycliffe. If it makes any difference ... I'm sorry, about what happened.'

She considered him distantly. 'I don't care.' A whisper, no more.

Leech stood aside to let them pass. Like mourners, he thought, just like a pair of mourners.

Gulliver drove steadily, resolutely. The car was unfamiliar and he found driving on the wrong side of the road distinctly unnerving, but it was better than letting her set off alone or stay at the house with Asanov.

Frances attended to her make-up – seemed to go through half a box of Kleenex. She didn't speak all the way to town and even then, when they dropped down into Hammersmith, the words were curt, the directions terse.

He found a meter in a parallel street and walked her to the door. She opened it without comment and left it hanging wide. He stopped, debating whether to follow, and decided he couldn't leave her yet. They got into the lift, crowding together, then out onto the landing. They paused at the door to her flat while she fumbled in her bag. He remembered then, and handed back the keyring. She opened the door and said: 'You'd better come in.' Despite the make-up, her face seemed old and gaunt.

'Coffee?'

'I'll do it.'

'I'm quite capable, thank you.'

He sat in a chair, listening to the sounds. A drawer grated, a cupboard door opened and closed, crockery rattled. He looked around him, absorbing the atmosphere. It felt clinical, cold. There wasn't much personality here, and no femininity at all.

Curious lady, Frances Wycliffe – cool, competent, a beautiful face carried like a mummer's mask. If it hadn't been for the car, he thought ... But the car gave it away, said a free spirit was lurking somewhere. It had gone like a white bullet.

'Sugar's in.'

He took the mug from her. 'Thanks.' He sipped thoughtfully, then placed it on a side table.

She settled on the sofa and watched him for a few moments, then indicated the cigarette box to the left of his coffee. 'Help yourself.'

'I didn't know you ...'

'For guests.'

Sobranies. Of all things, Sobranies. He lit one, savouring the unaccustomed flavour. Finally: 'I said I was sorry.'

'Yes.'

'Truce then?'

260

'Is it as easy as that?' Dark eyes held his, then moved restlessly away. 'I'm ... confused.'

'Understandable.'

'Don't say that. Don't say you know how I feel.'

'You love him?' The words came as a complete surprise – he couldn't comprehend their reason or origin.

'Probably.'

Probably. Just that, nothing else. As cautious as any other scientific evaluation. He stared wonderingly at her.

She gnawed her lower lip. 'I feel sorry for him –' a laugh full of cutting irony – 'is that the basis for a relationship? Tell me. You're the one with the answers.'

'I ... I didn't mean to pry.'

'Why not? It's your job, isn't it?'

'No, it's not my job, Doctor Wycliffe.'

Silence settled briefly. 'He's all alone.'

'Not really. He's with – he's okay now.'

'With friends? Is that what you were going to say?'

'I guess so. He needs us.'

'That's a neat inversion.'

He hesitated, then: 'Can I say something to you?'

'Go ahead.'

'I do know the way you feel.'

Frances' eyes widened and her mouth began to twist, but then she seemed to register something, seemed to identify the intensity in his face.

'I've been around quite a while, Frances. And the older you get the more you come to understand that there's very little that's absolutely good or absolutely bad. Instead, there's necessary evils and politic goodness.'

'Everybody has an angle? I have read Chandler.'

'Then try thinking instead of reading. Individuals don't have angles. I'm talking corporate: big business, commerce, the pragmatism of State.'

She cocked her head to one side and stared thoughtfully at him.

'You're very bright, Frances.' For the first time he realised he was using her Christian name. It hardly seemed to matter. 'But you misunderstood. You figured there was something out of kilter. Well, there was. But it wasn't a case of the good guys versus the bad, because there aren't any bad guys – just people, trying to do a job.'

261

'How can you say that, knowing what happened?'

'Because it's the truth. There was a non-combat fatality. Dmitri Asanov died because a component failed to perform the way it should. His dying didn't help us. It sent his father to the far corners of hell and half the worry of this job has been if he's still there.' He paused. 'We were trying to help.'

'Yourselves.'

'Cause and effect don't much matter when they come out the same.'

She sat erect again, swept the hair from her face. 'I don't know any more.'

'Seriously, d'you really believe Asanov was better off in Russia?'

'He was home!'

'Home's a state of mind. And his was long gone.'

She sipped her coffee. 'I don't understand you, Gulliver. I don't understand at all.'

'I'm not complicated.'

'A long time ago I asked what was your philosophy. You said you'd tell me one day.'

He shrugged. 'I exist. That's philosophy enough.'

'Not much of an answer.'

'The longer the answer, the stronger the voice has to be. Come the day you have the ultimate answer, you'll want to lead all the rest who haven't. They'll think you're taking them somewhere better. They won't realise they're merely loudspeakers, full of sounds that aren't their own.'

'You don't much care for your fellow man, do you, Gulliver?'

'No.'

'Why not?'

'I just said. They're so easily led – fattened up and herded along. They don't think, they just accept.' He shook his head. 'Sheep.'

'What does that make you, then? One of the butchers?'

'I'm supposed to be one of the shepherds.'

'Then we've not much chance, have we?'

The silence returned. She finished her coffee, then said: 'I won't tell him.'

'It's for his own good.'

'Of course it is. He's the luckiest man alive.' She paused. 'One last question. Is everyone ... malleable?'

'Yes.'

'You don't even have to stop to think, do you?' Her gaze slowly lowered. 'He was manipulated, Gulliver. Given a false choice – do this, do that, stay, go. Options. Except there weren't any.'

'It was his decision. He volunteered.'

'You believe that? Come on, look at me. Is that what you really believe?'

He breathed deep, exhaled slowly.

'No.'

TILGARSLEY
OXFORDSHIRE

Piotr strolled across the gravel and the lawns, made his way around the west corner of the house to where a patio gave off from the dining room. A white table and four white chairs beckoned. He sat down, looked beyond the miniature firs and troughs of heathers to the inviting expanse of water. They'd taken the covers off, cleaned it all out. He wondered why.

He sat for a while, watching the waters capturing the sun, playing and teasing, and then he set off again, going down from the terrace and past the rhododendron and azaleas, down into the gardens where they'd once walked, long ago. He stood in thoughtful silence, listening to the rustle of leaves, the distant chatter of the birds.

Footsteps rang out on the paving; he turned to see Hawkins loping towards him. His shirt was open and his sleeves rolled up; perspiration gleamed on his chest.

'Ah, there you are.' Hawkins smiled. 'Lunchtime. Want to eat in or out?'

'Whatever's easiest.' He yawned. 'Don't make a fuss on my behalf, Neil. I don't feel very hungry in this heat.'

'Same here.'

Hawkins lingered a few moments longer, then smiled again and walked back up the path.

Piotr watched the receding figure, then slowly followed. He reached the garden door and stepped into the coolness of a small corridor leading into the hall.

Everything was very quiet, very still. He yawned, feeling as though his limbs were draped in a warm languor. He found himself in the drawing room, moving idly, without purpose. The room seemed drenched in light. Unthinkingly, he crossed to the piano and pulled out the stool. He sat and contemplated the gleaming keys. Then his fingers settled gently, seemed to be drawn into the first configuration.

B major – white and black mingling together and the bass tracking gently – F sharp, E flat, A flat minor – treble now a gentle glissando trickling down through the octaves – then E major resolving into F sharp then returning to B major; and repeat and retard and into bridge and reprise and end.

'That's nice,' Hawkins said.

Asanov gave an embarrassed smile. 'I don't play well.'

'No? Pair of candles and Liberace'd better watch out.' Hawkins grinned. 'What is it, that piece?'

'You wouldn't have heard of it.'

'In that case, play it again, Sam.' He paused. 'What I really came in for was to ask if sandwiches would be all right. The larder's bare, unfortunately – no Owen.'

'Sandwiches will be fine.' He eased off the stool. 'How is Owen?'

'Doing okay.'

'He's back home?'

'Yes, convalescing.'

Asanov nodded. 'You will be seeing him?'

'I was going this weekend.'

'Good. I've bought something, for the children.' He walked to the centre of the room, then stopped. 'Where is everyone, Neil?'

'London.' Smoothly, no trace of hesitation.

'But Mr Leech was here –'

'He had to dash off for a last-minute conference. But don't worry, everything's all right.'

'And Frances? Doctor Wycliffe?'

'She's in London too.'

'She'll be coming today?'

'Maybe. Tomorrow, certainly.'

'I thought she might be –'

'Better go make those sandwiches, okay?'

Asanov nodded. 'All right. And I'll go and get those things for Owen's children, while I remember.'

Hawkins paused at the door. 'You and Owen – you've become ... close, haven't you?'

'I think I'm close to all of you. Friends, eh, Neil?'

'Yes,' Hawkins said. 'Friends.'

Piotr laid his suitcase on the bed and went through the contents. Sheer idleness, he thought, not to have unpacked yet. Shirts, jacket, pair of trousers, socks and underclothes – not much, really, to show for all the years. He shook his head. Travelling light, Piotr, he said to himself.

He fumbled with the small paper packages. Two wristwatches bought in California, one for each of Owen's children. Gulliver had done the shopping. A few dollars, the budget can stand it, he'd said. But Piotr had insisted on paying the American anyway, even though every last cent in his pocket had come from Gulliver in the first place.

Gulliver. Would he be coming over, for the test? He smiled a small private smile. The test. No conflict of loyalties, no doubts about the purpose or the setting – a complete absence of feeling now the bridge was finally crossed from one side to the other.

He closed the suitcase and carefully carried the two little packages out to the landing. He paused at the head of the stairs and looked down at the broad wash of carpeting, the graceful fall of the polished balustrade, the pattern of floor tiles gleaming around the skirting of the hallway.

I came as a pauper but I'm treated like a czar, he thought.

Click.

He frowned. Stood motionless, attuning to the noise.

Click-click.

Piotr turned towards the sound, a frown beginning to cloud his face.

Click.

He opened his mouth to summon Hawkins, then abandoned the notion. Quietly, purposefully, pulse quickening to the call of a ripening curiosity, he continued along the landing to the door at the far end.

Silence, unruffled and impenetrable.

He leaned against the door, pressed his ear to the woodwork and heard a distant squeaking, as of a mouse in a cage. He knelt down and placed the packages on the carpet. His fingers reached out to test the handle. The door swung slowly open.

He was in a rear bedroom with a view of the garden and the countryside beyond, but the furnishings were entirely unexpected –

265

nothing of any solace to any overnight guest.

Shelving ran around the walls, plywood struts and laminate facings supported ranks of files, folders and a jumble of telephone directories. A kettle and upturned mugs stood on a tray near the washbasin. In the middle of the room were two large trestle tables and two collapsible chairs and two tape machines. They lay flat on the coarse timber, side by side. Lights glowed in both but only the right-hand deck was active, the reels spinning in high-speed rewind. The machine must therefore be on automatic, the tape rewinding after reaching the end.

Click.

The spinning stopped. He bent forward. The tape had only rewound part distance. He identified the small counter, now displaying a series of number nines. Evidently it had overshot the re-set mechanism, defeating the inbuilt memory.

He hesitated, then reached for a set of headphones lying to his left. He grasped the jack plug, located it in the socket, then pressed the playback key. Reels turned in rhythmic accord, at some point in each revolution triggering the slightest of sounds – a high-pitched tell-tale sign of misalignment, like the squeaking of a mouse trapped in a cage.

He put on the headphones and adjusted the ear-pieces whilst continuing to stare in mute fascination at the mesmeric motion of the spools.

Mr Gulliver ... Piotr heard a crackling and rustling of fabric, a distorted sibilance created by the sensitivity of the pick-up. A woman's voice, familiar yet alien, speaking in a tone of exaggerated hostility; her respiration was painfully harsh. Then another voice: *What in the name of Christ is going on?*

The reels slowly turned.

Hawkins met Leech in the hall. 'You didn't have to rush back.'

'I can't sit around moping in the pub forever.'

'Trouble is, Martin, I told him you'd gone to London.' He shrugged. 'Well, I had to think of something.'

'Better tell him I changed my mind then. If he sees me now, he'll know I couldn't have made it there and back.'

'Doesn't matter,' Hawkins said. 'He's asleep again. Had his sandwiches, then went back up to bed.'

'Is he all right?'

'Well ...' Hawkins considered. 'He seemed bright enough to

begin with. Then he went kind of ... quiet.'

Leech nodded. 'He has a lot on his mind.'

They went into the drawing room. Leech flopped into a chair and didn't speak again. Hawkins wandered aimlessly around, then finally settled on the sofa. 'He's brought some presents back, from America.'

'Asanov?'

'Yes. For Owen's kids. Nice of him, wasn't it?'

Leech sighed. 'He's too nice. That's what's wrong with this bloody operation. He's like a big soft dog that – oh, Christ ...'

'What's the matter?'

'The tape's running.'

Hawkins frowned. 'I thought you'd turned it off?'

'I was going to, only ... Never mind.' He glared irritably. 'If you'd never switched the sodding thing on then –'

Hawkins stood up. 'I'll go turn it off.'

'No. I'll do it. You make the coffee.'

He missed the lock at the first attempt – a third of a bottle of gin was not a recipe for healthy co-ordination. At the second attempt, the key drove home. He turned it, felt an unexpected resistance, sighed in noisy exasperation, then tried again, wrist straining over to the left. Turn, you bastard, turn. He wrenched the key furiously this way and that, heard the tumblers click and catch, then free again. He moved into the room and closed the door softly, lest Asanov be disturbed.

He sat down at the table and gazed at the two machines. He'd have to erase that damn tape. The way things were acting up today, he'd probably pick the wrong one. Nothing going right, he thought, even locked doors behaving as though they were open all the time.

The hall clock was chiming the hour when Gulliver returned. He watched the Granada swing away then went into the drawing room to discover Leech half asleep, arms folded across chest, legs stretched out with feet resting on a leather stool. He nudged it with his foot and said: 'Where's Asanov?'

Leech opened one eye. 'He's resting. So am I.'

'Maybe you should try it on a permanent basis.' Gulliver sat down and fished a cigarette from the pack.

Leech shuffled upright. 'How is she?'

'Just dandy.'

'Meaning?'

'It's the happiest day of her life.'

'Yes, well, it ranks pretty high in mine, too.' He paused. 'Gulliver, about this morning ...'

'What about it?'

'No point in going to war over it.'

Gulliver paused in the act of lighting up and stared thoughtfully at his hand, at the small bright flame seeming to issue out of his fingers.

Leech waited for a little while longer, then looked away. 'She going to tell him?'

'I don't think so.'

'Oh.'

'She was talking,' Gulliver said slowly, 'about the test.'

'So's everyone else. It's been scheduled now.'

'When?'

'Saturday the ninth or Sunday the tenth. Depends on the target.'

'And what happens after?'

'Good question.' Leech fingered his jaw. 'We certainly can't stay here. They've sold it to the DHSS. They want it as a residential centre for higher management training. PSA were up yesterday sorting out the swimming pool.'

'What do they need a pool for?'

'They're very big fish.' Leech got up. 'I'll go check on Sleeping Beauty.'

Gulliver eased back into the cushioning and toyed with the idea of purloining Leech's foot stool. There were times, he decided, when you needed to pull the covers over your head and wait for the new day to dawn.

Leech cut abruptly into his reverie. 'Where's Neil?'

'I don't know. Why?'

'Sleeping Beauty – he's woken up.'

'Asanov?' Gulliver straightened up. 'Maybe he's gone for a walk.'

'Neil should've said, then.' Leech sighed. 'I don't know what's the matter with today.'

'Perhaps it changed sides.'

Leech frowned, then walked out again.

A bright star of ash caught the back of Gulliver's hand. He grimaced, moved across to the fireplace and flicked the cigarette stub into the hearth.

Leech reappeared. 'I've found Neil.' Irritation had yielded to anxiety in his voice. 'He thought Asanov was asleep, too.'

Gulliver gnawed his lower lip. Eventually: 'Let's go look, then.'

They walked out into the sunshine, clattered down the steps, then briskly across the gravel, footfalls crunching on small hard flints. The patio was deserted, the white table and three white chairs and the empty expanse of the pool making a tableau from which something seemed to be missing. Gulliver glanced around. Bushes and blossom fenced in the patio area from the rest of the grounds. He set off again, angling left past the dying candles of the azalea.

He saw Hawkins then, face entirely drained of colour, lips parted, trembling; he seemed to be having difficulty breathing. Gulliver pushed past him into a rectangle of cropped grass, stone paving along its borders, dividing line of bushes merging with the hawthorn barrier at the bottom, the right-hand quarter lost within the tree boundary of oak and birch marching back towards the house. There was something in the far corner, something pale.

He walked towards it, unaware of motion or thought, feeling oddly displaced. The pale object was a white patio chair, lying on its side.

He looked up then, and saw every detail of the high pierced canopy – the branches and leaves, the depth of shadow and the erratic flash of sky, the ramshackle fabric of a long-abandoned birds' nest, the unquiet face slowly turning.

'What time is it?' Leech asked.

'Twelve after six.'

'God.' He hunched forward and massaged the nape of his neck. He glanced at Gulliver, saw his grey pallor and the spreading stain of overnight stubble, then he went to the table, lifted the lid of the coffee pot and peered in. Empty. He watched the lid clacking up and down, up and down, as though controlled by fingers other than his.

After a while Leech said: 'You're certain we haven't missed anything?'

One eye opened. 'We've been looking for thirteen hours. I'm certain.'

Leech nodded slowly, then trailed wearily back to the sofa. 'No note, though.' Disbelief was still there, though its intensity had dwindled with repetition. 'No note.'

'Maybe he'd nothing to say.'

'At the risk of seeming flippant, he obviously had something on his mind.'

'So he'd no one to say it to.'

'What're we doing here, then?'

Gulliver sat up, stifling a yawn. 'The friends of Piotr Asanov,' he said.

'Doctor Wycliffe,' Leech said, 'he could've confided in her.'

'He never got to see her.'

'But what if she telephoned, if she –'

'What if she, what if he, what if, what if . . . Christ, Leech, let it drop, eh? We've been over it time and time again. I'm tired, I'm aching, and I'm sick of hearing it. When's Neil Hawkins due back?'

'Soon. When the report's ready.'

'I can't wait much longer.' He paused. 'Someone's got to tell Frances.'

'You?'

'Unless you want the job.'

Leech shook his head. 'No.'

'Then I guess I just got conscripted.'

'What'll you say to her?' Leech asked quietly.

'Just leave it to me, okay?'

'We'll have to match up.'

'Oh, I know that. Still, we've had plenty of practice – it's our job, it's what we do. Right?'

He closed his eyes when Leech didn't respond, heard the distant irrelevance of birdsong beyond the window. Dawn, he thought. Dawn. He clung to the word as though it was a raft, clung to it and stayed with it and drifted with it into sleep.

PATHOLOGY REPORT

NAME: ....N/A............ CHARACTERISTICS: Caucasian........

AGE: ......51............. SEX: ......Male...............

HEIGHT: ....5,10........... WEIGHT: ......128.............

SUMMARY OF FINDINGS:

(1) Marked depression around neck. Suspension point approximately one and one-half inches in front of angle of lower jaw bone.

270

(2)   Vital local changes and tissue damage as consequence of constriction.
(3)   Spinal fracture with one and one three-quarter inch gap and transverse separation of central cord.
(4)   Fracture, both hyoid wings and thyroid cartilage, left wing.
(5)   Fracture, larynx.

CAUSE OF DEATH:

Injuries to central nervous system and spinal column/cord consequent upon hanging.

DATE/TIME . . . . July 1st/0345 Hrs

LONDON

They drifted on an oil-smooth river coursing down to the sea, warehouses and wharves sliding slowly by, silhouettes cut into the pale night sky. Lighters murmured at their moorings, hawsers creaked. Now and then they caught glimpses of a hostile shore, of stooped stalks of streetlamps sprouting up from barren ground.

Owen Smith tightened his grip on the bow rail and half turned to look astern. Behind them, and receding, rose the domino towers of the city; coloured smears of traffic ran in slow tracery over the silent bridges. From one side to the other, he thought, crossing over.

Hawkins squeezed past him, stepping cautiously, uncertain of the decking beneath his feet. He glanced questioningly at Smith, but his gaze had travelled forward once more, beyond the escort launch, and he remained unmoving, unspeaking, staring at the herringbone pathway of the Thames tidal race, the ribs of water in arrowhead corrugation. The river wind chafed at his face, and with gratitude he blamed it for the moisture in his eyes.

The engines were dying – a brief reprise, then silent. The only sound was the slap of water against the boat's flanks.

Crossing over, Smith thought – and now this: a ceremony upon dark waters, strange, secret, surreal. A funeral for one who thought himself amongst friends.

The noise of the canister unscrewing was very loud. Hawkins held the lower half at arm's length, then inverted it, emptied it with a quick abrupt shaking of the hand, as though anxious to be done with the task. He screwed the canister together again, then relaxed his grip. It slipped from sight. The splash was the

271

loudest and the quietest of sounds.

They sensed movement behind them, turned, and found themselves staring into the faint luminosity of her face.

'Frances?'

'It's all right, Owen.'

The wreath rested indistinctly on her palms. Smith tasted the unexpected fragrance as the salt tang yielded to the flowers.

She stepped between them and braced herself against the rail. A second's hesitation, a blur of motion, and then her hands were empty and it was spinning in and out of the moonlight, going down into the dark. The sound of it falling to the water was soft, like the sibilance of a farewell kiss.

She turned away and, with a slight nod of acknowledgment, let Gulliver assist her down the short flight of steps into the cabin.

The engines restarted and water churned and foamed and the ripples travelled outwards to lap against the river banks. They passed the escort launch standing off, and then heeled around in a tight juddering turn and headed back along the Thames.

The cars sped along the Embankment, then turned north towards the West End. For a while she looked into the brightness of the restaurants and theatres, then lowered her gaze. 'Owen?'

'Yes?'

'It was a beautiful gesture. Thank you. All of you.'

Smith continued to stare ahead, beyond the driver's shoulders, through a windshield striped with the myriad reflections of passing lights. 'He brought the kids some presents. He didn't have to do that,' he said softly.

'It was his way,' Frances said.

'Yes, his way.' Weariness broke through, making his voice leaden. 'So, that's it.'

'Not quite. There's still the test.'

'You're going?'

'All this – it mustn't have been for nothing.'

Smith opened his mouth to speak, then reconsidered. 'Martin said it was a heart attack,' he said finally.

'He'd been through too much.' She hesitated. 'Leech told me he was asleep, it happened while he was asleep. He wouldn't have known anything about it.'

'Maybe that's the best way,' Smith said, 'not knowing.'

272

The lead car was turning left into a familiar street; they followed it and began to slow down. 'Home again,' Frances said.

'You'll be all right?'

'Hey, don't worry about me. You want to worry about yourself.'

'I'm okay.' A faint, sad smile. 'I'm going up to the house on Sunday. There's the clearing away to do.'

'I can't see you clearing anything away.'

'Supervising.' He paused. 'I promised the kids I'd show them where Dad used to live.'

The car stopped. Smith reached for her hand and squeezed it. 'Well, see you, Frances.'

'See you, Owen.' She kissed his cheek, then stepped out, only to pause in the act of closing the door.

'I'll always be grateful to you.'

'I didn't do anything, Frances.'

'You were his friend.'

She straightened up and walked slowly across the pavement. The car's indicators were flashing, bathing her in an erratic wash of amber light. Gulliver clambered out of the third car and came towards her. 'So,' he said.

'I hear you're not staying.' She smiled politely.

'There's no need, now.'

She extended her hand. 'Goodbye then, John.'

'Goodbye, Frances.'

His grip was unexpectedly gentle. He turned and retraced his steps.

She did not watch them depart, but instead crossed the deserted lobby, took the lift to the fourth floor, gained the sanctuary of her flat and closed the door. She leaned against it.

'Piotr.'

The wreath bobbed gently near the banking, made slow pirouettes beside the reeds. Then it responded to the tug of the tidal race, went dipping and cresting and riding the swell, moving on into the moonlight's silver gleam. Reeds like straws were borne alongside, and now a solitary rose broke free of the rest.

It surged and danced and swirled away, carried on the wide river towards the wider sea.

CHAPTER
NINETEEN

EAST ATLANTIC OCEAN

He sat at the chart-table, the seat of his chair cranked high, pen in one hand, glass of mineral water in the other, staring down at the litter of notepaper – pages begun but never finished, words that marched resolutely then stumbled and fell.

He took another sip from the glass and slowly shook his head. A futile exercise, this; he couldn't very well mail it and he certainly couldn't transmit it, so all he was doing was agonising over words that wouldn't hold together, like an actor who'd forgotten his lines.

Dearest Tanya: no, try again. *Darling Tanya*: false, too effusive. *Dear Tanya*: too remote – we're husband and wife, not mere acquaintances. *Tanya*.

He picked up a discarded page and read it once again. *There are so many things I need to say to you I don't know how to begin. I cannot phone you or be with you but you and Katerina are always in my thoughts. You have no idea how I miss you both. I keep remembering all the things we've done together, only the other day I was thinking about all the good times, you and I and then the three of us. We haven't lost those times, have we? They haven't gone. There's no reason why they should.*

His fist balled the paper into a hard wad, then dropped it to the floor. He started over, the pen moving slowly, almost warily, as though endeavouring to corner a quarry both elusive and insubstantial. Until now he had not realised that language was a vehicle requiring both guidance and command; it carried you on a journey, it mapped the route and dictated it. You began at the beginning and the words swept you onwards, and what they said defined both passage and destination.

After a while, he looked at what he'd written.

Tanya, I'm not very good with words, as you know. I don't even know why I'm writing this. I could mail it from Murmansk when we get back, we are always there a couple of days for debriefing, winding down, as you know, so this letter could reach you before ...

He set the pen down, massaged the taut hot flesh around the forehead with the back of his hand. No good. You know I know you know: so much knowing, so little knowledge. No good at all. The paper fluttered to the floor. He tried again.

After forty-five minutes Kiranovich came through on the intercom. 'Contact, captain.' He acknowledged, pushed back the chair, trudged the short distance to the door. He looked at the table and the debris. After forty-five minutes he had written the longest and shortest letter of his life. Two words, no more than that.

Tanya, please ...

RAF KINLOSS
MORAY FIRTH
SCOTLAND

Talbot squinted against the bright afternoon sun. The Nimrod towered above him, huge, awesome, a thing of limitless power even here, grounded on the shimmering concrete.

He turned to Daniels, followed the direction of the other's gaze. 'Well?'

'In the words of the song, sir, I've never seen anything like it in my life.'

Cradled upon five coupled trolleys, the sonobuoy resembled a kind of giant pear, its green-painted girth swelling and bulging to accommodate the folded arrays hidden within the casing.

'Yes,' the air vice-marshal said. 'It's certainly something.'

Daniels touched the smooth flanks. An air electronics officer, he thought, was supposed to know everything. But this – this *thing* created and fabricated so fast that two maybe three months ago not even the prototype existed – this almost defied understanding.

In time, you could learn the specifications by rote: the computer and the transducers and the EHE pack with its dozens of eight-inch batteries, cadmium cells with sintered nickel positives and negatives formed from plastics-bonded iron oxide steel substrate wafers ... By poring over the design manual it was possible to become familiar

275

with every bizarre aspect, from the hydraulic servo system through to the integral desalination and purifier plant.

You could stand around all day with the production people and sit up all night absorbing every last jot of data, but at the end of it all comprehension was still incomplete because a thing like this, so unpromising and inelegant, a thing like this could change the world.

He glanced up to where Ramsden was working within the maw of the aircraft's forty-eight-foot-long weapons bay. It was usually stocked with one-shot launchers and torpedoes, and sometimes even mail canisters, but not now. All the gubbins was being ripped out and the interior frantically modified to cope with the sonobuoy.

'It'll never fit!' he shouted.

Ramsden grinned. 'Have faith!'

Talbot began to walk back to the main building. Daniels lingered a moment more, then caught up. 'When will it be, sir?'

'Saturday, or Sunday – depends when the sub's in the target zone.'

'We'll never be ready.'

'As your friend said, have faith.'

They continued on in silence. Eventually Daniels asked: 'Pitreavie – is it co-ordinating?'

'Yes, with Fylingdales.'

'Fylingdales?' Daniels halted. 'How come they're involved?'

'They've a new relay centre for maritime surveillance – the works. Very impressive.'

'I didn't know. I've never been there.'

'Not many have.' Talbot set off again.

Daniels drew level. 'Will you be at Pitreavie?'

'Yes.'

'So who's liaising from Fylingdales?'

'Fellow called Koss. Reliable type, by the sound of it. Well, they all are. Have to be, considering.'

FYLINGDALES EARLY WARNING STATION
YORKSHIRE
ENGLAND

It was getting warmer now; the mist was rolling slowly off the moorland. Sheep bleated pointlessly in the bracken, a few standing silently, staring dull-eyed at the vista beyond, at the plain of dun-coloured earth.

The terrain undulated so that only the upper hemispheres of the duck-egg blue radomes appeared.

Koss was soon to come off duty, and glad of it. The new day awaited with all the cosy promise of summer. It had been a quiet Wednesday night, though, no real distractions until around 2.00 a.m., when Technical wanted a word and he found himself standing inside a 145-foot-high radome staring up at the asymmetric stitching of nigh on 2,000 hexagonal panels. He felt like a very small bee in a vast, deserted honeycomb. He'd stood in the shadow of the 124-ton radar dish, nodded patiently, understandingly, while Maintenance pointed out the repair work required to correct a fault in the lateral tracking, a flaw in the scales of the Dragon.

Dragons. Curious nicknames. Curious pets.

Things were exactly as they'd been before when he returned to the central control room, to the repeater banks and calm silent displays in housings of almost antiseptic whiteness. He sat down and examined the status board. Nothing: west and east hemispheres inactive. He glanced at two fellow duty officers – they were grouped about a desk, working on a report on the recent orbital degradation of a Soviet CK9 satellite, about the most exciting event all week.

His gaze meandered around the long, low room and finally settled on an incongruous focal point – a large, brightly-lit aquarium. No sign of the fish; perhaps they'd gone to sleep. Did fish sleep? He yawned, rubbed his eyes and considered the status board anew.

INCOMING:
OUTBOUND:
MINUTES TO IMPACT:

Beneath the legend BMEWS THREAT REPORT was a small rectangle of glass. He could just discern the single word etched upon its surface:

REAL

Sometimes, in the private hours, he thought so hard about the glass rectangle that the word seemed to glow, and then the adrenaline coursed, and his pulse quickened, and a momentary lunatic gratitude seized him.

Now, he strolled out into the sharp morning air and was temporarily stilled by a chafing wind that raced over the endless acres of emptiness. He checked his calendar wristwatch: 0630 hours, THURS JULY 7. Not much time left. From now on his duties would lie in a deeper, even more secret place.

He hugged his jacket to him. They had 150 million quids' worth of technology up here, but they'd still not found a way of improving the Fylingdales weather.

EAST ATLANTIC OCEAN

The great detective used a linen napkin to dab delicately at his lips. 'Well, Watson? What d'you think?'

'It's a rum business, that's my opinion.' The broad brow corrugated in a frown. 'Some sort of curse, what?'

'No,' Holmes stared at his reflection in the silver teapot, 'some sort of large ... dog.'

'A hound,' Watson said.

'Yes, a hound of Hell.' Slim fingers massaged the pointed jaw. 'And now it's loose, stalking its prey.'

Watson shivered. 'Used to like hounds.' He paused. 'I tell you though, something like this, a fellow can go off 'em pretty quick.'

Yevgeni pushed the crockery aside and eased himself up from the breakfast table. He crossed the wardroom to the teak veneer unit that ranged along one wall. The TV set switched off with a click and Baker Street and the Baskervilles vanished. He turned to the video recorder and ejected the tape. Sherlock Holmes, MosFilm style. Hit of the season, so everyone said; and as for that Watson – a brain like his wouldn't be out of place in the Kremlin.

He slid the tape into its box and wedged it in amongst all the other shelved cassettes: ice-skating, football, ice-hockey, variety show, travelogue – Albania, war film – *Cross of Iron*, science-fiction film – *Solaris*.

He yawned and glanced up at the clock: 0750 GMT. Two thousand five hundred and fifty kilometres to go before midnight berthing at Polyarno tomorrow. Soon be home, he thought, but then realised that the word 'home' had made him feel not cheerful, but apprehensive.

Yevgeni strolled out of the wardroom and along the mess deck, heard the familiar galley clatter of plates and pans, continued aft past the huge cylinders of the missile tubes, vertical shafts of gleaming steel like the vats of some fantastic brewery. The footway narrowed as it edged past the double-banked launchers, then broadened out at the access door. He ducked low and entered the launch centre.

Everything was serene, ordered: control staff monitored the screens, confronting antiseptic white modules starred with glowing beacons and multi-coloured buttons. Zeklin was hunched over the integrator desk, taking readings from the SINS link to the guidance master board. As the boat headed north-east, launch co-ordinates constantly changed. Without the electronic feed from the navigation computer you'd have a margin of error of hundreds of kilometres instead of a few metres.

He touched Zeklin's shoulder. 'Everything all right?'

The blond Latvian nodded. 'No problems, captain.'

'Where's the launch control officer?'

'I don't know.'

'Try and locate him by fourteen hundred.'

He climbed the steep, diagonal stairway leading to the upper reactor deck and paused at the top to look back. I have a weaponry officer, he thought, and I have a launch control officer, and both are used to dealing with equations. A pity that Bulgov chooses to practise Moscow and not Fleet calculus.

Measured footfalls took him silently across the rubberised tread of the catwalk. Soft light glimmered through the latticework; he stared down at the grey, squat bulk of the reactor and the span of umbilical cords connecting it to the cylindrical heat exchanger: so many cords, so many pipes, the thickest a weave of four coolant tubes that burrowed into the base of the reactor and looped in coils around the core.

Yevgeni tried to conceive of the unimaginable processes of infinite power, to imagine the scene at the heart of the nuclear furnace, but gave up, able to think of only a violent redness, the anger of a captive sun.

A winding staircase brought him down to the for'ard engine-room and the misshapen sentinels of the steam pathway housings, enormous junction boxes through which the coolant vapour fled on its headlong rush to the turbines and ancillary converters. The noise was much greater here, though not as loud as was popularly supposed; the average Leningrad factory made three times as much din. He threaded his way through the clustered groups of engineering

279

crew, thought how they looked like bakers, all dressed up in spotless white.

He gained the aft engine-room upper deck, a less cluttered though equally cavernous area, its far wall pierced by the enormous phallus of the sternward-thrusting turbine tunnel. Another spiral stairway took him to the lower aft deck, there to discover Svenchsky and two acolytes on hands and knees before the median shaft from the air-conditioning plant.

He hunkered down beside them. 'Any problems?'

Svenchsky shook his head; light gleamed on the bald crown. 'What brings you back here?'

'Sunday-morning constitutional.'

'All right for some.' A large screwdriver disappeared within a massive fist. 'Did you know, the Americans want jogging tracks installed in their boats?'

'I'd heard it was golf karts they wanted.'

Svenchsky carefully removed a semi-circular plate. 'No chance of you turning the con into an ice rink, I suppose?'

'It's a thought.'

'Be the best one you lot have had.'

He watched them for a few moments more. 'Well, better be getting back.'

'Aye, leave the workers in peace.'

He retraced his route, a leisurely procession through the aft and midships sections, nodding in acknowledgment to familiar faces. Like a Sunday-morning stroll, he thought, with the family.

Solokov intercepted him in the control room. 'It's nearly time, captain.'

He checked the clock: 0816 GMT. 'All right.'

They climbed the ladder to the lower sail-deck and waited while he punched buttons on the wall-mounted keypad.

'All clear,' Kiranovich answered.

'You don't know the question.'

'I do know the time.'

He chuckled and keyed again. 'Con.'

'Yes, comrade captain?'

'Time for the SINS update. Tell Shevelev, periscope depth.'

They ascended again, to the inner navigation bridge. Already he could discern the change in buoyancy as compressed air at 180 kilograms per square centimetre forced water out of the posterior casing vents.

He buzzed Sonar again. 'Anything?'

'Negative.'

Solokov confronted the periscope housing, dwarfed by the high, swelling cowl. 'Any minute now,' he said.

She broke into the glittering emptiness, sail rearing up, shedding foaming streamers from port and starboard planes. The sea surged and creamed around her bow, went sluicing back along the decking to swirl around the ebony tower and the spinal quilting of the silo covers. Spindrift clung to the multiple arrays on the smooth GRP structure, shimmered briefly on search and attack periscopes, whip aerial, ECM mast, search radar and intake and exhaust snorkels, shimmered then finally flickered away, an undulating chain of diamonds flung far and wide upon the wind.

Yevgeni reached the surface navigation bridge and breathed in deeply, oblivious to Solokov's labours as readings from magnetic North sensors were painstakingly compared with those from the gyroscopes and accelerometers of the SINS.

Eventually he turned to yell above the rush of the ocean: 'How is it?'

Solokov made a circle out of thumb and index finger. He smiled.

0832 GMT. After the astringency of the open air, the con felt muggy, cloying, and Yevgeni experienced the familiar impatience that always accompanied the final stages of passage.

They must be within range of Arkhangelsk Control by now, would have entered the secret sound corridor that ran all the way across Norway, Sweden, Finland and Karelskaya to the vast installation of the Fleet VLF transmitter. Their sixty-metre aerial array would be trailing behind now, twelve metres below the waves.

'Commcon ready,' Stukhov announced.

'Tell them: standard SITREP. Surface running, everything well. ETA confirmed 2350 GMT tomorrow night.'

'There's nothing out there then, comrade captain?'

'Not a thing.'

Silently, slowly, its bearings flashing briefly in the solar glare, the tracking gear moved about its axis, internal couplings making minute adjustments to pan and tilt.

The slender twelve-foot shaft nodded in response, settled and held at an inclination of 7.5 degrees as the lens focussed on the invisible point of heat that marked the boat's exhaust snorkel.

Data from the infra-red sensors poured into the central processing unit as the satellite continued on in geosynchronous orbit, always moving yet never quitting its parked position 820 miles above the Earth.

0910 GMT. Yevgeni glanced up from the signals log as Kiranovich paused at the cabin doorway.

'Contact, captain – twenty-three thousand.'

'Identification?'

'Not yet.'

He sighed and slipped the flimsy yellow sheets back onto the prongs of the folder. 'Tell Stukhov I'm on my way.'

When Kiranovich had gone, he crossed to the wall safe, slid the bound folder into its vertical slot, then locked the inner compartment. The safe door shut with a satisfying clunk, the combination lock spinning in automatic re-set.

On the way out of his cabin, he glimpsed the framed pictures of Tanya and Katerina, but with a faint chill of disappointment he turned quickly away from them and slammed the cabin door behind him.

Kiranovich's disembodied voice came over the intercom: 'Alpha contact bearing three three zero on one nine five, range twenty thousand and closing.'

Yevgeni's eyes flicked from the target-bearing transmitter to the time clock; numerals flashed and flickered in constant revision of the time–distance equation. Then he looked towards Solokov, hunched over the SINS desk, brow furrowed in concentration. 'Profile?'

'Clear, captain. For'ard scan level for ten thousand. We're on the edge of a shadow zone, too.'

He nodded, returned to the central island, and saw the anxiety on Stukhov's pallid face. Never seen a man who looked so worried, he decided; there were innumerable mysteries of the deep and the first officer deserved to be counted amongst them. He keyed through to Engineering: 'All ahead, two thirds.'

Kiranovich called out again. 'Contact bearing three three zero on one nine five, range eighteen thousand and closing.'

'Sector sweep?'

'Negative, captain.'

Could be anything up there – whaler, trawler; the fleets spread themselves all over this latitude. Except that was a hell of a speed to be going fishing.

'Fifteen thousand and closing.'

He turned to Stukhov. 'Any ideas?'

'No, comrade captain.'

One day someone somewhere would come up with a way of extending active sonar so that range and depth limitations were not so restrictive. But until then there was only the perennial combination of luck and technology, of subsurface sound channels and the efficiency of Kiranovich's passive systems, Kiranovich's ears.

Shevelev materialised at his side, fingers plucking abstractedly at his beard. 'Whenever I fancy a breath of fresh air you decide to submerge.'

'Shame.'

'All right for you, you don't spend your days in a bloody cupboard.'

'Thirteen thousand and closing,' Kiranovich called.

Yevgeni hesitated. 'Mark at ten.'

'At ten,' Kiranovich acknowledged.

He glanced at the transmitter again. The pulsing blip continued to trace a livid track across the radiating circles. 'Better get ready to take us back up,' he said to Shevelev.

'Alpha contact bearing three three zero, course one nine five, range ten thousand metres and closing.' Kiranovich, as deadpan as ever. A brief pause, then: 'ECM, ECM confirmed.'

No doubt of it then – not a random contact. Both on each other's screens as the two systems reciprocated, strained for the tell-tale signs of electronic surveillance. He leaned into the mike again: 'Identification?'

'Probability hostile.'

So, a single, surface vessel coming towards them at full speed with detection and counter-measure systems turned up high.

'Eight thousand and closing.'

'Can you identify now?'

'Have to be visual, captain. Sorry.'

'Very well. We'll go wide of it, take a look.' Yevgeni ordered the helmsman: 'Right ten degrees rudder.' Fingers jabbed the keypad. 'Engineering, reduce one third.'

'Contact still three three zero on one nine five, seven thousand and closing,' Kiranovich intoned.

He pressed another button to get through to Shevelev. 'Stand by to blow tanks.' He turned to Solokov. 'Scan?'

'Still clear. Thermal's fading, though.'

They were heading deeper into the Norwegian Sea, going further away from the Drift, speeding silently towards the most eastern area of the Atlantic – now a shining cradle for two vessels, one on the surface, the other below.

0930 on a quiet Sunday morning, and a strange dance upon an empty ocean.

FYLINGDALES BMEWS STATION
NORTH YORKSHIRE
ENGLAND

The escort halted them in front of a display bank. A ginger-haired man with florid complexion glanced up from the VDU. 'Ah, Sir Alec? Doctor Wycliffe? David Harvey, group captain.' He looked inquisitively at the final member of the trio.

'I'm Martin Leech, project security.'

They shook hands.

'So,' Harvey said, 'you found us all right.'

Kenyon nodded. 'Came up last night and stayed in Whitby.' He glanced about him. 'Pretty impressive, this.'

'Thanks.'

'Is this where it all happens?' Leech asked.

'No, this is TOR – Tactical Ops Room. You're going to the new section, ADR Con – Air Defence Region relay control.' Harvey paused. 'TOR's the surveillance hub, ADR Con's a duplicate but in a different comm chain. TOR's international, ADR Con's domestic.'

'I see,' Kenyon said uncertainly.

Harvey smiled sympathetically and wondered if the woman was going to speak. She seemed strangely subdued.

'Well,' Leech said, 'shall we get on?'

Harvey beckoned to a tall, middle-aged man dressed similarly in green military tunic and dark trousers. 'Squadron Leader Tucker. He'll lead the way.'

Tucker nodded to each of them in turn. 'If you'll follow me?'

284

They fell in step and found themselves trailing along a softly-lit corridor.

'Busy, squadron leader?' Leech inquired.

'We have been – just logged the twenty-thousandth item, out in the wide blue yonder.'

They halted before the blank doors of a lift. 'What was it?' Kenyon asked.

'A camera – Hasselblad; one of the Yanks lost it during Shuttle EVA on Wednesday night.' He shook his head. 'The amount of junk up there; the first scrap dealer in orbit'll make a fortune.'

Leech smiled. 'You identify everything?'

'Oh yes, we have to,' Tucker said. 'No use announcing a warhead's about to impact when it's really a camera or an astronaut's glove.' The doors opened and he ushered them inside, then thumbed the lower-level button. 'Be a daft way to start Armageddon, that would.'

'Is there a sensible way?' Kenyon inquired.

Frances stirred her tea. 'Oughtn't we to be doing something?' she asked.

'Expect they'll tell us.' Kenyon yawned. 'How long're you staying?' he asked Leech.

'An hour, maybe.' He set his cup and saucer down on the table.

'Are we safely delivered, Mr Leech?' Frances said with a grim smile. He looked at her, reminded himself anew that she still needed handling with care, that it was still only early days.

'All safe,' he said. He checked his watch: fifteen minutes since arrival; it seemed an age. He leaned back in the chair and tried to think of something else to say. Anything was better than the crowded silence of this underground suite, where they sat hemmed in by white walls and teak furniture.

The door suddenly opened then and Tucker reappeared. 'Your courier.' He ushered in a young, dark-haired man with a physique that strained at the confines of the white shirt and epaulettes.

The man made straight for Frances. 'Doctor Livingstone, I presume?' He gripped her hand.

'Wycliffe, actually.'

'I'm Harry Koss, flight lieutenant.'

'Pleased to meet you, flight lieutenant.'

'You'll find Harry easier.' The smile widened to embrace Kenyon and Leech. 'Welcome to the Cellar, gentlemen.'

'Hmm.' Kenyon appeared less than enthusiastic. 'You in charge?'

'I'm co-ordinating, yes.'

'What's happening with Pitreavie, then?'

Koss shrugged. 'They're like us, waiting for the target to reach launch zone.'

He turned back to Frances and registered the shadows beneath her eyes and the curiously concave aspect of her cheeks. Make-up had been expertly applied and in a different light, from another viewpoint, there'd be nothing to remark on apart from her obvious attractiveness. But here, in this fluorescent harshness, she reminded him of one who was ill, or in mourning.

She caught his gaze. 'Anything wrong?'

'Oh, no ...' He improvised hastily. 'I was wondering about this sonobuoy. Could you run through it for me? I need to be sure I understand what's going to happen.'

She breathed in, signifying her reluctance with a slow shake of the head. 'The buoy's in a twenty-four-foot canister. After launch it will fall to target depth and shed its middle casing. The inner shaft will then telescope, pushing the upper and lower sections further apart. The upper has the buoyancy chamber and comm link with command receptor. The lower has the DataCon computer, power pack, sensor feeds and command repeater.'

Koss nodded admiringly. 'That's as good as a press release.'

'Yes, well, I've had enough practice.'

Koss thought for a moment, then said: 'The shaft expansion – I take it that's hydraulic?'

'Yes. But on its own it isn't sufficient to maintain upper and lower separation, so there are six bracing cables.'

'I see.' Koss paused again. 'Tell me about the transducers. What's the configuration?'

'Six ELFTs in coupled pairs. They spring out from the shaft as soon as the waist casing is released.'

'Are they ECM sensitive?'

She nodded. 'The system's passive and active agile.'

'And what about this ACS thing?'

'An anti-cavitation system: without it all that power would produce nothing but bubbles. Think of it in terms of automatic braking on a car, where sensors detect wheel-lock just before it happens and initiate cadence braking. ACS does the same, sends out pulse bursts at milli-second intervals – cadence signalling.'

Koss gave a low whistle. 'Amazing.' He smiled at her. 'What happens to it afterwards? Surely you don't just dump it?'

'No. Each of the buoys has a radio beacon so we don't lose track. Battery life, in normal use, is seventy-two hours; when the system exhausts itself, it's a simple job to retrieve it and install a new power pack.'

'Isn't it a bit risky, leaving it lying around for anyone to pick up?'

She smiled wanly. 'First of all they'd have to find it. Then they'd have to dismantle it. That's not possible without frequency unlocking. Any other method triggers protective circuitry: an internal acid bath. All that would be left would be goo.'

'I understand.' Koss hesitated again. 'Final question. What has this got that other systems haven't?'

Frances shrugged. 'Portability, cost effectiveness, performance. They can be stationed like SOSUS or dunked by helicopter, dropped in one part of a surveillance zone then ferried to another. They can detect anything at any depth over one hundred square miles.'

'You're saying it can wipe out the submarine?'

'Well, I'd rather you didn't make it sound like a weapon.'

'Isn't it?'

EAST ATLANTIC OCEAN

The sheath spun silkily on its bearings, making a gentle hissing sound. Yevgeni held the crossbar lightly, maintaining a smooth and slow rotation through 360 degrees. Water still streamed from the lens – a blurred whiteness registered but nothing sharper. He turned the periscope two more points. He adjusted the elevation, using his left hand to alter the focussing as the perspective changed. A seagull planed by, a pale flash of orange and white. It was almost as good as actually being up there: the sea and the gulls and the following wind.

Two more points in the revolution: more gulls, quite a flock, came into view, feeding on the surface. Then beyond them, towards the horizon, he caught sight of a sleek grey superstructure and the black cowl of a funnel. Kiranovich called out for immediate confirmation, and the 'Quiet Alert' started automatically: no noise, panel lights on, steady, stage one to stage two, lights flashing rhythmically now.

Kiranovich's voice was perfectly calm: 'Hostile vessel, British Fleet, hostile, hostile.'

Yevgeni refocussed for range. Another course revision prior to ascent had left a healthy gap, but with the screen now filled by the magnified image, three thousand metres seemed not the best of margins. Not with a British destroyer.

It was a City type, Sheffield class. She was slamming out ECM at a hell of a rate and coming towards them at almost the same pace, matching her course to the target position displayed on her own target-bearing transmitter.

He held the final close-up a moment longer. A single word of identification was picked out in bright red letters beneath her helicopter deck: LANCASTER.

ADR CON FYLINGDALES

'Well,' Koss said. 'What d'you think?'

She nodded approvingly, let her gaze embrace the vast circular room. It must have been seventy or eighty feet wide, with a ceiling as high as a cathedral roof. She watched the duty crew at work, dozens of men in shirt-sleeves or sweaters, hunched over modular desks, staring at shimmering screens or talking quietly into their headsets.

Koss indicated a vacant rank of interlinked consoles to the left of the walkway on the second tier down. Remote terminals and VDUs sprouted from a swathe of white laminate that continued on in a sweeping curve.

'If you'd like to sit here,' Koss said. He stood aside to let her pass and motioned Kenyon to follow. 'Where's your colleague?'

'On the phone,' Kenyon said. 'He has to report that we haven't been kidnapped.'

Koss frowned, then stepped onto the third tier and positioned himself in front of Frances. She was still staring around her, stricken with the bizarre feeling of being in some high-tech theatre-in-the-round.

'Let's have a sort-out then,' Koss said. 'Before you is a notepad and pen; next to them, one red phone; facing you, the VDU from central surveillance system, so you can see everything as it happens.'

'It's quicker by Tube,' Kenyon said, winking at Frances.

Koss smiled uncertainly, then leaned forward to lift a headset from the console. 'This is what you'll be wearing most of the day, Doctor Wycliffe.' He handed it to her and reached sideways to grasp another set on the adjacent console.

'We're in multi-channel communication today. If you want a discreet conversation, press the orange button to your left, otherwise everything's open.'

She slipped the earphones into place and saw Kenyon doing likewise.

A voice bellowed in her head: 'Well I don't care who you are! I am Air Vice-Marshal Sir Kenneth Talbot. I am at Pitreavie. I am at Pitreavie because an exercise is under way. Now this may come as a complete surprise to Northwood, after all we've only been at it for the past four weeks and sent you copy signals every single hour of every single day . . . but no matter. You've a City type destroyer on station in the Norwegian Sea. I don't know which one it is and I haven't the faintest idea what it's doing there but I do have something to say about it. Kindly locate Admiral Heptenstall and tell him RAF's compliments and will he please arrange to GET THAT BLOODY SHIP OUT OF IT!'

She tore off the headset and rubbed frantically at her ears.

'Ah,' Kenyon said.

'They seem to be having words,' Koss said.

She sighed. 'Is this why there's a delay?'

'Yes. The Navy's trying to stick its – oh, my apologies, Sir Alec.'

'Don't mind me, young man,' said Kenyon airily. 'I opted out when steam came in.'

She sat back and contemplated the huge arc of the wall display – maps and clocks and status boards and an illuminated perspex sheet all of twenty feet wide on which was etched the continental outline of the US eastern seaboard, Europe, and the USSR. Small points of light glowed in a random scatter, some in the Atlantic, but most within the massif.

'It's a virtual duplicate of upstairs,' Koss said. 'You have to double up on everything nowadays, to be on the safe side.'

Her gaze came to rest on a curious kind of scoreboard centred between the perspex display and a panel of clocks marking different time zones.

INCOMING:
OUTBOUND:
MINUTES TO IMPACT:

289

Underneath were the words BMEWS THREAT REPORT. And below that was a small square of dark glass, the letters just discernible:

REAL

'Does that ever light up?' she asked.

'Not in earnest, no.' Koss hesitated. 'It comes on during systems test. Oh, and once because of the hang-gliders.'

'The what?'

'Hang-gliders. Local club down Whitby way: they like to fly over the moors. We've had to warn 'em off – there's a radiation belt around Fylingdales; over-exposure can cause sterility.'

She closed her eyes, experienced a sudden weariness of spirit. Something as harmless as that, she thought, wanting to be free as a bird.

'Well,' Koss said, 'could be awhile yet. I'll organise some tea.'

She remained lost in thoughtful silence, eyes squeezed tight against the vision before her, the arena and the lights and the simple, awesome words. Then a voice sharply intruded: 'Frances?'

She turned and looked into a familiar face. 'Gulliver!'

'The same.' There was laughter in the grey eyes.

'What're you doing here?' She followed the sweep of his hand, frowning incomprehendingly. 'Mr Schulmann ...?'

The gaunt figure nodded in acknowledgment. 'Hello, Doctor Wycliffe. Your people felt I ought to come, just in case.'

Kenyon was on his feet. 'Care to introduce me?' he said to Frances.

'Certainly.' She eased out of the chair. 'Sir Alec Kenyon, Max Schulmann, project director Searchlight Marine. They were the main contractors at Moffett.' The two men shook hands. 'And of course,' she added, 'you know who this is.'

'I do indeed.' Kenyon beamed. 'How are you, m'dear chap?'

'Fine.' Gulliver winced under the enthusiastic handshake. 'Just fine.' He extricated himself with evident difficulty. 'So, what's happening?'

Before she could reply, Kenyon said: 'They've pumped liquid coolant in under pressure. The ignition sequence should be under way.'

'The sonobuoy?'

'The kettle – they've just put it on.'

*   *   *

290

'This is Stratcon Pitreavie. Acknowledge please.'
'ADR Con Fylingdales. We acknowledge.'
'Roger Fylingdales. Destroyer has left the launch zone. Do we have go?'
'Affirmative Pitreavie. Everyone ready here.'
'Roger Fylingdales. Please stand by.'

'Stratcon Pitreavie to Kinloss. Over.'
'This is Kinloss.'
'We have go from ADR Con.'
'Roger Pitreavie. Please stand by.'

'Stratcon Pitreavie to ADR Con. Over.'
'Roger Pitreavie.'
'We have stand by from Kinloss. Over.'
'Advise when clear.'
'Will advise.'

'This is Stratcon to ADR Con. Over.'
'Roger Stratcon.'
'Kinloss is go.'

RAF KINLOSS

Ramsden ran her screaming towards the outer marker with the propulsion thrust ramming them hard back into their seats. She came out of the heat haze at the end of the runway like a giant white bird, hauled herself into the sky with body gleaming and wide wings shimmering in the dancing brightness; she shifted so fast she was clear to three hundred feet before the noise really came down in a screaming thunder fit to tear the day ragged.

And then she was gone, borne upon the power surge, rising high and higher through the fleece of cumulus, towards the cirrus's chalky scratchings in the brilliant blue beyond.

ADR CON FYLINGDALES

'You're through to the Nimrod,' Koss said.

Frances stared at the impenetrable green mist of the monitor screen and donned the headset. A rush of sound assaulted her ears.

'Doctor Wycliffe?'

'Yes?'

'This is Flight Lieutenant Daniels, air electronics officer Watchdog niner four. We're in position for the first launch.'

'Good.' She felt suddenly awkward, unsure of what to say. There was some sort of technology for exchanges such as this but the vocabulary entirely escaped her.

'You're at Fylingdales, aren't you?' Daniels said. 'Well, tell 'em not to shoot. We're friends.'

She smiled. 'I'll tell them.'

'Right then, ready when you are. On your word ...'

She inhaled steadily, conscious of the silence in the big room. People waiting, watching; she felt no sensation other than that of being the focus of countless strangers.

'On three, flight lieutenant. One.'

'One.' Acknowledgment echoing back over the miles.

'Two.'

'Two.'

'Three ...'

'Three. Buoy away! Launch time twelve twenty-four hours.'

She breathed out loudly. As though in response to a signal, the room erupted in noisy activity. People clapped, smiled, laughed, before returning to their consoles to punch buttons and check meters.

She waited for the monitor screen to come alive.

1225 GMT. Frances' headset blared. 'Watchdog niner four to ADR Con. Over.'

'This is ADR Con.' Koss responded before Frances could open her mouth.

'Give me Doctor Wycliffe, will you?'

She leaned forward and spoke into the microphone. 'Yes?'

'This is Daniels. Anything on your screen yet, Doctor?'

'No, nothing.' Her frown deepened. 'Aren't you getting a signal either?'

'Not even the transponder.'

'But ... But why?'

'With respect, Doctor, I didn't design it.'

'You're sure it's at its target depth?'

'Put it like this, it should be. It should be – hold on, Doctor ... Aw, Christ Almighty ...'

'What's the matter?'

'We've seen it.'

'The buoy?'

'The bits.'

1231 GMT: the telephone buzzed. Koss reached for it, listened briefly, then gestured to Kenyon. 'Sir Kenneth Talbot for you.'

Kenyon took the receiver. 'Hello?'

'What's going on, Alec?'

'I was just about to ask you the same thing.'

'The bloody thing's disintegrated!' The tone of shocked outrage suggested a gross display of bad sportsmanship.

'Yes,' Kenyon said, 'I heard.'

'That all you can say? Heavens, man, it's a disaster!'

Kenyon sighed. 'Well, it might've helped if your mob hadn't gone in like the Dam Busters.'

'What the devil's that supposed to mean?'

'They were required to launch it, not bounce it.' He turned to Frances. 'It's the Red Baron. Talk to him, will you?'

She accepted the phone. 'Sir Kenneth? It's Doctor Wycliffe.'

'Good day to you. Now listen to me. Is there some suggestion there that the RAF hasn't done its job?'

She forced back a laugh and said smoothly: 'No suggestion at all. It's just that from re-checking the data it's possible the buoy didn't go in clean.'

'And you're blaming us?'

'No, not in the slightest. I'm saying the entry point must've been wrong. Impact stress has occurred at the most vulnerable point – the axial release housing.'

'How d'you know?'

'I've had Watchdog ninety-four describe the bits they saw. They were actually the waist doors. They were meant to come off, though at target depth, not before.'

A lengthy pause. 'You don't sound very concerned, Doctor,' Talbot said finally.

'Well; I'm disappointed, but the buoy isn't lost; we can retrieve it later.'

'How? Is the transponder working?'

'Erratically. It seems to have been damaged, too.'

Another interval of silence, then Talbot declared: 'Hope you don't mind me saying this, but it seems to me you people didn't exactly do an outstanding job on the design.'

'Seems to me, Sir Kenneth, that we people weren't exactly given very much time.' She paused. 'Call your aircraft back, Sir Kenneth. The buoy isn't going to work now, not with positive buoyancy. I'm with a representative of the main contractor; we'll get to work on revising the launch parameters.' She handed the phone to Kenyon.

He sighed again. 'Kenneth? You get all that?'

'What did she say she was going to do?'

'Form a sub-committee. Appropriate, mmm?' He cradled the receiver and said to no one in particular: 'No sense of humour, that fellow.'

NORWEGIAN SEA

Yevgeni massaged his jaw. 'So you don't know what it was, then.'

'Well, some sort of surveillance equipment, obviously.' Kiranovich shrugged.

'Can't you be more specific?'

'We had a trace but it was too brief and too weak.'

Yevgeni stared thoughtfully around the sonar room, taking in the racks and tiers of counter-measure equipment. 'It just... popped up?'

'Dropped down, more like – my guess is it was aircraft launched.'

'And it's monitoring us.'

'Well, that's the odd part. I don't think it is. Obviously there's no way we can confirm without going active, and we can't do that at this range, but sonobuoys operate at predetermined target depths. Once down, they're sea anchored, whereas this thing seems to be moving. Its position certainly shifted between the time of initial registration and our pick-up of the R/F trace.'

'Meaning?'

'Tidal drift – it must be caught in the subsurface current.'

'And the radio signal?'

'I can't be sure, but it has all the hallmarks of a faulty transponder.'

'So it's something they'd like to retrieve.'

Kiranovich nodded. 'Whoever *they* might be.'

Yevgeni fell silent again. 'Curious,' he said.

Zeklin suddenly appeared in the doorway and said hesitantly: 'Comrade captain? It's thirteen fifteen hours. We're supposed to be preparing for the MTRE run.'

'So?'

'It ... it doesn't look like we're going to make it – the commissar has scheduled a messroom lecture for fourteen hundred.'

'He's what?'

The Latvian spread his hands, palms uppermost. 'Nothing I can do.'

Yevgeni swung round, grabbed the wallphone, keyed zero – all stations call. 'Commissar Bulgov to the captain's quarters immediately. Commissar Bulgov to the captain's quarters immediately.' He waited until Zeklin was clear of the sonar room, then turned to Kiranovich: 'Well, that's it. I've had all I'm going to take.'

'What the hell are you doing, calling the off-watch to the messroom without reference to me?'

'Political instruction, comrade captain. It is my duty.'

'Commissar, there's an MTRE run at fourteen hundred – or didn't you know?'

'But I checked Orders of the Day and –'

'Check again.'

'There's no mention of an MTRE.'

'There is of systems inspection; ATL it says – equipment appropriate to latitude.'

'That's right, a SINS update, a –'

'Not just SINS. We happen to be in launch latitude for the missiles.' Yevgeni stopped. 'Listen, comrade. OOD says Missile Test Readiness Equipment must be run, which means that the captain, the chief navigation officer, the missile control officer and the weapons control officer must all assemble together at the appointed hour. Not three or two or one, all four. All four keys, otherwise we can't activate the board.'

Bulgov stared at the floor. 'I apologise, comrade captain,' he said stiffly.

'It's a bit late for that. I've had to put the test back to sixteen hundred.'

'Oh, there's no need for –'

'Yes there is. I'm damned if the crew is going to be told one thing one minute and another the next. A command is decisive or it is not. Vacillation is the ultimate sign of weakness and I'll not let the crew get that impression of this command. So, you go ahead with your meeting. They think you've cleared it with me, which means you've committed me to it.'

'I didn't intend –' Bulgov said, then stopped. 'Please, accept my apologies.'

'No.'

'I assure you, it won't happen again.'

Yevgeni gave a brittle smile. 'You can count on that. You can also count on never setting foot aboard another submarine. I'm signalling Fleet about this, about why a crucial test had to be delayed because some jumped-up Party official likes to hear the sound of his own voice.'

'I wouldn't do that, comrade captain,' Bulgov said softly. 'I really wouldn't do that if I were you.'

The smile broadened. 'Run along, comrade. You've your speech to rehearse.'

ADR CON FYLINGDALES

They lunched in the office suite, eating from trays balanced awkwardly in their laps.

'Didn't expect to see you again,' Frances said.

'Schulmann had to come, so ...' Gulliver finished the last of the sandwich, shifted position once again as Tucker and Koss squeezed past in search of somewhere to sit. 'Anyway,' he resumed, 'how are you?'

'Not too bad. I wish he could have seen this.'

'How's it going?'

She nodded towards Schulmann's cadaverous form. 'We've nearly finished.'

'Fingers crossed then, eh?'

'Yes.'

He lit a cigarette and said: 'You've done well.'

'It's Piotr's achievement, not mine.'

'I didn't mean just the sonobuoy. Coming here today to face all this ...' The sentence hung unfinished. He had the feeling they were pursuing parallel conversations.

'He was worth something.' She shook her head. 'Worth a damn sight more than he ever received.'

'I know.'

'Do you?'

'Yes,' Gulliver said softly. 'I know all right.' He paused,

struggling to shift the focus of the exchange. 'Never stop, do they, these games? Them and us; they build something, we build–'

'I wouldn't know, I'm just one of the sheep.' She held his gaze. 'The sayings of John Gulliver Esquire.'

'Don't take it personally.'

'Why not? It's what we are. We don't do anything except follow. The only decision we make is to accept.' Her eyes suddenly misted over. 'I would've married him, you know?'

'Yes.'

Her lower lip trembled, shadows deepened on her face. 'I'm not even his widow.'

'Look ...' Gulliver said, then lapsed into helpless silence.

'Tomorrow it'll be a week since we – the river, when we ...'

'Hey.' He reached out, touched her arm. 'It's okay.'

She shrugged him away. 'Leave me, will you?' A whispered plea, no force or animation. 'Just for a while.'

He hesitated, coughed against the thickening at the back of his throat, then got up. 'I'll go have a word with Leech.' He moved uncertainly across the room.

'What's the matter with our friend?' Leech asked. 'Been exercising your fatal charm again?'

'She's upset.'

'Well,' Leech said, 'it's only been a few days, after all.' He sighed, then asked briskly: 'You here for the duration?'

'No choice.'

'Nothing's going to happen now.'

'Then why've you come?'

'Had to escort them, didn't I?'

'So you'll be hanging around too?'

'No.' Leech checked his watch. 'As a matter of fact, I'm off right now – by helicopter, courtesy the RAF. Couldn't bear the prospect of another journey with Sir Alec so I asked for a lift. This is the only time the chopper's available. Want to join me?'

'I can't leave Schulmann.'

'Of course you can. Besides, I'm bringing in a couple of extra bods tonight; they can look after your client as well as mine.'

'No.' Gulliver shook his head. 'Anyway, don't you want to see what happens?'

'To tell the truth, I've had it up to here with sonar and submarines and what have you. It won't be too soon if I never hear about the topic again.' He paused. 'This operation, it's been a right bitch.'

Gulliver didn't reply, but let his gaze trail back to Frances again. She was sitting up now, seemingly in polite conversation with Koss. 'You'll say goodbye to her, before you go?'

'I wasn't planning on –'

'She'd appreciate it, Leech.'

Inner debate, a sigh of resignation, then: 'All right.'

He walked over to her with obvious reluctance. 'Look, sorry to interrupt, but I thought I'd better say cheerio.'

'You're going?' She frowned.

'Something's come up.' It was near enough the truth. Something would certainly be going up soon. 'You know how it is.' He extended his hand. 'I'd have liked to stay around but...' Her fingers seemed cold within his. 'It's been a pleasure, Doctor Wycliffe.'

'You're not with us tonight?'

'Not personally, no. But there'll be a driver and back-up, same as usual.'

She stood up and said quietly: 'And after tonight?'

'No need.' He paused, bewildered by the anxiety in her eyes and voice. 'It's all over, Doctor Wycliffe. Finished.'

'What d'you mean?'

'I mean it's ... it's, well ... back to normality.'

'No protection?'

'You don't need it now.'

'No? What about this normality?'

He hesitated, beset by the alarming thought that if he wasn't careful she would lead him into a realm where language was dangerously cryptogrammic, signalling far more than it ever said.

'Yes, well,' he said awkwardly. 'All the best, and thanks.' He retreated gratefully back to Gulliver. 'That's that then,' he said.

'Mmm.' Gulliver seemed to be having difficulty returning from wherever his thoughts had taken him. Eventually he asked: 'Tonight, your people – Owen Smith wouldn't happen to be coming, would he?'

'No.' Memory dawned belatedly. 'As a matter of fact he's at Tilgarsley today, helping Neil, if that's what you want to believe. Day out for him, really. He's still convalescing.' He shook Gulliver's hand. 'Well, be seeing you.'

'Yes.' He watched the departing figure. 'Leech?' he said. 'Have a nice day.'

CHAPTER TWENTY

TILGARSLEY
OXFORDSHIRE

'What time is it, Owen?' Rhyannon asked.

He checked his wristwatch, eyes narrowed against the sun. 'Almost three.'

'Not getting any cooler, is it?'

'No.' He yawned and turned to stare at the pool, eyes beginning to water now because of the glare. David was doing an expert breaststroke, porpoising serenely across the glittering surface, while Sarah bobbed about in an inflatable duck-shaped belt.

'We should've come before,' Rhyannon said.

'Not allowed. Well, not until today.'

'Last day?'

'That's right.'

She rolled over on the sunbed. 'Owen? Why does the Department of Health need a place like this?'

He shrugged. 'Helps them run a better hospital.'

'I don't see how.'

'Nor me. But either they had it or the National Coal Board.'

Neil Hawkins emerged onto the patio, clad only in swimming trunks. He surveyed the scene with arms folded across his glistening chest. 'Beats the Bahamas any day.'

Rhyannon shaded her eyes. 'You've been?'

'Benidorm, anyway.' He looked down at Owen. 'How's the invalid?'

'Okay.' He shifted position on the recliner, tried to stop the discomfort showing through. 'How's the clearing up?'

'Everything's ship-shape, all ready to hand over to the new owners.' He moved to the white table, prodded the remains of the packed lunch and lifted a sausage roll for inspection. 'I think I'll save

299

this for later.' He grinned at Rhyannon. 'You swimming or posing?'

She removed her sunglasses and towel and stood up. 'All right, Owen?'

'Go on, enjoy yourselves.' He squinted at them through the brightness, then pulled the yachting cap further forward.

She ducked down to kiss his cheek. 'Poor love.'

The sounds of summer slowly receded as other images unfolded in his mind's eye, other days, other moments. He slipped into an uneasy half-sleep.

It was the silence which awoke him. He looked around: the pool was deserted, Rhyannon stretched out on the sunbed again.

'Rhy ...? Where're the kids?'

'Inside. Getting changed.'

'Had enough swimming?'

'They want to play.' She yawned lazily, languidly, felt the shifting caress of the afternoon sun. 'Clever, isn't it, the way they've laid this out? Pool and patio, garden, the bushes in between. I expect he was happy here.'

'Who?'

'Your ... defector.'

A shadow fell across the burning paving. 'I'm going into Tilgars-ley,' Hawkins said. 'The fridge is bare so I thought I'd raid the ice-cream shop. Pity the pub's shut, I could murder a pint.'

'Me too,' Owen said.

'Why not come for the ride, then? I don't know how you can stand it out here anyway; it's like an oven.'

'Which is why I've decided to go inside.' He eased himself out of the chair, moving cautiously, deliberately. 'Do us a favour, Neil, take the kids with you.'

'I thought they wanted to play?'

'I know, but I'd rather they didn't. Not here.'

Hawkins shrugged. 'Okay. I'll go round 'em up.'

When he had gone, Rhyannon said: 'Anything wrong, Owen?'

'It's the heat.'

'You're not in any pain, are you?'

'No.' He forced a smile. 'I'll go in, have a lie down where it's cool.'

'If you're not, you know, not a hundred per cent ... Perhaps we ought to go home.'

'What, on a day like this?'

RAF KINLOSS

'This is Stratcon Pitreavie to ADR Con over.'
'Roger Stratcon.'
'We have stand by from Kinloss.'
'Advise when clear.'
'Will advise.'

'Kinloss this is Stratcon Pitreavie. What's your situation?'
'Ready to roll.'

'Stratcon Pitreavie to ADR Con.'
'Roger Stratcon.'
'Kinloss is go.'

'Tower this is Watchdog niner four requesting clearance.'
'Roger Niner Four. Proceed to holding at zero three.'
They felt the power surge, heard the muted whine of the engines, the beginnings of the turbo-fans' rising scream. 'Second time around,' McKinney said. He rocked in his seat as the aircraft tyres thudded over the ground. 'They say it's always better second time around.'
'Maybe someone should tell Ramsden that,' Henderson said.
In the cockpit, Ramsden and Hutchinson concentrated on the instruments and the view ahead of the wide ribbon of runway, the chain of markers and landing lights slowly unreeling. The flat roofs of low buildings rolled by, then the broad sweep of yellowing grass, the colours flowing towards the soft ochre of the sand dunes by the Firth. Sunlight played on the windshield, brief reflections of the interior sliding across and out of vision.
Ramsden glanced at his co-pilot. 'This time, then.'
'Hopefully.'
'Well, everyone's allowed a practice run.'

ADR CON FYLINGDALES

Koss answered the telephone, then swung around in his chair and held the instrument out to Gulliver. 'For you.'
'Thanks.' He bent down. 'Yes?'

301

'This is Mission Control in Hews-Ton. How ya doin' all?'

'Ho, ho.' He saw the questioning look on Frances' face and said: 'Barnes. Check call.' He spoke into the mouthpiece again: 'And how is Mission Control then?'

'Comatose. What time you got?'

'Nearly four.'

'Nearly eight here. Nobody should be up and working at nearly eight.'

'Quit complaining. Where's Larson?'

'Not here.'

'Ah.'

A yawn transferred itself across three thousand miles. 'I only got in last night, from the Coast.'

'And?'

'We've a possible suspect, at the main contractor. IRS records don't fit with the guy's bank and credit accounts. He's spending more than he makes.'

Gulliver hesitated. 'As this is an open line, just tell me one thing. The friend I've brought with me this trip, he's not ...?'

'He's not the suspect.'

'Thank Christ for that.'

'I thought you'd be pleased. That's why I'm phoning.' Barnes paused. 'What can you tell me about things at your end?'

'Not a lot. They launched one unit but it broke up.'

'The cookie has crumbled, huh?' Another pause, then Barnes said: 'So what happens now?'

Gulliver smiled. '"So what happens now?" The number of times you've asked me that ... The day you die, I'm going to get that engraved on your headstone.'

'Don't bother. I should know by then.'

NORWEGIAN SEA

Yevgeni tasted the tingling scent for the last time, then turned away, eyes watering from the scouring of the wind off the Arctic. He crossed the surface navigation bridge with drunken gait; the boat was rolling unpredictably, lying almost dead in the water.

Shevelev glanced up as he squeezed into the crowded confines of Diving Systems, and asked: 'How's the weather?'

'Cold.' Yevgeni shivered, as though in emphasis.

'Why're we slopping along like this?'

'Almost sixteen hundred – I don't want to be too far off latitude for the MTRE.' He sniffed, then sneezed into a handkerchief. Rites of passage, he thought, the way the sinus reacts to sudden changes of temperature and environment.

'I don't know,' Shevelev grumbled. 'The distance we've covered this past couple of hours – I could've walked it quicker.'

'On water?'

'You don't appreciate how talented I am.'

They were waiting for him at the master board, three unmoving, unspeaking figures standing before the three-metre-wide panel that reared up vertically from the command console. On the far right, Bulgov; Zeklin in the middle; next to him, Solokov: Yevgeni looked down the line and nodded.

Bulgov tore open the slim brown envelope and removed the tissue-thin sheets of white paper. 'For today,' Yevgeni said, 'zero zero two four.'

Bulgov studied his sheets. 'For today, three one zero zero.'

Zeklin scribbled the activation access onto his pad and read it back to them: 'For today, three one two four.'

Yevgeni slipped the paper back into its envelope. 'Present keys,' he said.

Hands delved into pockets and extracted four key-chains that hung in a steel-sprung loop from the clasps of their trouser-belts.

'On my mark,' Yevgeni said. 'Three.'

Zeklin moved forward, right hand stopping before the waist-level locks. The one on the left was hidden under a small, circular impact cover; on the right was a double intersecting slot shaped like an X. Zeklin eased the standard key into the left-hand lock, turned it clockwise, withdrew it, then mated the male X-key with the female right-hand slot. The key turned twice, anti-clockwise.

A green light began to glow on the console. Beacons began to flash above it in the vertical display. 'Three,' Zeklin said.

When they'd all worked through the remainder of the sequence – one, two and finally Bulgov at four – Yevgeni said: 'Remove keys.'

With the simultaneous withdrawal from the X-slots, all the lights and beacons began to flash in unison and all the console meters turned a hazy green.

Kiranovich walked briskly into the room. 'Captain? A word.'

303

Yevgeni frowned, then followed him until they were out of earshot of the others. 'What is it?'

'That thing, whatever it is. We seem to have overtaken it.'

'Oh?'

'South-west, about thirteen thousand. Tidal current, running parallel with us. We just picked up its signal. Lucky we're surface running.'

'What d'you think it is?'

'A sonobuoy.' Kiranovich paused. 'Waiting to be picked up.'

While he thought, Yevgeni contemplated the panel and console again. The slim red bars moved from left to right under the glass, registering the pressure in each of the missile tubes; the analogue meters silently monitored stand-by power to the ignition systems. Lights flickered on and off in rhythmic procession as the system sampled each missile computer's memory bank in turn. The next stage would be cross-matching by the SINS computer, confirming that each missile held the correct launch co-ordinates for its pre-ordained targets. He turned back to Kiranovich. 'We can't do anything about it now, but can you work out a time–distance intercept for, say, sixteen-thirty?'

'I can try. There's no way of telling how the current will run, though.'

Yevgeni nodded. 'All right. Go back to the con, warn Stukhov. Signal Fleet we may be altering course to investigate.' He went over to Solokov. 'Kiranovich has a contact.'

'Yes?'

'He thinks it's a sonobuoy.'

Solokov stared blankly. 'So?'

'He also thinks it's retrievable.'

'Watchdog niner four calling ADR Con Fylingdales. Flight Lieutenant Daniels for Doctor Wycliffe.'

'This is Doctor Wycliffe.'

'We're on station, Doctor.'

She glanced at the clock: 1611.

'Launch when ready, then,' she said. She turned to Schulmann. 'Now.'

A brief lurch, a momentary lift in flight, and then the Nimrod levelled again, banking in a slow turn towards the Arctic. Bombs away, Daniels thought – except somehow it wasn't like that, this time.

304

All the excitement had been and gone with the first abortive launch.

He studied the anodised aluminium inset containing the additional instrumentation for the sonobuoy. Next to it was the flat, twelve-inch-square screen. Two switches beneath it: BDIS – Buoy Display, and SECDIS – Sector Display.

If they'd got it right, there were only a few more seconds to wait.

Descending silently through the depths, its bubble cloud vanishing as quickly as a shoal of frightened herring, light briefly dappling before the shadows took it, the Asanov sonobuoy . . .

At target depth – fifty feet – the antenna motor whirred and the filament telescoped, breaking through the waves like a glittering needle. Pressure sensors triggered the release mechanism: the waist doors separated, splitting like a walnut, and cartwheeled away. It waited, a strange, misshapen insect with huge wings folded flat upon the spinal cord, the endo-skeleton of a new species.

Fifty feet and the sonobuoy was holding almost rock steady; a slight bobbing, but not much more, caused by wave disturbance transmitted from the surface commcon mast to the rest of the structure.

Twenty seconds elapsed as the computer assessed and confirmed position and angle, and then secondary separation was initiated. The upper and lower sections parted even further, hydraulics extending the shaft, silently, slowly; and the lower section withdrew even more, the six slim cables stretching to the limit of tensile strength.

Forty seconds later, the transducer faces began to bloom.

Daniels pressed the transmit key, fought to keep the elation out of his voice. 'We've got the status signal, Doctor.'

'Here too.'

A simulated graphic shimmered on the screen: the outline of the sonobuoy, perpendicular, steady at target depth. 'So far so good,' Daniels said. 'Congratulations, Doctor Wycliffe.'

'Thank you.' Her voice seemed to echo in his headset. 'Could you go to SECDIS now?'

'Roger.' He flicked the nearest of the four orange keys. The graphic yielded to a grid of lines displaying the sonobuoy's position and its location relative to the submarine.

'Sonobuoy, middle of screen; target, top right-hand corner. Justifying for target,' he said, and thumbed a concave button engraved

305

with the letters JUS. Instantly the grid shifted so that the sonobuoy was now at the extreme left-hand bottom corner, the target at the centre.

Two little lights separated by over three miles of ocean – the gap between them would widen as the submarine continued north-east, pursuing a diagonal across the screen to vanish finally out of the top right-hand corner. When that happened, the sonobuoy's computer would get a return signal from the aircraft and within seconds the aspect ratio of all the receptor screens at Pitreavie, Fylingdales, and on the Nimrod would alter to accommodate the increased range.

Her voice interrupted his reverie. 'Are we still on passive?'

'Yes, Doctor.'

'What's the target doing?'

'Well, we had a visual when it was surface running. Now, though, it's dived.'

'How long d'you think we can hold on passive?'

'You're the expert,' Daniels said. 'I wouldn't have thought much longer. You'll have to go active very soon.'

'All right, Mr Daniels. Stand by.'

ADR CON FYLINGDALES

Frances removed the headset and nodded in acknowledgement to all the smiling faces. To her left, Koss said: 'You're not switching to active, then.'

'We're a bit too close to the target. No point in letting their ECM pick us up just yet. As long as we stay in passive ...'

'... they can't see us,' Koss finished for her.

'Well, they certainly can't define anything, not with all that clutter on sternward scan. Their own transit is causing the worst disturbance.'

She stood up, squeezed past Schulmann and went out into the aisle. Kenyon stepped down from the upper tier to shake her hand. 'Well done, m'dear.'

'Still early days, Sir Alec.'

'I have every confidence, every confidence.' He smiled broadly. 'Now, if you'll excuse me?' He turned and climbed back up the steps.

She hesitated for a few moments, savouring the quiet joy of the moment, the relief of aftermath.

Gulliver beckoned to her from his position directly above

Koss and Schulmann. 'Congratulations,' he said, as she settled into Kenyon's vacated seat.

'Where's he gone?' she asked.

'Men's room – must be all the excitement.'

She smiled. 'I don't know how he'll cope when we switch to active. That'll be the true test, when we find out the real extent of our range.'

'I hope you get the opportunity.' He spoke quietly, gaze fixed on the SECDIS image again.

'What d'you mean?'

'The range.' He nodded towards the screen.

She frowned. 'What about it?'

'It's shortening.'

NORWEGIAN SEA

He made his way at a brisk pace from launch control to the con, past the SINS desk and Solokov and then into near collision with Bulgov.

'Comrade captain?'

'Not now.'

'I only wanted to –'

'Go back to your station. Help Zeklin.' He moved to the central island and said to Stukhov: 'You've changed course, then.'

'Kiranovich was very quick.'

'Must've been.' He punched the keypad and leaned into the mike. 'Sonar? Well done. Range and position, soon as possible.' Yevgeni glanced at Solokov: 'For'ard scan?'

'Still too much clutter.' The small man shrugged. 'You'll have to go up and get a surface bearing when it transmits.'

'Except we don't know when it will.' He spoke into the microphone again. 'ECM?'

'Nothing,' said Kiranovich flatly.

'But it's been signalling.'

'Only a location pulse – radio.'

'Even so, it could be transmitting on passive.'

'To where? There's no other traffic, surface or subsea. The signal is from its transponder, there's nothing else.'

'Yes, well, I'm not taking the chance. Cancel active scan.'

'But its ECM isn't functioning,' said Kiranovich doggedly.

'You don't know that for sure and neither do I.' He straightened up to confront Stukhov's predictable anxiety.

'We'll be running blind, comrade captain.'

'Hardly.' He motioned towards the overhead speakers relaying the rushing of sound from the acoustic bow cones. 'If anything's heading –' He felt the lightest of touches on his arm and stopped abruptly.

Bulgov smiled apologetically. 'I see you have everything in hand, comrade.'

'What do you want?' said Yevgeni coldly.

'Our previous conversation –' the big man moved even closer, assuming the posture of a co-conspirator in some as yet unguessed-at plot – 'the signal you were going to send . . .' Thick lips parted as the smile broadened. 'I think we should both forget our little –'

'It's already gone.' Yevgeni took a deep, steadying intake of breath. 'And now, comrade commissar, do as you're told. Help Zeklin with the shut-down.'

The smile was still in place, as though tacked into position, but within the rest of Bulgov's face, muscles were beginning to tauten and contract. 'Gone?'

'Yes. And if you waste any more time I'll send another.'

Bulgov's gimlet eyes glittered briefly. 'You talk to me about wasting time, comrade?'

'Commissar . . .' The warning note carried like a current of freezing air.

'You accuse me of wasting time when you've just turned this boat around on some fool's errand –'

'Go to your station, Bulgov.'

'– some fool's errand, and for what? A trophy? A souvenir? We have to go back the way we've just come because you want to make an impression?' His lips curled and his voice became a snarl.

Yevgeni closed his eyes. 'I won't tell you again.'

'Because you don't want to waste any more time?' The bullet head snapped back and laughter thick with venom racketed all around. 'Ah, comrade, comrade, just who do you think you are?'

'Bulgov!' The whisper seared the space between them. 'Go to your quarters!'

'No.'

'That's an order!'

'I am a ranking officer, I don't have to –'

'Problems, Yevgeni?' Shevelev, a mere two or three paces away, had appeared, a genie suddenly conjured out of the ether. He stood there smiling idly, but the expression was denied by his posture: body taut, legs splayed, fists clenching and unclenching.

'Go to your quarters, commissar.' Yevgeni, still whispering, struggled to stifle the outrage within. 'You're relieved of duty.'

'I'll escort him,' Shevelev said.

Bulgov pivoted. 'Stay out of this, comrade.'

Shevelev continued to smile; fingers plucked carelessly at his beard. 'Captain ...'

The small figure of Solokov came towards them, moving quickly from the SINS desk. He halted beside Shevelev. 'We'll escort him,' Solokov said.

ADR CON FYLINGDALES

'Watchdog niner four to ADR Con. We have an anomaly on sonobuoy transmission.'

'Roger niner four. This is Flight Lieutenant Koss. What is your position?'

'Twelve thousand and holding, west of launch zone.'

Koss turned his head and glanced up at Frances, who nodded and adjusted her earphones.

'This is Doctor Wycliffe. Have you run a systems check?'

'Affirmative. There doesn't seem to be anything wrong.'

'But the target ...?'

'It's definitely come about. We're going to go down and try for magnetic scan.'

She hesitated, then told Daniels on the Nimrod: 'Switch the buoy to stand-by mode – no more signals or sampling.'

'Roger. Into stand-by ... now.'

She tugged off the headset and leaned towards Schulmann. 'What d'you think?'

'I don't know, Doctor.'

'Could the buoy have been detected?'

'Seems unlikely.' Schulmann paused. 'Not only was it in passive mode, the target doesn't seem to be using active ECM either.'

'But why?'

'It's as though it suspects there's something out there, something that can detect its ECM.' He shook his head. 'I don't understand ...'

'Me neither.' She sat up, put the headset back on and spoke into the mike: 'This is Doctor Wycliffe at ADR Con for Stratcon Pitreavie.'

'This is Stratcon. Go ahead.'

'You'll have seen what's happening. We've put the sonobuoy into stand-by mode, no signalling, no electronic activity. The buoy display won't function now, but SECDIS will still hold on simulation via Watchdog ninety-four.'

'The buoy isn't transmitting at all, then?'

A voice cut in: 'This is Sir Kenneth, Doctor. Have we been spotted?'

'I don't know.'

'The target's heading back.'

'Is there anything else out there it could've locked on to?'

'No, nothing.'

She sighed. 'Well, something's gone wrong, somewhere ...

NORWEGIAN SEA

A length of silver cord uncoiled as Shevelev's palm opened, the assortment of oddly-shaped keys slipping between his fingers. 'You want me to take these to Zeklin?'

Yevgeni shook his head. 'I'll do it. I've got to go there to help close the MTRE.' He pocketed the keys. 'Yuri, thanks.'

'I was in his report anyway,' Shevelev said.

Yevgeni crossed to the SINS plotter and touched Solokov on the shoulder. 'When we get back I'll –'

'Forget it, captain. Like Yuri said, we all got a mention.'

'Even so –' he squeezed the narrow frame – 'I'm grateful.' He went off in the direction of the sonar room, where he found Kiranovich lost in thoughtful silence, staring at the quiet screens. 'Everything all right?'

'I don't like it. I feel as though I've been blindfolded.'

'Just a little longer, that's all.' Yevgeni leaned against the lip of the console and smiled sympathetically. 'Look, you know better than anyone else what's been going on. From the time we set off up to this very minute we've been targetted. But now it seems ... well, that they've made a mistake. I want to get to that buoy before they do. Besides, you said yourself it's retrievable.'

'Yes, but, if we used active scan –'

'Why risk it? You've worked out a rough position; we'll surface as soon as we're within visual range. Come on, have faith. Wouldn't you like to sneak this one out from under them?'

Kiranovich nodded uncertainly. 'We have done it before,' he said.

'So we'll do it again. Who knows? This might be some type of surveillance equipment we haven't heard about.'

'I still don't like it, captain.'

Yevgeni sighed and looked around the crowded room. The junior sonar officers met his stare, then returned to the shimmering serenity of the inert monitors.

I know, he thought, I know. Flank speed at this shallow depth, surging westwards at nigh on forty knots, every centimetre of the boat alive with the power of the nuclear furnace. At this pace you had to be certain you weren't heading into trouble, otherwise you'd wind up like Prubin last year, making a fast transit of the Irish Sea, everything clear one second, then bang, embroiled in the trailing gear of a trawler, net catching and shredding as it fouled the casing. Damn near sank it. Another entry in the chapter of accidents which every year, on at least a dozen occasions in these waters alone, saw near collisions and even actual impacts as submarines transited between east and west or surfaced at the most inappropriate places.

These things weren't supposed to happen, but they did, even when your ECM was running full-tilt, when every screen danced to a white electronic storm; accidents were never supposed to happen, but try telling that to poor Boriedev, who rammed an anti-submarine barrier half-way up a Norwegian fjord and found himself stuck firmly in the middle of a NATO/US propaganda war. Running blind – in the final analysis, that's what you always did.

He glanced up at the clock: 1627, three more minutes.

ADR CON FYLINGDALES

'Watchdog niner four calling ADR Con. Watchdog niner four calling –'

Daniels' voice had an urgency she had not previously detected. She frowned. 'This is Doctor Wycliffe ...'

'We've just picked up a signal from the buoy.'

'What?' She stared wide-eyed with disbelief at the console repeater screen: still the dull simulation of the sonobuoy, the brighter point of light of the submarine, now captured by the

Nimrod's magnetic anomaly detectors. 'But it's on stand-by!'

'It's the first sonobuoy, Doctor.'

Frances' thoughts skittered in a wild helterskelter. The first buoy, the bits – she had completely forgotten it. She shook her head in vigorous reflex. 'What d'you mean, the first buoy?'

'Must've been caught in a sub-surface current. The transponder's still dicky, but we got enough of the signal. It's drifted straight into the launch zone.'

'ADR Con to Stratcon Pitreavie.' Koss spoke quietly, urgently.

'Roger ADR Con.'

'We have non-operational unit in target area.'

'Affirmative here. What's your assessment?'

'The target must've picked up the transponder signal during surface passage.' He half-turned to Frances for confirmation. She nodded.

'You think it's gone to investigate?'

'No other reason for heading south-west.' Koss paused. 'We're not sure if it's positively acquired either sonobuoy. It could be running blind.'

Beside her, Gulliver said: 'You watching the screen?'

'Yes.' The buoy was a constant light in the middle of the monitor, while the target light flared, faded, then flared again a few centimetres further down the invisible diagonal.

'It's heading right for the second buoy,' he said. 'Jesus Christ, what speed's that thing going at?'

'About thirty-five knots – forty miles an hour.'

'But they're going to hit!'

'We can't tell, we can't –'

'Damn it, Frances, do something!'

She spoke into the mike: 'Flight Lieutenant Daniels? Can you compute intercept?'

'Sorry, Doctor, no way.'

'The sub's still on course?'

Frances paused for a moment, eyes closed, and heard the drumming thunder of her pulse. The situation had become numbingly dangerous. 'We'll have to warn them,' she said finally.

Silence coursed across the miles, hissing in her earphones, then Daniels, slowly, reluctantly: 'You want to switch to active?'

'We've no choice.'

'We've no guarantee that they'll see it, either. If the sub killed its ECM for the same reason we did, it'll stay blind whatever we do.'

A familiar voice interrupted the exchange: 'Doctor Wycliffe, this is Talbot. You've no evidence the target's at the same depth as the sonobuoy, it could easily –'

'The target's still being held by the Nimrod's magnetic sensors,' Frances broke in wearily. 'That places it at almost exactly the same level as the sonobuoy.'

'But if the damn thing's going to miss, why betray our position?'

'You don't know that it *is* going to miss.'

'And you don't know that it is going to collide. No, Doctor, leave the buoy in stand-by mode, understood?'

'Sorry.' She paused, surprised by her own calmness. 'I can't do that.'

'I'm ordering you, Doctor, you hear me? Leave the buoy –'

She removed the headset and leaned forward over the console. Koss was still occupying her original position, hands spread out over the keys and buttons of the over-ride panel. 'Bypass,' she said.

'Doctor Wycliffe, I'm not –'

'I'll take responsibility.'

She watched him intently, seeing the turmoil working in his face, registering the trembling of his hands and the first faint indecisive movement of the fingers.

Then he slowly nodded, with the air of one given no choice, and the dull light at the centre of the screen suddenly blazed and across the SECDIS a word abruptly shone: ACTIVE

NORWEGIAN SEA

Kiranovich's voice came over the intercom: 'Sixteen-thirty.'

Yevgeni glanced up to check the control-room clock. 'All right, activate ECM and for'ard scanning.'

The repeater screen came alive under his gaze – shimmering circles and drifting smears of illumination. 'Anything?'

'Not yet.' There was a brief silence, then: 'If it's non-functioning, or even if it's in passive mode, we're not likely to –'

A dazzling brightness suddenly exploded in the middle of the monitor. Yevgeni recoiled involuntarily. 'What the –'

'ECM! ECM!' Kiranovich's ragged shout echoed around the con.

* * *

313

The starboard sail-plane slammed hard into the upper lip of the sonobuoy, then sliced into the central shaft, driving forward, cartwheeling it down, impetus dissipating fast in the medium of the sea, but still great enough to hurl it against the lower sail.

Primary impact: damage to superior structure, upper lip sheared off; cables three and four snaking wildly, lashing the bubble cloud issuing out of the fracture in the buoyancy chamber.

Secondary impact: destruction of transducer C as the vertical blade twisted against the sail of the sub, as though struggling to free itself; the shaft's rotation continuing remorselessly, shivering the blade and ripping it like cloth.

The final release of energy left submarine and sonobuoy intertwined in a thrashing filamental tangle of wires and cables and torn steel.

'Blow main! Blow auxiliaries!'

'Main auxiliaries.' Shevelev's voice came back hoarse, dazed.

'Blow safeties!'

The blare of the crash-dive klaxon melded with the shattering clamour of the proximity alarms, high-toned bells punching out sound in vicious bursts. Stukhov was yelling, words lost in the din, yelling and waving his arms, and then an ear-splitting thunderclap broke directly above.

Yevgeni clamped his hands to his ears, stared up at the unyielding steel, tried to visualise, to comprehend the jangling, grating caco-phony overhead. The floor tilted then, as air released in an explosive rush and the ocean came surging into all of the tanks.

Twenty metres, twenty-one, twenty-two; the depth-gauge was unwinding like a broken spring; twenty-three, twenty-four, twenty-five, twenty-six; the tilt getting steeper by the second; twenty-seven, twenty-eight, twenty-nine; every beacon on , every panel lit, and still the klaxon's shriek pierced through all the other alarms.

Its buoyancy chamber flooded, the sonobuoy tilted over and down into the narrow cradle between the safety rail and lower sail of the sub. The angle of dive was increasingly acute, but the sonobuoy's natural rate of descent was not as rapid as the sub's, so the structure began to jolt and jar, grinding back along the starboard decking, a grotesque parasite with broken wings and writhing tendrils slither-ing towards the stern.

Thirty metres, thirty-two, thirty-four, thirty-six; the sonobuoy was spiralling again, so that cables two and five were wrenched out from the bottom lip, the central shaft retracting in violent recoil and mangling three transducer faces in abrupt unison.

Forty metres, forty-five, fifty: the sole remaining transducer was still secure, but the sonobuoy turned once more, cabling and antennae looping and flexing, and an elliptical fragment of jagged steel at the tip of one of the spiralling hawsers locked firm within the throat of the boat's for'ard vent, tensed, tightened, stretched taut and was trapped by the increasing sternward drag and the downward pressure of millions of tons of ocean.

Sixty metres, sixty-five, seventy; the buoy's computer struggled to compensate as sensors registered transmission loss, augmenting the power along the feed to the last remaining transducer. Seventy-five metres, and the lateral force of the trapped cable combined with depth pressure to strap the transducer against the upper surface of the boat. Eighty-five metres, ninety, ninety-five, and the bond was complete, final, unbreakable, the face squeezed flat between shaft and spine.

One hundred metres below the waves and in turbulent darkness the acoustic interface was finally born.

ADR CON FYLINGDALES

Frances jolted in her seat as the tumult of voices assaulted her, but her gaze was captivated by the screen, its glass no longer bright but opaque, dead, the surface reflecting nothing but her own spectral features. No lights, no display, nothing. Dead.

Koss was flailing at the console, tapping keys up, down, back and forth in search of a response, but there was none.

'This is Stratcon, Stratcon. Clear all channels, this is Stratcon, Stratcon. Clear –'

Koss was shouting: 'Contact lost. Repeat, contact lost. ADR Con to Stratcon Pitreavie –'

And a stranger was yelling from miles away in an aircraft still pointlessly circling through the sky: 'The buoy's gone!'

NORWEGIAN SEA

They were going down, the descent accelerating with nothing to impede it ... And nothing to prevent the spreading isonification, nothing capable of obstructing its path because a six-metre track through the hull counted as nought: after Krakatoa in 1883, the self-same sound waves travelled three times around the world.

The signal plunged through the lower register, penetrating steel and plastic and tissue and bone, and beginning to provoke an answering response.

Yevgeni reeled away from the command island, staggered backwards into Stukhov and the two of them went into a sudden tripping, stumbling pirouette. Vision whirled, steadied, then whirled again; the floor underfoot lost substance, then regained it; the sensation of something grating and trembling, but no longer above, nor even below – something was starting to shiver within.

As the signal strength rose through 150 decibels, an infinite pulse beat passed along the outer auditory canal, with pressure shock impacting deep inside the eardrum. 200 decibels, and the membrane vibrated sympathetically, relaying the rhythm to the middle ear. The intermediate aural structure tried to reduce the overall amplitude, but still continued in its natural task of increasing the signal strength, providing greater perception, increasing it five-fold, ten-fold ...

Acuity declining, orientation slipping, room going around and around in a spinning vortex of darkening red, bone, muscle and tissue beginning to shriek, whistle, vibrate near its own natural frequency ...

'Stop it! Stop it!'

Yevgeni could neither hear nor feel his own voice. Pain was flash-firing in the pit of his stomach. With one last convulsion of nausea, he voided and crumpled.

He tried to drag himself up off the deck.

One step, two step, left foot, right – like a blind man dancing. Shevelev, wide-eyed, lurched alongside, head shaking wildly, holding his jaw. Then somehow Yevgeni was out of the control room – Stukhov, Solokov and all the others left far behind, like Shevelev, bobbing past on the tortured tide.

The ADP siren called dimly, dully: automatic depth correction to 140 metres.

Amidst the sensory terrors came belated cognizance of the

message and its meaning: ADP, 140 metres, which meant the central tactical computer was still linked to launch control. The boat was automatically re-trimming because of MTRE mode, stabilising temporarily at red-line depth – the maximum depth for missile launch ...

Blind man dancing, onwards into the red red womb. They are doing this to me, doing this to my boat, my command.

They are not going to do this, they are not. Blind man dancing, going forward, going on ...

Kiranovich was half in, half out of the sonar room, lying on his back thrashing like a fish on the bank. Their eyes met. 'Yevgeni ... Yevgeni ...'

They are not, they are not ... After everything that has happened, all the pressure, all the pain flaring wide within. On again, left shoulder banging against the silos, sliding, banging, colliding again.

He sprawled into the wide wide room, then crabbed along on hands and knees, seeing through the heat haze the dials and panels and screens. Zeklin still sat at his station, pointing up with outstretched fingers: *Hatches, blow the hatches!* He watched the words being formed by Zeklin's trembling lips, watched and understood.

Yevgeni clipped back the impact cover and slid the master key home. Zeklin was out of reach, but he must be synchronising because the third-tier metering changed from green to amber; then the second-tier metering came alive, alert, needles deflecting in fourteen rectangles of shimmering glass as silos repressurised in sequential parade. Blow the hatches, blow them, throw them, my Latvian friend! Images of pain and fire and hatred engulfed him. He gripped Bulgov's keys in his right palm. So much for you, my bold commissar. Zeklin was pitching from his chair, rolling out of vision. ACCESS COMPLETE. So much for all of you.

The first-tier metering came on. Now every single little face was bright and vivid red. Beacons flashed, winked, pulsed, and the whining cadence of the alarms still came as if from far away ...

Fingers in her hair, soft as fine thread. 'Do dna! Do dna!' Standing in the doorway with the little bear hanging limp. 'It woke Mischa.' Oh, Katerina, forgive us, child, forgive me, Tanya, Tanya ... They are not going to do this, they are not.

He hunched forward and pressed the first button, middle tier, watched the beacon beside it flashing white. He pressed the adjacent key to complete the circuit, watched its beacon begin to flash red. His

317

hand tracked to the right, and then the pain burst and he was driven to his feet, rigid, electrified. Every muscle was in spasm, every nerve in shock, but his fingers still squeezed in amongst the spaces and then his thumb crashed hard down and the triggers went in all the way.

LAUNCH

Guidance reconfirmed true north in crossmatch with the SINS input, then the hatch cover blew off in a silent gale and the exhaust slowly pushed it up and out of the silo, into a lethargic ascent through the still, dark water. The aft-mounted fins unfolded and the forward tabs trimmed as momentum increased.

When it smashed through the surface tension of the ocean it was already climbing at thirty-three feet per second, on a journey that could span half the world.

Silo nine blew six seconds after silo three. The hatch cover slashed through the retaining mesh and the Asanov sonobuoy tumbled away.

ADR CON FYLINGDALES

People moved, stood, shouted, telephones rang, bells shrilled, klaxons whooped.

Upon the perspex wall the continental outlines began to glow, overlaid now by a series of circles radiating outwards like ripples in a pool.

Two stars flashed. Two stars amid all the others, but this pair winked side by side over the Norwegian Sea. And amid all the lights and all the sounds, one word clamoured and shone bright:

REAL

NORWEGIAN SEA

No further request was addressed to launch control, so the MTRE over-ride now deactivated, sending the bow down, letting it pursue the descent it had so arbitrarily disrupted.

External pressure was at one ton per square inch and increasing, but without haste, without fuss. The submarine was a soft feather fall, sinking with a sigh. Within the graceful form, pretty lights still beckoned. Digits skipped, totalizers spun, numbers scampered behind all the shining glass.

One thousand metres, and the electronic carnival still went on, unchecked. Screens applauded out of sterile tiers of whiteness, computers engaged in silent dialogue, shifting thoughts and sharing memories.

At 1,150 metres, the initial pressure burst and the stern weighed down. At 1,170 metres, the tanks ruptured, the hull splitting in sudden fissure. Ten metres deeper – implosion.

At 1,200 metres – nothing left at all, only the dense, freezing dark.

ADR CON FYLINGDALES

Gulliver yelled in her ear; Frances spun around, saw confusion, fear, disbelief in his face. 'What's happening, Frances? For Christ's sake, what's happening?'

REAL

The headset distracted her, metallic voices of remote, efficient strangers suddenly cutting in through the static.

'This is Clarion One. All stations alert. Hostiles confirmed UK Domestic zero seven niner. Repeat, hostiles confirmed.'

'Torch Control to Zulu One over. Advise status LOS.'

'Negative, Torch. Repeat, negative, line-of-sight tracking.'

REAL

The control-room loudspeakers abruptly came alive, crowding out the din in her ears: 'Launch confirmed, two hostiles UK Domestic. Repeat, launch confirmed. This is not a simulation. This is not a simulation.'

In the tier immediately beneath her, Koss was swivelling out of his seat, standing up, turning to face her: 'You can't stay here, either of you. You can't –'

The loudspeakers interrupted again: 'All unauthorised personnel clear the area. All unauthorised personnel clear the area.'

REAL

Sound blared anew through her headset: 'This is Torch Control all stations, Torch Control all stations. Hostiles identified two,

319

repeat two, submarine-launched ballistic missiles. Probability Sawfly class, repeat, probability Sawfly class.'

Koss reached for her hand. 'Doctor Wycliffe ... Please.'

She was unable to move, mesmerised by the shining circles on the perspex screen, the ripples spreading outwards.

REAL

Trajectory re-set as the SSN 18 veered northwards for the Pole and approached the roof of the world, an SLBM with six independently-targettable thermo-nuclear warheads, each of them capable of creating a blast twenty times greater than Hiroshima.

The shining star headed remorselessly towards the Kill Corridor, the American death zone around longitude 100 degrees west. Four independent warheads were destined for release along the north-south axis of North Dakota, South Dakota, Nebraska and Kansas, the other two for Colorado at 105 degrees west and Missouri, 92.5 degrees west. 120 Hiroshimas cruised towards the silo complexes in the sleepy fields, towards the heartland of a nation that still believed in the day after.

Far behind and below it, the single-warhead SSNX 22 cruise missile switched to contour mapping and began its flight over the United Kingdom.

There was too much to comprehend: a huge screen to the right of the status boards abruptly lit up in ghostly animation; a red beacon blinked rhythmically above it; a two-tone siren rang out, punching again and again like a hammer at an anvil. Even as she struggled towards understanding, words flickered then steadied on the shimmering display:

STRATSITREP 1636

2 (TWO) HOSTILES LAUNCHED UK SECTOR:	CONFIRMED
HOSTILE ONE, POSITED TARGET:	NOT KNOWN
HOSTILE TWO, POSITED TARGET:	NOT KNOWN
EVALUATION: PER CENT AGGRESS:	PENDING
PER CENT ERROR:	PENDING
CENTACTCON RESPONSE OPTION:	STANDBY

She turned to Gulliver. 'Response ...?' But her speech seemed robbed of all strength.

320

The display fragmented, then instantly re-formed:

CENTACTCON RESPONSE OPTION
POSITED HOSTILE TARGETS, WAVE ONE:

ABOVYAN	ARKANGHELSK	DNEPROPETROVSK
KAMCHATKA	PENINSULA	LENINGRAD
MOSCOW	MINSK	PLESETSK
TYURATAM	VLADIVOSTOK	

STANDBY FOR POSITED HOSTILE TARGETS, WAVE TWO

A thin sound of denial came involuntarily to her lips. But the machinery of retaliation already seemed to be in remorseless motion; cities in a distant land were now targets etched upon a wall of glass.
'No!'
But the noise hammered on and the screen was still bright, and in the midst of it all the word still shone undimmed:

REAL

Koss herded Schulmann into the aisle and urged him up the steps. The gaunt man moved as though in a stupor.
'Doctor Wycliffe, Mr Gulliver ...' Koss paused at their level, then seemed stricken by a belated realisation. His gaze ranged desperately over the shelving tiers. 'Where's Sir Alec?'
'He went to the –' Gulliver broke off, confronted by an absurdity too black to articulate. 'He's outside.'
Koss's breathing was quick and shallow. 'You'll have to come with me. You can't stay here.'
'No.'
'But Doctor Wycliffe ...'
'*No.*'
Gulliver stared from one to the other, too surprised by the unexpected collision of wills to do anything but observe.
Frances said: 'I have to talk to Pitreavie.' Her gaze flickered back to the display: it had re-set the evaluation equation, but the analysis was still pending. 'It's an *accident.*'
Koss debated a moment longer, then began to climb the steps, pushing Schulmann out of the erupting electronic arena.
She adjusted the headset, eyes still fixed on the display screen. There came a crackle of static, then a voice announced: 'This is Colorado Vigilant. Colorado Vigilant. We have acquisition hostile

321

one. DefCon Two instituted three minutes fifteen into event. Hold for intercept.'

She glanced questioningly at Gulliver to see if his headset had picked up the same message. He nodded. 'Norad –' a humourless smile – 'the Voice of America.'

'They're intercepting?'

'They're trying.'

The disembodied voice resounded again: 'This is Vigilant. Silo clearance three minutes thirty-five, intercept now twenty-two seconds and counting.'

Four parallel scratches suddenly scored the perspex screen, lengthening with astonishing speed, homing in on the pulsing star of the SSN 18.

'This is Vigilant. Six seconds to intercept. Four seconds, three, two, one ...'

Brilliance blossomed. She thought of all the screens in all the war rooms in all the secret places of the world, all the computer-enhanced simulations of ABMs flaring out in silent explosions of ultra-violet.

By her side, Gulliver let go a prolonged shuddering exhalation, and used the back of one hand to wipe at the sweat on his face.

Her gaze swung back to the perspex screen and the rippling circles. But there were only the circles – nothing more.

She heard herself say: 'Where's the second one?'

Air whistling through its intakes, it cruised three hundred feet above the wave-tops, ram jets blazing a short, fiery tail. Within the nose section, guidance systems continued to update the target co-ordinates as terrain monitors adjusted for altitude, whilst ECM detectors spun and stalled, then spun again.

One SSNX 22 missile bound for Dispersal Point A7 of the Greenham Common defence system, travelling above the North Sea but below the radar screens.

'This is Vigilant to Torch Control. What is your status, hostile two?'

'Negative, Vigilant. Repeat, no contact.'

'Roger, Torch Control. We're going for infra-red scan. Please stand by.'

The small VDUs on their consoles came alive as the different comm links integrated.

322

On the wall of glass, the second wave of projected targets silently materialised.

'Pitreavie for Doctor Frances Wycliffe. Acknowledge please.'

'This is Doctor Wycliffe. I was just about to –'

'We have the air vice-marshal for you.' Frances felt her pulse quicken as Talbot's voice boomed in her ears. 'Doctor Wycliffe. This is Kenneth Talbot. There isn't much time, so listen carefully. The missiles – nothing in any of our scenarios accounts for the sub's behaviour. I take it there's no possibility that when the buoy went active it could've triggered the launch system?'

'I can't say what's possible and what isn't without more information. All I know is –'

'I'm grasping at straws here, Doctor Wycliffe. We're in the middle of an attack evaluation and either it's an error or an act of aggression, and unless someone comes up with some answers –'

'It's an error.' She stared at the display, at the mundane words that seemed now to thrust a vast weight of responsibility upon her: PER CENT ERROR: PENDING. PER CENT AGGRESS: PENDING. 'It's an *accident*,' she insisted.

'You're certain?'

She hesitated, then started over with a fierce desperation. 'Listen, the prototype malfunctioned on test. The power output sent everything haywire and –'

'But there hasn't been a malfunction *today*. The thing worked perfectly!'

'I know that, I know, but there has been a collision. What I'm telling you –'

'What I'm telling you is, the feeling here is electronics *alone* just can't do this.'

Frances fought down the fast-rising edge of a brittle panic, closing her eyes against the glare of the screens, the blaring of the klaxon and the siren, the swirling kaleidoscope of a hostile technology:

'The isonification, if there was an interface . . .' She was stricken by an inexplicable breathlessness, unable to speak, almost unable to think, struggling to find some last reserve of strength to go on: 'Infra-sound is highly unpredictable. If there was an interface, the

323

infra-sound could have disorientated the people down there, un-balanced them –'

'Unbalanced?' Talbot was scathing in his disbelief. 'Unbalanced them? Good God, they'd've had to be half crazy in the first place to even contemplate this! That's a submarine down there, Doctor Wycliffe, professionals, trained professionals –'

'You don't know what the pressures were!' Frances was shouting now, letting it all go as something suddenly snapped deep inside her.

'Dammit, woman!' Talbot's self-restraint was fragmenting, his words flying at her like shards of glass. 'Facts! I want facts! *What caused all this?*'

'We did!' Frances screamed, unable to contain the bitterness any longer, the anger jolting from her in vicious spasm. 'We did!' She tore off the headset, hurled it at the VDU and pitched forward with hot tears spilling from her eyes.

'Frances!' Gulliver was half out of his seat, yelling and reaching for her shoulders, twisting her towards him. 'Talk to them! Tell them! For Chrissakes, Frances, make them understand!'

She opened her eyes and stared pointblank into his panic; and that was the most paralysing thing of all. He released her, heard himself shouting, spitting into the lip mike: 'Damn you, you stupid bastards, listen to her! Will you *listen* to her?!'

But Talbot's voice was already distant, as though he had turned to someone else, and then the channel clicked and died and words unintended for Gulliver's ears went clamouring through his head: 'Get 'em out of it, get those bloody civilians *out of it!*'

A belated message came up on the small console VDUs:

```
COLORADO VIGILANT STAGE ONE ALERT
INFRA-RED CONFIRM: HOSTILE INCURSION
   UK DOMESTIC SECTOR 4
STANDBY
```

The image on the wall display flickered, then held:

```
STRATSITREP 1641

INCURSION:          MIDAS AFFIRMATIVE
                    SAMOS AFFIRMATIVE
IDENTITY:           SUBMARINE-LAUNCHED CRUISE
                       MISSILE
TYPE:               SSNX 22
```

324

WARHEAD: SINGLE TACTICAL
POSITED TARGET: NOT KNOWN
INTERCEPT: NEGATIVE
MINUTES TO IMPACT: NOT KNOWN

EVENT IMMINENT

Silence. It washed over her in a sudden tide, then ebbed away, leaving her cold and spent and possessed only of an aching emptiness. Silence. The screaming and shouting, the see-sawing of the siren, all the mad tumult cut off, ended.

She glanced at Gulliver, not knowing what to expect. His face was averted. Without understanding why she reached for his hand and squeezed it. 'It's all right, John.'

'What?' He turned towards her, eyes downcast, unable to meet her gaze. 'They wouldn't listen to me. They wouldn't listen to a . . . a civilian.'

'Welcome to the fold, then,' Frances said.

'Fold?'

She stared at the grey eyes in the grey grey face, missing the light that used to be there. 'Doesn't matter,' she told him gently.

A stark and simple message appeared on the screen:

STRIKE

The secret sphere at the heart of the warhead suddenly shattered under the stabbing thrust of shards from the beryllium and uranium 235 casing, the ten-kilogram plutonium core pierced and riven by a frenzy of darting neutrons.

The first plutonium atom split within a billionth of a second, breaking in two as the beryllium and uranium neutrons smashed through. As it split, two of its own neutrons were released; they escaped and cannoned into adjacent atoms, and divided them in twin simultaneous bursts of energy. With each sequential act of fission, the heat began to climb an unimaginable exponential curve so that after a hundredth of a second the core temperature was scaling 100 million degrees centigrade, and rising.

The thermal trigger fired the nuclear gun: lithium deuteride, a compound of deuterium and lithium 6, now underwent the act of fusion, sparked by the blaze of the atomic furnace. Lithium isotopic atoms fused together in a burst of heat and energy infinitely greater than anything that had gone before.

The sun exploded shortly before 1643 GMT. Three thousand million megawatts of pure energy sent heat and blast waves radiating outwards and pushed up the surrounding air temperature from twenty-nine to five million degrees centigrade. The fireball blossomed to an instant width of 606 feet and began rising at 212 feet per second.

TILGARSLEY
OXFORDSHIRE

Hawkins sighed and slammed the driver's door shut. No sign of Owen's kids, no sign at all. Couples were strolling about, families ambling, kids being shepherded away from the traffic – but no David, and no Sarah. He gazed down the steeply-shelving hillside and tried to discern them in amongst all the little figures weaving in and out of the ferns. No good. Shaking his head, he turned around to study the perimeter of the forest across the asphalt.

As Neil Hawkins wondered and waited, the sunlight sharpened against the nape of his neck and the brightness suddenly intensified and the world abruptly became a beautiful, bedazzled place and all the trees had shining haloes.

The ultra-violet destroyed all colour then. With eyes liquefying, he fell to his knees and, in an attitude of prayer, began to burn.

'It's mine!' Sarah shouted and fled from his grasp, laughing and running back towards Prior Hill, towards Uncle Neil, arms flailing and legs pistoning, but her fingers never relaxing their grip on the biggest fir cone of them all.

Excitement imbued her with a recklessness of almost hysterical abandon, but then a serpentine root uncoiled underfoot and she tripped and sprawled heavily and the cone bounced away out of sight. David stopped and knelt beside her.

'Sarah? You all right?'

She winced and reached down to touch her ankle.

'Let's have a look,' David said.

She leaned towards him as he moved closer, and they melted into each other, and thence into the earth.

Rhyannon yawned and pushed herself up from the sunbed,

struggling against the afternoon languor. Everything looked serene and warm, bright and enticing. Blue water, white furniture, green grass, red brick, brighter than ever before, then suddenly over-bright, over-exposed – no hue, no texture, no shadow or shape, only whiteness, bleaching it all away.

Book in his hands, the bed accommodating his shifting weight, Owen Smith was reminded of a long-ago morning in Leningrad, when the sun came out of the clouds and the pages beneath his gaze seemed to shine.

The memory was so forceful that he was experiencing it again, here within the somnolent house, eyes narrowing against the sudden intense daylight that came flooding into the room.

The words on the page burned clear away as the heat wave continued south.

The blast moved at 1,150 feet per second through the tame places and the wild. Whatever had withstood the atomic dawn would fall before the dusk, the darkness created by a searing wind carrying upon it the debris of forest and field.

Cottages bowed, bulged, flattened, houses turned and twisted into themselves; the hotel, with its candles and flowers, vanished in momentary conflagration; the eaves of the coaching inn undulated like bats' wings, masonry crazing, timbers soaring free, thatch borne aloft on a furnace wind, scouring clean a place soon to be re-christened Ground Zero.

ADR CON FYLINGDALES

Systems shutdown – the electromagnetic pulse effect had smashed like a hurricane through the invisible web of comm links, blanking out screens in rapid succession as data feeds cut in abrupt amputation.

One missile, one warhead, and for eight impossible, unbelievable seconds there was nothing at all – screens blank, headsets dead.

And after all the wild affray of thoughts and emotions, Frances too felt a numbness spreading over her as the brain, like any other overloaded system, switched itself out, leaving only stillness and silence, touching a chord in her memory that reverberated softly.

If we could do all that, the finbacks could hear each other across four thousand miles. Can you imagine it? Can you imagine what it would be like to give them ... silence?

The screen seared with sudden incandescence:

```
STRATSITREP 1643

EVENT:                              0010
TARGET:                             SQUIRREL DISPERSAL A7
EVALUATION: PER CENT AGGRESS:       PENDING
            PER CENT ERROR:         PENDING

CENTACTCON RESPONSE OPTION:  STANDBY
```

'Squirrel?' Frances stared mesmerised at the display. 'Squirrel dispersal ...?'

'For your own cruise missiles.' Gulliver swallowed. 'Dispersal site – safe place in the event of ...'

'But nobody's supposed to know where –'

'Get a map, pinpoint the high ground within a radius of the base.' He seemed suddenly angry. 'A child could do it.'

'Where is it, though?'

'Anywhere –' a despairing shrug – 'could be anywhere.'

Her own anger kindled briefly. 'What's the use of having them if everyone knows where they are?'

'Yes,' Gulliver said, 'what's the use.' His gaze moved from her and ranged across the wide, still room, beyond the frozen figures at their silent consoles to the perspex screen and the shimmering display.

An echo of a familiar voice seemed suddenly to call from close by, and for a moment he almost believed that Barnes was there beside him. Then he slowly shook his head.

No, my friend, don't ask what happens now.

```
STRATSITREP 1646

EVENT:                              0138
EVALUATION: PER CENT AGGRESS:       50
            PER CENT ERROR:         50

CENTACTCON RESPONSE OPTION:  PENDING

HOLD            HOLD            HOLD            HOLD
```

AUTHOR'S NOTE

The Oxfordshire village of Tilgarsley no longer exists. Its inhabitants fell victim to a sixteenth-century natural disaster – the Black Death.